THE MEMORY THIEF

THE MEMORY THIEF

STREETS OF NOX VALAR, BOOK I

C.D. CORRIGAN

DEDICATION

Not a single step on the weird journey that led me
to write this would have happened if not for the
support and encouragement of my incredible wife.
Matti, you're my favorite human.

TABLE OF CONTENTS

CHAPTER 1

The body heat was missing.

That's what was off about the place, Cypress realized as she wound through the throng of bodies. Patrons sang, laughed, drank, danced; they reveled and made merry, packed to the rafters of the Wayward Friar. But the air was too cool. It lacked the cloying, muggy closeness of life pressing in, the hot breath and sweat to match their jubilations.

Cypress wondered if she was the only one to notice. *Doubtful.* The older souls, more wan and frayed around the edges, looked better able to immerse themselves in the experience—the finer details of life having long since slipped away from the ever-crushing onslaught of the now, so that one rarely thought to miss them.

The newer arrivals were easy to mark if you knew what to look for. Fashion was a poor indicator, of course. Nox Valar teemed with the myriad dead of the cosmos; trying to discern anything about a soul from their garb was a fool's errand— something Cypress would have pointed out to her apprentices, once. Now that thought brought only a hollow pang of loss.

What marked the newly dead separate from the seniors was in their stares, the slightly bewildered dissonance that sat behind their eyes as they joked and drank. It was starkest in places like the Friar, where souls flocked to while away eternity, chasing the verisimilitude of life, but never *quite* finding it.

Nox Valar, the city of the dead, offered many wonders to those who walked its stormy streets, but living again was not among them. One could come close—one could, in fact, find many things in the Sunless Crossing that were denied to them in life—but they could never feel alive. Not here.

The old souls had found a small mercy in forgetting, Cypress mused as she slid over to one of the Friar's several bars. Dressed as she was in a voluminous gray-brown robe, wearing the scruffy, weathered old man's face she'd picked to be unremarkable in a crowd, it took a moment to be served. A comely bartender, a tall elven woman, smiled as she finally noticed Cypress. They exchanged a few mixed copper coins for a tankard of, allegedly, mead.

It tasted like mead, sweet and potent, as Cypress nursed it. Vultha would have called it a fine batch, she reckoned. But like the merrymaking that filled the oversized public house, it wasn't perfect. An ashy aftertaste followed each sip, bitter and chalky in the back of Cypress's throat, the same permeating char that followed every morsel the dead consumed. She didn't know if it was a fundamental taste in all food and drink in the Crossing, or if the charcoal chaser came from within. She hadn't met anyone who knew either, and the longtime residents rarely understood the question.

What minutiae would Cypress forget if this purgatory lasted a decade? A century?

Cypress flipped her hood up, surreptitiously studying the barkeep as the elf flitted about, chatting and teasing the regulars as she poured, deftly scooping coins off the bar as she delivered imbibements, rarely bothering to count the currency as she went.

The elf's voice was melodic, lilting, a bit strained when she tried to speak over the din. Her features were delicate, and she had dimples, but a habit of speaking askew so that one was more pronounced. She wore a bemused smirk most of the time, except when she furrowed her brow at a mumbling customer. Cypress noted the fluidity of her movements, that effortless elven grace; a hard modality to learn, but one Cypress had practiced many times.

The barkeep would do well enough for what was needed.

She gestured as the elf made her rounds again, sliding a few more coins onto the bar and finishing her drink.

It tasted like mead, if you didn't remember mead very well.

It couldn't come to that.

"My friends have arrived," Cypress told the barkeep in the gruff, salt-scratched voice of a sailor she'd once known, gesturing over her shoulder. "I'd like to treat them. Seven more, please. And do you have a platter I could carry everything with?"

The barkeep nodded, flashing her a crooked smile that Cypress committed to memory. The elf twirled and began filling tankards from the great cask set into the wall, planting them on a thin wooden tray with practiced efficiency. When she was done, she hoisted the whole thing up onto one shoulder, holding it in place with one hand and scraping Cypress's coins off the bar with the other.

"Sure you don't want me to carry it out, love?" she asked as Cypress reached to take the burden.

"No, thank you! You seem very busy here."

The dead elf laughed. "Not like anybody's in a rush."

"I suppose not, but I'll take it all the same." Cypress shrugged.

"Suit yourself." She delicately transferred the platter over the bar. Cypress shouldered it as she'd seen her do. The barkeeper watched for a nervous moment, but as Cypress stepped away and the drinks didn't immediately tumble to the floor, she turned her attention to other guests.

The Wayward Friar, like many venues in Nox Valar, was a large establishment sized to accommodate lingering crowds with few imperatives to leave. Cypress wound through her fellow souls, working her way to the distant back wall of the building, allowing the tray of drinks to tacitly encourage others to make way. Some instincts held strong in death. The desire not to get doused in sticky beverages was one of them.

When Cypress reached up with her free hand and pulled her hood down, she looked out at the crowd with the smirking visage of the elven barkeeper. A subtle twist of the wrist flipped the hood's fabric from the nondescript gray-brown exterior to a bright, cheerful emerald lining, which she deftly pulled forward to resemble a high collar. A few flicked clasps had her robe flowing open, and she eased from the old sailor's hobble into a confident, sashaying gait as she went.

The bouncer could have been any other patron if you didn't know to look for him. A big fellow with orcish blood stood leaning against an unassuming door, idly holding a mug that he never drank from, and few would notice was empty. Cypress made for him, flashing the elf's cocked grin when the bouncer clocked her approach.

Her path was interrupted by a diminutive human who shambled up to the bouncer while Cypress was still a few yards away. The man reached into his shirt and pulled out a small, neatly tied bundle that he passed to the orcish doorman. He reached for the door, but an orcish hand the size of his head reached out and stopped him cold.

"Hold up," the bouncer said. "Need to check your cover."

"T-they're good," the man stammered. "I was told that should—"

"'Ravel what you were told," the orc grunted, dumping the contents of the bundle into his palm. He squinted at them before rolling his eyes and flicking a trio of shiny coins unceremoniously back at the would-be entrant.

The man made a sound of protest as they bounced off his chest and clinked to the ground. One rolled a few feet as he scrambled to recollect it.

The bouncer sighed, something like long-worn pity in his eyes. "Lasters won't get you in here, no matter how many you bring. Someone was putting you on."

The man grumbled in meek defiance and shuffled off, disappearing into the crowd of the Friar once more. Cypress approached the door.

"Ceil," the big man greeted her. "They got you working downstairs tonight?"

"Covering for a bit. Didn't hear why," Cypress responded in the musical voice of the barkeeper—Ceil, it seemed.

He shrugged and opened the door, holding it wide so as not to jostle the tray of drinks. "Always some damn thing," he commiserated.

Cypress made a noncommittal noise and went through. You don't talk unless you have to when you don't know your face. The door closed behind her.

Beyond, a short hallway led to a wide stone staircase that spiraled down out of view, gently lit with ebbing mage-lights. Flanking the top of the stairs was a pair of doors, one closed and one ajar; Cypress ducked into the latter. It was a private lounge with a few cushioned chairs around a central table. Likely a place for higher-stakes rounds of Purgatory Poker or clandestine conversations when the need arose. For her, it was a convenient place to ditch the drinks and shift.

She'd spent two days considering what face to wear into Paradise. She had a few that would suit, plucked here and there from her life before, but Anastasia had won out. She could appear every inch the haughty, aloof noblewoman when it suited her, and then unleash her mischievous inner trickster like taking off a mask. She was Cypress's paramour and oldest friend; not a face she liked to wear for a job. Anastasia had been the first person she'd ever known who had been enthused with Cypress's true self, instead of regarding her with fear or disdain, and she'd always been thankful to her for it.

But what Cypress needed now was the cold, entitled surety that Anastasia wielded like a scalpel, carving her way through the tangled, backbiting web of high-societal goings-on through sheer force of will. Cypress allowed herself a bittersweet smile as Anastasia's fuller lips replaced the barkeep's hunters-bow.

She missed her.

Cypress reworked her clothing as her limbs morphed, swapping the elf's natural delicacy for Anastasia's calculated elegance. Her clothing was made for this sort of work, consisting of a series of fine, reversible sashes that could be flipped, pinned, and tied in a range of silhouettes; from the shaggy bulk of a traveler on the road to a slinky socialite's gown. It was never perfect, of course, but it needed only not to strike casual observers as out of place. Next, she reversed her robe and clasped it around her waist, creating a floor-length emerald skirt that allowed an occasional flash of Anastasia's calves as they moved. Anastasia was a tall woman—another point in her favor tonight, as it would have been impractical for Cypress to secret a second pair of shoes away on her person. Much simpler to hide her feet and let height do the work. Anastasia herself had come up with that trick, a lifetime-and-change ago.

Cypress tied her top into a simple wrap, looping over her shoulders and behind her neck, creating the general effect of a ruffled evening dress. She pulled Anastasia's long, dark hair into a tail—no time for anything elaborate there, but her goal was to pass unnoticed, not attract attention.

Less than a minute after the smirking elf had slipped into the deserted backroom, a striking young noblewoman emerged, turning hard on her heel and marching down the staircase to Paradise as if the thought that the lowly bouncer at the door could have turned her away had never even occurred to her, and ought not to have occurred to anyone else.

CHAPTER 2

Light came first.

A pinprick exploded into the frigid void, shattering the boundless dark that engulfed the cold embers of her awareness. It was a tiny mote, a candle's flame alone in a universe without stars, made awesome in its singularity. The slumbering notion of her essence drifted toward it, propelled on cosmic tides she could not think to question, nor even perceive. Such was the nature of eternities—freed from time, one tended to get where they were going. Eventually.

Before any part of her roused enough to know the light, it was all around her, and the chilled nothing she had spent an infinite moment drifting through faded to the quickly-scoured memory of a dream. The light surrounded her, stunned her, blazing and bright and as endless as the dark before, and the echoed whisper of her mind had no choice but to perceive it in its fullness and writhe without form against the weight of forever.

Noise followed.

It built by infinitesimal degrees, so slowly that she scarcely noticed until it was a constant, battering roar. She did not think to question whether it, like the light, had always been there, for all things were, weren't, would-be, and had-been in this place that time touched so gently.

The noise was the cacophony of worlds, of every breath, shout, moan, and whisper, every footstep and every hoof-beat and every breeze and every hurricane and every volcano, condensed into a keening instant experienced forever and not at all.

Some instinct, sluggish from oblivion but still primal and reactive, thought that the noise should be so great as to simply unmake her, or that any light so bright should burn her from existence with its simple magnitude, and that the very act of *being* within such a place was a contradiction that merited alarm. But in her formless transcendence, she had no eyes to blind, no ears to deafen, no heart to stop nor body to crush, and thus bore mute witness as her soul passed through the annihilation between all things and carried on.

Then she fell.

The onslaught of light and sound attenuated, morphing as her mind began to knit itself together. There was speed now, a sense of merciless tempo. The light dimmed, then vanished, but it was not the deathless void of before. This darkness held texture and nuance and lacked the unfathomable depth of endlessness.

A light—not *the* light, but mighty in its own way—seared a jagged line across her vision for an instant and vanished. A crash of rolling sound gave her the word for it: lightning. It arced around her in flashes, casting strobing glimpses of roiling, angry storm clouds. She would have believed the storm was as boundless as the light, the void, and the noise she was already forgetting, but as she streaked through the lead-dark mist, she began to catch glimpses of other things, far below but growing closer. She was no longer formless, and though she was not yet so defined as to know her ends, she had ceased to be a sprawling filament of a thing stretched across the cosmos.

Then she was through, bursting from the storm in a blazing streak of silver fire. She hurtled toward an ashen plain covered in fields of delicate golden vegetation that glittered far below. There was a somber beauty to it, she thought, save where an angry gash rent the landscape like a festering wound.

The ground rushed at her, but she felt no fear. This, she was certain, was inevitable. And inevitabilities did not merit alarm. Not here, not now.

When she struck the ground, it was as a thing of weightless energy that splashed amongst the golden wheat like a drop of honey-thick liquid sunlight. Then her wispy tendrils of molten soulfire began to coalesce, refining themselves into bones, muscle, and sinew, taking on the curves and planes of a mortal form. She had been scattered for a flickering infinity across the every-nothing, but she was Here and Now in this place, and to the universe that meant she must also Be.

She kneeled in the swaying wheat. She saw calloused hands resting in the crimson-and-cream fabric of her lap, crisscrossed with scars and porcelain pale. She saw them not with the flitting dream-sight that had marked the fall from above that she was already forgetting, but with mortal eyes that blinked and darted and focused as her attention shifted. She felt the pressure of her weight on her knees, pressing them into the strange soil. She felt a mass against her spine and found a warm wooden haft when she reached back. Curious, she drew it around and found an intricately carved hammer, its head shaped into the screaming likeness of a bird.

Raven, she thought, unbidden, and was startled by the presence of her inner voice. She did not know the hammer, and yet she did—it felt familiar in her hands, like an extension of her body that could be manipulated as easily as a limb.

She contemplated it, intrigued by this faint recognition, and snatches of feeling came to her. There was old fear and well-trodden exhilaration, both distant. There was an under-current of *must-do* that she knew as duty, but she lacked any context of what it meant, and that frustrated her.

There were raw feelings too, flashes that caught in her throat as she turned the glinting raven hammer in her grasp, surprised by their potency. A sickening twist in her gut that felt like betrayal. A hardened hollowing in her heart of trust burned up and replaced with outrage. That fed into fury, so incandescent that her chest heaved as her body lived the memory of it, and her new-made but familiar limbs trembled with the electricity of demanded action. She didn't know where these feelings came from, didn't remember any more than the hammer in her hands and the impulses it sparked, but they were real and visceral and with no other memories to insulate her mind, they threatened to overwhelm her.

A shriek echoed through the field.

Her gaze snapped up, locking on a gangly form tearing through the wheat toward her with ferocious intent. The plants obscured it, but she caught glimpses of sloughing, sagging flesh, over-articulated limbs, and a gaping maw lined with rows of mismatched, jagged teeth. It thundered toward her, salivating and slashing through the stalks, a glowing set of ember-orange eyes fixed on hers.

Instinct drove her where memory failed. She sprang to her feet and charged, Raven twirling into a ready position in her hands. A spindly limb tipped with boney talons swiped at her as she closed with the creature, but she swatted it aside with the butt of Raven's haft and arced the movement around into a two-handed strike. Raven bit into the creature's mis-shaped head, driving it down into its torso even as its skull split open. It staggered, tumbling forward in a heap from its own momentum. She side-stepped and sprang at its back, bellowing wordless defiance as she finished the thing with a devastating strike to the back of its neck.

As Raven cleaved through the creature's bones, its flesh blackened and peeled back from the blow. It crumbled to ashy dust as it fell, leaving a mound that steadily diminished with every stirring of the breeze, the particulates so fine that strands of them hung in the air like wispy smoke.

A soft rustle, barely audible over her heavy breaths, was her only warning. An arm lashed out from behind, wrapping around and trying to crush her throat. She twisted, snapping her head back and feeling the *crack-spatter* as it connected with her attacker's nose. The strike bought her space, and she slipped loose of the attempted grapple and took her assailant's feet out from under it with Raven's haft before bringing the hammer back down for a killing blow. This one had been a man, she saw in the instant before he turned to dust, though his sightless, milky eyes and rotting skin did little to convey any hint of life.

Another shambled through the wheat field, a bloated corpse with a gaping, distended jaw. She made a knife of her fingers and drove them through its rotted face, exploding through the back of its soft skull in a shower of innards-turned-dust.

More came, and still more again, as if the sound of each dispatched monstrosity attracted two fresh horrors in turn. No two were alike—some were recognizable, animated mockeries that might once have been something like her, while others wore twisted, decrepit forms of rot, sinew, fangs, and madness. She battered each down all the same, Raven describing deadly arcs that ended with shattering blows and showers of dust. Soon there were more enemies visible than there were stalks of golden wheat around her, and she slewed sprays of vanquished corpse-dust around with every surefooted step.

She bellowed defiance as more came on, trying with the low cunning of a horde to rush in and pin her down with the weight of numbers. She bashed them back, Raven whirling against a deathly tide that broke upon it in waves of dust. Whatever they were, they sought to harm her, and she would not let them. Wherever she was, whoever she was, they could not have her. If she had to carve a path of destruction from this field through the end of time, she would do so gladly before she permitted these wretched un-things to devour her.

She remembered rage.

CHAPTER 3

Every soul in Nox Valar tried to grapple with death in its own way. Some, upon learning that the City-In-Waiting was not their final destination, found a second wind of piety in their un-life, striving to find and more fully embody whatever virtues (or vices) they thought would guarantee their acceptance in the afterlife of their choice. Others sought to make the most of their time betwixt, delving deep into hobbies, studies, or esoteric pursuits they'd had neither the time nor means to engage with in life. Most simply waited, mourning their demise and hoping for a second chance at life or a hastening of their final passage beyond.

Still others found … something else.

Nox Valar held many wonders. For a certain kind of soul, most of those hid in Paradise.

Cypress-Anastasia descended the final steps, fingertips tracing the curve of an ornate, polished banister as she turned to take in the view with cool disregard.

The first level was a great ring-mezzanine hundreds of yards in diameter, and at least thirty from the foot of the stairs to where one could stand at the central edge and gaze below. The chamber itself, deep within the city's mesa, was a vast, smoothed-rock cavern, lit by a soft white-gold glow set at its apex.

Private rooms and semi-private alcoves pocketed the outer wall, interspersed with the occasional staircase identical to the one Cypress had emerged from, radiating outward like the spokes of a wheel. Many of the alcoves were occupied, some with souls enjoying one another's company, but most hosting mortal souls blissfully bewitched by one of Nox Valar's darker denizens. From afar, Cypress saw a gorgeous and statuesque infernal accept a handful of gleaming coins from a hooded patron before coyly leading them away.

Cypress strode as if she had all the time in the world, studying the scene with the aloof detachment Anastasia would affect when she was at her most dangerous. The mezzanine itself was plush, with thick carpets and luxurious seating arrangements scattered about, but these were just waiting areas.

Entertainers of every description prowled like sharks through the scattered patrons, snaring any who would be enticed for a private moment in one of the perimeter booths. Exotic foods and liquors were on full display at island bars staggered throughout the space—some, it seemed, even imported from the living world, a prospect that Cypress had to honestly pause to consider trying. She reminded herself that it wasn't what she was here to do. Maybe some other day.

A pair of entertainers surprised her as she tore too-hungry eyes away from a display of succulent grilled meats and vegetables she couldn't even name. They appeared as towering, horned figures immaculately chiseled from marble, one blue-white with veins of glittering silver, the other polished onyx shot through with gold. She almost mistook them for gargoyles, the animate stone-folk native to the Crossing, but something wasn't quite right. They would have been the most alluring gargoyles she'd ever seen, for one, all elegant proportions and fluid, delicate grace—but that wasn't what tweaked her perception. Gargoyles were stone through and through. These two were more like stone shells; their eyes and lips betrayed an organic softness, their motions the subtle stretching and twisting of flesh.

The duo were infernals, not gargoyles or fellow dead. She identified them as incubi, and they were dressed like they had only a vague notion of how clothing worked and lacked any notion of modesty. The white-and-silver fiend flashed an alluring smile, kissing the back of Cypress-Anastasia's hand and promising they could be whom- or whatever she desired … for a reasonable price.

Cypress fought down a knowing snicker at the suggestion and fed them one of Anastasia's charming denials. Getting tangled up with hungry demons was a dangerous game in the best of circumstances; today it could be catastrophic.

"Low on Coins?" The onyx figure purred in her ear, a languid fingertip gliding down the side of Cypress's neck, drawing an involuntary shudder. "There are many forms of payment in Paradise, my love…"

Cypress's eyes fluttered, and she forced herself to take a step back. Incubi had a way of making any price seem trivial. "I'm here to meet someone," she managed, putting some of Anastasia's steel into their voice. "I'm spoken for this evening, I'm afraid."

The onyx figure looked unconvinced, but immediately dismissed her as he spied another target, an elderly gnome in merchant's robes looking around the mezzanine with wide-eyed wonder. The fiend moved off without another word, his features shifting toward cherubic and his stature diminishing with every stride.

The white-marble incubus lingered, leaning in close as if sampling Cypress's perfume. "A shame," he growled. "I think we could have fun with *you*."

Cypress-Anastasia swallowed.

"Another time, perhaps," his lips brushed her cheek, a farewell peck that sent a spasmodic jolt down her spine. "Happy hunting." He winked and stalked off to join his kin.

Cypress did her best not to stagger the rest of the way to the mezzanine's overlook, where she leaned heavily on the railing. The banisters were carved to resemble a flowing ocean of ecstatic mortal forms, no two alike and doubtless inspired by millennia of encounters like the one she'd just, barely, refused. She took a moment … several moments … to gather her wits and focused on the levels below.

Paradise formed a vast bowl beneath the mezzanine, divided into a series of terraces upon which glimpses of every kind of worldly delight were visible from above. The immediate next level was flush with banquet tables piled high with delicacies from across the cosmos; sections divided by raised stages upon which performed otherworldly dancers and angelic musicians. Even from this distance, their ephemeral movements and flowing notes resonated deep within, teasing at the ghost of a heartbeat Cypress barely thought to miss anymore.

The next terrace was a series of crisscrossed causeways that separated a multitude of small, sandy arenas. Cypress had learned of these while preparing for this heist. Each ring was bewitched to mitigate all harm to the paying customer and make them mighty within its confines against challengers of their choosing. Souls from all walks of life basked in borrowed martial prowess, striking down the conjured likeness of hated foes, squaring off with one another to duel without fear or limitation, or even challenging monsters and living out unfulfilled dreams of heroism. Cypress spied one customer, a slight, frail-looking thing, punching craters into a dragon's scales with their bare hands. The beast stumbled, fell, and disintegrated as it hit the sand, the victorious soul bellowing in primal victory. They reached into their robe and threw something shiny to the arena's attendant, and the sand began to churn, rising and forming the outline of a new great beast Cypress didn't recognize.

Cypress stepped away from the railing and made her way to the stairs down. Her objective would be farther in, away from the simple delights of lust, gluttony, and glory. Paradise catered to all appetites—but no one made the angel's list for such routine indulgences.

She made her way through the banquet ring and fighting pits with little issue. The mezzanine was full of predators that would weed out the aimless or easily swayed, but down here, the dead moved with purpose. Souls did not make it to Paradise's lower rings by accident, and the house had no need to convince those who were already eager to line up and pay. None of the staff here were souls either. The dead were permitted to serve refreshments as far as the mezzanine, but all of Paradise's offerings beyond that threshold were managed by creatures happy to take payment in more than just Crossway Coins. Cypress had no doubt that a fair bit of Anywhere's merchandise started with a pleading soul in Paradise, desperate to grasp at one more sensation and willing to go into debt with the Guild of Vices to do it. Not that anyone could prove that, of course. Paradise maintained an immaculate façade of legitimacy.

Beyond the fighting pits, she found the possibility peddlers. Not a venue for *true* memories—lest they invoke the wrath of the Godless Monarchy—but the chance for a soul to remake themselves as they desired, and frolic for a time in an arcane simulacrum of their choice. Cypress dismissed this as underwhelming at first, until she noticed that most of the souls here were of the older, more worn cohorts. She realized that for everyone who came here to soar as a bird or roar as a dragon, there were a hundred more who were bartering anything they could just to relive a cherished moment or revisit a regretted choice and take a different path.

The next ring was shrouded from view by spans of black and crimson silks stretched between a sea of wooden poles, arranged so that no one above nor outside could see or hear what happened within. Cypress had to navigate a winding pathway through the outermost silken walls before she found the staircase down. She was close now.

The transactional, opportunistic debauchery on offer in the mezzanine seemed prudish compared to what she found within—as if the marble-skinned incubi above were mere apprentices to the true masters within the ring of silk. Devilish beings, beautiful to the point that they were painful to behold, danced and swayed on stages set at waist height, around which enraptured souls crowded.

Cypress stalked through, leaning into Anastasia's persona as a mental crutch, a pry bar with which to wrench her own eyes away from the performers. She scanned the audience, looking for her target.

The mood of the room felt balanced on a razor's edge. A thrumming, reverberating music filled the air, all notes of charged anticipation and sensual rhythm—but the onlookers were near silent. Instead of cheering or applauding, they gawked in muted awe. Occasionally, one stepped forward and scrawled something onto a piece of vellum set at the head of each stage.

Cypress didn't understand until she had been in the silken ring for almost ten minutes. One soul, a bedraggled man in tattered clothes, wrote something on the vellum sheet belonging to a stunning woman with angelic wings. Her feathers had been blackened and burned and were shot through with hot embers that flared as she danced. Her eyes skewered him as he finished writing, though she could not have seen his message from where she stood.

"My, *my*," she crooned, ending her dance and beckoning him forward with a crooked finger. "What an offer."

Hesitantly, the petitioner stepped up onto her stage, and she flashed a wolfish grin as her ruined wings wrapped around them both. Then they were gone in a torrent of smoke and cinder, and the stage was empty. The rejected onlookers grumbled, shaking heads and rubbing eyes as if emerging from a daze, and began to disperse, seeking other performers.

It took some time for Cypress to comb the area. Offers were made frequently at most stages, but acceptance was rare. Not all performers were as private as the fallen angel. Cypress saw one, a devil of some fashion, drag three onlookers onto his stage at once, and proceeded to demonstrate to the remainder what they were missing with ecstatic delight.

A fourth person attempted to rush the stage as the group began tearing garments from one another, but a column of black-and-red silk lashed out from somewhere high above, cocooning the interloper and dragging them screaming back into the dim heights. Their shrill cry of alarm ended abruptly. The stage's occupants did not even notice the disturbance.

Cypress hurried onward as soon as she realized what was unfolding, though the sounds made by the winners mixed with the permeating music and followed her long after she had left the scene behind.

Not every performer offered such carnalities, though that was the norm. Cypress caught sight of another patron as he stepped onto the stage of a woman who looked near mortal, save for the star-speckled, abyssal voids that cut holes in reality where her eyes should have been. She leaned in close to her charge and whispered no more than two words into his ear. He collapsed to his knees, sobbing uncontrollably—with anguish, joy, or relief, Cypress couldn't be sure, but the void-gazed seer held his wracking shoulders impassively for a time.

Finally, Cypress spotted the general.

General Edwin Harson was a bald, muscular older man in a gray-and-cobalt robe, with a distinctive scar line carving a fierce furrow from one milky eye up and over most of his scalp. He was scribbling a long entry onto the offering sheet of a stage, where an enchanting fae woman danced, twirling a shimmering ribbon and weaving between an arrangement of ornate standing mirrors. Whenever the ribbon or the mirrors would have obscured her directly from her audience, one of the reflections would step from a mirror into full life, and the dance would continue uninterrupted. On certain notes, more than one of her would occupy the stage, dancing in enticing duets or trios before spinning hypnotically away to merge with the reflections again.

General Harson finished writing and snapped his expectant gaze up to the mirror-dancer. Cypress saw the muscle bulge in his jaw when he realized the performance was going to continue unabated, and *felt* rather than heard the bilious curse he uttered under his breath. Another applicant shouldered him aside, snatching a quill from a slot set into the stage and beginning to write themselves.

Harson looked like he wanted to strike the impudent soul down, but a fuming glance upward had him clenching his fist and storming away. He'd seen the silken security in action too.

Cypress followed him at a distance. He stopped to regard some of the other performers for moments here and there, but it was clear from his coiled posture that he was still fuming. His path took him toward the perimeter of the ring, a circuitous route that avoided straying too close to any other stage.

Cypress began to get a measure of him. Edwin Harson, it seemed, was a man for whom the sting of a spurned offer outweighed the pursuit of alternatives. She doubted the general had many successful bids under his belt. Not here. Paradise would gladly trade your Coins for tastes and thrills, but the deeper rings sought more personal sacrifices. The powers that ran such places had no use for Coins beyond the walls of Nox Valar. Given what she'd just seen, and what the angel had shared, Cypress imagined General Harson as a man happy to offer up plenty from others, but very little of himself. No wonder the ring of silk frustrated him.

Easy enough to exploit.

Cypress closed the distance as the general neared the exit. As he reached the outer wall and began winding through the shrouded path, Cypress stepped close.

"My dear General Harson," she said in Anastasia's honeyed voice. "Want something you can offer up next time?"

The general whirled. "Who are you?" he snapped. "I don't know you!"

But Cypress had already stepped away, off the clear path and into the space between the fabric walls. She didn't turn back as the general demanded answers and kept walking.

She heard him follow, curses muffled by their surroundings. Cypress stayed just ahead of his progress, making sure he caught a glimpse before they went around another bend. Between the vague proposition and the shock of being recognized here, Cypress wouldn't have been surprised if he started sprinting and tearing through the walls to get answers.

That wasn't necessary though. She only needed him out of the immediate sight of passersby. And besides, she had no wish

to delve so deeply that their presence antagonized whatever force protected the sanctity of the silk ring.

General Harson stepped around another twist in the flowing path, berating the mysterious woman who had the audacity to address him here without the barest hint as to her identity or intention. She was a mortal like him, he was sure of it, not like the maddening occupants of the—

A small doll sat in the path before him, the woman nowhere in sight. It was simple, a rough-spun and sawdust-filled thing stitched together by inexpert hands, and...

...and he knew it.

He knew the stain on its leg, where he'd dropped it in the mud by the barn. He knew the mismatched stitch that held its imperfectly stuffed arm in place when it had torn and his ma had patched it with the only thread they'd had.

He knew the charring that consumed one side of it, scorched and blackened from the fire, from the night the men with horses and axes had come...

Cypress-Anastasia stepped back into view, surveying the man. He had collapsed, eyes wide and pupils shrunk to pinpricks, his mouth working wordlessly as he stared into nothingness. He'd fallen in a heap, one arm pinned under himself, and Cypress rolled him onto his back. She wasn't sure if loss of circulation affected the dead, but the man would be out for at least a few hours. No point in being cruel.

Cypress kneeled and studied him as he lay there, twitching and gaping. She half-shifted parts of Anastasia's face absent-mindedly, trying to capture the intricacies of Harson's distinctive scarring. Proper asymmetry was tricky to get right; no point in wasting the opportunity to study a new face up close.

When she was satisfied that she'd committed Harson's form to memory, she stood and gingerly retrieved the curious little doll. She wasn't sure exactly what memory it had taken from Harson, but they were rarely happy ones. She caught a mental glimpse as the magic faded, sensory snatches of screaming, crackling, wood-smoke mingled with the acrid stench of burning hair, the iron tang of blood ... and then it was gone, as she wrapped the toy in rune-stitched spellcloth and tucked it into her pocket once more.

Time to go see the angel.

CHAPTER 4

"Well, that's … new," Secan drawled as he surveyed a crater.

It wasn't a particularly impressive crater, maybe as deep as his thigh and a couple yards long. But craters, impressive or otherwise, didn't crop up in the Ashen Fields with much regularity. More troubling still, in Secan's estimation, was the half mile of broken wheat stalks and torn-up soil he saw on the opposite side of the crater, describing a jagged path through the fields.

The disturbance was new, he was sure. Sometimes it was hard to tell in the Fields, without a proper water- or solar-cycle to weather churned-up turf like one expected, but he'd passed this way often enough that he felt he would have noticed a man-deep trench blasted into the ground, or an acreage of broken and torn-up wheat all around it.

That wasn't a pleasant thought. "New" was troubling, out there. "New" tended to mean something had gone wrong, and that could get hairy for a Shepherd trying to track down a soulfall by himself.

The problem was, "new" *also* wasn't much to go on. The Nyxian Guard weren't likely to ride out here and investigate a kinda-weird hole in the ground or a bunch of battered crops nobody was farming, anyway. They'd ask what made the crater, and Secan would have to admit that he had no idea, and they'd say that they couldn't promise when they'd get to it without more information, and he'd be standing right back here a round-trip later tracking down the same soulfall that he was now, no better for the attempt.

He considered trying to wrangle another Shepherd or two to watch his back, but dismissed the idea as soon as it came. There was no telling how long he'd be sitting in the Junction waiting for another Shepherd to happen by with an unexpected abundance of free time, especially not one seasoned enough to help him if they ran into an actual problem. Which would be preferable to dragging a senior Shepherd out here for nothing because he was perplexed by a hole.

"Nothin' for it then," he huffed, hopping into the crater.

He poked and prodded the walls of the trench methodically, but truth be told, they weren't telling him much until he found a trio of parallel furrows that *might* have been claw marks.

"Hells," he cussed, before biting the word off. On reflex, he looked over his shoulder to see if Ma or Pa had heard his slip-up—they'd never approved of colorful language—but of course, there was no one there. Just fields of ashy soil and golden wheat sprawling into the stormy distance. Secan wondered if Pa had known that his soft-spoken, disappointed lectures on dignified conduct and "not let'n Ma hear that kind of talk" were going to condition him well into his afterlife. That had probably been the intent.

He moved on and kneeled at the base of the ditch, examining it. There was a layer that might have been soul-dust at the bottom, but it was so mixed in with the surrounding soil that he couldn't be sure. He chewed his lip and stood, worried that some horror from the Chasm had run a freshly fallen soul to the ground.

He closed his eyes and did his best to still his thoughts. The sense had never come easily to him, and with his mind eagerly turning over the curiosities before him, it took a few beats longer than usual, but eventually, he was able to make out a soft glow, as if he had turned his closed eyes toward a bright light in the distance. The soul was still here somewhere.

That was that then. He hadn't given up on a new-fallen soul yet, and he didn't intend to start today. He wasn't the most elegant at Shepherd-craft in the Crossing, that was true, but he got the job done just the same.

He picked his way up the opposite wall of the crater, catching himself with his walking stick when he slipped and almost went tumbling back in. The tubes holding Ori's scrolls poked into his ribs as he jostled, pinching where he had them strapped to the side of his pack. It was an irritation, but one he found comfort in, due to familiarity.

"Stickman Secan," he muttered, sparing a wistful thought for his older sister's go-to tease whenever he was clumsy, awkward, or "too gangly" in her presence. He clambered over the lip.

A different picture emerged as he followed the trail that led away from the crater. "Somebody put up a fight," he said, as he noted multiple piles of soul-dust strewn about one area of shattered wheat stalks. The Ashen Shepherds would have noticed any recent mass soulfall, which meant most of the mounds had to belong to entities that had already been in the Fields—which, in turn, made it unlikely that he was looking at the aftermath of one undead or eldritch abomination ambushing a crop of fresh souls. The opposite, in fact: he was looking at one or a few souls brawling their way through numerous attackers.

He was looking at a battlefield.

His confusion grew as he pressed onward. He'd have known about a mass deployment or an incursion near his destination before he'd set out. Shepherds were independent operators, sure, but not so isolated that he thought he could have missed news that big. Whatever had caused the carnage around him, he didn't think the common authorities of the Crossing had been involved.

He stopped by one pile of soul-sand, more distinct than most. A footprint was pressed into the mound, humanoid, wearing a flat-soled boot or sandal. Secan had never been a tracker—even when he'd helped Pa hunt, he'd relied on sitting quietly and waiting for animals to come to him—but after a decade or three herding souls around the Crossing, he'd picked up some basics. Once he had the first print, he was able to follow the flow of less-distinct impressions around the area.

Whoever had left them hadn't been retreating, he concluded. Their path consistently turned to meet the scrabbling trails of various bestial markings head-on, usually with a mound of soul-dust a few paces away from the initial contact.

The mystery fighter was smaller than him, or at least smaller-footed, but he couldn't draw many conclusions there. One of the senior Shepherds he knew, Caustus, was a diminutive gnome who had spent his life as the highest-paid caravan guard in the Entwined Cities. Secan had no idea where that was, but it sounded very exclusive, and he'd seen Caustus lay out rowdy souls and Ashen monsters with contemptuous ease more than once. Secan had learned not to judge anyone or anything in the Crossing by their size.

Secan followed the trail farther, bewildered by the number of dispatched attackers he was seeing. They converged on the footprints, sometimes one at a time, but in other places, they came in twos, threes, or more. Each ended as a pile of dust, struck down by their intended target and scattered back into the fabric of the Crossing.

The path wove on through the wheat, a ragged wound in the otherwise uniform height of the field. He studied what new details he could, but gleaned little insight. A frustrating quirk of the Crossing, he ruminated—soul-dust left a lot less to mull over than corpses.

Secan followed the trail until he lost it. Gradually, the patches of disturbed foliage and churned turf became less distinct and farther apart, until he couldn't find another. He stood in the last fight scene he could clearly distinguish, pondering what he saw while scratching his head out of habit.

"Maybe they finally got 'em," he wondered aloud, trying to see if one of the dust piles might have been the fighter he'd begun to root for. "Or they ran out of bodies to throw at—"

A susurrus of fabric and the *whisk* of rushing steel were his only warnings. He whirled just in time to see the head of a hammer hurtling toward his skull with deadly intent.

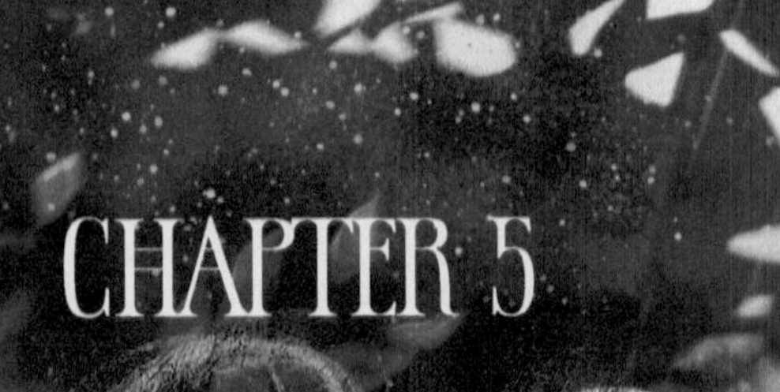

CHAPTER 5

Cypress kneeled on the cool cobblestone, her head bowed and hands clasped. A dozen cream-yellow candles were placed against the wall before her, a few flickering but most long cold. One stood out, crimson red and extinguished, but she did not reach for it yet. With gnarled, knobby fingers, she reverently picked up one of the white candles and lit it from the wick of another.

She wore the face of an older woman, creased and weathered, that she had learned in a marketplace long ago. She held the candle close, mouthing a pantomime of prayer; she didn't believe anyone was watching, but she would never take that for granted while she worked.

This was an alley shrine, one of many that dotted Nox Valar—crude expressions of simple devotion for the souls of purgatory. A symbol of a deity Cypress didn't recognize hung above the candles, crudely etched into the exterior wall of a building that bore no relation to the shrine.

Not every god in the cosmos merited a space on the Road to Eternity, but their followers still found themselves here as often as not. Even faiths with robust representation within the city couldn't keep up with the endless tide of souls, taking devotion and giving sermons in the same manner as everything else in the city: at the end of a line. Thus, the alley shrines—nooks where the faithful could offer their prayers without difficulty, delay, or production.

For Cypress, the shrines were a place to fish.

As she returned the mundane, cream-colored votive candle to the others, she palmed her swath of spell-cloth and deftly scooped the crimson candle into her sleeve. An observer would have been hard-pressed to note the movement; one moment, the crimson candle was there, then an old woman prayerfully placed another beside it, and then the red one was gone.

Cypress hobbled away from the shrine with the exaggerated gait of a soul that had lived with an injury so long it had haunted them after death. Had she known of the Crossing before her own death, she would have wondered why such a soul would wind up here and would have worried that such a distinct disguise would compromise her. Ostensibly, the Crossing was a waystation for souls who may, someday, walk the world of mortals again before their final rest. But in practice, that applied to a great many unlikely candidates—even the very old or chronically infirm might be resurrected after death if they possessed the right connections or influence. Or knew the right secrets that someone may come searching for. And so, Cypress walked, wearing a mask of great age, and no one in Nox Valar marked her as out of place.

She made her way into the shadow of a breezeway between two slate-colored buildings, huddling into the corner. Safe enough from prying eyes and hidden from any Gargoyle who might be passing above, she shifted, calling up the visage of Rydan, a young blacksmith she'd known in life. Her back straightened, the wispy gray strands of hair that hung down into her face darkened and retracted, and her atrophied frame filled out with the muscled tone of youth. With a few quick adjustments and reversals of her manifold robe, she cut a completely different figure than who she'd entered as.

She waited until a few other souls had passed through the breezeway, just in case someone had been watching for the doddering old woman to reemerge, and then slipped out as Rydan. She moved swiftly through the city, though she was careful never to take a direct route toward her ultimate destination. Rydan stopped to ogle at strange or exotic wares in storefronts, stared bewildered at the teeming mass of myriad dead moving through the most crowded thoroughfares, and gawked openly when he passed the soul of a warrior bedecked in intricate, ornate battle armor. Rydan, the blacksmith, had no aim in Nox Valar beyond taking in sights far beyond anything he would have experienced in life. The fact that his wanderings took him closer to Madrigal's was, to any outside observer, pure coincidence.

Madrigal's was not a fine establishment. It was not, from the outside, even clear that it *was* an establishment, or what kind it could be. But it was a curious one, and curiosity was a motivation that few would find difficult to ascribe to the doe-eyed Rydan. The building itself was of the same black-and-white marble as most of the city, with a distinctive saddle roof that the periodic ashfall had left streaked with soot, pierced by a great crooked chimney that sputtered occasional gouts of oily smoke up into the leaden twilight sky. The frosted windows of Madrigal's flickered with inner firelight, though these frequently skewed too far toward sullen reds or curious blues to come from a normal lamp or hearth. A simple pennant above the door declared the name of the place in Celestial, Infernal, Draconic, and a handful of common mortal tongues, though none of them elaborated on what goods or services were offered within. If you had to ask, Madrigal's wasn't the place for you.

Cypress-Rydan slipped inside, bypassing the common room in which a quiet, eclectic collection of souls and other entities drank, spoke, and smoked at a handful of tables around a great central fireplace. Cypress made instead for another door, tucked out of sight around the corner from the entryway. She heard a groaning creak of wood as she approached and felt the small pass-charm in her pocket warm as it worked. The door swung inward by the time she reached it and groaned again when shut, swelling tight against its frame.

A more intimate lounge lay beyond—the true heart of Madrigal's, open by invitation only to those with something to offer. A handful of regulars hunched around one table, bickering over a card game. Madrigal herself stood behind the bar opposite the door, tail flicking as she scanned Cypress.

Cypress found the half-devil attractive in the same way she could appreciate a finely wrought weapon; beautiful in form, perhaps, but dangerous first and foremost. Mads was the scion of mortal and infernal parents, six feet of muscle-laden, scaled crimson. She sported another foot of goat's horns on top of that, and a leathery wingspan twice as wide as she was tall. Madrigal eyed Cypress curiously as she entered, head cocked to one side.

"That you, Cy?" she asked, and Cypress saw her ember eyes flash with cold blue ghost-light as Mads tapped into her gift for true sight. She quirked a smile as she confirmed her guess. "New face?"

"Old one." Cypress shrugged. Mads was already pouring a slug of flavored rye liquor into a pair of tumblers as she approached the bar. Cypress took one and clinked it with Madrigal's before they both downed the shot. It didn't shy away from the ashy flavor of the Crossing, and as a result, Cypress found it one of the less distasteful libations available.

At least it was honest. "Trying not to be the same person in the same place too often."

Mads scanned Cypress-Rydan up and down, whip-thin tail swishing with eagerness. "Does that mean you've brought me something good? I smell something…"

"Maybe. I haven't had a chance to look at it yet."

Mads flashed a hungry grin. "Well, let's get to it then." She looked over at the table of card players. "Hmm. Maybe in the back."

Cypress arched an eyebrow. "Think one of the regulars is a rat?"

Mads laughed. "Don't want a competition."

"You get dibs on the first offer, Mads." Cypress chuckled, following her into a small storeroom behind the bar. "Deal's a deal."

"Damned right." Madrigal closed the door behind them and threw a deadbolt for good measure. "Now let's see it, sister. Whatever you're holding smells *good*."

The room was tight; between the shelves of liquor and sundries and Mads's folded wings, they were pressed close as Cypress revealed the red candle. Mads *cooed* with anticipation.

"Let's see what we caught," Cypress said, unwrapping the spellcloth and gingerly placing one finger against the wax. Mads did the same, and Cypress focused on relaxing her mental defenses. It was almost like meditation; trying to maintain a state of deep relaxation to allow the feathered touches of a foreign mind to seep into hers.

The red candle, painstakingly inscribed with sigils and runes hidden beneath the outermost layer of re-melted wax, was all one really needed to snag a memory, as long as they were patient. An object unusual enough to be noticed, but mundane enough to avoid scrutiny—in this case, a crimson candle in a collection of cream—might spark a memory in a passerby. If they touched the trap, or even got close enough, the magic would do its work, pruning the memory from the victim's mind and coiling it up tight inside the arcane labyrinth inscribed within.

The runes Cypress had devised were nowhere near as potent as the angel's, even with Mads's instruction. Her candle would not have knocked out its victim, and might have been passed over by a hundred shrine-goers before any reacted strongly enough for the spell to sink its hooks in. Whereas tokens like the doll the angel had prepared were bombs to be lobbed at a specific target, Cypress wove traps of subtle bait to be laid and checked later, to see what they had captured.

She never knew what she would get though. Trapping a random memory in this fashion was one part cunning, two parts luck, and the result could often be a meaningless noth-ing-thought that was unlikely to net her much profit. But as Mads touched the candle, her breath caught and her feline pupils widened to gaping voids, and Cypress judged that she might have snagged something good.

She fell into the memory a second behind Mads. She saw her hand, young and tanned, running through the dark curls of a lover's hair. She felt silken sheets swirling around them and smelled the cedar smoke of a low-burning hearth in the room. They rolled. He was above her, backlit by the hearth light that glistened on their sweaty skin. She laughed, joy bubbling up in her chest. She saw candles on the headboard, candles he had eagerly shown her when he returned from the market that afternoon. They were unusual, dyed beeswax instead of the typical raw tallow. The candles flickered as the headboard began to rock, and she felt—

"*Ohh,*" Mads gasped, breaking the spell on both of them. She looked at Cypress with a distant, glazed expression. "You snagged that from a shrine trap? You lucky bitch."

Cypress didn't bother to suppress a smile. "Had to get a good one eventually."

Mads licked her lips, her prominent canines flashing. "You've got to sell me that one, Cy. I'll give you a fair price."

"You get the first offer before I take it to the table," Cypress reiterated. "But you know I need to get as much as I can for it."

"Isn't your stupid pretty-boy paying you enough for whatever you two are cooking?" Mads huffed, but there was no real venom in it. "Let me think. I've got a couple good spots coming up on the Road to Eternity I could part with."

It was a decent offer, but still a lowball, and they both knew it. Cypress shook her head. "You know Azlaru will beat that for anything with a—"

"He'll pay extra for smut, I know, I know," Mads grumbled. "I don't think he's got any Coins for the Horsemen though. Not that he's shown lately."

Cypress chewed her lip. The currency of Nox Valar, like most societies, was based on scarcity—but among the dead, it was the scarcity of moments, not the scarcity of minerals, that gave coinage its value.

In the City of the Dead, home of uncountable souls waiting indeterminate years in limbo, myriad paths to wonder and power existed… but there was a queue for everything that mattered. Lines to speak to greater powers. Lines to learn of your afterlife. Lines to learn of *anything*. Lines even to speak to the living, or at least strike a deal with entities that might deliver portents, omens, or signs. In this place outside of everywhere, no fate was immutable, no secret unknowable, and no wish unfulfillable—so long as a soul had the cunning to chart a course, and the patience to see it through.

The Crossway Coins were tokens. Placeholders for a spot in one line or another, backed by the might and magic of the Godless Monarchy, the House of the Dawn, and every other

Power of note in Nox Valar. For the average soul, Coins were the only currency that mattered.

It had taken Cypress some effort to reckon with the system, an economy where the most valuable coinage—holding spots at the front of the most in-demand lines—had a fixed expiration date. It made everything fluid, relative. But then she reframed it not as cold currency, but as a more elegant barter system, and it made more sense. So long as a soul wanted something, *anything*, within Nox Valar, there was a Coin that would help them get it sooner. Conversely, some souls were required to hold a place in a specific line, by law, decree, or necessity, but they never wished to reach its end. From such a web of desires, commerce of a different sort could be conducted, where not only were the prices debatable, but the value of the Coins themselves ever-changing in the eyes of each beholder.

Of course, Coins weren't the only thing of value in the Sunless Crossing, if a soul was willing to take risks. Cypress looked down at the candle trap, imagining the stolen memory locked within.

"I could throw in a half dozen fivers," Mads added as Cypress considered. "I know they're not what you're looking for, but..."

Fivers—Crossway Coins that were coming due in the next five years—weren't the *most* valuable Coins in Nox Valar, but they *were* highly transferable. They were in a sweet spot: close enough to their due dates that they would be worth something to the right soul in a reasonable timeframe, but not so immediate that their holder ran the risk of missing the date or failing to find a worthwhile trade. Or of attracting less savory souls intent on taking them by force. If she couldn't cut a deal that got her what she really needed, amassing fivers was a good way to stash value until a better deal came along.

Cypress let out a slow breath. "I don't know, Mads."

Mads was looking at her with a quizzical expression. "Bit stressed there, Cy?"

Cy was about to ask what she meant, then realized her voice had shifted away from Rydan's cheerful naïveté. She chuckled when she looked down and saw Anastasia's long fingertips holding the candle and spellcloth.

"Sorry," she told Mads as she completed the shift. "Long day. Guess my mind wandered."

"This one's a *snack*," Madrigal said with approval, appraising her with a swishing tail.

"Old friend."

"I bet."

Cypress smirked. "Anyway. I think I need to take this to the table."

Madrigal groaned and hung her head, defeated. "*Fine.*"

"Sorry, Mads."

"Yeah, yeah. Come on then," she led Cypress out of the storeroom, loosing a sharp whistle to get the attention of her regulars. "Listen up, degenerates. Our friend has a fresh haul for us."

CHAPTER 6

Secan hit the dirt with a collection of curses that would
have made Ma blush.

"Hey now! Hey now! There's no need for—" he was cut off
when he had to make an awkward prone scramble-lunge to
avoid another whistling hammer blow.

The hammer-wielding woman snarled an incoherent
battle cry and arced the weapon around again, carrying the
momentum of the rebound into a follow-up attack. Secan
got one leg under himself and leaped, seeking to put as much
distance between himself and his attacker as possible. She
hounded him, slamming two more thunderous blows into the
ashen soil that he barely managed to twist and avoid. Finally,
he managed to scramble back to his feet, interposing the
length of his walking staff between them.

The fact that she was the combatant he'd been seeking
was obvious. Her white-and-crimson robes were disheveled,
stained with the ash-dyed sweat that streaked her face and
arms. Her breath was ragged, coming in heaving bursts as if
she had been sprinting for hours. Her dark hair, near-black
with a reddish cast in the Crossing's wan light, had been pulled

back into a braid, but now rogue strands spiraled loose from the knots in chaotic tufts.

Her eyes, a cool slate-gray that matched the soot on her face, were wide, but fixed on Secan. She hefted the hammer—a full-sized maul, Secan saw—and circled him warily.

"Peace, please," Secan beseeched. "I ain't here to harm ya'."

She cocked her head, as if struggling to register his speech. *"Who?"* she rasped after a moment, her voice hoarse.

"My name's Secan, miss," he answered, though he kept his stick up to ward her off if she turned again. "Ashen Shepherd, here to guide new souls such as yourself."

Her brow furrowed. *"Where?"* she pressed, a faint wag of her chin indicating their surroundings.

"You're in the Crossing. The Sunless Crossing," Secan replied. "The Ashen Fields, specifically. Name speaks for itself once you've had a chance to look around."

Her expression didn't change, but she paused her slow pacing around him. She glanced down and kicked at a pile of soul-dust with a booted foot. *"What?"*

Secan looked meaningfully at the half-dozen mounds he could make out from their current position. "Well—I can't be specific, you understand, since all the leftovers look more-or-less the same, but—if I had to guess, you ran into a pack of unraveled souls. Maybe some worse things. Awful luck, really, and you have my sympathy. I've never seen so many attracted to one soulfall before."

She eyed him for a moment. Then, with a prolonged exhalation, eased her stance and let the hammer rest on the ground. Secan could practically see her muscles uncoiling, like the tension being eased out of a bear trap.

"Well, I'll call that progress." Secan relaxed, bringing his walking stick back to a more practical position and leaning on it. "May I ask your name, miss…?"

A curious, distant expression crossed her face. "I do not know."

Secan frowned. "...Alright then. Do you know why you're here?"

She shook her head. Secan huffed out a breath.

"Well, it's been a rough start, for sure." He unslung his pack, pretending not to notice when she tensed up at the motion. He unclipped a water skin and offered it up. She eyed him with mistrust.

"You should probably drink," he explained. "And there's not much water within an easy trek of here. I always bring extra, so drink up."

She set her jaw and stepped forward, eyes locked on him, and she tentatively reached for it. Secan made an extra effort to remain still and think unthreatening thoughts. She snatched the water skin away and scurried back, unstopping its neck and giving it a cautious sniff.

Instinct took over, and she was greedily pouring its contents into her lips seconds later. Secan took the opportunity to close his eyes and focus. A bright, warm glow showed through his eyelids, as if a bonfire burned where the woman stood guzzling water and rinsing the ash from dry, chapped lips. He hadn't doubted that she was the new-fallen soul he'd been searching for—any other explanation would only have been stranger—but he was nonetheless perplexed. He'd shepherded all kinds of souls through the Crossing before, but he'd never had a first encounter quite like this.

She finished the water, something like relief washing over her face for just a moment. She stepped forward and offered the skin back to him, which he took with a polite smile.

"Is more danger near?" she asked.

"Hard t'say," Secan admitted. "Things can always surprise you in the Fields. But I expect that everything near enough to notice you would have come to check out the scuffle already."

She nodded, looking around.

"You sure know how to handle that hammer," Secan ventured.

"Raven," she corrected, apparently on instinct.

"Raven," Secan agreed. "Good to have a name for a piece as fine as that. How did you come by it?"

"I do not know."

He frowned again. "There's a bit of a pattern emerging there. You remembered that it was called 'Raven' though? Or at least that it resembled a raven?"

She shook her head. "I held it and it just ... *felt* like Raven." She gestured toward him. "What is yours?"

It took Secan a moment to realize what she meant. He held his walking stick up for inspection. "I suppose I just think of this as 'stick.'"

She nodded. "Raven and Stick. We will fight if they return."

"Can't fault that logic."

"You said you are a soul shepherd."

"I did."

"So, am I a soul?"

"I suppose we both are, technically."

"But only you are the Shepherd."

"I'm one of many Shepherds, miss. But I showed up here just like you at first. Took the Shepherdin' job later."

She nodded to herself, analyzing everything he was saying. "I do not know how I came to be here," she stated, her tone blunt and matter-of-fact. "Or where I was before. Do you?"

Secan doffed his cap and rubbed his scalp anxiously. "I can answer part of that," he began. "We all wind up in the Crossing for a reason. It's kind of a between-place. Some souls need to stop here on their way from one plane to another. A little detour."

"Between where?"

He huffed. He would have preferred to slow-play the typical "bad news, you died" speech with this one, at least until he was sure she was feeling less hammer-y. But keeping her in the dark wasn't going to help anyone.

"Between your life and whatever's waiting for you after, miss."

He waited for the pin to drop. And waited. She just stared at him, as if expecting him to continue.

"Erm... which is to say, you died, I'm afraid. Condolences."

She looked down at herself, then up at him as if he was a simpleton. "I seem alive."

"Yes. Here. Because the Crossing manifests us as... you know, sorry, this is my fault. I usually have a whole explanation for new souls. I got off-script, as it were, and maybe I'm jumbling you up. Let me put it this way: what's the last thing you remember?"

She looked around at the mounds of soul-dust. "Fighting?"

"Before that."

"Raven. And before... falling."

"Of course. And do you remember what happened before your fall?"

"No."

"Try."

She considered, then shook her head. "I fell. I was attacked. I met you. There is nothing before."

"...Nothing?" Secan faltered.

"Nothing." She told him with confidence.

"Oh."

"Oh?"

"That ... may be a problem."

CHAPTER 7

"A delicious dalliance," Nexil bubbled, leaning back from the table. The fiend's mandibles clacked with what Cypress had learned was contemplation. "Such tender emotions. Savory. Sweet."

"Is there an offer coming?" Madrigal pressed, tail thrashing with annoyance. Nexil vented steam in hissing irritation.

Bartering with devils, Cypress had discovered after arriving in Nox Valar, was a tricky process.

When she'd been alive, the sight of any of Madrigal's regulars would have sent her running to rally the nearest order of holy warriors. Denizens of one Hell or another, all of them, with eons of violence, torment, terror, and temptation behind them—directed against one another as often as mortals like her. If her agents had brought her word of even a half-devil like Mads, Cypress would have scrambled to activate well-rehearsed protocols and ready her forces for the worst... but here, she considered Mads almost a friend. *Oh, how death changes the living...*

That wasn't quite right, she realized as soon as she'd thought it. Death hadn't made her more comfortable breaking bread with fiends and angels. The Crossing made those creatures something she *could* break bread with. As always, the simple act of being in this peculiar place changed all the rules.

Not, she mused, *that it makes it any safer.*

Nexil finished grumbling a half-hearted retort to Mads, the bloated, fleshy larva-like demon's many eyes rolling slightly out of sync with one another. Nexil liked to pontificate, to ponderously weigh every potential transaction, but it rarely made any offer. As near as Cypress could read it, Nexil enjoyed bartering more than acquiring—much to the annoyance of Mads and the others, though Cypress had no issue with the grub-fiend driving up her prices.

"Thisss is paltry fare," S'lizh complained from the other side of the table. "We are not interested."

Cypress shrugged, unsurprised. S'lizh was something less than corporeal; she perceived it as a cloud of ink-dark whisps of smoke, though she gathered that it appeared different to others. S'lizh's taste was for the esoteric—their most lucrative offer to date had been for a fragmentary jumble of fear and anxiety that Cypress and Mads had barely been able to decipher as a partial memory capture. No one had expected the peculiar dread-fiend to bid for an experience as physical as the red candle.

Gryort barked a negative as well. Cypress had never been able to make sense of his form; all fur and teeth and extra joints—something between a hyena, a lycanthrope, and an octopus. All she knew was that it paid well for violent memories and raged when anything else was brought to the table. She coached herself through an implacable façade as Gryort bristled and snarled and flecked the room with frothy spittle, until Madrigal snapped a series of harsh commands in his native tongue that seemed to pull him out of his impending spiral. Gryort settled back down, beady red eyes burning and snouts twitching, disinclined to pay the transaction any more mind.

"I could be persuaded to part with some of my collection," Tilla purred, locking eyes with Cypress even as Gryort sputtered through his last aftershocks. She was another half-devil, deep violet compared to Madrigal's blazing crimson, though Cypress had heard faint mention that they were related. Mads had refused to confirm it.

"I'm listening," Cypress replied.

"Sweet Mads would have already offered you something savory," Tilla mused, tapping a taloned finger on her chin. "With a sweetener, before she let you back out here. Hmm."

"I hate it when you do this," Madrigal growled.

"Hate you more, dearest, kiss-kiss," Tilla said without even looking away from Cypress. "How about ten Fivers to start," she continued over Madrigal's audibly grinding teeth. "And ... a favor."

Cypress's eyebrows shot up, and she heard Mads suck air through her teeth, even as the others tittered in amusement. Ten Fivers was a good bit of bartering power to stow away for a rainy day, if not the immediately useful trade she might have hoped for. But the favor... the favor was interesting, and terrifying.

There was every possibility that Tilla could immediately solve Cypress's problems. A well-connected fiend in Nox Valar had access to networks of resources no mortal soul would ever see, which could no doubt be leveraged to accomplish a great many things—but there was a reason you didn't ask devils for favors. Even Madrigal had never offered anything of the sort, which Cypress figured was about the closest expression of friendship she could expect.

Still, it was a potential shortcut around the angel, around Nox Valar's infinite lines, before it was too late ... and all Cypress would need to do would be to out-negotiate an eons-old devilkin to ensure the fine print of the agreed-upon favor didn't invoke some unforeseen consequence. Which it almost certainly would.

"Azlaru. Will. Speak now." Croaked the final member of Madrigal's table. He looked like an old man, impossibly stretched and emaciated, so spindly as he squatted into the chair that his knees folded well above his hunched shoulders, and his tucked elbows resembled knobby wings where they stuck out behind him. Azlaru wore a fine, tailored noble's outfit that looked as if it had been abandoned in a moth-infested, dusty attic for a century, and he spoke in a broken, raspy whisper.

The sightless, void-dark pools that should have been his eyes scanned the room in a ponderous sweep. Gryort's mane shuddered beneath Azlaru's attention, and even Tilla seemed to shrink when it was her turn. From what Cypress knew, the spindly devil was something twisted and old even by the standards of his peers, and she had never seen any of them direct their frequent sniping or petty barbs his way, even once.

"Azlaru knows. What. The shifter. Wants." he declared. Cypress must have shown surprise on Anastasia's face because he continued, "Azlaru knows. Many things. These others do not. See. They play. In many games. But Azlaru plays. *Most* games. And Azlaru. *Watches*. Even more."

"So … what is your offer?" Cypress asked, unable to keep the slight waver from her voice.

"Azlaru likes. This morsel. It is. Sweet. To Azlaru. But it is not. Worth the end. Of the shifter's. Suffering. *That*. Is sweet. As well."

Cold dread washed over Cypress, a sense of marching needles prickling along the inside of her skin. She did not like the idea that a being like Azlaru was enjoying her predicament. Not at all.

"But. The shifter. Should not. Take. The Tilla's favor. It is … succulent poison. It will end. With the shifter. Becoming one of. The Tilla's. *Playthings*. This. Will bore Azlaru."

"Fair point," whispered Mads.

"Azlaru. Will offer. A chance." His spindly fingers rolled, and a gleaming coin clattered to the tabletop. "One coin. *The* Coin."

Cypress's eyes locked onto it. The insignia was unmistakable—the Pale Horsemen. The number was shocking. It would come due in a matter of days.

"You're offering that?" she asked, her voice a whisper nearly matching his.

"No."

A brief flash of anger born of desperation flared in her. "What, then?"

"Azlaru will. *Wager*. This coin. Against your. Sweet morsel." He waved his too-long fingers again, and a deck of cards appeared on the table. "Will. You. Play?"

CHAPTER 8

General Edwin Harson's head swam as he bolted upright, sucking air like a drowned man and trying to shake the fugue of sleep from his eyes. He rolled, spurred to panicked, undirected action by the wave of adrenaline that had woken him—and fell unceremoniously to the floor.

He did not recognize the room he was in. It was dimly lit, with a round table and a handful of chairs. A platter of drinks had been knocked to the floor when he fell, and a lukewarm honey-and-ash-scented puddle was seeping into his shirt. Apparently, he'd been unconscious on the table.

He staggered to his feet, feeling as if his heart was beating out of his chest. He hadn't felt this panicked since—

His first campaign. Their orders were to find the rebels hiding in the village. Someone had attacked them. There was still an arrow lodged in his shield. It had barely missed his head! Bastards, bastards, bastards all! They should burn the whole lot of them—

He hacked and hacked as the cobbler screamed, hot blood spraying his face as his companions shouted. Funny. He'd never expected his sword arm to tire. You just didn't think about that. He heard a whimper in the next room, and tightened his grip—

Edwin doubled over and dry heaved.

His mind was swimming in images of blood, fire, and cruelty. Every ragged breath dragged up a flash of himself, panting, screaming, *laughing* as he drove steel through flesh. He saw a hundred burning skylines, mountains of the dead and rotting; some heaped in grim rows upon battlefields, but more—*so many more*—clumped into frantic piles amid town squares and courtyards.

"*It will be okay, Edwin.*" A voice, no louder than a thought, whispered into his mind.

He ordered his men into the building. Several were weeping, the sniveling weaklings. He expected his orders to be obeyed. He gave strict instructions to the lieutenant—any man who did not engage as directed would join the prisoners at the gallows, and their unit would be lashed until bloody—

He knew them, these vistas of horror. Knew them all. They were memories. He had lived with them for decades, added to them year after year. But now he lived them all anew, each fresh and visceral.

"*I'm sorry it has to be like this, Edwin.*" The voice pressed. "*But you need to See.*"

He dismissed the council, the lackeys, and lickspittles. He brooded over the maps as they filed out of his command tent. They begged him to win a fucking war, and then they had the gall to question every damned move he made to do it... There. There, a city a day's march out, already encircled. The siege would be in the terminal phase by now. He could order a push, and they'd take the walls by dawn before these simpletons even got wind of it. Then he'd march the command elements straight up to the aftermath tomorrow, make them walk through the rubble, see the shit and the blood and the bodies. Then he'd know who really had the stomach for war, and who was playing at it. A grin spread across his face. Where was that courier...

Where once he had looked back at his life with grim satisfaction, a detached sense of duty done, now his knees buckled and his heart fluttered at the onslaught. Each scene was like a hot iron he struggled to wrest from his consciousness, a burning thing he could not bear to let sit and yet could hardly force himself to handle.

"*You See now, Edwin. You See clearly,*" the voice continued; a breath of calm in the tempest of his grief.

Another vision crept in, and Edwin wept before it even resolved itself: a black sword, suspended in darkness. There was no light to discern its shape, but he saw it clearly, an inky void against the pervasive dark. Harson realized with a ragged sob of relief that *this* thought was something cool, a locus of relief that his fraying psyche could latch onto.

The grisly tableaus returned in force, but he held tight to that fleeting image, the black-on-black blade, and it gave him strength. The soothing darkness was a refuge he could retreat to, a respite where he could convalesce for a fleeting moment before the cacophony of memories pressed back in.

"*A man is coming for you, Edwin.*"

He wasn't sure how long he lay there, sobbing and writhing in that forgotten room. The things he saw, the things he *remembered*, made him want to scratch out his eyes, split his own skull, and rip them from his mind. But that lone point of calm kept him sane, gave him something to rally to.

"He's in here," a muffled voice said. At first, Edwin thought it was another memory coming to haunt him, but he heard footsteps as well. A slash of brighter light split the gloom as a door he'd hardly noticed swung open, revealing a pair of figures.

"They brought him up an hour ago. Not sure how long he'd been down there before that," the speaker continued. Edwin saw a stocky orc pointing toward him as he spoke.

The other figure with him was a tall, gaunt man dressed head to toe in grays and blacks, with stiff black hair framing a hawkish face. He dropped a handful of gleaming coins into the orc's palm and said something quiet. The orc shrugged and left.

"Go with him, Edwin. It will be all right."

"Please," Edwin whimpered. "Please."

The tall man cocked his head, looking down at him. "Please what?"

"I don't know," he sobbed. "Something's wrong. Can you help me?"

The tall man kneeled beside Edwin, who curled into the fetal position as he neared. He reached down with a gloved hand and hooked Edwin's chin, turning him up to meet his gaze. Edwin felt as if he was being studied.

"I can't help you," the man said matter-of-factly. "But I'll take you to someone who can try."

"Go with him, Edwin." The voice sounded as if it was moving farther away. *"Go with him. But do not trust him."*

CHAPTER 9

Ominous silence settled over the room, and Cypress felt as if her vision had tunneled—as if the rest of Madrigal's backroom had dimmed, leaving only Azlaru, the coin, and the cards shining vibrantly in her eyes. She nodded once.

"Good." Azlaru beckoned to Tilla's seat, across from him. Tilla vacated it without a word. The others stood and stepped back from the table as well.

"The. Madrigal. Shall deal. Is this. Fair?"

"Yes. That's fine," Cypress managed through Anastasia's clenched jaw.

The Crossway Coin Azlaru had wagered, representing a nigh-immediate meeting with the Pale Horsemen, was everything to her, and the devil knew it. The Horsemen were the messengers of the Monarchy, the only reliable way for the dead to contact the living, the only way for Cypress to warn Anastasia—the *real* Anastasia—about the backstabbing conspirators who'd taken her life before...

Cypress steeled herself. She knew that devils didn't make bets they weren't certain would work in their favor. But that coin could—*would*—save people. Save Anastasia. Getting to the Horsemen had never been the problem, but getting there before too much time passed in the living world…

She had to win.

Had to.

Madrigal assumed the dealer's position, standing beside the table between them and taking up the deck. She flicked through a cursory inspection of the card faces, shuffled the cards with a deft flourish, then placed them in front of Cypress. Cypress cut the deck and Mads whisked them back.

Purgatory Poker was a big deal in Nox Valar, a ubiquitous pastime indulged by nearly every soul in the city. Anything *could* be wagered, but the only thing with universal value to the legion of souls-in-waiting was time, and so Crossway Coins were the chief currency. Most games were played at the House of the Dawn, an upstanding casino that operated with the Monarchy's blessing and maintained its reputation for fairness with the ruthless efficacy of jealous gods.

But with legitimacy came oversight. Standards. Rules. One could not walk into the House and wager a soul, a curse, or a memory—not without drawing the ire of the Monarchy. And so, Nox Valar had a second, quieter circuit of venues, like Madrigal's.

Black market games had their own rules, spoken or implicit. Some offered twists on the standard game. Others were simple threats. Cypress had played here before, but only against other mortals looking to wager in contraband. She'd never dared dance with the devils at the high rollers' table; a venture even the other fiends in the room had acknowledged as supremely foolish and never put much effort into trying to coerce.

"Private game," Madrigal announced to the onlookers, assuming her role. "Both members are in good standing. Set ante. House fee waived from the first hand. Requests?"

They could each make two requests that the dealer would enforce, so long as both parties agreed. They also each got one veto of the other's requests. The dealer had the right to refuse any request that made the game unwinnable for one party, but it was rarely needed.

This was the first real test in backroom Poker. Asking for anything that would grant a clear advantage would result in a veto—and wasting one request. It was a psychological game before the first card was even dealt.

Cypress wasn't foolish enough to try and out-trick an ancient infernal like Azlaru. She decided to try to enforce fairness with her requests. "Scales," she said at once. Mads looked to Azlaru, who accepted the request with an incline of his stretched-out head.

Madrigal snapped her fingers, and a shower of embers burst from them and scattered across the tabletop. In short order, they congealed and began to grow, assembling themselves into a set of wrought-iron merchant's scales, accented with brass hardware that gleamed in the low light of the room.

Cypress viewed them with satisfaction, her chief concern playing against Azlaru satisfied. The most contentious part of backroom Poker was often agreeing upon the value of the wagers. Mortal players could bicker and debate the worth of this-or-that coin, but only fools engaged in that with an immortal. So dealers like Madrigal had devised enchanted scales as a service offering: they would provide a general assessment of value for anything wagered.

No two dealers' scales were exactly alike, and the criteria they used could vary from one illicit game to the next. It was nothing near as consistent or agreed-upon as the House of the Dawn, but at least within a single game, all bets were weighed the same and backed by the dealer's reputation.

"Request from Azlaru?" Mads asked.

"Infernals. High." he said. Mads looked to Cypress for her approval.

Cypress arched a brow at Azlaru. The request didn't affect the game, simply the ranking of suits in the event of a tie.

"Pride," the fiend explained with a shrug and a slow, snaggle-toothed grin. Cypress indicated to Mads that she accepted the rule.

"Dealer rolls," Cypress offered next.

"Foolish. But. Accepted." Azlaru stroked his pointed chin with over-long, spidery fingers. "Weight. Of. Sacrifice."

Madrigal pressed her lips into a thin line and looked to Cypress.

"I ... don't know that one," she admitted. Tilla tittered behind her, but Cypress ignored her. Whatever she lost by admitting ignorance in front of the fiends, it paled in comparison to the risk of agreeing to an unknown condition.

Mads's eyes softened a fraction, but she stayed silent.

"The Tilla. May. Explain. For her. Outburst." Azlaru granted, his tone bemused.

Tilla's mocking laughter cut off, and she switched to a clipped, matter-of-fact cadence as if chastised beyond Azlaru's words. "Madrigal can't offer any advice as the dealer, sweetling. It would compromise the integrity of the table."

"Explain. The. Request." Azlaru's tone didn't change, but the room felt *darker* for a moment.

"Oh, I didn't—yes." Tilla cleared her throat. "Azlaru has requested a modification to the scales. Instead of appraising the general value of a wager, they'll appraise... well, *you*, sweetling. They will weigh your potential relief at winning the pot against your pain at losing."

"Azlaru. Does not. Need. To stand. In lines." Azlaru elaborated, dismissing Tilla with a disinterested flick of his fingers. "I wish. For us to see. How you might. Suffer."

Cypress thought for a moment. Exercising her veto now was a huge risk—Azlaru had just demonstrated that he could make requests she hadn't even known were possible, and there was no way of knowing what he would submit without the threat of a veto. Modifying the scales hadn't actually changed their utility to her either. She'd wanted a way to impartially assess the value of the pot—and she still had one.

"Accepted," she told Mads.

"Requests are in. Scales used, infernals high, dealer rolls, weight of sacrifice. Ante up."

Cypress placed the crimson candle on one side of the iron scales. Azlaru reached forward and placed the Pale Horsemen's coin onto the other side with a soft *click*. The scales wobbled and then tilted decidedly in favor of the coin, the brass needle swinging to point toward Azlaru.

"Your joy. In acquiring. This coin. Is far greater. Than what you lose. In parting with. That sweet morsel." Azlaru grinned wider. "But we. Knew this. The temptation. It is why. You agreed. To play."

"Ante accepted." Madrigal removed both offerings and placed them in front of her station. Then she dealt four cards out, alternating between Cypress and Azlaru.

Cypress gathered her pair before her. The card backs were a dark, luxurious crimson velvet of some kind. She tilted them up to peek.

An ace of infernals—an excellent card, given Azlaru's first request—and a ten of ghosts. A strong single card and a decently high backup, but nothing solid yet. It would come down to her roll.

Azlaru did not look at his cards. That wasn't unheard of: their hands were only partially dealt at this point. Some players took the view that the cards didn't matter until they were all present.

"Azlaru has the higher ante," Madrigal announced. "First roll to him." The crimson half-devil produced an ivory pyramid the size of Cypress's thumb and presented it to the players for inspection. Cypress had seen her use the die many times, and gave it no more than a cursory glance, instead studying Azlaru for any reaction. Had he been mortal, he'd have looked bored, even dismissive, as he waved his approval for Mads to proceed.

Madrigal dropped the pyramid into a gilded cup, covered the top with her hand, and shook it so that all heard the bone die rattle around inside. Then she flipped it onto the table, pulling the cup away. The "one" side of the die pointed up.

Cypress felt a pang of hope deep in her chest but checked it. She could just as easily get the same result. Madrigal scooped up the die and repeated the process, announcing the roll for Cypress.

When Madrigal pulled the cup away, Cypress allowed herself a small gasp. A four!

"Azlaru rolls one. Cypress rolls four," Madrigal narrated. She dealt a singular card to Azlaru, who speared it impassively with a fingertip. Mads flicked four fresh cards to Cypress.

She had to clamp down on any outward expression of hope as she reviewed her cards. There was every chance Azlaru could still win, but she had gained a huge advantage in odds. Both had to assemble the best pair they could from their hand, but she was choosing from six cards, while Azlaru had only three.

Her ace of infernals and ten of ghosts had been joined by a six of ghosts, a two of gargoyles, an eight of celestials, and a ten of gargoyles. She set aside the six and the two immediately; matching suits were fine, but matching numbers were better. That got rid of the eight too. The ace was her highest card, but the matched tens were a winning hand, even in the lower suits. She discarded the ace as well.

She placed her pair of tens face down in front of her and passed the four unused cards back to Madrigal.

Azlaru had not checked his cards; not in any way she could see. He slid one of them back to Mads.

Is he picking at random? she wondered. *Or does he know what he got?*

"Azlaru has the disadvantage. Check or raise?"

Another coin appeared between Azlaru's fingers, rolling across his knuckles, and he drummed them. He placed it on the scale, which tilted in his favor once more.

Mads's eyebrows shot up. "Azlaru raises. Keepers' coin. Ten year term."

Cypress stared at Azlaru, though she couldn't bring herself to meet his pitch-dark eyes directly. Souls waited a century to see the Keepers of the Eternal Sands, sometimes more. The scale didn't tip as far as it had for the Horsemen—the Keepers held no *immediate* value to her—but cutting nine decades off a line was certainly something she could use to fuel any bargain she needed throughout Nox Valar.

He's not going to give anything away, Cypress realized as she tried and failed to glean anything from the fiend across from her. She couldn't read him like another mortal; he was too alien, too inscrutable. She had to press him or leave it to luck.

"I'd have played just for the ante," she ventured. "Why offer anything that valuable?"

Azlaru's terrible grin widened, and he leaned back in his chair. "Why. Not?"

"You haven't even looked at your cards."

"They. Do. Not. Matter to. Azlaru."

"You're the one who wanted to play."

"And Azlaru. Is having. So much. Fun." His grin showed more gnarled teeth than should have fit in his head, she thought.

"We could have flipped a coin if you just wanted to play at chance."

"Do not. Be. *Reductive.*" The room flickered darker, just for a moment. Cypress saw Mads flinch. "Ah. But you do not. Understand. Us. How could you. Understand. Azlaru?

"The cards. Are not. *Interesting.*" Then he was looming over the table, impossibly craned forward so that the tip of his nose was almost in line with the scales. He skewered her with an empty-void stare and gestured with his horrible, reed-fingered hand. "What you. Will risk. *That.* Is interesting. *That.* Is delicious. The play of hope. Of chance. Of misfortune. The *sorrow* it breeds. It is. Succor. It is. Vitae."

Cypress closed her eyes. She had to bet something close to par with Azlaru's Keepers' coin, or Mads was bound to reject it and award him the whole pot. Or she could walk away, forfeit the memory trap *and* her chance at the Horsemen's coin rather than risk any more.

He'd made a good choice in terms of value, she had to admit as she reached for her coin purse. The Keeper's tenner was worth enough that matching it would hurt. But not so much that she'd forfeit. He'd known that. He must have.

She pulled two fivers from her pouch—one was her winning from a previous game against another mortal member of Nox Valar's underworld, the other she'd pulled off one of the angel's targets—and placed them on the scale. They were shorter terms, but not for anything nearly as valuable as the Keepers. The scales tipped back toward the center. "Call."

Azlaru chuckled, a broken, halting sound that she'd have mistaken for illness had she not been staring at his smile. "Raise," he said, pressing his thumbnail into the flesh of his fingertip until a dollop of thick, black blood rose. He dripped it onto the scale, where it remained as a perfect sphere of glossy darkness. "Azlaru bets. A truth."

"What truth?"

"A lie. Revealed," Azlaru explained. "The shifter. Hunted liars. Told. Lies. But Azlaru. Knows. One lie. The shifter never. Suspected."

The scale wobbled, uncertain. "It's hard for me to know what that's worth. I was a spy. I dealt with liars every day. Some of those lies may not matter to me anymore."

"Azlaru. Does not. Speak of. Your. Life." He shook his head. "Azlaru. Knows liars. In the Crossing. Liars. Who will. Hurt. The shifter. Stop. Her."

Cypress fell silent. The scale tipped slowly toward Azlaru.

She contemplated her coin purse for a moment, then put it away. She could put her whole collection on the scale, she realized, and it wouldn't tip her way. Every coin in there was a means to one single end. If Azlaru knew a secret that would foil that, they were all worthless.

"What do you want in exchange?" Cypress asked, unable to hide the dread in her voice.

Azlaru hacked a wheezing, airy laugh for a long moment before responding. "A. Favor."

On some level, she'd known. When you dealt with fiends, that was what it would always, always come to. A bargain that dragged you deeper in, made you desperate for the next one.

"Why should I deal in favors from you when we all knew it was a terrible idea when Tilla offered one?"

"Tilla. Offered. A gilded. Chain. It is. Her way." Azlaru spread his arms wide, gangly limbs encompassing half the table. "Azlaru. Has no. Need for. Thralls. Azlaru. Will not. Perform a favor. For the shifter. The shifter. Will perform one. For Azlaru."

"That's worse."

"It is. Not."

"What's the favor?"

"That answer. Is not. Part of. The wager."

"What could you possibly need me for that you can't do yourself?"

"The shifter. Still. Does not. Understand. Azlaru."

Dread crept into her thoughts, her subconscious alarms screaming that she'd already been trapped, but she didn't know the extent of the damage yet.

Azlaru didn't care about the details. Azlaru cared about the suffering. The favor wouldn't be about the utility, it would be about making sure it hurt her.

"I have conditions."

"Good." Azlaru leaned in again, that grin so wide she thought his whole head might split. "You become. More interesting."

"Your favor cannot affect the living. You cannot invoke it before I am able to send word to them."

"You begin. To learn." He nodded. "Go. On."

"If you don't call it in within a year from this moment, it's voided."

"Ten. Years."

"Two."

"Ten."

Cypress hesitated. "Five. Against all my better judgment, you'll take five years, or I'll forfeit this match right now. You can keep the smut."

Azlaru nodded to Madrigal. "This. Is. Acceptable."

Mads gave Cypress a pitying look and produced a delicate brass needle. Cypress took it, pricked her fingertip, and squeezed a drop of crimson onto the scale. It balanced once more. "Call."

"Enough. Fun," Azlaru declared. "Call."

Cypress picked up her two cards but waited before she flipped them. "One question," she said. "You said I was foolish for letting the dealer roll. Why?"

"You. Made requests. To keep. The game. *Fair*." Azlaru's smirk didn't fade as he explained. "It was. A waste. Azlaru. Does not. Cheat. It spoils. The flavor. You have to. Have. A real chance. Or your sorrow. Is hollow."

"Why your requests then?"

"Azlaru. Makes requests. That make. The game. More fun. For Azlaru."

"Duly noted," she muttered, trying to ignore the pit in her stomach. She flipped her hand unceremoniously onto the tabletop. "Pair of tens."

"A decent. Hand." Azlaru slowly flipped his cards over and splayed them out for all to see. "It seems. Azlaru. Was dealt. A queen of ghosts. And. A queen. Of angels."

Cypress's heart fell through the floor.

"Delicious."

The scales vanished in a flash of embers, as did the cumulative pot.

"An interesting. Game. Shifter." Azlaru collected his card deck from Madrigal and began to shuffle it with great deliberation. "Azlaru looks forward. To playing. Again. But now. You have. A visitor."

The gnawing despair inside her seemed to dampen by degrees as she heard footsteps from the hall. By the time the door opened, the sting of the loss to Azlaru felt almost like a distant memory, rather than an immediate fear.

The angel had come to Madrigal's.

CHAPTER 10

Secan was having a bad day.

Jagged talons frayed the hem of his cloak as he dove to the ground. He tasted ashy grit as he struggled to catch his breath, hauling himself away from his attacker in an undignified scramble.

The nameless soul he'd come to shepherd slammed her way into the fray, Raven sweeping up into an underhanded strike that sent the taloned death-beast reeling. She pivoted, letting the hammer's momentum carry her into a fluid downward blow, bashing it across its malformed, hulking shoulders.

Secan didn't have time to admire her prowess. A swarm of fist-sized, oily blobs were rushing at him, the only feature creasing their iridescent slime-skin a gaping maw lined with razor teeth. He backpedaled and put the newly dubbed Stick to work, swatting at the horrid little things as they charged, intent on ripping chunks from his flesh. Each of them popped when struck, exploding into sticky globules of sludge that only transitioned to the dry ash-sand of death when it finally hit the ground.

A gurgling moan sounded behind him, and Secan caught a spray of particulates across his back as his companion dispatched their larger quarry. The swarm proved the greater threat though, surrounding them and pressing in against the pair's frenzied attacks.

"Damnation!" Secan cursed, ripping a precious scroll from where it hung secured to his pack. He broke the wax seal as he did, snapping the parchment to unfurl it and present it to the oncoming horde like a declaration. He spoke the arcane word Ori had taught him, and the faint glyphs embedded in the parchment flared to blinding life.

Lightning erupted from the parchment, blazing forth into the crowd and raking at the onrushing monstrosities with a thousand snaking tendrils of plasma. Then the scroll blackened, starting with the lines of the glyphs and burning outward until the whole thing crumbled to flaky embers that fell from his hands.

A handful of the blob-mouth monsters escaped the blast, but his nameless companion was quick to dispatch them with a series of satisfying stomps.

"That worked better than Stick," she observed, wiping sweat from her brow with one grimy hand. It left a streak of soot in its wake.

"Well, Stick doesn't catch fire after I use it," Secan replied. "And it was a lot easier to come by." Not as trivial as it was when he was alive, given the relative absence of forests in the Crossing, but he wasn't going to complicate the point.

"Do you have more?"

"Scrolls? Some. Not all of them for lightning and whatnot though. A friend of mine made them, but they take a lot of work."

His charge nodded. "For rare use then. That is fine. We have Raven."

"And Stick," Secan reminded her, mostly for his own amusement, when she returned an unironic nod of affirmation. "We should come up with a name for you, since we've already covered the inanimates."

She gave him a quizzical look. "I do not remember my name."

"I understand that, miss, but surely it would still be useful to agree on something to call you? Even if it's just for the time being."

She considered this for a moment, then nodded. "It would be more efficient, I believe."

"Agreed, then. Let's put our heads together and come up with one you like as we walk now. I think we need to get away from here."

They talked softly as Secan led the way through the golden grains and ever onward. Twice in the next hour, he bid them lie low as things rustled through the wheat, and several times more he adjusted their path to avoid shapes glimpsed in the distance.

He'd never had this much trouble getting a soul across the Fields before. The Chasm had flare-ups when it would disgorge a blight of abominations that caused havoc across the plane before the forces of Nox Valar cleaned them up. But this was beyond the pale—the beasts they'd dealt with so far seemed drawn to them like filings to a magnet, and they were unlike anything he'd encountered in the Fields before. Most of the feral horrors one could stumble across out there were of a type: spirits, banshees, and their related ghost derivatives. These were...

Well. "Squishy," he thought.

The consistency of their tormentors aside, they were far from the Lightless Chasm—as far as one could reasonably be, at least. When manifested souls were taking metaphysical pilgrimages across liminal dimensions, time and space got the slightest bit fuzzy, but concepts like "near" and "far" still held enough sway to make that true—and so the sheer concentration of attackers they'd been faced with was alarming.

"Rasa," she said at one point.

"Rasa-what?" Secan asked, distracted by his thoughts.

"I think, for a name: Rasa." She frowned, and a look of uncertainty came over her for what Secan thought might have been the first time since they met. "It's not... not wrong for a name, is it?"

"Not at all," Secan reassured her. "Plenty of names in the Crossing. Souls from all over the cosmos come through here, you know. I think Rasa will fit just fine."

She flashed him a small, satisfied smile. "It's done then. I am Rasa. Unless I remember a better name, of course."

"Well then. It's a pleasure to officially make your acquaintance, Rasa. And we'll try to see to that memory of yours soon."

"Is that where we are going? A place of memories?"

"Kind of," Secan demurred. "We're heading for the Atonement Grove. It's a place for a soul to reckon with its life."

"I do not understand what that means."

"Welcome to the club," he muttered. "It's different for everybody, is what I mean to say. You see reflections of your life, the lives you touched. How ... you died."

"I ... see." Rasa looked pensive.

"It doesn't have to be horrible. Often isn't. How it's presented to you can vary, and the Grove isn't trying to hurt you. It's trying to provide closure."

"I will see my memories?"

"That's the idea. Can't really see how it would get around that. But we have to go there regardless."

"Why?"

"Because a Shepherd's job is to make sure you get where you're going. And the Grove is the first step, even when your memories aren't in question."

"The first step?"

Secan nodded. "We died, Rasa. All of us. That's what the Crossing is, mostly: the place where some souls go between their lives and their afterlives. I don't know where you are on that path yet. Some folk move fast, some folk stay here a long time. But while we're here, we try to make the next steps easier."

"Ah. And atonement is part of this process, I gather."

"It's not quite as dire as it sounds." He shrugged. "Not always, anyway. You get to sit and work through the truths of your life. Can be cathartic, revealing. Guess the gods wanted us to work through the messy bits on our own before we wind up in their pockets."

"Hold." Rasa cut him off, unslinging Raven and pointing skyward. "On guard, Shepherd. I spy more enemies."

Secan followed her gaze, gripping Stick tight and running through which of Ori's scrolls he still had in a mental checklist. He relaxed when he found Rasa's target.

"Looks like a couple of Gargoyles," he told her. She looked to him for an explanation but relaxed her stance somewhat to match his. "Probably headed to the Quarry."

Far above, against the ever-roiling vortex, a pair of humanoid shapes flew past, their great bat wings stretched wider than their bodies were long, bobbing periodically in the storm's unpredictable winds.

"Other souls?" Rasa asked.

Secan shook his head. "They're kind of the locals here, as a matter of fact. One of the only things native to the Crossing. 'Sides the wheat, I suppose. Friendly folk, for the most part. You'll run into a few once we get to the city."

They watched the Gargoyles sail by, their path describing a lazy arc across the sky. The moment was short-lived, however. Secan frowned when he saw the pair bank sharply, then dive, gathering as much speed as they could and vectoring in the opposite direction from where they'd been traveling.

"Something spooked them," he muttered.

The something was revealed in a short time, as they spotted a swarm of smaller shapes darting in and out of the clouds, pursuing the fleeing gargoyles.

"What are those?" Rasa asked warily.

"That, Rasa, I do not know." He gestured for her to get down, and together they made their slow way into the cover of a thicker patch of wheat, their eyes fixed on the drama playing out overhead. The Gargoyles looked to be the faster fliers and soon outpaced the newcomers. The unidentified creatures formed an agitated cloud, the shape morphing and bickering over their lost prey.

"What do we do?" Rasa asked in a deliberate murmur.

"Wait," Secan replied in the same manner. "Whatever they are, they can't have seen us. That, or they don't care for us. So, we just wait for them to go on their way, and then we go on ours."

After a few tense, silent minutes, they did just that. The foiled swarm began to migrate away, dipping in and out of the storm as they fluttered along the edges of the clouds.

"Alrighty. I think we can—" Secan couldn't even finish his thought before the trailing edge of the flock pivoted, a dozen distant specks tumbling into a controlled dive that brought them hurtling toward the Ashen Fields—and directly toward where they were hiding.

"How in the hells did they see us?" Secan growled, frustrated. Rasa provided no insight but moved farther to one side and readied Raven with grim determination.

Secan glanced around for anything he could leverage into an advantage. Whatever these things were, they were flying, and they were coming *fast*. His instinct was to burrow; to get down into a depression or gully and force them into a narrower approach, but such things were few and far between on the plains of the Crossing.

"Sorry, Ori," he muttered to himself, ripping another scroll from his pack. It was one of the first she'd gifted to him years ago, and he'd never foreseen a reason to use it until that moment. So much for a keepsake.

He tore the scroll open and muttered the activation word, pointing the face of it at the dark soil in front of him and focusing on the desired result in his mind's eye. The precious ink of the glyphs blazed bright, and nothing happened.

Rasa shot him a skeptical look. "Perhaps Stick may be more helpful than the papers, after all."

"Wait for it," Secan said, even as the paper started to char and flake away. Sweat beaded on his brow as he held tight to his focus. He tried to ignore the fluttering shapes that were getting bigger in his peripheral vision at an alarming rate.

Just as Rasa opened her mouth to shout a warning, the ground beneath them bucked, and a great mound of ashen soil bubbled up, forming a steep berm almost a dozen feet tall that wrapped around them in a crescent. The spell took hold not a second too soon, as they heard the first of the flying creatures impact on the far side of the berm with a series of wet, muffled thumps.

Secan picked up Stick and threw himself against the newly formed wall, eyes up for what he knew was coming next. Rasa joined him, and in moments they were beset. Any beast that had been aloft enough to avoid impact scrambled to adapt to the unexpected barrier between them and their prey. Most waved off, losing momentum and fighting to regain their altitude even as they circled and sought a better direction of attack. Several landed hard on the berm, clawing their way over the lip to seek the pair out.

It was then that Secan and Rasa got their first clear look at the monsters. Their bodies were twisted, emaciated knots of gristle and sinew, short and unpleasant torsos that were little more than a host for the gnarled joints it took for their limbs to function. Their legs were scrawny, digitigrade things that ended in small, clawed feet. That was in contrast to the enormous fleshy wings that burst from their shoulder sockets, their span wider than Secan was tall. The creatures that landed folded them back and up like hellish sails, skittering forward on their stubby legs and the clawed joints in the middle of the wing-limbs.

Their faces were what horrified and transfixed Secan though. They were human, or humanoid—from the nose up, they looked for all the world like any resident soul of Nox Valar, their eyes bloodshot, wide, and horrified. But from their upper lip down, the flesh gave way to the skull of some great predator, bare-boned and fleshless save for the oversized tendons required to gnash and tear and a long, leathery tongue that lashed to and fro as they vocalized guttural, chirruping nonsense at their intended feast.

"Shepherd," Rasa called as she sent Raven whistling through the skull of the first one that came within reach, smashing it to ashy powder. "I do not remember much. But I am beginning to think I do not like this place."

CHAPTER 11

Radiance washed through Madrigal's back room, much to the displeasure of its denizens. A thrumming chord of awe reverberated in Cypress's heart, but she pushed it down, grappling with a primal urge to fall to her knees and worship. Such impulses did not go well with business meetings. And that wasn't the kind of impression she wanted to give the fiendish regulars of Madrigal's regarding her personal inclinations—though she had to admit that it was a decent balm for the lingering despair she felt after her loss to Azlaru.

The fiends around Mads's table flinched away from the glare, their expressions a mixture of irritation, dread, or hatred. Only Azlaru seemed untouched, as the gangly old monstrosity continued to shuffle his deck of cards.

"Turn the lights down, pretty boy," Madrigal snapped after a moment, squinting toward the door and scrunching up her nose like she smelled something foul.

A warm chuckle replied, the tone resonant and comforting. "As you wish, Madrigal of the Black Bells."

The light eased by degrees, as did the sense of wonder it inspired in Cypress. She had seen the trick before, of course, many times now, and it lacked some of its initial impact upon repeated exposure. But the chord it struck was deep, as if calibrated precisely to affect mortal souls. A cynical part of her suspected that it was, in fact, just that.

Striding into the room with an air of beneficent grace was Dimereial, Angel of Redemption. He wore a simple shift of white silks, belted and broached with delicate strands of gold. Great white wings folded behind him as he walked. He fixed Cypress with a welcoming smile, as if she were an old friend he hadn't seen in ages. "Once more unto the den of sin, eh, dear sleuth?"

It was one of his preferred monikers for her. An odd quirk in a city of oddities; the angel had no qualms about hiring her services as a thief, infiltrator, or spy—but he preferred to couch it in the terms of investigation and discovery. She wondered if perhaps it was too contrary to his nature to openly admit the tawdrier side of their dealings.

So be it, she thought. A client was a client, and Dimereial paid better than anyone.

The angel pulled over a chair and sat beside Cypress at the table, as if he were joining in on any casual gathering of friends and not cutting in on a game among his immortal foes. Cypress found herself sitting between the softly glowing angel and a glowering Madrigal.

"As always, warm greetings to all of you," Dimereial began. "I am sure I am not alone in thinking that I find myself in strange company once again. And I will greet you as I always do, with an offer."

"Go 'ravel your offer," Gryort barked through bared teeth, a shudder running through his spines. Cypress registered mild surprise at hearing the frothing demon employ the common slang of the city. Perhaps he socialized more than she gave him credit for.

"Uncalled for, Tenth-From-Eldest," Dimereial scolded with a wry smile. "But I understand your sentiment. As I know you understand mine. We all have our ways. And so I remind you all: even the wretched can be redeemed. You will find rest and succor in my halls, if only you come to ask."

Gryort made a wet, snorting sound that must have meant something to immortal ears. Dimereial's eyebrow went up a notch. "I haven't heard anyone called *that* in an age. Perhaps I should come by more. It's enriching."

"The road travels both ways, you know." Tilla purred, ember eyes glowering at him. Her tail lashed against the floor, then coiled into a serpentine, contemplative pattern. "We have plenty of kin who used to have feathers."

Dimereial frowned for the first time since entering. "Careful, youngling," he warned. His tone was gentle and carried all the more terrible weight for it. "One pathway to redemption is the *scouring* of sin, you know. Let us not salt old wounds."

He turned to Cypress, a dismissal of the others by simple omission. "Ready, dear sleuth?"

She nodded, looking to Mads for confirmation. The crimson half-devil shrugged, her wings mirroring the motion in her shoulders. "All yours."

Cypress followed Dimereial across the room, to the rear-most corner. Set into the floor there were a series of concentric rings, the widest perhaps ten feet across, and the innermost several feet less. Each ring was less than the width of her pinky, and each was made from a different material. The largest ring was pure silver, the next was sullen lead, then brass, then gold, cold iron, obsidian, and so on; ranging from precious metals to simple bedrock to a few that Cypress could not identify. Each served as a bulwark against a different school of magic or metaphysical concern, all anchored to glyphs, wards, and runic engrams scribed beneath the floor of Madrigal's.

Mads made it known that she was more than happy to unravel any soul who tried to suss out her proprietary formulations. To Cypress's knowledge, she'd done exactly that at least twice. It did not pay to meddle with the businesses of devils.

Dimereial flicked his wrist, and a layer of barely seen dust banished itself from the surface of the rings before he took up a position in the middle of them. "If you would do the honors."

Cypress nodded, producing a concealed dagger from her belt as she joined him, and pricking one of Anastasia's slender fingers until a welt of blood rose to meet the steel. She reached down and touched each ring as she crossed it, imbuing each with an investment of will and vitae.

She felt their workings snapping closed around them like a series of heavy doors, each muting and muffling the world outside as it activated. By the time she touched the last ring and stood, the innermost circumference was the only thing she could see, hear, or even smell.

The angel's gaze held on a point over Cypress's shoulder for a moment, toward where she realized Azlaru remained seated.

"I'll grant She of the Bells this thing. This sanctum is well wrought. Even the old one's presence is but the faintest stain from here." He nodded, apparently satisfied.

Madrigal's privacy-circle-for-hire was guaranteed against any manner of scrying, eavesdropping, intrusion, thaumaturgy, transcription, surveillance, and a dozen other things Cypress couldn't remember or make sense of. What she knew was that everyone in Nox Valar's underworld who was connected enough to know about it trusted her workings implicitly, and that included the Angel of Redemption.

Dimereial frowned as he turned his gaze to Cypress. "What troubles you, sleuth?"

She sighed in response. "I just lost a bet that I think is going to haunt me."

"Such always flows from dealings with devils. Even here." He looked sympathetic.

"I know, I know," she huffed. "But he offered a Horsemen Coin coming due this week. He knew."

Dimereial frowned. "Have you lost faith in our deal?"

"No, nothing like that," she assured him. "But I can't afford not to take every contingency I find either. I could fail one of your jobs. I might not be fast enough."

The angel looked at her with pity in his eyes. "You're lost in the wilds here, sleuth. And I have asked you for faith in She of the Bells' den of infamy. I understand how hard this must be. But I'm afraid you've only harmed yourself."

"Yeah, well. It would have been worth it if I won."

"T'was ever thus." The angel shrugged. "What's done is done, dear sleuth. We must look forward."

"Yeah," Cypress agreed. A wry smile crept onto her face. "First, though, I have to ask about the Bells thing."

Dimereial rolled his hand in a *how do I explain* gesture. "There are a few billion devilkin named Madrigal, or some close variation, when you begin dealing with the greater cosmos. The titles help narrow things down."

"Are there actually bells somewhere though, or is that just arbitrary?"

"Oh yes, very much so. The Third Greater Ring of Black Bells, down in a not-so-quiet corner of a very unpleasant set of Hells. Awful place. It's where she grew up."

"They all have names like that then?" Cypress couldn't help herself, her old spymaster's instinct to acquire and horde trivia against future utility kicking in.

"Their full titles could get a good deal longer, sleuth, but the shortened versions would be: Madrigal of the Bells, Tilla of the Splintered Towers, then Gryort Tenth-From-Youngest-Who-Feasts-Fifth-By-Right. And I'm afraid Nexil and S'lizh have proper names that your ears aren't equipped to hear, so you'll have to make peace with that."

Cypress nodded, fascinated. "What about Azlaru?"

She thought she saw the angel wince when she spoke the word. His eyes darted back over her shoulder again, just for an instant. "That *is* the old man's name. Just that. Please don't say it again. Not in here."

Cypress paused, weighing the implications of that. She was still upset about losing their game, but … maybe it would be best not to do anything that might miff Azlaru, anyway.

"You have it, of course." Dimereial held a hand out.

Cypress reached into a deep pocket sewn into her many-layered robe and pulled out a bundle of spellcloth. "You have this installment of my payment, as well?"

"Do you have to ask?" Dimereial grinned like he'd told a delightful joke. "*Ahem.* Your Queen Anastasia is healthy. She learned of your unfortunate passing several months ago and was distraught, of course, but has comported herself with grace at court. Her inner circle is not part of the plot against her."

Cypress took in each fact as he delivered them, nodding solemnly. She handed him the bundle.

He partially unwrapped it, peeking at General Harson's doll and nodding with satisfaction. "Go on then, ask. I know curiosity is killing you."

Cypress shrugged, admitting the point. "Why a doll?"

The angel held it up as if studying it for hidden meaning. "General Edwin Harson is a vile man," he began. "He has butchered kingdoms for gold, for infamy, and for glory. And now his soul waits in Nox Valar, primed to be inflicted again upon the world if he is resurrected, or to be dragged to a torturous afterlife for his deeds. There, his wicked soul would be another fleck of kindling for the fires, a scrap of fuel burned up to drive the darkest forces in the multiverse. Things that your friends out there know plenty about."

"And so, the doll…" Cypress started, not following.

Dimereial smirked. The expression seemed too coy on his beatific features, too knowing. "The good General dressed up his actions as the duty of being a statesman, but it was never really about that. The fact is, dear sleuth, that as a young man Edwin Harson was hurt, badly. His home was taken, and his kin slain. Edwin saw it all. It burned vividly in his mind's eye, always. A rarer soul may have turned it into a catalyst for grace and empathy. But it was not thus for Edwin. As a leader of men, he acted out the crimes committed against him again, and again, and again, this time casting himself as the butcher instead of the meat."

He wrapped the doll again, tucking the cloth neatly into itself and slipping it away into his robes. "Edwin is a strategic genius, Cypress. You were a spymaster. You know what kind of resources can be found when a king needs to win a war. Edwin Harson will live again, sooner or later. But now he will go forth without this memory, *the* memory, eating at his heart. He will see his deeds for the barbarity that they were. And before his soul next walks the streets of Nox Valar, he will have had every chance to atone, make peace, and be *redeemed*."

"And that's worth the trouble, is it?" Cypress pressed. "You. A celestial. Skulking around Nox Valar's underworld, risking— what, exactly, if the Monarchy catches you trafficking in memories? All to save one soul?"

Dimereial's lips made a grim line, his features drawn. "I know what I'm about, Cypress. Do not think this business is a triviality for me."

Cypress held up her hands in a placating gesture. "Sorry, sorry. Spy, remember? Old habits."

Dimereial inclined his head ever so slightly. Cypress took the hint and let it drop.

"Do you have another job for me?"

"Of course. Five was our deal. Harson was your third."

"Who then?"

Dimereial produced a small leather pouch, cinched with silver thread, and handed it to Cypress. She looked inside without spilling the contents. The inner surface of the leather was painted with intricate, glittering runes. Nestled at the bottom was a small medallion, molded in the shape of a raven with its wings spread wide. It would have appeared silver once, but most of its surface was pitted with tarnish and wear, belaying a more humble material. It had the patina of something well-worn and oft-handled.

Dimereial held out a hand, palm up, and motes of arcane energy flitted into being above it. They coalesced as Cypress watched, forming into the face of a scarred middle-aged woman. Vivid crimson hair was pinned back out of her face, and her gaze seemed to hold Cypress in reserved contemplation even through the illusion.

"High Herald Vessa Theramay. She is a member of the clergy at the temple of the Harbinger, on the Road to Eternity. The 'Bastion of Endings,' they call it. Dear Vessa is a holy woman with some unsavory secrets, who deserves to be unburdened."

"The Road?" Cypress asked in surprise. That was the apex of worship within the city of the dead. It was where things like... well, like Dimereial spent their time. It would make her job exponentially more difficult.

"Is that a problem?"

"No," she said quickly. "Just a surprise."

"Good. Now, your fee."

"You can skip the installments if you just carry my message to—"

"A deal is a deal, my dear sleuth. Five jobs, and then I will ensure you can deliver your words to the living. You have my personal assurance that it will not be too late for your queen." He smiled, but it inspired none of the usual reciprocal warmth in her heart. "Have a little faith."

"Fine." She'd known what his answer would be, the same as it had been for the last three, but she had to try. "Three questions then, answered in total truth."

"Indeed."

"First question: will the army stand by the queen?"

"I suspect you would know that better than I already, spymaster, but I will find out."

"Second question: who of the queen's bloodline is involved in this plot against her?"

"A narrower approach. Interesting." It was a subtle jab at a broadly worded early question, which Cypress didn't find very angelic of him. But she wasn't dwelling on that now. She had enough information for the queen to act on already, if she could only get the message delivered. Duty was satisfied. It was time for other answers, like the one she'd been wracking her mind for since the moment she fell to the Ashen Fields and realized she lived no more.

"Third question." She took a deep breath. "What is the name of the person who had me killed?"

Dimereial's brow rose. "Finally," he said with approval. "You don't wish to know who held the knife?"

"I do," Cypress's words felt bitter on her tongue. "But it may have been a hired job. Some professional. A meaningless name. I won't risk wasting the question."

The angel nodded again, offering no further comment. "Your answers will be ready by the time you complete your task."

"Thanks," Cypress muttered, stowing the spell-pouch he'd given her and moving toward the nearest ring set in the floor, ready to dispel the privacy screens. She'd learned what tone he used when their business was concluded, and so she was surprised when he spoke again.

"Cypress?"

She turned. "Yeah?"

"You asked if it was worth it. The risk. This … *skullduggery*." He looked contemplative. "For the *right* souls, dear sleuth. To redeem them, it's worth anything."

CHAPTER 12

"Finally," Secan breathed, pointing ahead. On the horizon, a burst of varied vegetation broke from the rolling fields of golden wheat and ash. "Atonement Grove, *dead* ahead."

Rasa gave him a blank look. "It looks to be slightly off our previous path of travel, in fact."

"S'fine. That joke was for me," Secan muttered.

The last miles to the Grove were mercifully quiet, a contrast to every other step in their journey thus far. Secan had never seen anything like it; occasionally something dark and predatory wound up in the fields, or something slipped out of the Chasm and got by the Nyxian Guard, but he felt like they were being *hunted*. The things that came for them were nightmares of a kind he'd never even heard of before. Most held some trace of mortal form, but were twisted and warped to monstrous ends. It made him queasy when he wondered at the beasts that held no trace of mortality he could see—were they something Other, or just further gone?

It had been harrowing, to be sure, but not beyond them. They'd carved a path of cindered monstrosities across the Fields, with no sign of aid or any activity at all from the forces that were supposed to respond to such things. He was bruised, battered, and cussing at the loss of so many of Ori's irreplaceable scrolls.

Even Rasa was beginning to flag, though from the way she'd conducted herself thus far, he was willing to bet his last Crossway that she'd been a warrior of some accomplishment in life. Her cream-and-crimson robes were streaked with soot, grime, and sweat, and she bore the multitudinous minor abrasions that were inevitable from close melee. Secan doubted he looked any better—he was certain he'd fared worse, in fact—but he'd avoided checking himself over too thoroughly.

He hoped that their troubles were close to an end. The Grove was a major locus in the Fields, which meant other Shepherds, other souls, and regular monitoring by the Nyxian Guard. Even if some major incursion was underway, the Grove should be a safe enough place to rest for a spell.

"This place will help me remember, you believe?" Rasa asked, chewing her lip as they neared the outer perimeter. He thought it might have been the first time she seemed apprehensive to him.

"One way or another, I hope," he said.

"How does it work?"

"Well, it's part of the whole path us Shepherds help souls like you along. You might be in the Crossing for a long time, or you might only be here for a few days. All depends on your luck and your fate, and I don't have a say in any of that. But while you're here, we—and that's not me personally, but the greater forces that run this place, you understand—we try to make sure you're ready for whatever comes next."

"What comes next?"

"Oh, I dunno."

It took a moment for him to realize that she'd stopped walking. He turned to look back.

"I am beginning to be very frustrated, Shepherd."

Secan frowned. "I wasn't trying to frustrate, Rasa. Apologies."

"You say I am dead. I say I feel alive. You say I am a soul. But I sweat, bleed, thirst, and hurt. You say I am to be prepared for what comes next. I do not know what came before. You do not know what comes next." She huffed a great sigh of consternation, blowing a rogue strand of hair from her face as she did. "You see why this is aggravating, yes?"

"I do, I do." Secan nodded. "And we haven't had a chance to clarify anything yet, we've been fighting for our lives so much."

He gestured to a great tree at the edge of the Grove. Though the Sunless Crossing lacked just that—a sun—the nature of the Grove still lent the tree's overcast pseudo-shade a refreshingly crisp coolness. He sat down, leaned against a trunk, and gestured for Rasa to join him. She hesitated before finding a prominent root and taking up a position at his side.

"We should be safe enough here for a while," Secan explained. "Well past time for me to do some proper Shepherd work, I think. We've covered some in bits and pieces, so I say go ahead and ask your questions and I'll answer them as best I can."

Rasa collected her thoughts, her eyes wandering from him to study Raven, then the tree line as she did.

"I am ... dead," she started. Less a question, more a confirmation.

"Afraid so."

"As are you."

"A while now, yeah," Secan granted with a sad smile. "My baby sister will be older than I was, I reckon."

"I suppose this is not what I think death should feel like."

"What makes you say that?"

Rasa gestured to a bloody abrasion on her forearm that she'd earned diving under a swipe from a gruesome unraveled horror a few hours earlier. "Bleeding. Fighting. I don't remember my life. But these things feel very *alive* to me."

Secan tossed Stick back and forth between his hands, an idle gesture while he considered his words. "I don't mean to get sidetracked, but that's something interesting right there, Rasa. You're speaking from experiences that you can't remember."

"Is that important?"

"I don't know," he admitted with a shrug. "But I think it means that you aren't as memory-free as you feared. At least not as much as you *could* have been. You know how to talk. How to fight. You're pointing out things that don't match your expectations. But the way I figure, you have to *have* expectations to get there."

"What does that mean?"

"I think that your memories aren't that far gone. Maybe someone could bring them back to the surface right quick. I don't know, really. Never dealt with a thing like that before. Just observin'."

She huffed, but nodded. "I suppose that's something then."

"Back to it though. I understand what you're saying. I thought the same when I got here. I'm dead and gone, but I'm still walking around in my body, and it still hurts when I fall down; hardly seems different."

Secan spotted something that brought him a bit of comfort. He got up, walked over to a bush, and came back with a variety of plump, ripe berries. He gave half to Rasa. "Here. Best part about coming to the Grove. Fruit's always ripe, and it tastes like the best you ever had. Eat your fill; it's some of the nicest chow you can find in the Crossing."

Rasa furrowed her brow, then popped a strawberry into her mouth. Her eyes widened, and she tossed another in right after. Secan chuckled as he retook his seat, cradling a shirt-tail full of blueberries.

He ate a handful and sighed to himself, the taste strumming a bittersweet tune on his heartstrings. To him, they always tasted just like the ones on the farm.

He continued, "The Crossing is a special place, Rasa. Not every soul who dies winds up here. Maybe not one in a million. But you and I and everyone you'll meet here did."

"Why us?"

"We don't have a lot of the answers, Rasa—" He held up his hand to forestall her frustrated protest. "I'll tell you what the common thinking is. And what some pretty smart folks I know think. But I just want you to know that there's room around the edges and some people are still trying to make the pieces fit. Fair?"

Rasa chewed her lip before letting out a long sigh. She threw back another handful of berries before she answered. "I will take what you can offer, I suppose."

"The Crossing is a place of waiting, as best we know. For all the souls that don't have such a straight path from life to afterlife."

"I ... don't understand."

Secan laughed, not at Rasa but at the world in general. "I don't think many people do, if that makes you feel better. But from what I'm told, it was like this: gods, fiends, other big powers in the cosmos—souls are important to them. We're supposed to go somewhere when we die, most of us. This afterlife or that. Maybe you're pious, or damned, or cut a deal with a devil, but you're headed somewhere, you understand?"

Rasa shrugged. "The words make sense, I suppose."

"Yeah, you're missing some context there. We'll try to see to that. But the salient point is, souls are headed somewhere. But if that somewhere isn't clear cut for you, if maybe the cosmos hasn't decided where you're headed yet, or you're fated to a resurrection or two before you find your hereafter, or maybe you're due for some third and fourth thing I don't know about—well, then you wind up in the Crossing until you're all sorted out."

"So was the Crossing made by those powers? Gods? Or was it just ... here?"

Secan inclined Stick toward her as if he were a fencer acknowledging a point. "Haven't the faintest," he said through a mouthful. "Know some wizard type folks who've been trying to figure it out for ages. Some of Ori's friends. Might be they can talk to us about how your memory got compromised too. We'll see."

"Alright. So we are dead. And ... here. In this between place, full of those things that hunt us."

"Hardly perfect. But those things are new to me, actually. Going to have to talk to some folks about that. But I gather we're still better off here than some of the alternatives."

"For how long am I to remain here then? Where will I go next?"

Secan barked out a laugh. "I have not the foggiest beginnings of a clue, friend. Something I know for sure is that, for one reason or another, one way or another, there is a *chance* that each soul in the Crossing might wind up back among the living for a spell. Just a chance, mind. Most of the time, it never happens, and the soul moves on once that chance is no longer in play. But so long as there's a chance, we wait here."

"How long *could* that take?" Rasa paused in her chewing, a ghost of dread seeping into her features as she stared blankly back at the path of horrors they'd blazed to reach the Grove.

"Longest I've heard of is a couple centuries," he told her, wincing when her eyes widened in shock. "I know. Big thing to swallow. But usually it's not that long. And the Crossing is a lot more than just the Fields. Plenty of souls never see them again after a Shepherd gets them set up somewhere more comfortable. So don't fret quite yet."

Rasa let out a slow breath, visibly relaxing the tension set into her posture one muscle at a time. She turned to face him directly.

"This has been a fine story, Secan, but what does it have to do with running and fighting and eating berries? Granted, very good berries," she paused, "I think. I don't remember berries. And now you say I have started with the best berries. Secan, you have cursed me to be disappointed by all future berries."

Secan started to reply, then stopped. "Hells, I didn't think of that," he admitted.

"I will consider forgiving you if you get to the point. Why am I ... this? Why do I bleed?"

"Right. Well. I figure souls can't just sit around in jars forever while the universe sorts us out. Maybe we spoil. Or maybe we need to be doing something like living so we can sort ourselves out. So this place came with rules. One of those rules is that you're basically *you*. Almost like you were in life."

"...Almost?"

"Almost," he confirmed, his tone somber. "There's little differences. You notice them less once you start to forget."

"I have a head start there."

"You certainly do!" He laughed. She had a knack for breaking melancholy with blunt observation that he was coming to appreciate. He wasn't sure if it was a quirk of her state or a deep-rooted sense of humor, but he enjoyed it either way. "And if you're ready, we can go see if there's something to be done about that."

Rasa stood and indicated that she was ... after she secured another handful of fruit from the bushes and branches around them. Secan led them deeper into the Grove.

"What should I expect?" she asked, munching on a pear.

"Within the Grove, there is a pool," he explained. "It's special. You'll see your reflection there."

"And that is not a normal thing for water."

Definitely a joker buried in there, he thought. "Your reflection will be... well, 'alive' isn't really the right word, all things considered, but *aware.* It'll talk to you if you talk to it. You sit and have a conversation."

"With ... me."

"With a version of you that's, and I'm quoting the Shepherd's guidebook here, 'free from bias, self-deception, or ego.' It's a version of you that can't lie about your life."

"I assume from context that many souls lie to themselves about their lives."

"I think we protect ourselves in memories," Secan mused. "Life isn't perfect, and you still have to get up every day. So, we see things in ways that let us carry on. But here, we're done with that part. We have a chance to reflect and reexamine."

"That seems uncharacteristically peaceful for the Crossing."

"It's more in line with what most souls get." Secan tossed Stick between hands as they walked, considering his words. "I think ... if it was the gods or the angels or something else that made this place—whoever it was that said, 'No, actually, we should have a Grove with some pretty good fruit and a nice bit of water'—I think they wanted us to have this chance. To see things clearly and make our peace about it all. Then maybe we're a little less changeable about where we're going to wind up afterward. And maybe the time waiting doesn't feel quite so bad."

They walked for a while, the Atonement Grove wrapping them in a comforting, cool embrace. An air of serenity permeated the trees, of finality, purpose, and closure. Secan didn't mention it, but the Grove was a big part of why he'd accepted becoming a Shepherd. The Fields were trying, and he never knew what to do with himself in Nox Valar. But the Grove made sense to him. And there was fruit.

"You think that this reflection of me will have answers?" Rasa asked, a nervous edge in her voice.

"It could. I've never had an amnesiac before," he admitted. "It'll be interesting, that's for sure."

They wound their way through the Grove's meandering paths until they could no longer see the gold of the Fields, and even the ever-swirling sky above was closed off under a ceiling of delicate leaves. Secan kept an eye out for other souls, other Shepherds, but they were alone. That was alright. When he crossed paths with others here, it was always toward the outskirts. The Grove had a way of guiding everyone to a place of solitude within, so that they might undertake their contemplations without distraction.

The path wound on for a while before it deposited them on the bank of a vast, placid pool. It seemed larger than it should have been, given the Grove's external footprint, and Rasa wondered aloud how they hadn't seen it as they approached; but it was always so here. Secan made his way over to the large rock set back just out of earshot from the shoreline. The Grove seemed to know he liked to sit a polite distance away when he brought his charges here. There was always a rock, a log, or a convenient stump.

Rasa approached the water with tentative steps. Secan tried to imagine the prospect from her perspective and admired the bravery there. On the one hand, she must be burning for answers. On the other, she was more-or-less a fresh mind. How would it feel to walk up to a threshold that promised to rewrite everything you knew about yourself? Even more so than the typical visit to the Grove, Rasa was facing down the very *idea* of who she was. There was every chance that she would turn from that water a completely different—

Secan realized Rasa had, in fact, already turned from the water, and was beckoning him over. He frowned and moved to join her.

"I don't normally like to intrude on this part," he started.

"I just need to know how to begin," she explained.

Secan furrowed his brow, not following. "What do you mean?"

She gestured to the water's surface. "You said I would speak to myself. How?"

"I..." he trailed off, seeing what she meant. The normally mirror-perfect surface of the pool was disturbed, simmering as if placed in a great kettle. His reflection was jumbled, a barely distinguishable silhouette, but Rasa's was fully occluded. Murky clouds of silt were billowing up from deep within the pool, covering what little of Rasa's image could be made out with a dull layer of churning mud that disturbed the surface further.

"That's new," he said, kneeling for a closer look.

Then the water reared up and tore him from his feet.

The Bastion of Endings was one of the smaller complexes on the Road to Eternity, hunkered toward the periphery of that venerable route through Nox Valar's heart. But a runt among titans was still a giant, and despite her deeprooted desire to be done with Dimereial's bargains before it was too late, Cypress conducted her surveillance with the level of deliberate precaution she'd once reserved for the most dangerous enemies of her home.

Cypress Monroe had not been a thief in life, skulking about to snatch valuables and trinkets. There had been skulking, sure, she'd be the first to admit that—but high-brow skulking. *Professional* skulking.

Cypress had been a spy. And a damned good one.

Her first pass of the Bastion had been as an elderly man, indistinguishable from the throngs of aspirants who filled the Road at all hours, making their long-awaited appointments at this temple or that or, for most, collecting their day's Lasters and leaving the Road one or two near-worthless Coins richer.

Cypress joined them, going so far as to collect a Coin from the Temple of the Academician before turning back. She kept her expression flat as the Adherent at the outer gate passively handed her the next Laster in the stack, but allowed herself a sigh of disbelief when she glanced at the date marked. Those who sought an audience with the faithful dedicated to learning and knowledge, it seemed, would be waiting near-enough a century. Not the longest line in Nox Valar, but not one for those with an urgent question either.

Over the following days, she found that such waits were more on par for the Road than she'd realized. Every few hours, she would don a new face and make her pseudo-pilgrimage to another of the Road's myriad temples, all chosen solely because they sketched a plausible route from a starting place in the wider city past the Bastion of Endings.

She never wore the same face twice and took care to avoid any that she had picked up since coming to the Crossing. Further, Cypress never stared overlong at the Bastion. She decided the level of "gawkishness" that each face would display on their trip down the Road with a series of coin flips and was strenuous about maintaining it. If Galm, the orcish caravan guard, was a new soul stricken with awe at every mighty edifice in the city, then she spent as much time ogling the Abbey of Reflection or the Hall of the Unsung as she did the Bastion. But if Kester, the impish card shark, was a jaded man with a singular task and no patience for distraction, then she spared no more passing glances at the Bastion than she did for any other sight along the route she walked.

It was arduous work, but necessary, and death brought with it a certain amount of patience. It was unlikely that the Bastion or her target, Vessa Theramay, were alerted to her coming. But if anything went wrong, the scrutiny brought down in the aftermath would be colossal, and Cypress would take no chances. Not on the Road. Not with so much at stake.

Between her excursions, Cypress read. The Harbinger was not a faith known to her, but that didn't mean much. The Road to Eternity was filled with worshippers of gods she had never heard of in life, and the Road was reserved for only the most prominent from across the cosmos—or those with the most weight to throw around in the Crossing's politics.

Nox Valar was a nexus of lives, afterlives, planes, and information. The godly were all too willing to share their dogma with the curious, so that was a simple starting point. Throw in a few Coins to brokers of less available tracts, and Cypress had acquired a decent collection of scripture and theological musings on, by, and for the Harbinger's tenants.

The Harbinger was not what she would call a warm god, but neither did it seem malicious or cruel. It—the deity's gender was rarely specified, and then, contradicted—was a god of omens, strife, and perseverance. It concerned itself with times of great turmoil, prophesied their coming, and carried messages of preparedness and fortitude. When great events were due to reshape a region or people, the Harbinger stepped to the fore, staying prominent during the transitional period before its presence began to wane, often in time with unfolding events on some other frontier. Its popularity ebbed and flowed across time and space as Cypress peeled back the years of history she'd collected, in time with the fortunes of those who wrote of it.

The Harbinger often expressed neutrality, the religion positioning itself as a messenger and source of prophecy. But Cypress was skeptical the more she read. The Heralds—the leaders among the faith—marked the dying of paradigms, true. But they were not impartial, looking at their long history. Most often, they sided with the downtrodden against the powerful, thumbing the scales toward more favorable outcomes.

In the oldest scraps of her collection, the Harbinger had all the trappings of a war god; not only a herald of coming strife, but its catalyst, with the faithful taking to the field of battle to defy and dismantle the order of their age. And Cypress noted with faint amusement that, in those eras where a self-serving echelon of Heralds accumulated power within the church, the prophesied seismic changes of the day tended to focus on their own demise and the reformation of the faith. There was something of a "getting your own house in order" undercurrent to the whole thing that she appreciated.

The more recent dogma had a protective tone, indicating some shift toward palatability within the faith a few centuries past. Cypress saw nothing to suggest whether that had been due to an edict by the Harbinger, or a desire that emerged among the faithful. Regardless of the root, the modern Harbinger was a tempered thing, more prone to guidance than force compared to its early days. Today's tenants preached that change was always on the horizon, and it was the duty of mortals who held that knowledge to prepare others for times of uncertainty. The modern Heralds took on roles as planners, stockpilers, and teachers of resilience and adaptability within their communities.

That was their public face anyway. As Cypress made her painstaking passes of the Bastion and dug into her less-circulated tomes, there was another story emerging between the lines. Some internal sects within the faith had never lost touch with their martial spirit. Cypress saw stronger hands at work in guiding them, perhaps, but no loss of zeal when they were unleashed.

She didn't have a name for this militant wing of the Heralds, and she wasn't sure how they were organized, nor how official or informal they might be. Not yet. But they were there in the margins, she was sure of it. When the church took an interest in events unfolding one way or another, they were not above throwing blood and steel into the fray.

In one singular tract, she found a name. "Proclaimers," she read, attributed to a group of Heralds that had tipped the scales of a conflict in a place she'd never heard of. The text was a journal, translated at least twice, of a common soldier who had fought against them. She wondered if they had ever imagined their words reaching a place like this, if they even had a notion that a place like the Crossing *existed*. She chuckled to herself when she considered it.

With a burgeoning notion of whom she was dealing with, Cypress planned her more direct approaches on the Bastion. Her first move was a simple matter; she donned the guise of an old bookseller and joined the trickle of souls collecting their Lasters for the Harbinger's temple. Collecting a Coin was rarely an illuminating experience, but it was a perfectly acceptable way to get a taste of what lay inside.

The complex, like nearly all of Nox Valar, was an elegant edifice of storm-dark marble. A gently curving wall surrounded the perimeter, funneling all comers to a broad, circular portal that faced the Road to Eternity. As Cypress passed under the grand arch of the gatehouse, she noted a fan of iron rods folded into either side of the gate; a clever, scissoring portcullis that could be dropped down into an interlaced mesh, sealing the entry closed. Massive doors of iron and a wood that she couldn't readily identify were swung wide to the inner courtyard, sturdy things operated by more than simple manpower.

The courtyard was tight, but beautiful in its bleak way. It consisted of an array of small islands, connected by a lattice of fine stone bridges. A surface of smooth, dark water filled the space between them, quietly flowing from some unseen source around the foundation of the main sanctuary and slipping away through grates set into the perimeter wall.

The bridges were arrayed as branching paths, so no straight line through the islands existed. Several other structures filled the courtyard along the shores, but none of the visiting souls made their way toward them, and so Cypress did not either. She followed the majority through a specific path across the bridges, emerging at the stairs of the main building after a minute of wending and winding.

An acolyte in crimson-and-white robes greeted each soul that crossed the final bridge. "Heed the Harbinger, know the change," he said, bored by repetition as he held out a fresh Crossway Coin. Cypress accepted it with a gnarled, elderly hand, bowing her head. She followed the last soul along the shore to another bridge and began following the circulating line along the twisting path back to the gate.

She closed the distance to the next soul as they went, timing it so she was within a few feet as they exited the Bastion. "A beautiful courtyard, wouldn't you agree?" she asked.

The soul glanced back and grunted when he realized Cypress had addressed him. "I s'pose."

"Did you know the Harbinger in life? I confess, I had not heard of the faith until my later years."

The man, who had the look of a fisher or seaman with his leathered skin and wide, soft hat, nodded. "Aye, miss. They founded a temple in my town in my pa's younger days. Preached that the sea was dying. Not a popular lot, in a port city."

"I see." Cypress smacked her lips idly. She did enjoy playing with her older personas. "What brings you here now then?"

He looked downcast, fidgeting with the Coin he'd acquired just before her. "They were right. Nets came back emptier and emptier the last few years. No crab, no shellfish neither. Turned so salty you couldn't hardly swim in it anymore. Neighborhood got rough, people desperate... n'any case, here I am."

"I'm sorry to hear that, young man," Cypress croaked.

"Is the way of it." He shrugged. "My daughter, she listened. Joined the Herald's lot as soon as she was out of the house. We felt betrayed, cussed her for it, but she was stubborn like her old man. Set right to it. Told me 'Da, da you don't need to like it, but you need to be ready...' I should have heeded her. Would have turned out different."

"You couldn't have known."

"That's what I told myself, my first while here. But that's not true, is it? I was warned." He sighed and pocketed the Coin. "Came here to pay my respects. Offer... offer whatever services they might use an old hand like me for. I didn't listen to them in life, but they were right. Maybe I can do something worthwhile here, make up for the squandering. Maybe I'll be here when she comes through someday. Tell her I was sorry."

Cypress patted his shoulder. She felt for the man; she'd paid her dues to Regret since coming here too. "Bless, lad."

Their routes diverged, and she bid him farewell.

Cypress paused once she reached a secluded alley, a place she'd scouted on a previous pass and identified as a good spot for a change of face. Back in Anastasia's form, she leaned against the wall and exhaled for a long, long moment.

She heard a lot of heartbreaking stories in the City of Souls. The old fisherman's wasn't even one of the most harrowing. Hells, it wasn't even the worst thing she'd heard when she was *alive*, not by a long shot.

But sometimes the weight of this place seemed to press down all at once, and it took a moment to pry her spirits back up off the soot-stained stone.

She reflected on the fact that she'd taken Anastasia's form again. When had she started doing that? She used to switch from one face to another, based on the needs or whims of the moment. It was unusual for her to be defaulting to anyone. Dangerous even. Was this some quirk of being dead for too long? An effect of the Crossing itself?

She dismissed the notion as soon as she had it. She'd developed a tic. A comfort form she reverted to in times of stress. And she had been stressed since she'd started working for Dimereial. She missed her younger days with, and as, Anastasia. That was all.

And at least this way, she still got to see her. In a fashion.

"Back to it then," she whispered, pushing herself off the wall and heading toward the street. She plucked a face from her memory at random and made her way back to the Bastion of Endings for another Laster and another look around the place.

It took four days. Four days of careful scouting and observation. Four days working her way closer and closer, studying the guards, the acolytes, and the regulars in the line and on the street around the Harbinger's enclave. Four days of retiring to one of her safe places to study, to learn all she could about the doctrine, lingo, and beliefs of a religion that had developed for thousands of years in places she had never seen. Four days to select the right faces, learn the right habits, and plan the right routes.

On the fifth day, everything went wrong.

CHAPTER 14

"And you just woke up in the Wayward Friar?" Pel Solimo asked again, arching his brow at the subject.

"Yeah. That's the right of it," said the man, not bothering to meet his gaze. When he spoke, his voice was hollow and raspy, and an air of dejected horror radiated from him. A gruesome scar haunted the soul, ripped through a milky eye and up across his bald pate. It lent him a fearsome appearance that his current manner just didn't match.

Pel frowned and flipped through his notepad. "Mister Harson, my colleague told me you were a general?"

"That's true, sir. I think."

"You think?"

"Well…" He scratched the back of his neck absentmindedly. "It's… I don't know what's true anymore, do I?"

"What makes you say that?"

The general shrugged. "It doesn't feel … *right*, I s'pose. You said my memories have been tampered with, yeah? So maybe that's part of it. Maybe someone is trying to make me think I was someone else."

"What doesn't feel right about those memories, sir?"

"I..." The man hesitated, and his gaze fell farther. "I remember all these awful things. Horrible things I saw. Things I did. But I don't remember ever caring."

"I think that may be true for a lot of souls who lived lives like that," Pel said, trying to keep him going.

"Aye, sure. But I can't imagine doing some of those things now. I can't fathom it. The idea makes me ill. So how can it have been me? For so long?" He looked at Pel with a pleading eye. "So it can't have been, right? My mind's been bewitched, somehow?"

Pel placed his stylus in the spine of his notebook and closed it. "That's possible, sir. It's possible. That's all I can say right now."

"Do you know what happened to me?" he asked. "You people are with the Monarchy, right? Can you fix it? Can... can you make these horrible things go away?"

Pel shook his head, rising. General Edwin Harson followed his lead, a timid gesture from a man who seemed lost. Pel showed him to the door, offering a comforting pat on the general's shoulder. "It all depends on what we find, sir. I don't want to offer any false hope. But the Monarchy takes matters of memory very seriously, and I want you to know that we're going to be looking into this closely. We'll see what can be done when we know more. In the meantime, perhaps some of the temples in the city can offer some comfort?"

"Aye, that makes sense. Thank you, Mister Solimo." Harson stepped into the corridor and shuffled down the hall. Pel watched him go from the doorway.

Thrace was in his office when he turned back. Pel didn't jump; he was too used to his partner's unexpected comings and goings to bother. But Pel hated it when he did that.

"Liar," Thrace chuckled. It was an unpleasant, wet noise.

"Cynic," Pel shot back, taking his seat again and kicking his feet up onto the desk. He flipped his notebook open and thumbed through the pages without reading them. It was an idle habit he indulged in when he was thinking.

"You know damn well nobody implanted anything in that old bastard's head," Thrace pressed.

"It's possible."

"It's fucking *not* and you're full of shit."

Pel fixed him with a deadpan stare. "There is no optimism left in any scrap of that husk, is there?"

"Say I'm wrong."

"Say you really don't understand why I don't want to crush our best witness's entire sense of hope before we at least have something to *tell* him."

Thrace glowered. Pel matched him.

They were certainly a pair, Pel told his colleagues. Classic odd-couple: the gumshoe and the fucking nightmare.

Pel had been in his mid-forties when he'd come to the Crossing. A lifetime city watchman, he'd spent his last decade of life as an investigator in Tumblefray. Out of uniform, Pel looked every bit the average man you'd share a story and a pint with at any tavern; a few extra pounds for his years, a haircut that didn't quite hide his bald spot, and kind blue eyes that encouraged conversation. Unassuming, pleasant, and non-threatening. Paired with his ravenous appetite for puzzles and a whip-sharp intellect, Pel had *excelled* in his new career.

The Godless Monarchy had recruited him within a month of his arrival in Nox Valar. As far as any soul on the street was concerned, he was Pel Solimo, just another Pale Horseman—the innocuous messengers and general gophers of the real Powers That Be. Only the privileged, or exceptionally criminal, knew about the *other* Horsemen within that mundane bureaucracy. The ones like Pel. Those who moved unseen through

Nox Valar, the Crossing, and beyond in secretive, siloed teams tasked with the unseen business of the Monarchy.

Pel was not sure even *he* knew what every cell of the Horsemen was tasked with. For his part, he was an investigator, and he was Thrace's handler. Aside from that last bit, which was admittedly a mixed bag, Pel thought there was simply nothing better to do with his afterlife than to continue to pursue the calling he'd felt in life.

Thrace was ... a unique complication.

Thrace was a monster. There was no other word for it. A monster on the side of the angels, sure, *usually*—Pel would grant him that. But Thrace was a soul stitched. What was left of his mortal essence was rattling around in an ever-deteriorating patchwork shell of other souls he'd consumed and assimilated to keep himself going.

Thrace was a *mistake*. A flaw in the cosmos. An undead soul smashed into the crossing by furious divine energy, leaving a collapsing vortex of an anti-mortal that couldn't leave, couldn't move on, and couldn't exist without annihilating other souls. The stitched should never have been a possibility. They were an oversight in the fundamental fabric of the Sunless Crossing, and no one could convince Pel otherwise.

Thrace was a lanky man, a full foot taller than Pel, with stringy gray-black hair that looked like it should snap off in a stiff breeze, and hawkish, avian features. He swathed himself in grays and blacks, always layered and sleeved to hide the telltale malformations that grew more obvious every year. Everything about Thrace was calculated to help him fade into the background, until he wanted your attention. Which, when he did, he got.

For Thrace to exist, he had to obliviate others. That was a fact. If he stopped, he ended. When Pel first learned of those like Thrace, he thought they were among the vilest things in creation.

Then he started learning about what constituted criminality among the already dead. And he'd had to begrudgingly admit that—so long as they were properly directed—having a couple stitched like Thrace around was a net positive. Or at least, a lesser negative.

Trace broke their mutual glowering off first, to Pel's quiet satisfaction.

"Think he's a security risk?" the lanky stitched asked.

Pel tapped his stylus on the page, considering. "I don't," he admitted. "He was so out of it when he got here that he barely remembered meeting you. Thinks we're some bureaucratic sub-department of a department within a department within the Monarchy. I've got Carlow taking him the long way out too. He won't have much to tell anyone besides 'I woke up feeling weird and talked to somebody somewhere.'"

"Fair enough," Thrace grumbled. "And I suppose it doesn't hurt if we wait to tell him that there's no way someone implanted a whole *lifetime* of memories without turning his mind to soup. Not like he's on a deadline."

"We are though," Pel said, accepting the parlay and moving on. It was like that a lot, with Thrace. He'd pick a fight just to fight, but the wind came out of his sails just as fast.

He was a grump.

"I'm assuming you heard the whole interview. What do you make of it?"

"What's this, the fourth one? Fifth?"

"Fifth we know of," Pel said. "Doesn't mean that's all of them."

"Are you suggesting that there might be things happening in a population of fuck-all infinite souls that nobody wants to talk to the fire-and-brimstone death-police about?" Thrace whistled. "*Weird.*"

"Helpful."

Thrace leaned forward and steepled his spidery, gloved fingers. "Wayward Friar's something."

"Is it? Never came up before."

"The Friar's got a staircase," Thrace said simply.

"To Paradise?" Pel flipped through his notes, frowned, and jotted down an addition. "Didn't know that," he admitted.

Thrace stared into the middle distance. He never took notes, but his memory was ironclad. "That's two near Paradise," he said.

"You're talking about … S. Moore? Victim two, a year back. Found near the Copper Welp entrance."

"Yeah. Might be worth another interview with her, see if she and the General have anything in common."

Pel leafed through papers, shaking his head when he found the addendum to that case log. "No good. She's gone."

"She got 'raveled?"

"Nah. Resurrected, three weeks ago."

"Fuck me."

"Not for all the Coins in the Crossing."

"She was here for what, a century? One twenty? And she gets rezz'd a month before she might be useful to us? Fucking Nyxia's got a sense of humor, Pel, I'm telling you."

"Mm, probably," Pel muttered, reading through his notes on the older cases. "Hells, vic three is gone too. Six months ago. Resurrected."

Thrace ceased his ramblings, locking onto Pel with a glare the detective always likened to a dog spotting a steak. "*That's* interesting."

"Ain't it just?" Pel was pulling files from shelves now, tossing them to Thrace, who spread them out on Pel's desk.

"Vic one's gone," Thrace confirmed as Pel continued to dig. "Eight months back."

"I want to look at the 'possible' files."

"Yeah, the maybes. Already doing it." Thrace was reordering stacks of paper as they talked, discarding some with a grunt and nodding as he added others to the growing spread. "Here. Cleric with the fucked name."

"Razamar'tak."

"Your saurian is awful, and that's why I don't even try. But he popped off a week after Dominic and Luslo talked to him. They closed the case before anything else happened."

"That's before our first victim, right?"

"By a full year. Three ... four more possibles in that pile. Three rezz'd. The last one vanished, presumed unraveled."

Pel looked over his work, pointing to one category Thrace hadn't commented on yet. "What about these?"

"Useless. Moved on."

Pel frowned. "Wait. That can't be right." It was the biggest pile on the table.

"Why not?"

Pel began to thumb through the stack. "What's the average time a soul sits in the Crossing before they get to their afterlife?"

Thrace shrugged. "Depends. Days to centuries. No real control over it."

"Yeah, but practically speaking?"

The soul stitched drummed his fingers thoughtfully. "Decades for most, I'd say. Don't know if anyone's done a proper census."

"Someone up in the House has, for sure. You're welcome to fill out a requisition form if you really want to know, but I think we're fine with the broad strokes." Pel sorted the afterlife stack into several sub-categories. "Look. All of these were possible memory victims, we knew that. But here," he tapped one pile, "all resurrected, died again, and then moved on within a year."

"Unusual," Thrace muttered. It sounded like a growl.

"Here," Pel continued, "same story, but all gone in six months. Here, three. Here, weeks."

"All of these folks maybe had a run-in with our memory thief, *then* got resurrected in short order, *then* died again, and *then* went to their afterlives in record time? When the fuck does that happen?"

"That, Thrace..." Pel sat back in his chair and began fidgeting again as he thought. "That's the right fucking question."

CHAPTER 15

Rasa roared as she whirled Raven above her head, then around and *through* the thing that had swallowed Secan. A spray of water followed the hammer's head like a comet's tail, and she had to strain to arrest the unexpectedly retained momentum.

It was like a waterspout sculpted into a lumbering, ogroid form; a whirling vortex of rushing water in the vaguest shape of limbs and a torso, the details merging with themselves and the churning surface of the pool as the thing moved.

Secan kicked and thrashed within the elemental's mass, flipping and tumbling as if caught in roiling rapids. If she didn't save him soon, he would drown, and then she would be alone and hunted in this strange place. She didn't need more than the past day's memories to know *that* would be a much worse situation for her.

Besides, the Shepherd was a decent fellow. Drowning seemed like a poor reward for his efforts.

The elemental lunged, sending a whirling column of water slamming her way. She sprang aside, and the impact splintered a tree trunk with the force of a battering ram.

She dashed along the water's edge with the elemental in hot pursuit. It lashed at her with whip-quick tendrils that crashed against her like cudgel blows when they splashed across her back. Occasionally it reared back and sent another battering pillar of force her way, but that attack was slower, and easy to avoid if she saw it coming.

None of this helped Secan. Precious seconds were slipping by as she ducked and dodged. Raven was a useless weight in her hands, though she never considered dropping it.

She growled in frustration as she slipped another flurry of blows. She was reacting, stuck on the back foot. Her instincts screamed at her to take the fight to her enemy, charge the thing and force a resolution—but she didn't know how to hurt it.

A wolfish grin flashed across Rasa's face at that thought. "I know someone who might, though," she said to herself.

When next the tree-shattering column of water thundered into the shore, Rasa pivoted and charged.

The elemental did not react as a flesh-and-blood enemy might have as she raised Raven to strike; why should it? They both knew the blow would pass through its form without effect. But that's what Rasa was counting on as she heaved the long-handled maul straight through its mass. She wasn't aiming to strike the elemental with Raven's head. She was aiming for Secan.

She saw his eyes widen in alarm the instant before Raven connected, and she had to suppress an annoyed *chuff*. She clearly hadn't sent the hammer's head hurtling his way; a fact made clearer as he folded around Raven's haft and used the momentum of her charge to wrench him free. A little faith wouldn't have been out of order.

Secan hit the ground with a damp *crunch* and a fit of coughing, either from the waterlogging or getting socked in the diaphragm. Probably both.

"Can you kill that?" Rasa asked, dragging the Shepherd to his feet and hauling him bodily back up the bank.

Secan was too busy emptying his lungs and trying to keep moving to answer properly, but he reached back and grasped at where his pack usually hung. It was gone.

Rasa spotted it lying on the ground where they'd initially approached the water and pointed as they ran. "You have a scroll there?"

Secan nodded, but anything he was about to say next was lost. She shoved him away and jumped back as another column of water lanced out, scouring a furrow in the ground where it struck. Secan managed to dive into the tree line, gaining distance and cover from their attacker.

The elemental pursued Rasa as she rushed toward the discarded pack, mud and debris clouding its form as it left the water's edge behind.

Rasa ran, dogged by the monstrosity. Secan's pack was twenty yards ahead. She dodged a crushing blow. Fifteen yards. One of the quicker tentacles broke across her back, droplets spraying past her as she reeled from the blow and fought to keep her feet. Twelve yards. Nine. She heard the elemental's stormlike churn roaring in her ears, felt its spray on the nape of her neck, and juked aside as it lashed out again. Five yards.

Rasa dove the last few feet, tucking into a roll that let her scoop Secan's pack wholly and regain her feet with minimal loss of speed. She spotted the waterlogged Shepherd on the path they had followed through the Grove, beckoning to her with clear alarm.

She sprinted to him, and he was running down the path even before she neared. He was taller than her, downright lanky, but whatever Rasa had been in life, she held the clear edge in athleticism. She caught him soon enough, shoving the pack into his arms in a running hand-off as she glanced behind them.

The elemental had slowed slightly as it left the water, and that had brought them some distance, but it was still giving chase. Rasa had hoped they would be free of it if they could simply leave the shore far enough behind, but they had no such luck. This thing was determined to pursue them, and she had no way to hurt it. She was counting on Secan's bag of tricks to deliver.

Secan, for his part, was tearing through his belongings as they went. A scatter of camping implements and creature comforts clattered to the path behind them as they went, bid farewell by a stream of curses Rasa knew he'd chide himself for using in a less fraught moment.

Rasa felt a spray of water and saw Secan go sprawling as a stone the size of her fist skittered off into the trees. She made to go for him, but another stone whistled past her head, and she had to backpedal.

Peeking from behind a tree trunk, she saw a constellation of stones and branches tumbling around in the elemental now. It raised a pseudo-arm in her direction and propelled another rock on a jet of water. It *cracked* into the tree she was sheltering behind like a slinger's shot, forcing her down. She heard the elemental closing on them.

"Run!" Secan coughed, out of her sight. "Split up!"

Rasa growled but complied, bolting into the trees directly away from the downed Shepherd. Stone shots ripped through the woods, showering her in splinters as she ran. She hooked Raven to its place across her back—might as well, for all the use it was in this fight—and leaped into a depression, dragging herself forward on her elbows as more stones whizzed by above her head.

She reached a tree large enough to stand up and risked a glance. No sign of Secan. The elemental was closing on her, spewing volleys of projectiles to slow her down as it approached. Another ricocheted off the tree she was behind, and she flinched.

"Rasa!" she heard Secan's hoarse voice shout, somewhere perpendicular to the track the elemental was taking. "Have something!"

She didn't bother with any back-and-forth. Rasa launched into a dead sprint, hurtling over undergrowth and shattered branches as she went.

Despite the danger, despite the frustration, something about this felt *right* to her, as if she were most at home in her body when she was pushing it to its limit. While they walked and Secan explained the ways of the Crossing to her, she felt helpless and frustrated. But when they were in the thick of it, sweat pouring and blood pumping, she was at peace. Her muscles knew what to do. Her mind had only to will it, and she was unleashed, a being of instinct and surety.

Of course, she preferred it when she could *hit* the things that were hunting them, but it seemed that was not always a guarantee.

She spotted Secan on the path, scroll in hand. She ran to him, the elemental rushing after her. It was close now, barely a dozen yards away. Secan waved her past him as he raised the scroll, and the rune-etched paper blazed to life.

A thundercrack echoed through the Grove, and a searing flash of lightning impacted the elemental. It recoiled, its surface boiling in a burst of billowing steam.

Then the spell faded, leaving a blurry afterimage in Rasa's vision. The elemental slowed, its cohesive form in turmoil. Then it began to reconstitute itself and advance once more.

"Shit," Rasa hissed.

"Run," Secan panted.

"I assumed," Rasa sighed. And they both ran down the path.

Fewer stones whizzed by them now; whether as a result of the lightning or for some other reason, Rasa couldn't tell, but she wasn't going to question the small favor. They were nearing the edge of the Grove, if she was any judge of distance. Secan continued to riffle through his scrolls, glancing at the markings on each with a growing stream of profanity as he put one after another back into his bag as fast as he could.

"Gats-daym sonofa-twobit thricefucked on a merry preacher's porch—" Secan cut himself off with a howl of triumph as he tore a scroll free from the rest. He ripped the wax seal off with his teeth, snapping it open and spinning around so fast that he fell unceremoniously on his ass. As he sat up, he presented the scroll in the elemental's direction like he was issuing a royal decree.

Rasa skidded to a halt, doubling back to snatch Secan back up if his magic didn't work. She saw fractal runes blaze through the parchment as Secan whispered a mantra of arcane syllables, outlining cascading, angular patterns in blue-white light. The elemental bore down on them, its muddy mass terrible and immediate.

A blast of frigid air cut through Rasa's cloak like a knife, chilling her to her marrow. The air between Secan and the elemental flash-froze, jagged icicles bursting into existence and transforming the tranquil path into a mesmerizing landscape of crystal. The ice grew into, out of, and through the elemental, which cracked and shattered under its own forward momentum. One minute, a sentient waterspout was bearing down on them, and the next they were being pelted with a flurry of hailstones. The main mass of the thing remained more coherent than its extremities, but already cracks were spreading. A piece as tall as Rasa cleaved off as they took in the scroll's effect, and she had to drag Secan back so it didn't smash down on top of him.

"That one worked," Rasa observed, helping him back to his feet. "Use more of those."

"There are no more of those." Secan looked forlorn as the scroll crumbled to ash in his hands, flaking off in bits that were carried away on the wind. "Ori only left me the one."

Rasa patted him on the back, surveying the frozen shrapnel of their kill. "I would like to meet this Ori and thank them, I think."

"She's not around anymore, I'm afraid," he said, a hollow edge of loss in his tone.

"Oh." She wondered if she would have known what to say even with her memory intact. Somehow, she doubted it.

"Well. That was informative," Secan said, his melancholy buried for the time being.

"How so?"

He pointed to the ice. "Elemental, not a soul. Didn't turn into ash after death."

"Also, it was a water monster."

"You're catching on." He chewed his lip. "No elementals in the Crossing though. Had to come from a totally different place."

"Ah. That is informative," Rasa agreed.

Secan looked surprised. "You put it together too?"

"Not even slightly."

He blinked. "Then why—"

"I think I might be funny," she informed him with absolute sincerity.

He was baffled for a moment before a racking cough-chuckle bubbled up from his chest. She cracked a smile in response. "Hells. You just might be."

"What is your revelation then? That this thing came from far away?"

Secan touched the tip of his nose. "Even better. Someone had to bring it here."

CHAPTER 16

"Heed, Loren." The guard nodded as she approached. "What news?"

Cypress returned the greeting, plastering the young acolyte Loren's features with apprehension. "Messages from the gatehouse."

Her plan had begun to form after two days of visiting the Bastion of Endings in different guises. Those without an appointment never made it past the line for Lasters, but the faithful of the Harbinger could be seen circulating the compound from time to time.

The key was the messenger network. Whenever someone outside the Bastion needed to send word to one of the higher-up Heralds, a written message was sealed and left with one of the guards at the outer gate. It didn't take Cypress long to identify the path these messages took; every hour, one of the lower acolytes gathered the waiting messages and took them through the compound, distributing them to their intended recipients. If there were no messages, the acolyte remained at the gatehouse until the next hour.

It was practically a tailor-made opening for her. She focused the final days of her surveillance on that avenue of attack, learning which acolytes performed the duties on which days, what paths they took, and who they talked to. There were portions that she wasn't able to observe, of course. She could time her visits to the Lasters line to coincide with the messenger's rounds, but she couldn't see into the buildings. Still, she was able to determine what buildings they entered, in what order, and how long they spent in each. And, most importantly, she discovered a point of entry.

Because of the peculiar paths of branching bridges that filled the Bastion's courtyard, the message carrier didn't have a direct path between each building in the compound. They had to cross like everyone else, following a circuitous but practiced route. That route intersected with the line of souls seeking each day's Laster for the Bastion.

It took timing, and a bit of luck, which Cypress was never thrilled with. Moreover, it took three tries. But finally, she was in the right place in the line, ten past the hour, when there were no messages to deliver, and acolyte Loren remained at the gatehouse.

But the guards inside had no way of knowing that.

As the crowd of listless souls wound their way through the queue, she'd separated herself from the knot at one of the crossways and walked briskly to the nearest building. Anyone observing the line from that side simply saw acolyte Loren push through, as he did several times a day, carrying a bundle of folded letters. Anyone observing from the opposite side simply saw a slight jostle in the line; hardly a rare event as they picked their way through the confusing network of islands and bridges.

Cypress had walked with purpose through the first building, a mix of offices and archival rooms, always projecting an air that she was on her way to deliver the next letter, but never actually stopping to do so. She was killing time, getting the rough lay of the place until it had been long enough for her to plausibly head to the next structure. It was an efficient layout; several connected hallways with roughly similar rooms between them per each floor, all with modest decoration paying homage to the Harbinger or some significant event of the faith. The only real affectation that gave her pause was the peculiar statues on each floor, depicting mastiffs with the heads of giant ravens.

Some kind of divine servant for the Harbinger? Cypress wondered. *Or just an animal from some world I've never heard of?*

She was careful to follow the route she'd seen Loren take before, as best as she'd been able to determine from the outside. She modified it very slightly to avoid coming within the line of sight of the gatehouse itself.

And so it went, one building after the next, until she'd finally been addressed by a guard several floors beyond the main sanctum, as she left the sanctuary and angled for what she assumed were the Herald's offices in the wing of the building furthest from the courtyard.

The guard gave Cypress-Loren a cursory examination as she stood and waited. A heavy, dark oak door blocked the way, and Cypress hadn't located another path deeper into the building that wouldn't have involved scrambling up a wall and through a window—not something she thought she could do without drawing some attention.

After a moment that felt longer to Cypress than it probably was, the guard grunted and tugged the great door open.

Cypress allowed herself an exhalation of relief as the door closed behind her. Getting this far had not been a given. But now came the dangerous part: she had no idea what to expect this far into the Bastion of Endings, and there was no room for error.

It would have been preferable to lure a target like High Herald Theremay out into the open, instead of hunting her down on her home ground, but Cypress had not come up with a viable way of doing so within any reasonable timeframe. The Herald seldom left the Bastion, and Cypress worried that any event she contrived to draw the Herald out would have created numerous opportunities to hunt her down afterward.

No, she told herself. *It has to be here. If I do it clean, no one will even know anything happened.*

She made her way into the Bastion's back rooms, a series of plushy appointed marble halls trimmed in the whites and reds of the order. The walls were lined with numerous tapestries and paintings, some threadbare and ancient, others freshly made. They depicted great events; always with figures in cream-and-crimson leading throngs of common folk. Some were battle scenes, with armored Heralds anchoring fighting formations and leading charges. But others were more domestic; the faithful securing a home against a coming storm, leading caravans away from a burning city, administering medicine in a plague ward. Always, the servants of the Harbinger appeared as beacons of calm amidst calamity, someone who the fearful could follow for guidance, and the survivors could rally to afterward.

It was a curious faith, Cypress thought as she went. She could view it through the eyes of an idealist; a god and its followers devoted to the perpetuation of order despite inevitable chaos. They did not seek to defy the changing world, but to prepare for it, and ensure that society trended toward prosperity as it emerged from each cycle of turmoil. There was a need for such forces in many places, Cypress thought. Hells, there would *always* be such needs in any given place, eventually. She was enough of a student of history to know that.

She could, however, also turn a cynic's lens on the Harbinger and its flock. By nature, they positioned themselves as figures of importance during the most desperate times. Their creed meant that they did not have to see to the needs or wants of the common folk around them; they needed only to be prepared when calamity inevitably came, and they would never exhaust their welcome. From what she'd read, the Harbinger's church rarely emerged from a transitional age worse than before. It was one thing to act selflessly to help the helpless; quite another to assume—or ensure—that others would be helpless without you. Even after all her research, she wasn't sure which side of that line the Heralds fell on.

A bit of both, probably. But Cypress was *also* enough of a student of history to know that "trust me, I'll keep you safe" was the opening line for every ten-copper tyrant there had ever been.

The halls became busier as she went, but no one paid Cypress-Loren any mind. Other acolytes rushed about in ones and twos, chasing after some task or another. She passed a few Heralds in more elaborate robes, trailed by gaggles of their juniors, to whom they dictated memos or assignments as they walked. She kept her head down and made sure her handful of fake message envelopes were visible, and no one interrupted her. Just another junior acolyte going about a task.

The commotion was a wrinkle she had not foreseen. The Bastion, from the outside, looked as somber and tranquil as any other temple on the Road. Cypress wondered if she'd raised an alarm somehow, but that didn't track. Something had kicked the Bastion's inner circles into motion, but it lacked the frenzied quality of a fresh alert. The Heralds and their assistants were moving with a deliberate pace, not a rush.

They were working on something.

Cypress-Loren had little trouble blending into the hubbub, but it was complicating what she'd hoped would be a methodical search. Dimereial had given her a decent description of Vessa Theramay, but after five minutes of combing the halls and peeking into as many open doors as she could, Cypress hadn't spotted anyone fitting the bill. She strode around for a few minutes, projecting a demeanor of rushing to deliver her next message, stalling for time. She was growing nervous. The Bastion was large, but this was a confined area with a lot of activity. It would only be a matter of time until someone noticed that acolyte Loren was wandering in circles, doing nothing.

Eventually, she had to take a risk. She spotted one of the acolytes, standing off from the rest as he jotted down a hasty series of notes. She gestured to get his attention, bobbing her head in greeting. He returned the gesture without any dawning look of familiarity or warmth, which was great. If she'd stumbled onto Loren's best friend, she'd have been doomed.

"Heed the Harbinger," the acolyte said automatically, eyes flicking between his unfinished notes and Cypress-Loren.

"Apologies," Cypress replied. "I have a message for High Herald Theramay, but I can't seem to find her."

The acolyte held out a hand. "Heading her way now. I'll take it."

Godsdamned fuckity fuck, Anastasia's favorite expletive echoed in Cypress's head.

She feigned nervousness, which wasn't a difficult thing to sell in her current situation. "I'm afraid I was told to give it to her directly."

The other acolyte arched an eyebrow at her, annoyed. From his attitude, he either held some internal rank far senior to poor gatehouse-Loren, or he was an arrogant twat.

"Fine." He sneered, folding up his note and handing it to Cypress. "Messages from Herald Rine and Lieutenant Thomlin. You can give them to her too. She's down this hall, last door on the right. As usual."

Cypress flashed an embarrassed grin and scurried away without another word. People like that were all too happy to believe their orders were being followed without delay, in her experience.

As she rushed off, she stole a glance at the first note the other acolyte had handed her:

Per Herald Rine: no sign yet. Violence in the Fields; forces near the Grove repelled. Nyxian Guard alerted, engaged. Search parties expanding.

Cypress furrowed her brow. It didn't mean anything to her, but her spymaster's instincts tucked the words away. Perhaps she could use some detail there if she needed to bluff any further today.

She reached the indicated door and steeled herself. She didn't hear voices within, which was a good sign—it was crucial she caught the High Herald alone.

"Enter," a stern voice commanded after she knocked.

Cypress did so, surreptitiously closing the door behind herself without waiting to be asked. The room she found herself in was large, divided into several smaller areas by functional arrangements of furniture. There was a sitting area directly before her, a couch facing two chairs upholstered in deep blue leather. The area beside the door was taken up by a set of bookshelves laden with well-worn tomes and various curiosities. And set against the opposite wall was an imposing, heavy desk, positioned beneath a stone relief of the Harbinger: a cowled figure flanked by a trio of ravens.

Seated at the desk was a red-haired woman in the cream-and-crimson robes of the other Heralds, with additional embroidery along the trim to denote rank: High Herald Vessa Theramay. She beckoned Cypress to the desk without looking up from the sheaf of parchments she was reviewing.

Cypress scanned the room as she approached. They were alone, though from the scattered minor disturbances about the room Cypress gathered that the place had been used as a meeting place often enough. The Herald's desk was cluttered with stacks of hand-scrawled notes like the one she'd been handed in the hall, all piled atop a woodcut print map of the Sunless Crossing that took up most of the surface area.

"What news, Loren?" Vessa Theramay asked.

"H-Heed, high Herald," Cypress stammered, embracing the low status Loren had been treated with by his colleagues. "Messages from the gatehouse, and a report from Herald Rine."

"Read the report for me," she instructed. Her tone was curt from efficiency. She shuffled a stack of papers out of the way as Cypress narrated, nodding and making notes directly on the map.

"That's something, I suppose," the Herald mused to Cypress-Loren.

"You've a parcel as well, ma'am." Heart thudding in her ears, Cypress placed the ensorcelled pouch with the raven amulet Dimereial had given her on the desk. This wasn't going to be like trapping the arrogant General Harson in an underworld brothel. If things went wrong in here, it would take a miracle to get her out of the Bastion in one piece.

The High Herald frowned at it, then fixed Cypress with an interrogative gaze. "What's that?"

"I'm not sure, High Herald. Something found during the search, I believe." Cypress was taking a risk by bluffing, but she needed the Herald to open the pouch herself. If she tried to just fling the ensorcelled memory totem at the Herald, it was just as likely that her attention would be too fixed on Cypress to trigger the magic there. Even the angel's spells required the target's focus before it could start plucking away memories.

"I see." The Herald plucked the pouch from the desk and tested its weight. "Do you think this might give us a clue as to what the Pale Horsemen are doing out in the Fields?"

"I can't say, Herald."

"Of course not." She stood, taking the pouch and turning to regard the Harbinger relief behind her desk. "Because Loren doesn't know what we're doing back here, nor are the Horsemen doing anything in the Fields. And he would never deliver an unknown package to this room. So, clearly. You aren't Loren."

Cypress's head snapped up, eyes wide with alarm. The High Herald placed the pouch in the beak of one of the carved ravens, which snapped closed as if it was a live bird taking a morsel. The eyes of all the ravens in the carving began to glow with baleful arcane fire.

The High Herald shrugged. "Nice try though."

Searing light flooded the room, and Cypress screamed as she felt her flesh flay away.

CHAPTER 17

"Oh, thank the *gods*." Secan exhaled as they crested a small hill.

A great mesa broke the horizon ahead of them. Rasa regarded it with confusion. "That was not there before."

Secan nodded. "It's always there, but you weren't ready for it. Now you are."

Rasa shot him an exasperated look. "I don't have anything to compare this to, but that seems like nonsense."

The Shepherd shrugged. "We're dead. The Sunless Crossing feels like life most of the time, but it isn't. Everything we see and touch and feel is one part Thing and Place, and two parts Memory or Idea. Or just 'Cosmic Decree.'"

"And this explains why a giant mountain has appeared where there was an empty field a moment ago?"

"It's a mesa, technically. Maybe a plateau? S'pose it doesn't matter much."

"Secan."

"Sorry, sorry." He held his hands up. "Tryin' to keep things light. That right there is Nox Valar, the city of the dead. It only shows up once a soul like yourself is ready for that part of the Crossing. Usually after a long stop at the Grove."

"So the city moves?"

"Nah, it's just really far away until you get closer."

"Is that not how most things work?"

"Ah, no. Nox Valar is far away until you get closer to the *end*, not the city. The city didn't move."

"This is becoming more confusing."

"I hear that a lot. Best advice? Don't fixate. City shows up when you're ready to see it. That's the salient point."

Rasa pinched the bridge of her nose. "It's informative that I do not remember visiting a single other city, ever, and yet I still find this one vexing."

"Not an entirely unreasonable opinion of the place," Secan muttered. "This is good though. I was worried our interruption at the Grove was going to throw things off, but it looks like you spent all the time with your reflection you needed."

"I did not have a reflection at the Atonement Grove. I had muddy water that turned into a monster and tried to drown you."

"And yet, there's the city."

"So, what does *that* mean?"

"Haven't the slightest notion."

Rasa threw her hands up and took several steps away from him. Secan chortled.

"Believe me, I'm none too thrilled with our lack of explanations either, but this is progress. I'm hoping once we get there I can find someone who will make sense of all this."

"We are going to the city then," Rasa stated.

"Best option right now. Normally I'd take you to the Junction—that's a place where Shepherds like me can gather up new arrivals and get you all acquainted with the ins and outs, see—but I don't want to risk staying in the Fields at this point. Nox Valar should be safer."

Rasa frowned as she caught the tentative note in his voice. "Should?"

Secan scratched his head. "Should. It seems like something is after you, in particular. Out here in the Fields, all sorts of things can happen to a new soul. But in Nox Valar, there are rules. Order. Witnesses. Guards. Plenty of powerful folk who don't much like others summoning rampaging elementals or marauding undead monsters to smash things up."

"But you only think we *should* be safer."

"Well. There's every chance the source of our problems is *in* the city too."

Rasa arched an eyebrow and drummed her fingers on Raven's haft. "You seem concerned about that, Shepherd. It sounds like an opportunity to me. Lead on."

Rasa thought they'd reach the mesa after an hour or two of hiking, but in reality, it took much longer. At first, she figured this to be some other trick of space within the Crossing, but it turned out that Nox Valar was simply much farther away than she had initially thought—and much, much larger.

By the time she could pick out the buildings and features encrusted on the mesa's surface, it dominated their field of view. Glittering waterfalls cascaded off its edges and down its sides, lending the ashy air wisps of chilled vapor near its base. The city was perched atop the mesa like a prize on a pedestal, a glittering field of black-and-white marble. As they drew closer, even the tallest spires slipped back behind the lip of the mesa from her view, so far above were they.

"What are the statues?" she asked as Secan led them around the vast perimeter. There were thousands dotted around the circumference of the great edifice. The lowest was almost fifty feet up, and she could see rows and rows of them climbing up toward the top, all winged figures facing outward.

"Good eye," he replied. "Fallen Gargoyles, all of them. Their body reverts to stone when they end, and they are placed here to keep watch forever. It's how they honor their dead."

"I thought all the souls here moved on to some afterlife at the end of their stay?"

Secan shook his head. "Gargoyles aren't mortal; don't have souls like you and me. They're sparks of ... existence, I suppose. Energy that found a body and decided to *be* for a while. When they're done, that energy fades back into wherever it came from."

Rasa was curious but had trouble articulating it to Secan. It frustrated her; she constantly felt there was something at the tip of her tongue or the back of her mind, but it always slipped away as she reached for it. She lacked context for so much. Something like the gargoyles would pique her interest, but without a life of mortal memory to compare them to, she couldn't fathom where to even begin.

"Here we are," Secan announced. "Hope you're ready for a climb."

Coming into view around the curve of the mesa was a tremendous archway set into its base. The apex of the arch was carved in the likeness of a gigantic gargoyle, its wingspan extending down and blending into pillars that supported the structure. As they drew near, she saw that these, too, were intricately carved; studded from ground to wing with lifelike faces of dozens of races. Some she recognized—elf, human, dwarf, orc, and more—though she knew not from where. Others appeared alien to her, with proportions she couldn't make sense of or features she found surprising.

Something sparked within the recesses of her mind, and she reached up to touch her own ear. It was smaller than the elven carvings in the pillars, but not entirely as rounded as Secan's.

Secan's brows shot up at the motion. "Didn't even occur to me," he admitted. "If I had to guess, I'd say you have a little elf blood in you. Maybe not from a parent, but a generation or two back."

"Huh." She paused. "That's ... interesting."

"How so?"

"I am not surprised by it."

Secan looked at her in askance.

"I have been noticing things as we travel," she explained. "Some information surprises me. Things about how this plane works. Things about souls, things about afterlives, the city. I have no basis for comparison, but they surprise me."

"Think I see where you're headed."

"Other information—that I am part elven, for example—feels normal. It is not new to me, though I did not know it until just now."

"Might be something to that," Secan mused. "It might be that your memories aren't gone. They're suppressed. Hidin' in your mind."

"I thought the same," she huffed. "I am not sure what to *do* with that thought yet. But I am paying attention to these moments. Perhaps a use for the information will reveal itself."

They passed under the archway, into a wide, sloping pathway that tunneled through the mesa upward. It was lit by burning mage-light at regular intervals, and while not notably darker than the sunless fields behind them, Rasa felt as if the air was markedly cooler beyond the threshold, as if the very idea of winding underground pathways were linked with a sense of cloying mists in her mind.

Secan named the path Ascension Row and explained that it would take them into the city above. She tensed when she saw other figures moving on the path ahead of them, but relaxed when she identified them as other souls making their own pilgrimage into Nox Valar. Whereas the path had seemed lonesome moments before, as they climbed, the crowd thickened, and soon she could not imagine where so many souls had come from without her noting their approach. But Secan didn't comment on this, and so Rasa did not raise an alarm. Perhaps it was related to the city's habit of appearing only to those who were ready.

Most souls were headed upward, but others passed them, coming down the slope toward the fields. She saw groups dressed as soldiers, monitoring the crowd or headed out on patrol. Rasa saw souls like Secan, guiding others and explaining their surroundings. Some wore looks of wonder, of despair, of bewilderment. Others betrayed simple resignation.

The crowd held all kinds. She saw merchants, beggars, nobles, priests, the young and old, all pressed together and marching up, up, up.

Finally, they emerged into the diffuse un-light of the Sunless Crossing once more. They entered a wide plaza, surrounded by the glimmering marble structures of Nox Valar. Through the gaps between, she could catch glimpses of the vast gold-gray fields they had just spent subjective days crossing, but the city dominated her field of view. The pervasive hustle and noise of other souls, though diffused compared to the press of their ascent, was more jarring here for its ubiquity. After days with only the noise of Secan and herself, adjusting to the background buzz of a metropolis would take a while.

Rasa looked at the structures she found herself among. There was a striking uniformity to them; each hewn from the same soot-streaked black-and-white marble, each designed with the same architectural sensibilities and flourishes. The whole city lacked any distinctive marks of craft, as if each roof and wall had been grown fully formed from the bedrock beneath their foundations. Where there were features like seams in masonry or rows of roofing tile, they appeared as if elements of decoration instead of necessity. It was a subtle difference that Rasa would have struggled to articulate in the moment, but the cumulative effect left her with the notion that this city was not a construct, but a fundament—something primordial and foundational to the world, permanent and unmoved by the procession of transient souls that filled its streets like lifeblood.

"Nox Valar, city of souls. Sure is something," Secan said as she took it all in. "No place like it, not anywhere."

"Eh, I've seen better."

Secan's head snapped around, but he found her grinning. "Heh. Got you."

"Gods help me, you really might be funny. Come on then."

"Where to first?"

He pointed at a large, fortress-like structure that squatted at one end of the plaza. It bristled with towers, each in turn studded with myriad alcoves and balconies. An iron sword and shield of titanic proportions hung suspended above its main gate.

"Crag Veil, headquarters for the Nyxian Guard. They need to know about all the trouble we ran into out there, especially that thing at the Grove."

The outer gates were open, and Rasa eyed the point of the great blade as they passed beneath it. Beyond, a throng of soldiers in uniforms like she'd seen on the climb into the city filled a broad courtyard, drilling or exercising in squads or passing by in ones and twos on errands unseen. For the first time, she saw the Gargoyles up close: tall stone-skinned humanoids with bat-like wings. They intermixed with the other soldiers or filled the sky above. She saw the purpose of the towers then, as many flew between the various archways, or stopped to rest in the external alcoves.

Secan seemed to know where he was going, and while she spotted some of the sentries keeping an eye on them and the handful of other non-soldiers in the courtyard, none confronted them. She wondered if that would change should they veer off the path the Shepherd had set. It mattered not though, as Secan led them through the iron-banded doors of the main hall.

The entrance to Crag Veil was cavernous, lined with rows of columns that rose to support a ceiling many times taller than the room was wide, so high that additional rows of torches were required to light the recesses far above those illuminating the ground level. These were necessary though, as Rasa saw additional arches and balconies far above the floor, open to parts of the structure beyond. As a pair of armored gargoyles emerged from one such opening and flew across the hall to another, she realized there was an entire secondary network to the fortress accessible only to those who could fly. A few dozen yards in, even the distant ceiling vanished, and Rasa looked up to see a diminishing tunnel lined with flickering lights and spots of the Crossing's not-daylight shining through. They stood beneath one of the fortress's many towers; this one at least being mostly hollow to allow for rapid ascension or descent of the flying soldiers. Fascinating.

Secan stopped before a pair of soldiers seated at a desk in the center of the hall. The desk itself was a heavy, dark wood thing piled with neat stacks of logbooks, devoid of adornment save a simple painted rendition of the sword and shield that hung outside the fortress. A half dozen other soldiers flanked the desk, standing casually but forming an implicit line. This, then, was as far as the public was welcome within.

One of the seated soldiers glanced up from the tome she was writing in as they approached. She appraised them with a quick glance. "Shepherd. Citizen. How can the Guard be of service?"

How she identified Secan, Rasa wasn't sure, but for his part, he did not seem surprised. "Sergeant. I've just returned from an extended trek across the Ashen Fields. We encountered hostile creatures I can't identify, including one in the Grove that cannot be explained by random incursions of undead…"

Secan went on to produce a map from his pack, marking their approximate path of travel and the sites they had been accosted. Rasa wasn't quite sure how navigation worked in a place like the Crossing, but the sergeant made dutiful notes while her partner copied Secan's descriptions onto a similar map of their own.

"Patrols have already been stepped up," the Sergeant explained as Secan finished his tale, and the second guard took the report to be delivered somewhere deeper into Crag Veil. "Unusual activity has been noted, but it sounds like you took the brunt of it compared to the other Shepherds. The elemental from the Grove is particularly concerning."

"No surprise there," Secan agreed.

The sergeant's partner returned and handed her a piece of parchment. Her brows shot up as she read it.

"You can tell the other Shepherds that we're tasking a platoon to secure the Grove for now. There was already one headed for the Junction, and they're being redirected as soon as we can get a message out. You'll probably see them next time you're in the area."

"Thank you kindly, Sergeant. That wasn't an ordeal I'd care to repeat."

"Of course, Shepherd. Seems like we already had units in the area, so with luck, you'll be the only ones who got caught unawares," she replied, a hint of sympathy softening her tone.

"Someone else already put in an alert?"

She shook her head. "One of the temples from the Row has been sending people out and asking for our assistance. They had enough pull to get soldiers into the Fields on a request. All I know is your report got flagged immediately as relevant."

Secan looked at Rasa, who shrugged. She was well beyond her limited experiences, but the commotion was exciting to watch.

"That's ... odd. Which temple was that, did you say?"

"Someplace called the Bastion of Endings. Not one I'm familiar with."

"*Well...*" Secan chewed through the word with a particular drawl that came on when he was deep in thought. "That's something, ain't it?"

CHAPTER 18

er heart thundered in her ears as she felt hot blood flowing between her fingers, the drops flicking away into wisps of soul-ash as they speckled the corridor in her wake.

Cypress lost her balance as she sprinted around a corner, and she gasped in white-hot agony as she slammed into the wall with her wounded shoulder. She scrambled to keep her momentum, the shouts of the Heralds just behind her.

An acolyte emerged from a door ahead of her, carrying a stack of scrolls. His shout of alarm was cut off as she tackled him back inside, clamping her good hand over his mouth. He bit and struggled, but she gritted her teeth and bore him down into a well-practiced submission.

She studied his face as he struggled. It wouldn't be a perfect replication, but she was in a hurry.

His eyes widened with panic as he looked back at her. High Herald Theramay's arcane ward had ripped Loren's face from Cypress and left her reeling in her natural form. The acolyte she had pinned beheld a blank, amorphous humanoid with translucent, flowing skin and only the barest hint of facial features—save two large, dark, lidless orbs for eyes.

Cypress had been mistaken for many things in her natural state. An undead, a demon, even a golem: all monsters. She hadn't let anyone see it in decades. Hells, she hadn't even gone without a face in private for many years. And the Herald's trap had ripped it out for all to see in an instant.

She had what she needed in a few seconds. She stuffed the terrified acolyte's mouth with a wad of his own cloak and rolled, slipping him into a lock and pinching the artery in his neck that fed his brain. Cypress hadn't had the occasion to practice that trick since coming to the Crossing, but she figured that the manifested soul-forms here behaved like flesh and blood for all other purposes, so … *there*. The acolyte went limp in her grasp.

She threw the unconscious man unceremoniously behind a bookshelf and ran to the slim window across the room. It was too high for her to jump from, but she heard raised voices coming down the hall outside. She threw the window open as she struggled to assume the acolyte's form. Loren's face was lost to her now, magically burned from her mind, but luckily all the acolytes of the Bastion of Endings dressed almost identically. This fellow would do.

He would have done anyway, but whatever spell she'd been hit with was still holding sway. She felt her flesh morphing, rippling with the innate transformation that had been as second nature as breathing to her since birth, but cried out as a burst of pins-and-needles frisson erupted across her nerve endings before the change could take hold. She staggered—the pain was *incredible*—and collapsed to her knees.

The door burst open, and a pair of armored guards in the Bastion's colors stomped into the room. Forcing herself to think through the pain, Cypress embraced the pain and doubled over, burying her face in her knees as if she'd taken a blow to the gut.

The guards barked overlapping questions at her. "The window!" she croaked, gesturing behind her. "The window!"

The guards rushed past her to peer outside. They spoke among themselves, and one ran back out of the room, shouting for a search of the exterior.

The remaining guard reached for Cypress. "Are you injured—" She didn't wait for his reaction to her natural form. She sprang from her place on the floor, driving the heel of her palm into the hollow of his throat with the strength of her entire body behind it. He careened backward and crashed to the floor, wide-eyed and wheezing. With a grimace, Cypress delivered two swift kicks to his head, and his eyes rolled back. She watched him for a dreaded moment, but nothing more happened. Good. She hadn't wanted to unravel the poor fool.

With the frenzied activity, warm blood had soaked her sleeve and was dribbling onto the floor in a steady stream. On instinct, she tried to shift again, but her nerve endings lit up with electric pain before her features had even begun to distort.

"Damn," she cursed. "Damn, damn, *damn*." She flipped her acolyte's hood up and stalked out of the room, keeping her head cast down.

The sanctum wing of the Bastion resembled an anthill that had just been kicked. She was able to lose herself among the crowd of rushing acolytes and Heralds, avoiding scrutiny by always moving with the greatest flow of people, never lingering in any one person's perception for long.

That got her to the inner gate, but that wasn't nearly far enough. The guards who had waved Loren through earlier were scrutinizing every person leaving that wing of the Bastion, despite the protestations of several high-ranking Heralds.

"Damn," she cursed again. In stolen glances from beneath her hood, she spotted a cleric beyond the guards, reciting some incantation and anointing one of the raven-dog statues she'd seen on her way in. She paid little attention to his actions at first. But as she was scanning the crowd for a viable escape route, the statue began to move.

Oh, she thought. The creature looked more lifelike by the second, stepping forward from its alcove and shaking a peculiar mane of feather-fur as if to dislodge the dust. With each step, it became less a thing of stone and mortar, and more a beast of flesh, blood, and claw. It began to sweep the room, its motions a disquieting blend of birdlike darting and head-cocking, and houndlike scent-hunting.

It snapped its beak up, its dark gaze locked directly onto her. The ruff of feathers around its throat prickled as it croaked in a deep, almost-whispered bass, *"Foe."*

Oh, fuck.

The hall erupted into chaos as the horse-sized animated bird-hound erupted into motion, charging straight toward her with no regard for the other souls in the way. Bodies were tossed aside like rag dolls; the beast's mass not much changed from its stoney slumber. She saw one soul ashed immediately upon bone-crunching impact with a column, and another screamed as they were brutally gored by the snapping beak that barreled toward her.

Cypress threw herself to the side as the raven-hound slammed into the wall, showering her with fragments of shattered marble. It croaked and thrashed as it freed itself, lumbering to turn around in the crowded hall.

Small favors, it's not agile, she thought. But it was *fast* in a straight line, and it looked like it wouldn't take much for it to crush her flat.

A fast unraveling was almost her best-case scenario at this point, grim as it was. Her soul would probably come back in the Fields without too much damage—and so long as the Heralds didn't have enough to identify her already, she might be able to make it back to the city undetected. Of course, if they *had* found a way to identify and intercept Cypress—or worse, if they managed to capture her without ashing her—she'd be hauled off by the Monarchy as a memory thief, toward a fate she would barely allow herself to contemplate.

Still. If she could take herself out fast. Put on a fresh face before a Shepherd found her. Make her way back...

If it worked, it would still cost her time. So much time.

Time Anastasia didn't have.

"Chaos is an opportunity." She had told her pupils year after year, training new spies to go forth and protect Anastasia's realm. "If no one knows what's happening, no one knows you're out of place."

The crowd of acolytes and Heralds waiting to exit was in disarray, having scattered to every side to avoid the guardian's charge. Cypress dove in among them as the raven-hound lumbered to course correct, making to help some to their feet while in actuality tripping and hobbling as she went.

One caught sight of her face—her true face—and cried out in alarm. But then the beast declared again, *"Foe,"* and she heard screams as it launched itself once more. It slammed into the knot of clergy she'd inserted herself into, sending souls scattering, and the man who'd tried to inform on her was battered down.

She saw the cleric who'd animated the statue running frantically in its wake, reciting a ritual and waving a glowing raven pendant around at the loose guardian. Others were scrambling, retreating into the halls of the inner sanctum, or fleeing past the guard checkpoint. The guards, for their part, were reeling to shift from screening the crowd to responding to this apparent renegade animation in the scant seconds since its first attack.

It was messy, but it might be her last chance, she saw in an instant. She rushed forward with the other fleeing acolytes, sprinting past the guards and into the broader complex beyond. She made a point of looking over her shoulder as she went, keeping her eyes on the raven-hound and her face turned from the guards as she approached. She sailed by without any outcry beyond the general bedlam of the scene.

"*Foe.*" She heard behind her.

Well, hells.

Cypress juked at the first intersection she came to, sprinting as fast as she could down the corridor before swerving down another hall. She heard the beast thundering after her, slamming into walls and grinding against them at full speed as it failed to completely make each turn.

Blood soaked her entire side now, the wound the High Herald had landed on her before she escaped her office gushing freely. Cypress knew she wouldn't be able to maintain this pace for long without properly dressing it. But stopping would mean accepting certain ashing or worse, capture, and so she rushed on. She had to do *something* to change her odds.

She ran through her scouting of the Bastion of Endings in her head. The courtyard and gatehouse would be a death trap by now, locked down in the commotion and likely alerted to her coming before she had any hope of reaching them. The scant secondary exits of the compound were always secured, as far as she'd seen—perhaps if she were able to use her shifting, but for the time being, she could not rely on it. A knot of dread and bile sank in her gut at the notion that the effect might be permanent; an eternity deprived of her innate power, her birthright, cursed to wear a form she'd never bothered to grow comfortable in. She pushed it aside for now. There was no point; if she didn't escape the Bastion, her long-term prospects were bleak, regardless. The Monarchy annihilated memory thieves, noble intentions be damned. And there was no telling what the Heralds might do before they turned her over.

Cypress came to a staircase and dashed up it. The floor she was on was even with the courtyard, though a drop off in the terrain meant that the side of the building opposite it was already several stories from the ground below. The mastiff might pursue her still, but she hoped the move would confound the Heralds themselves, who likely expected an intruder to make a beeline to the nearest exit. Perhaps she could even maintain the impression that the raven-dog-thing had gone wild, though that seemed unlikely to last once the Heralds overcame the initial chaos and began to coordinate.

She went up another flight of stairs and already heard the beast stomping up the set below. She estimated she was about level with the top of the courtyard wall now and rushed away from the stairs and down another corridor. She almost fell when she saw another raven-mastiff, before she realized that this one was still an unawakened statue.

Cypress tried a door at random, a string of violent curses spilling from her lips as she found it locked. She tried the next with the same result. The pounding feet of her pursuer, and the shouts of its handlers, reached the same floor behind her. A third door: locked.

She was about to dash away, find another route, when she heard a *click* from another door in the corridor. She snapped her attention to it and found it slightly ajar. Without pausing to assess her luck—she'd take divine intervention, at this point—she barreled through and slammed it shut, throwing the latch.

The room was empty; a contemplative chamber lined with bookshelves, writing desks, and several worn sofas. A row of windows filled the opposite wall, high and tall to make the most of the Crossing's meager storm-light. She rushed to them and had what felt like her first stroke of good fortune for the day: they opened.

There was commotion in the hall, muffled by the door. She had seconds to act. She scrambled through the window, smearing blood-ash on the sill and glass as she went. A narrow ledge awaited, hardly wide enough for her feet.

The top of the outer walls greeted her, half a story below her level and several yards to the side. If she jumped and missed, she would fall into the courtyard below, be terribly injured, and be set upon immediately by the guards. If the fall didn't outright ash her. But if she stayed—

Splintering wood and an angry shout from inside made the choice for her.

Cypress leaped.

CHAPTER 19

Madrigal of the Black Bells—Mads, to her friends—leaned on the polished onyx bar top of her VIP room, tail flicking back and forth with agitation. The high rollers had made themselves scarce, and that didn't bode well. They all had places to be, of course, but one or two of the old haunts could usually be counted on to fill a chair. As it was, the room was empty save for a pair of imps bickering in one corner, and a couple of mortals Tilla had her hooks into gambling among themselves. Mads wondered if they knew they were screwed yet, or if Tilla was still stringing them along with hopes and promises.

Speaking of: Tilla *was* there, but Mads didn't count Tilla as a customer. Nor was she a guest. More of a house pest. The kind that found its way back inside after you were *so sure* you'd finally rid yourself of it. That wretched breed of pest that was so abominably persistent that eventually you threw your hands up and said "Fine!" and just let the damned thing stay, as long as it didn't chew on anything particularly important.

"Where are all our friends, sister-mine?" The purple half-devil whined, striding up to her. "I was hoping to rob them blind over a couple hands."

Mads bit down a reflexive snarl. "Don't know. Not their keeper."

"Honestly though, when was the last time Gryort went two days without coming in here to lose his proverbial shirt, at least?"

"The March, probably." Mads found a spot on that bar that was slightly less pristine than it could have been and scrubbed at it with a rag.

"Madsy, the March of Claw and Gore was thirty years ago."

Mads ground her teeth so hard she was sure the patrons heard. "Don't call me Madsy."

"Well, you've proved my point, dear. Our cute little furball doesn't have anything better to do when he's not slaughtering something. And we'd have heard if the Pack had been called up."

"'Cute?' Ick."

"Don't be a prude."

"You are not seriously saying *Gryort*—"

"It takes all kinds, dear. You never know what you're missing until you take a little taste."

"You are absolutely the most disgusting being on this plane."

"Love you too, Madsy. Kiss-kiss."

"I swear on the pit the next time I kill you I'll make sure it stick—"

"Mistress," a small voice behind the bar croaked. Tilla laughed and sauntered off, pleased to get a rise out of her half-sister.

Mads regarded a short, toad-faced imp with a complexion like rotted corn. It was one of her least useless staff in the main, public taproom. "What is it, Bix?"

"Someone on the list is here, Mistress. I came as soon as he entered."

Ah. Ah-ha. Now things are making sense.

She bid Bix to attend the VIP bar, with strict orders not to serve Tilla anything she requested, and left him there, cutting through the back to emerge behind the public bar.

Thrace was sitting down as she entered, the gaunt, black-clad soul stitched granting a nod of recognition as he saw her.

Showtime.

"How can Madrigal's help the Monarchy today, Thrace?" She projected her voice as if greeting a favorite colleague.

He rolled his eyes as several patrons began to not-so-discreetly pivot toward the exit. "Fuckin' smooth, Madrigal. Practically clandestine."

"Why would I want to be clandestine when greeting a loyal customer in a legitimate place of business?" Mads asked, feigning confusion.

"Cut the shit. You know I wouldn't be in here for petty stuff."

"Yeah? How's your handler feel about that?"

Thrace gave her a deadpan stare that only corpses could really manage. "*Pel* is a straight shooter, Madrigal, and that ain't always a fuckin' bad thing to have around. But when it comes to the gray areas, let's just say that Pel works his leads, and I work mine, and nobody needs to give him details he doesn't ask for."

Mads frowned. She and Thrace weren't exactly on good terms, but they respected each other's place in the complex weave of intrigue that was Nox Valar. Usually, that meant a degree of selective blindness from the savvy, pragmatic stitched agent, so long as Mads didn't stray too far across any bright lines and kept her clientele select.

There would always be an underworld to the underworld, and the city could do a great deal worse than places like Madrigal's—and they both knew it. That's how the game was played. For him to be coming in here blatantly, and speaking well of Pel Solimo, no less...

"What's wrong?" she asked.

"Got a place we can chat in private?"

"Can you be a blind amnesiac for two minutes?"

"Deal."

Mads led Thrace through the back and wove a hex of blindness and deafness over him before they entered the VIP area. "Didn't realize you were being fucking literal," he grumbled, but didn't resist. Tilla looked agog at her when they entered, and so Mads mimed a rude gesture her way and marched Thrace over to her privacy circle. Once each layer was engaged, she dismissed the hex.

Thrace blinked and looked around. They stood in a cylindrical slice of the back room, but all sensation from beyond the circle's perimeter was cut off. "Hell of a circle," he said.

"Literally."

"Fair enough. I'll get right down to it. We both know things make their way through here that ain't strictly permissible in the Monarchy's eyes. I don't care about that. You and I also know that, from time to time, a stray memory might find a buyer in a room full of fiends."

Mads opened her mouth to protest, but he held up a hand. "Don't care about that either. That's one of those gray areas, Madrigal, where a different agent or a strait-laced proper Horseman might take issue. But I'm not a Horseman. I'm Covenant. They don't keep me around to run down the little stuff. There's some shit in this city that would make *your* skin crawl, lady. Give your worst clients nightmares."

"That's ... debatable." She thought of Azlaru. She doubted this once-man thing *really* knew what her regulars' worst looked like, but she could see what he was getting at.

"My point is I don't have time for the gray areas right now. I *live* for the fuckin' gray. So I don't give a shit if you're sucking down little Kenneth's fond farewells to gam-gam as a delicacy back here. There's some big shit happening, and if it goes how it's going, you're all just as double-fucked as we are. Clear?"

Well. This is new.

"You've got my attention."

"Good. Listen to me: someone is fucking with the cycle, and it's tied into the memory market somehow."

Mads frowned. "What does that even mean?"

Thrace shook his head. "Still putting the pieces together. But we glimpsed enough that I decided you and I needed to come to an accord, sooner rather than later. So, we're going to do this proper. Get a contract."

Madrigal's eyebrows shot up so far they threatened to take off. "You're *kidding.*"

"You a devil or no?"

"My contracts are for souls, Thrace."

"Got plenty."

"I don't even—not to put too fine a point on it, but *which* soul would I even be taking as collateral?"

"Freshest one I got. Six months from now."

"That's insane."

"You're a part-devil. I'm soul soup. We un-live in death's waiting room. Where's all this fucking sanity hiding, Madrigal? Can you do it, or not?"

Mads was, uncharacteristically, baffled.

"Hells with it," she said after a moment. A piece of parchment appeared in the air before her in a flash of hellfire and brimstone, a quill hovering just above it with a drop of blood-red ink beading on its nib. "What did you have in mind?"

"You put me under a geas not to pass along anything I learn about the workings of your *specific* establishment. You agree in turn to feed me or Pel information relevant to the case we're working, if you learn about it. You need to do it in a timely manner too. Same day. You allow the geas to be lifted in instances where those two things conflict. And you can't tell anyone about our case without my explicit permission first, indefinitely."

Her quill scrawled as he spoke, framing the intention of his request in robust and binding legal terms. On instinct, she willed it to elaborate on definitions and contingencies based on what he was driving at—she knew Tilla would have skewered him for failing to define "day," as the Sunless Crossing technically had no night, but she inserted it for him. This was one of the most peculiar situations she'd encountered since coming to Nox Valar, and she wanted to see where it was going.

She presented the contract to him for inspection. It was shorter than most, but he still read it in record time. Had he been the kind of wide-eyed, desperate mortal who signed most infernal contracts, she'd have thought he was skimming it to his detriment. But Thrace had never struck her as careless. He'd come here as a calculated move, and as fast as he went, she saw him reading and registering every line on the page. He requested several revisions; all clarifications, which she granted. When he was satisfied, he plucked her quill from the air, stabbed it into his fingertip to draw a bead of blood, and scrawled a looping signature on the end.

"I think you'd better tell me something about this case," she said as the contract vanished. Usually, a fresh contract was a cause for celebration or at least satisfaction... it was rare for her to feel as if she'd gotten in just as deep as the signatory.

"We've been digging through the Keepers' archives for days, and there's a pattern. At least a hundred we've found in the past decade, and for every one we know there's probably five more we're never going to fucking piece together."

"Every one *what?*"

"Every weird res', Madrigal. Always on someone who just got their brains scrambled in the Crossing."

"What are you telling me right now?"

"I'm telling you that someone is moving pieces that no one *should* be able to move. Victim pops up as a possible memory case. Common enough. They get raised back to life right after. Weirder. Then they're *back* here, again. Some of them, sure, that makes sense, but it's *all* of them. Every case. They never stay flesh-side more than a year; usually, it's *weeks*."

"That's all strange, Thrace, but I'm not seeing the alarm yet."

"That's because I'm not fuckin' done. The last part is what's got Pel slamming reports up the chain and two-thirds of me remembering what the cold sweats are like." He locked eyes with her. "Every one of those cases? Second time they hit the Crossing, they're off to the happily ever after as soon as you can spit. Months, in the older cases. Weeks, for most of them. The latest ones are getting down to *days*."

"Some souls move fast. So?"

"Nah, no, not like that. If it was only a few here and there, call it chance. But this is manipulation. It's *escalation*. Somebody found a new lever to pull. They're fucking around with who goes where, and it's starting to make waves."

"That ... is interesting, I'll grant you."

"It's not fucking *interesting*, Madrigal, it's *terrifying*," Thrace snapped. "The entire point of this place, the *entire fucking point*, is to have neutral ground to park all these mortal fucking souls while their business gets wrapped up. It's what keeps everyone behaving. It's why you can have a bar full of fiends a block away from a shrine full of angels and nobody starts calling down plagues. What do you think happens if this gets out, Madrigal? How long does it take some second-order deity or an archdevil or some fucking wannabe outsider to figure out that there's a cosmic fuckload worth of souls up for grabs?"

"Yet here you are, blabbing to a fiend yourself," she chided, without any real venom in it. The kind of cosmic energy heist he was describing was well above her abilities, but the information might have been worth plenty to the right buyer.

Thrace arched a brow and shot her a piteous look. "You know as well as I do that you'd get trampled in the stampede if you open that door. Besides..." There was an arcane *thrum* in the air that felt like Thrace had struck a harp string anchored to her sternum. He'd turned his magic senses toward the contract that bound them. "You got me, I got you. We're in the same boat now."

"Fucker," Mads spat. Keeping his confidence had seemed a minor concession a moment before. "Alright. You don't want it getting out. Fine."

"Seems like a quick way to turn Nox Valar into a battlefield."

"Ah, yes, very noble. Not to mention that soul stitched don't have the *best* life expectancy outside of the Crossing." Mads shrugged. "So it's probably good for you if everyone around here keeps playing nice too."

Thrace blinked. "Was that a 'life expectancy' crack?"

"I almost went with 'quality of life.'"

"I'd say 'good one,' but it happens to be true."

"Yeah, Thrace, you've sold me. It does sound bad. Now draw a line for me—what's it got to do with my little watering hole here?"

"Only lead we've got right now is that all the souls start this little detour after a memory snatcher. Need to know if anything new is happening on that front. Something that doesn't fit the pattern."

Madrigal considered. There were about a dozen memory merchants she dealt with at any given time. They all operated more or less at Cypress's level; a couple of passive traps around the city, places they wouldn't get noticed, and they'd circulate through the backroom when they snagged something juicy to sell.

"Most of what comes through here is small time," she explained. "Solo operators. Work almost like fishermen. Only show up to market if they catch something worth selling, so they're sporadic. No one goes back as far as you're talking about. Most only do a couple of deals and either get pinched, move up to a bigger racket, or vanish."

"No bigger players? An operation? Something coordinated?"

She knew of a few big fish, but they took their merchandise straight to Anywhere. Those were the players most likely to run afoul of Horsemen like Pel. Madrigal deliberately kept out of those circles and didn't welcome them here. If a fiend wanted to take the trip down to Anywhere and buy something premium at full price, that was their prerogative—hells, she indulged herself once in a while, when business was good—but it attracted far too much heat to get involved. She said as much.

"Damnit. I'm going to have to go to Anywhere, aren't I?" Thrace cursed to himself.

"I can probably arrange that," Mads offered. "Since we're under contract and all."

"That'll save me some time," Thrace admitted. "Let me circle back with Pel and see if he's shaken anything loose. If not, I'll be back to take you up on that. No more than a day."

Mads, as per her new obligations, provided Thrace with a few tidbits of information that might have borne a passing relevance to his inquiry, but they agreed it was all thin and probably worthless. She affirmed that she would keep her ear to the ground and keep him apprised of any strange goings-on in Nox Valar's underbelly that might be connected.

As she prepared to hex him again, one last question occurred to him. "Any of your clients stand out lately? Someone who doesn't seem to care about the status quo as much as the rest of us?"

"I've got a damned celestial coming in to rent out this circle every couple of weeks, and that's ruffled plenty of feathers. Pun intended."

Thrace paused. "Which one?"

"Dimereial. Hall of Tempered Innocence."

"Don't know that one."

"Lesser redeemer cult. Don't think they've made it to the Road."

"What's he do here?"

"Defeats the point of the circle, if I know that. Goes in with some mortals and they chat for a few minutes. Recognize a few, others are new to me. He pays well enough that I make the regulars put up with it."

"The mortals ever say what they talk about?"

"Nah. And I don't ask. That's the business."

"Sure, sure." Thrace sighed. "Well, wrap me up."

Mads finished her spell and felt the blinding, deafening hex snap closed on Thrace. She deactivated the privacy circle.

Tilla stood at the bar, eyes wide and looking at Madrigal. On the bar, a bloodied, battered humanoid lay, its breathing labored. Its eyes were closed, the only prominent feature on an otherwise near-blank face.

"What the fuck?!" Mads demanded.

"I don't fucking know!" Tilla shouted back.

CHAPTER 20

"There's that, then," Secan declared as he handed her the Crossway Coin. "Keep this safe."

Rasa looked at the metallic disk—the Crossway Coin, he'd called it—in her palm. On one side the insignia of the temple they stood in was stamped, an arrangement of hourglasses, filigree, and writing in a language she did not know. On the other, a peculiar glyph that made her vision swim. She could not read it, whatever language it was, but it left her with an indelible impression of a date nearly a century hence.

"That coin holds your spot for a meeting with the Keepers," Secan explained, gesturing over his shoulder as he led her out. The marble temple was set at the base of a gigantic tower, tall enough to be visible across the city. An enormous pane of glass was set into each face of it, through which could be seen a slowly rising pile of sand. "They keep the clock around here, but that ain't all they work on. Every soul gets a meeting with them, and they'll tell you how long you're due to stay here."

"In the city?"

"In the Crossing. They know when you're on track to get to your afterlife."

Rasa nodded. "If they know, why can't they tell me right now?"

"Meeting takes a while. They need to spend some time with you to figure it all out proper. Here, come look at this." He took her around the corner, away from the grand entrance of the temple. There, a line of souls stretched away from a side entrance and snaked down the street, before disappearing around the corner of a block. Rasa spotted a handful of acolytes in similar robes to those she'd seen inside walking up and down the line, issuing instructions and keeping the waiting souls organized.

"What's that for?" she asked.

"Today's crop of appointments," he said. "Most of them have been waiting decades for the meeting on their Coin. Today they find out how much longer they have here."

Rasa nodded. "So they have the most valuable Coins right now?"

"Can't recommend going down that path." Secan held a cautionary hand up. "Look there."

She followed his gesture and spied a soldier's helmet gleaming from a nearby rooftop. Then another, and another. Then a squad standing in the arch of another building, watching the line, and a pair of gargoyles flying overhead.

"Thieves snatch good Coins all the time, but not right in front of their destination. Mugging people outside every major line in the city would be a level of anarchy that the Monarchy isn't inclined to allow."

"I wasn't suggesting it as a course of action. More wondering what prevented it. Now I know. Is there any other way to get a faster Coin?"

"Lots," he replied. "They're the main way folk trade here. *This Coin's worth more to me, that one's worth more to you, let's swap; I'll give you two of these for a taste of real pastries you managed to get brought in from the living world,'* that kind of thing. Or you get good at Purgatory Poker and start betting your way up."

"Purgatory Poker?"

"Card game. Trust me, you won't be in the city long before someone ropes you into a hand. Just don't start gambling more'n you've got to lose, and you'll be fine."

Rasa took it all in, filing the information away for later use. "Well. Assuming I don't want to just sit here and wait for a century. What do we do next?"

Secan scratched his chin, an unconscious gesture of thought. "Normally, I'd point you toward somewhere to lay your head and cut you loose, come check on you in a week or two."

Rasa whirled around to shoot him a look of alarm. He made a placating gesture.

"Now, now, I said 'normally.' Ain't been nothing normal about your circumstances. So, I'm going to stick with you until we get some answers. Been considering where to go with that."

Rasa relaxed by degrees. She was surprised at how much the notion of Secan's departure disturbed her. She had no desire to try to navigate this place with no lay of the land *and* precious little life experience to draw from. *I'd be better off in the Fields,* she thought.

"You have a plan then?"

Secan rolled his head in a little *kind of* gesture. "A starting place, maybe. We're headed to the Belfry."

Exora's Belfry, as it turned out, was back at the edge of the mesa. Even after Secan pointed out the tower against the skyline, Rasa had plenty of time to take in the sights of Nox Valar before they reached it. Even without a base of comparison, the city was peculiar to her. It had the hubbub and bustle of life; souls passing to and fro, merchants hawking their wares, and deliveries being made. She thought nothing of the non-mortals moving among them, as it never even occurred to her that a celestial or a fiend going about their business or trying to catch the attention of passing mortals was an odd sight at all.

What struck Rasa was the absences. Things she had expected of any large group, on some instinctive level. There were no families in Nox Valar, and precious few children from what she saw. There was no marked difference between the young and old when it came to how they organized and conducted themselves, and she realized then that *if* a child wound up in the city, they might very well be here far longer than their mortal years before they'd even met with the Keepers of the Eternal Sands. She said as much to Secan.

"Happens sometimes, yep," he confirmed. "Gotta be a kid with the connections to potentially get brought back to life, mind you, and there aren't as many of those. They tend to skew toward royalty or wealth when they show up here. Few I've known wind up just as scared about being resurrected as they are about crossing over. They turn into some of the city's most stubborn residents. Don't want to leave the familiar."

The Belfry spanned one of Nox Valar's rivers, built atop a bridge perched just above the precipice where the water tumbled off the city's mesa toward the Fields far below. Rasa's gaze followed the tower up and up, toward a chamber high above that housed a large, black metallic object she could barely see. *A bell, one assumes,* she mused, then wondered why she knew that.

"The Belfry is a collective of arcane types. Place where souls who lived to learn about magic gather to keep learnin' as much as they can. Lots of crossover with the Academicians—you probably don't know who they are, huh—but I'm hopeful we can find someone there who might know something about your condition."

"Will we need to get a Coin and wait to see them too?" Rasa asked.

"Usually." Secan flashed her a crooked grin. "But I think we can jump the line today. Got a feelin'."

The central hall of the Belfry was a vast library, with a continuous spiral of bookshelves that wound along the inside circumference of the tower itself. It almost reminded her of the Gargoyle routes within Crag Veil, except that the Belfry boasted a wide mezzanine that followed the books, complete with regular terraces filled with desks and study areas. Globes of amber mage-light levitated along the central axis of the tower, one at each level, each boasting an orbit of smaller lights that floated closer to the stacks and desks.

Rasa saw no way to reach the stacks from the ground floor however. Secan approached a teller's window set into one wall, where an enormous, elephantoid soul sat. They were squinting at an ancient tome on the desk through comically large spectacles, tracing the lines as they read with their trunk.

"Hey there, Borssa," Secan said in greeting.

Borssa glanced up from their reading as if they hadn't seen Secan enter. "Stars and sigils!" they boomed, their voice echoing and reverberating up the tower. Rasa spotted a mild commotion among the lowest tiers. "Secan, is that you?"

"Last I checked."

The elephant-person made a pleased trumpeting noise and rose, pushing the entire teller's desk easily out of its mountings and stepping through the opening to sweep the Shepherd into an exaggerated, trunk-powered embrace. Spying the oft-splintered edges of the desk and noting how it came away from the opening with minimal resistance, Rasa gathered that this was hardly the first time Borssa had simply forgotten to find a door.

"It's good to see you too, Bor." Secan laughed, wheezing a bit as they put him back down.

"I haven't seen you in the Belfry since Ori ... left." Borssa's tone fell as they caught up to what they were saying. "Sorry, Secan. We all know how close you were."

"Yeah, well. That's the deal, isn't it?" Secan's tone was unusually level, as if he was making an effort to keep it flat.

"What brings you by then?!" Borssa was clearly trying to push past the moment. "Not that a social call would be unwelcome, you know. You've still got friends here."

Secan pressed his lips together and dropped his gaze, nodding once. "Appreciate that, Borssa. I won't forget it again."

"Good. You twerp."

"I'd like you to meet my friend here. This is Rasa. We think."

"Greetings, Borssa," Rasa said.

"I need to consult with someone. Open to recommendations," Secan went on.

Borssa's brow furrowed. "I'd love to help, Secan, really, but you know the rules. You need to make an appointment or get a spot in line from someone else."

"I thought you might say that." Secan smiled at both of them. "But you're going to make an exception, Bor."

"I am?"

"You sure are. You know why? Because someone is going to volunteer their time."

"They are? I know I just said you had friends, Secan, but there's still a procedure—"

"They are, Bor, because my friend Rasa here is a genuine, first-in-the-Crossing mystery, and I think the bellflies are going to be crawling over each other to get the first crack at solving it."

A smile crinkled the leathery gray skin around Borssa's eyes, the ridges magnified to canyon scale by their enormous lenses. "I suppose you'd better tell me all about it then, and I'll spread the word. But first, would you two like some tea?"

Borssa led them through the fresh hole in the wall with a "Don't worry, the novices need to practice their mending spells," and into a cozy study beyond. It was cramped with the three of them—Rasa imagined it was cramped even with just one Borssa—but they squeezed in, and Borssa set a kettle boiling over a small fireplace.

"This is why I stay down here on desk duty," they confided to Rasa. "Only a couple of offices get a real chimney. The bigger ones all have to use magical heat. It's just not the same."

Rasa grinned as the giant pachyderm "whispered" to her at a level just below outright shouting. Not because she had any opinion on magically-heated versus fire-boiled tea kettles, but because Borssa was so obviously delighted in the choice. It was contagious.

The kettle set, Borssa shuffled around the perimeter of the room and scrunched in behind an enormous desk, piled high with tomes and parchment. They gestured to two oversized, overstuffed armchairs opposite the desk. "Tea will be up in a few minutes. Best tell me what this is all about then."

Secan and Rasa sat, and Borssa listened intently as they recounted their journey to Nox Valar. They interrupted only to ask for clarifications, and after a few moments shuffled some papers around and began taking notes.

The kettle whistled as their story approached the Atonement Grove, and Borssa bid them keep talking as they shuffled back around and delicately distributed teacups, leaves, hot water, and honey to their guests.

"Hells, is this real honey?" Secan blurted out after his first sip, interrupting himself mid-thought.

Borssa raised their cup to him with their trunk while and kept writing with their massive hands. "Some of the bellflies pool our resources to get proper tea and related supplies from the mortal realms. We have a club. Another reason to visit. But please, continue."

Borssa's much-magnified eyes went wide as they described the elemental attack in the Grove.

"You know what that means?" they asked, intent.

"I reckon I've got the outline of it, yeah," Secan confirmed.

"It had to be summoned, right?" Rasa asked.

"Indeed." Borssa scribbled more notes. "And in the Grove, no less. The location isn't trivial. Nor is the fact that you found your way here, even after interference at the reflecting pool. This is going to throw Manuel's computations on determinist relativity and perceived space in the Crossing into disarray. It's a completely new set of variables to account for. He'll love it!"

"That about brings us to now," Secan finished. "We made it to the city about a day after we left the Grove, nothing too unexplained there. My big concern, as you can guess, is Rasa's memory. I'm not even sure how to begin with something like that. Think you can help us?"

Borssa thought for a moment, then reached up and tapped on the rim of their glasses once, twice, three times. Each time they did, the lenses took on a different vivid tint. Borssa kept their eyes on Rasa as they cycled through the colors a few times. Then they tapped them again, and they returned to their typical magnified clarity.

"I might know some folks who'd be interested. You mind waiting down here for a few minutes while I round them up?"

"Not at all, Borssa. Thank you."

Rasa nodded her agreement. "Truly. Thank you."

"Haven't done anything yet," Borssa muttered as they squeezed back out of the room. "Unless you meant the honey, in which case, you're welcome."

CHAPTER 21

Cypress cried out as a bright lance of burning pain shot through her arm.

"Suck it up," a woman's voice scolded.

"Shut up, Tilla," another chided. *Mads?*

"Mortals are so dramatic."

"So we're half dramatic?"

"Father wasn't like *that*."

"Father was a sociopath."

"You're bringing back fond memories."

"Shut *up, Tilla*."

Cypress tried to open her eyes, but her vision swam into bleary streaks of nonsense-colors, and the voices faded as everything went dark again.

The next time she came to, she saw Mads's face looking down at her, lines of concern creasing her brow.

"Heh," Cypress croaked. "Made it."

"Not that it isn't always great to see you, Cy, but what the hells are you doing here? And what the fuck happened?"

"Job went sideways. Where is here?" She looked around, finding the dim room unfamiliar.

"Back of the house," Mads explained. "The real back. We won't be disturbed."

"Sorry to barge in." She tried to sit up and failed. "I'll pay you back. Keep our accounts square."

"Tilla wants me to put you under contract for the inconvenience."

"You may not wanna do that."

"No shit, Cy. *Somebody* kicked a hornet's nest over on the Road, and I'm not going to get caught holding a contract with anyone involved. If you were. Which I don't know. And you should not confirm."

Cypress slumped back. "I hear you. Next three traps I pull in are yours, no charge."

"I get the first choice of your next *five,* no charge, and we're not square until I pick five good ones. You can sell anything I pass on. *Then* we're square."

"Deal." Cypress held up a smooth, near-translucent hand. Mads shook it.

"Uh-huh. Now, what's going on with your new look?"

Cypress tried to shift but shuddered as a fresh wave of needles-in-nerves pain rippled across her skin. "Got hit with a spell. Trap, ward, something. Didn't get a chance to examine it. Can't shift. Feels like I'm being skinned when I try."

Madrigal's eyes flashed with a telltale glow of arcane vision. "So that's what that is. Saw something hanging on you, wasn't sure what I was looking at."

"Is it permanent?" Cypress didn't try to hide the fear in her voice.

"Eh. Doubt it. It's got some divine backing though. The magic may be a long time fading—"

The room darkened, as if every candle had suddenly flickered down to an ember, and suddenly they were not alone. Mads jumped back from her view with a snarled curse, and

Azlaru's grotesque, stretched-out face filled Cypress's vision. That gnarled, fetid grin split his features and continued to slowly widen by agonizing degrees.

"Azlaru. Will. Help." Cypress's eyes widened in fear, but found herself unable to marshal the energy to move.

"How the fuck did you get in—" Mads began but cut herself off. Azlaru ignored her.

"The Cypress. Tweaked. The Harbinger's. Beak." Azlaru chuckled, waves of hot garbage and rot stench washing over Cypress's face as he did. "This. Amuses. Azlaru. But. The Cypress. Owes. Azlaru. A favor."

"Y-you can't call it in yet," she protested.

"No. But. Azlaru will. Make sure. The Cypress. Can. Deliver." His enormous hand blocked her vision, and she felt his elongated spider-fingers wrap around her skull with crushing force. Mads cursed.

Cypress screamed.

She next awoke in a cold sweat, panting heavily. She clawed at her face with such urgency that her fingernails drew blood before Mads could intervene. The half-devil firmly pulled Cypress's trembling hands away from her face, stained with smears of crimson.

They were Anastasia's hands.

"Oh... oh gods and..." Cypress wrenched herself free so she could double over and vomit. "What did he do? Where is he?"

Mads sat back as Cypress pulled herself together. "No clue on both fronts. But the curse you walked in with is gone. Give it a whirl."

Cautiously, Cypress reached for her shifting. Anastasia's skin darkened, then reddened, and horns sprouted from her head. A wingless Mads faced the original.

"Fuck, I'm pretty," Mads said appreciatively, looking Cypress up and down. "You missed some bits though."

"Never could do wings," she explained. "No tails either. Any limb I don't normally have just … doesn't come out right."

With that, she shifted back to Anastasia and took comfort in wearing the familiar shape once more. Mads feigned disappointment.

"Thank you for the help, Mads. Really."

Mads scowled at her. "There are no thanks required, *Cy*, because you're a client in good standing who has already arranged payment for this unexpected service."

"...Which is exactly what I would tell anyone who ever asked," Cypress continued, catching the subtext. Infernals didn't exactly have a reputation for charity—and didn't want one. Maybe especially the infernals with mortal lineages. "Which, of course, they won't. Because who would even tell them it happened? Not me."

"Correct," Mads said. "And you're welcome. Now, what are you going to do?"

Cypress had already been trying to piece that together. "Don't think I was followed, but can't just stay here. Need to find out what the damage was. Think I need to cut one more deal with you."

"Oh?"

"Yeah. Need a ticket to Anywhere."

Pascal approached the vendor's stall, a simple awning stretched between the walls of an alley and wrinkled his nose up at the stench. "Hells of a thing to import," he said to the fishmonger, looking with disdain at the stinking piles of half-thawed, half-recognizable fish piled on the table.

"You'd be surprised. Flavor's flavor," grunted the old man from his seat atop a pile of cushions.

"Flavors can be bad," Pascal said.

"Not like it'll kill you twice."

"I've already died twice. Just looking for a place to wait it out."

The fishmonger nodded and moved to the next part of the script. "Got a place in particular in mind?"

"Can you recommend Anywhere?"

"Come inside. Quick-like, while the street's clear."

Pascal limped around the fish table, and the vendor gestured to the fabric rear wall of the stall. Pascal pushed through, and a few feet beyond found a black marble wall just like any other alley in Nox Valar, save for a peculiar symbol marked in chalk.

He produced his own stick of chalk from his pocket and finished the symbol with three swift, precise lines, completing the shape: a stylized, half-open door. The stone of the wall rippled like the surface of a pond at a sudden breeze. The stick of chalk dissolved in Pascal's fingers, flaking away to ash as the particles fell to the ground.

Pascal stepped through.

It was thick, like pushing through six inches of half-damp mud, but left no residue. Beyond was not the interior of the building, but an open plaza filled with row after row of kiosks and merchant's stalls.

Today, Anywhere was in a desert, and Pascal-Cypress was momentarily shocked at the sensation of baking sunshine beating down on her. She stood there for a moment, dazzled at the unexpected sensation. She had been to Anywhere several times since coming to the Crossing, and while the market itself never changed, its location was always new. Previous trips had taken her to a night market amid a vast city she'd never seen, a snowy bazaar set among alien steppes, and a damp, misty morning shrouded in fog so thick she'd barely been able to see two stalls down. But today the sky above was a clear, azure blue, the distant horizon blurred with heat-haze.

There were no walls around Anywhere, but she felt its boundaries in the very bedrock of her soul. Within the marketplace, she could wander, barter, and peruse as she pleased. But no matter where Anywhere settled today, she could not leave it. Straying too near the invisible edge of the pocket-realm filled mortal souls with sheer, animal panic. She had heard rumors—*everyone* had heard rumors—of souls being forced beyond the line or rushing it themselves in some desperate defiance of their fate. Those that had seen such incidents gave differing stories, but never spoke of a pleasant result. The powers that had defined Anywhere had not been inclined—or able—to create a back door to the Crossing. Cypress sometimes wondered if that was where some of the beasts that crawled out of the Lightless Chasm started out.

She limped along in Pascal's form, spending most of her time in the stalls dedicated to mortal food, all a good deal fresher than the festering catches of the fishmonger. Despite the exorbitant prices, Cypress found herself tempted more than once, simply for the chance to taste something real, vibrant, and free from the ashen overtones of the Crossing.

In one stall, Cypress overheard a horned, purple-skinned devil in garish silken robes making arrangements for a public banquet in a month. *Come for the free food, stay for the pitch on the merits of damnation,* she thought. The amazing thing was, it worked well enough to be worth the effort.

The trade of mortal food into Nox Valar was a vibrant one in certain circles. Most of the vendor's stock each month was bought up by immortals stationed in Nox Valar, as an easy and nigh-universal means of bartering with the mortal dead. The devil was hardly the first to put together something like that—in fact, there was a whole backroom circuit in the city where savvy mortals could taste the delights of the cosmos as they were plied and tempted by celestials, infernals, and other powers with an interest in cheap souls. The problem was, eventually everyone fell for a sales pitch.

The food vendors were the least of Anywhere's offerings, and the least illicit. Anything a soul could imagine was available for sale in the underworld's black market, including things no one should ever want. Where Paradise was a cornucopia of sensation and experience, Anywhere was a warehouse without rival. Forbidden texts, cursed artifacts, the rarest reagents, hallucinogens, and spellcraft that would give a balor the high of its existence: these were but a question away for any who could pay their price, and still just the tip of the iceberg.

There were goods and services for sale here available nowhere else in existence. Covens of hags focused their entire attention on bending the strands of fate at the behest of clients they met here. A blind cartographer sold maps to worlds unseen, marked with all the places the veils between planes were thinnest. One infernal traded in luck: great fortune found his customers for an agreed-upon duration, after which it was taken back, with interest. Why someone would agree to such a deal, Cypress had never been sure, but she had never seen the chair in front of his stall empty.

One stall sold keys, a new one each day, displayed in a simple case with a price tag affixed to it that Cypress had never even been able to decipher, and provided no further information. All Cypress knew of it was that a silent crowd of infernals, celestials, and other Things gathered outside the stall each day when the newest key was unveiled and bid ferociously to take possession of it.

The most infamous trade in Anywhere, at least from Nox Valar's standpoint, was in memories. Memories were the lifeblood of the dead. A soul's memories of life, of experience, of *being* were what gave them substance in the Crossing, and what let them "live" nearly unchanged. Snatch a stray thought or idle reminiscence as she did with her traps, and the victim wouldn't lose much—the damage was no worse than finding a new gray hair or developing a touch of pain in your joints; a bit of wear and tear, but nothing that would unmake a soul. At least, that's what Cypress told herself.

The memory butchers of Anywhere were not interested in so light a touch. They would bind a soul and tear it apart, sifting through its existence to rip the juiciest, choice cuts of sensation, emotion, and impact from the victim. Infernals, psychophages, and worse flocked to Anywhere for these psychic feasts, and the cartels were all too happy to provide. What was left of the mangled souls, if it was anything coherent, were beasts best destroyed or committed to the Chasm.

Cypress knew enough to avoid the scene here. This was turf; dominated by organized cartels who had no issue unraveling a free agent that crowded in on their business. The Monarchy raided the market from time to time, when they could predict its ever-shifting doorways, but they rarely netted anyone more than bit players and cutouts.

Cypress had sometimes spotted Pale Horsemen milling through the stalls—nominally, the Monarchy's messengers and couriers. It wasn't implausible that their business would often carry them to a gathering point of so many extra-planar creatures and objects. But the rumor in Nox Valar's underbelly was that the Horsemen had more ... *direct* duties too. In their presence, the cartel merchants made themselves scarce, presenting only mundane and uninteresting wares in their stalls if one happened by. It was a façade they didn't bother with in the presence of actual angels, and that alone was enough for Cypress to avoid the Horsemen who found their way here on principle.

Still wearing Pascal's face, she wound her way through Anywhere's many wonders and did her best to skirt around its terrors. She'd arrived early, but killing time there was not a problem.

When she estimated the appointed time was close, she found her way to a simple kiosk on a less-trafficked aisle of the sprawling marketplace. The structure was as much a tent as a stall, its opening closed by a hanging swath of canvas. The fabric walls of the tent were a brilliant blue, matching the shade of the blessed desert sky above. Despite the daylight, a single lantern hung from a hook outside its entryway. The flame within flickered a gentle green.

Cypress parted the tent's flap and limped inside. Her knee ached badly, wrenched somewhere during the desperate flight through the Bastion of Endings and subsequent leap from the perimeter wall down to the Road of Eternity. She was bandaged and patched as well as Mads had been able, but she needed rest and a proper healer. For now, at least old Pascal's twisted frame matched the pain she felt with each stride.

Dimereial waited within, brow arched as she tottered toward the runic circle inscribed on the floor. He waved his hand, and they blazed to life.

"If I wanted to use one of these rudimentary privacy-for-rent places, sleuth, I wouldn't be paying she of the Bells such a high retainer." The angel's tone was laced with disapproval. "I had to correct several basic mistakes in the scrying wards myself. This can't be the best Anywhere has to offer."

"It's not," Cypress explained in Pascal's grizzled voice. "But it's cheap enough to be beneath notice for anyone looking into a major incident, and Madrigal's might be compromised right now. And I trusted you to add whatever extra measures were needed."

"You failed to secure the Herald's memory, I take it?" Dimereial sounded unsurprised.

"I was expected, it turned out. They laid a trap for me. I barely escaped."

He frowned. "Tell me everything."

She did, recounting her entire operation starting from her first surveillance pass to her frantic, wounded escape through the city, trying to balance a circuitous route to avoid pursuit with an expedient one to get to Mads before she keeled over and unraveled there in the street. The angel sighed as she finished.

"This is unfortunate, Cypress, but I do not think you were at fault. Somehow, the Heralds caught wind of my intention. This operation was doomed from the start; I asked too much, and I am impressed that you managed to escape at all. It was bold."

Though she was clinging to her sense of professionalism while conveying the matter-of-fact report, relief washed over her at his response. She hadn't realized just how much she'd been dreading reporting her failure to her celestial client.

"What now?" she asked. "I need to recover or find a good healer. But I need another job as soon as I can. You know my timetable."

"You won't recover fast enough, dear sleuth. The window of time to save your dear Queen Anastasia will have passed if we wait that long."

Cypress felt her pulse thundering in Pascal's ears. "Then we'll start immediately. If you have targets that aren't in such a secured—"

"Peace, Cypress. Be at ease." Dimereial held up a hand. "One way or another, you have become known to those I seek. I will not risk all I've achieved, all *we* have achieved, by sending you out again. There is too much at stake." There was a glimmer of warm light in his palm, and he held it out. Two items sat there: a simple platinum amulet, circular and without design save for a hole in the center, through which a leather loop was affixed, and a Crossway Coin. Cypress took them.

Her heart hammered louder as she looked at the coin. It was for the Pale Horsemen, and it was due the next day. "D-Dimereial…"

The angel smiled, and the sight filled her with reassurance that everything would be okay. "You did great things for me, Cypress. For the Balance. Souls were saved by your actions. I'll not see your hopes dashed due to bad luck. Our work is at an end, and this is your payment—a little earlier than expected, but well-earned nonetheless."

He clapped her on the shoulders, beaming with pride. "The Coin, you know. Keep it secret, of course, but I have faith that you can handle a valuable Coin for less than a day."

"The medallion?" she whispered.

"A personal mark. The Horseman that Coin grants you an audience with is known to me. Present the mark to him, and he will know that your payment has already been made in full, and that your message must be carried to your queen with the highest urgency."

"T-thank you, Dimereial." Tears blurred her vision, and she fell to her knees as a sob of relief shook her chest. "I thought… I thought that I'd fail her again. Thank you. Thank you."

"Dry your eyes, little one." He helped her back to her feet. "Such loyalty should be commended. You know, it wasn't your abilities that led me to you. It was your sense of duty. Your drive to do what you had to in order to save those you loved, even from beyond the grave—that's what caught my attention, dear sleuth."

She nodded, not trusting her voice. Anastasia would be warned. Anastasia would be *safe*. She hadn't failed her oldest friend, her only love. Even in death, she would protect her.

"I trust you already know what your message will say?" The angel smiled again. "If not, you've got a couple of hours to hash out a draft, by my count."

"I know. I'd better go. I can't miss this." Cypress matched his smile. "Thank you again. I'm glad we did some good."

"As am I, dear sleuth. As am I."

CHAPTER 22

Pel Solimo restarted his circuit of the room, triple-checking his notes. "They looked like this acolyte, Lori?" he asked again.

"Loren, investigator. As I said." The High Herald sighed. Pel made a mark next to that line in his notepad, a simple symbol he used to indicate that the witness's story had remained consistent.

"They approached you at your desk," he continued. "What were you working on?"

"I was studying the scriptures," Vessa Theramay said for the third time. Indeed, the huge desk in the office was clear, save for a large, illuminated tome and a smattering of blood. The scarlet droplets were sprayed across a two-foot arc, clearly from someone standing in front of the desk. A slender, bloodied dagger small enough to hide up a sleeve had been neatly placed at the edge of the desk, ready for inspection.

Pel tapped the tip of his stylus on the page. "And the object the intruder gave you?"

"It appears to be a simulacrum of a charm I had as a girl."

The tarnished pendant had fallen to the floor, its spellcloth pouch crumpled and discarded to one side. Scorch marks traced the pendant's path from where it lay up into the stone beak of a raven motif set into the wall. The beak was shattered, its edges charred. "Powerful enchantment on that thing," he observed.

"Indeed. It takes a lot to destroy a sentinel ward like that."

"I meant the … what did you call it?" Pel jotted down another note. "Sentinel ward. Looks like it completely dispelled a memory totem. Not an easy thing."

"If you say so, investigator."

"Do you have many wards like that, Herald?"

"High Herald," she corrected. "Every ranking clergy member on the Road has protections and protocols in place, Pel. You know that."

Pel tapped his stylus a few more times, then closed his notebook. "You're right, Vessa, I know that there's wheels-within-wheels on this side of town. I probe because it shakes loose more information. And I need information if I'm going to do my job. So help me out here."

Vessa Theramay's expression hardened to the imperious mask he knew she wore for all official duties. Or on-the-record conversations. "The Bastion of Endings endeavors to provide all the information required of it by the Godless Monarchy, investigator Solimo. If I can be of further assistance, you need only ask."

Pel glared at her, annoyed. "Fine, High Herald Theramay. What else was on your desk during the incident?"

Vessa's expression flickered. "What are you talking about?"

"The blood spray, Vessa. All the droplets cut off along a straight line. Something else was on your desk; you or your people removed it before I got here, but you still took pains to make it look like the scene was unchanged. Which has me wondering more about what you were hiding than who attacked you, because what are the odds those things are going to turn out to be related?"

Vessa Theramay sighed and made her way over to one of the plush armchairs in her office. She gestured for Pel to take the one across from her. After a moment, he complied.

"Off the record," she insisted.

"We'll see."

"I'm serious, Pel."

"And so am I, Vessa. I'm working on a case that ties into this, and I don't have time for cloak-and-dagger Road crap. Not this time. So either tell me what's going on and trust me to focus on what needs doing, or I'm going to call up a task force to pull up every floorboard in this place until I piece it together myself."

Vessa stared at him, surprised by the intensity of his response. Then, she reached down and flipped a subtle latch in the end table beside her and swung a compartment open. She reached in and produced a crystal decanter of amber liquid and two matching tumblers.

"What's going on, Pel?"

"I can't, Vessa."

"Show me yours and I'll show you mine."

Pel gave her a deadpan look. She poured both glasses.

"What? A little humor."

"Just because we know each other—"

"I think we're a little beyond 'knowing' each other."

"That was a long time ago."

"We're dead, Pel. Be less rigid with your carefree summer flings." Vessa held out one of the tumblers.

"You're supposed to be a holy woman," he muttered, accepting the drink.

"Haven't seen a thing in the doctrine about my personal life."

"Dammit, Vessa, I'm not here for your personal life."

She contemplated the liquid in the glass for a moment, swirling it around. Then she raised it in a mock toast to Pel and slugged it back. His brows shot up.

"We lost someone," she explained as she poured herself a refill.

"In the attack?"

"No. Well, yes," she corrected, "but before that. We were expecting a visitor. Another Herald. Living. We'd made arrangements. But something happened. We think they were killed. So, we're looking."

"You think they wound up in the Crossing?"

"Yeah, I do. But I also think they should have had a dozen different ways to contact the Bastion days ago. So, I think whoever offed them is working both sides."

"Shit." Pel hesitated, then sipped his drink. "Damn, that's good."

"It would be better for me if this stayed quiet," Vessa told him.

"If it doesn't matter to my case, it will," Pel said. "What was on the desk?"

"Maps. Reports. The sum of our recovery efforts."

"And you hid those because…?"

"Someone's working both sides, Pel. And I had a shapeshifter in my office."

He stared at her.

"I didn't know it would be you who came." She shrugged. "And I still had to make sure it *was* you."

"Someone like that couldn't infiltrate the Horsemen."

"I'd have said the same thing about my office, yesterday."

Pel sat back in the chair and took another swig. "Shit."

"You said it." Vessa leaned in. "Is Thrace working on it?"

Pel instinctively glanced around.

"We're in private, here," she assured him. "And, I'm hoping, still off the record."

"If such a person existed," Pel began, "I'd say he was working his contacts. The ones I don't ask about."

"Isn't that your whole job with him? To ask about things?"

"It's Thrace, Vessa."

"Yeah, the Blackfire Lich," she said. "He didn't give *himself* the name, Pel. He earned it."

"That was a long time ago," Pel replied. "Lot of souls since then. He's ... mostly just Thrace, now. He's an obstinate, foul-mouthed asshole..."

"Oh, but now I'm just thinking about how much I like him."

"... But he's on the level. And even if he was slipping, he's contained enough that he can't go rogue. Beyond that, how much I hover over him is really a matter of how miserable I want to make both of us."

She nodded, acquiescing. "So how bad is it?"

"I don't know. Thrace was really freaked out, but he tends toward the dramatic."

Vessa waited. Pel sighed, exasperated, and continued, "We were tracking a string of possible memory thefts. Thought they were isolated. Some big hits, some small ones. Typical Anywhere stuff. But then we picked up on a pattern. Followed it back through old cases. *Way* back. Found a ton of possibles. We spent a week just piecing together the timeline, figuring out what fits and what was just noise."

"You found something that alarmed you?"

"There's enough there to think it's an organized effort. But not cartel stuff. Nothing really turns up on the market to match the thefts."

"So the goal isn't profit."

"Not here, anyway. Maybe there's an angle I'm not seeing."

"What'd Thrace think?"

"He focused on the other half of the equation: what happens next."

"Which is?"

"The vics usually get resurrected soon after the attacks. Then they're back here before long. And cross over practically immediately."

Vessa furrowed her brow. "That's odd. You could work it with some agents on the mortal side, I guess. But why?"

Pel took another sip. "You're going to love this part."

"Oh?"

"Most of their destinations change."

Vessa stared at him. Alarm bells began to sound in her mind. "What do you mean by that? Spell it out, Pel."

"When they come here, they're like anyone else. Afterlives lined up based on their lives, faiths, pacts, whatever. Maybe a few of them cut a deal in the Crossing, find religion, get a new direction. You know how it goes." He set his drink down, still nearly full.

"That's a minority of souls," Vessa confirmed. "A couple here and there."

"Yeah, well. Every case we pulled as possibly related? We were just looking based on likely memory theft victims, mind you. Didn't start looking into their outcomes until we had a huge collection of them… Damn near every one of them wound up in a different afterlife than what was expected."

Pel and Vessa sat in silence for a long moment.

"You're not as alarmed as Thrace?" she asked.

"I don't like to jump to conclusions."

"I think I'm with Thrace on this one."

"Never liked it when you two got along."

Vessa stood and strode toward the door. "Come on, Pel."

He followed without complaint. The High Herald led him through the twisting corridors of the Bastion, pointing out the path the intruder had taken after the failed attack on her. She pointed out the room where an acolyte had been found throttled into unconsciousness, and how the wards in her office had likely disabled the intruder's shifting abilities. She pointed out the damaged walls and marred stonework caused by unknowingly releasing a guardian statue right on top of the intruder, and the path it had blazed out of the inner sanctum and through the higher floors. Finally, she brought him to where the intruder had leaped from the window, injuring themselves further when they scrambled down the perimeter wall below.

"Sounds like they were hurt pretty bad. Surprised they didn't 'ravel themselves on the jump. When will your spell wear off?" Pel asked.

"When it's removed," Vessa told him. "That was a divine ward. The list of people who can undo it is short, even in Nox Valar. I know most of them. Your shifter isn't going to be looking too pretty for a while, and I'll hear if someone starts asking about getting a curse like that lifted."

Pel wasn't so sure. He didn't doubt Vessa's knowledge of the power players on the Road, but she didn't have as much experience with the illegitimate side of Nox Valar. There were plenty of beings in the city's underbelly that could pull off something like that discreetly … for a price.

"Don't count on it," he told her. "Next question is the big one. Why you?"

"I'm listening."

Pel blinked. "I wasn't being rhetorical, V. This was targeted. It's possible the other attacks were too, but we've never gotten to interview a victim before they were hit. So why would someone go after your memories?"

"I don't have a clue, Pel."

Pel glowered.

"No, really," Vessa insisted. "Hand to the Harbinger, the secrets I've got are mostly professional."

"Mostly?"

"Well, you wouldn't want me telling people abou—"

"Point taken! Point taken."

She winked before continuing. "The things I know that might attract espionage came with my position. If I were neutralized, the next High Herald in my office would have access to all the same information."

"You're saying that this couldn't be personal? Someone exacting payback, or someone with a vested interest in altering your fate?"

Vessa held up her hands, puzzled. "I suppose anything's possible, but I can't think of anyone I pissed off *that* bad. Alive or dead. It could be a shot at the faith through me? But that takes us right back to the same question."

"Yeah, 'why you?' Had to be easier targets related to the Harbinger than the dead center of the Bastion." Pel paced the room observing the trail of ash smeared on the door, across the carpet, and to the windows. "And on top of that, if you were going to take a shot at the Bastion, would you do it with one person?"

"I wouldn't try that at any temple on the Road," Vessa confirmed. "But that Bastion struck me as a particularly bad idea, yes. Being that one of our tenants is preparation for inevitable conflict."

Pel tapped his stylus in his notebook. He was circling around an intuition, just out of reach. He just needed that extra push...

"If you were taken off the board right now," he began, putting it together as the words left his mouth. Yes, there was something here. "What would go wrong?"

Cypress gazed up at the Onyx Requiem in quiet awe.

It was impossible not to have seen the mammoth structure before, of course, with its titanic domes, arches, and spires that stood as the central focal point over the whole city's skyline. It was the throne of the Godless Monarchy, the seat from which all the many factions and cosmic, necessary functions of the crossing were coordinated as best as the mortals, celestials, and Other Things within could manage. But Cypress had never been so close to it, never had the time nor reason to trek all the way to the edge of Nox Valar for simple sightseeing.

From the moment she'd arrived in the Crossing, murdered and disoriented, every moment had been dedicated to this mission. To find a way to send word back, and do it fast. She was one of the few souls in the city who simply didn't have the *time*; not yet. Once Anastasia was safe, the real Anastasia, her childhood friend, her love, her queen, there would be all the time in the world. *Then,* she could kick back and enjoy being dead, as odd as that sounded, and notions like sightseeing or seeking enlightenment or studying the accumulated, flowing knowledge of the multiverse wouldn't seem like frivolous distractions. No more ticking clock, no more dirty deeds in the underworld—though she'd probably still play cards with Mads, if she were being honest—just finally, *maybe*, something like peace.

She clutched the Coin that Dimereial had given her, his final payment. She was so close.

The Pale Horsemen had a presence throughout the whole city, but the Coin was for here: a small office set into a large barracks, a block away from the gargantuan Requiem. It didn't surprise her that Dimereial had a Coin that brought her so close to the proverbial heart of things, but it could have been a satellite office on the edge of the Chasm for all she cared. The important thing was that it was *time*.

She'd worn a face she'd avoided since coming to Nox Valar: Lizabeth, a flame-haired half-elf she and Anastasia had grown up with. The visage seemed fitting. Lizabeth had died young, a casualty in another bout of palace intrigue gone wrong. It had been a sobering moment for Anastasia and Cypress, a loss of innocence. It was the loss of their friend that had put the mischievous pair on the paths, Anastasia to the throne, and Cypress as her ever-present watcher in the shadows.

Cypress couldn't risk wearing Anastasia's face here, nor any other she'd worn since coming to the Crossing. The Pale Horsemen were messengers, sure. But Cypress had spent enough time around Madrigal's and crawling through Nox Valar's underbelly to hear the whispers about their other duties. The secret departments, the undercover agents, the way the fiends of Madrigal's always made themselves scarce when certain "messengers" were about. Cypress didn't know what was true when it came to all that—but she wasn't taking risks today.

Lizabeth would do.

Cypress presented her Coin to the attendant outside a gilded black-iron door and was directed inside. The structure itself was grand, but the Horsemen's section was a practical, utilitarian thing. Wide corridors, several stories tall, with vaulted roofs connected wings lined with offices that branched off of them at regular intervals. Symbols she didn't recognize, but that had the bearing of heraldry, decorated the walls and floors in the most public areas, but the majority of the place was no more ornamented than whatever embellishment bare marble and fine furniture lent the space by default. For much of her life, she'd have thought that luxurious... but in a city hewn from the stuff, it was practically nondescript.

Her Coin got her into a waiting area, where a prominently displayed hourglass and dial mechanism, the tower of the Keepers cast in clever miniature, ticked down the final few minutes. Cypress tried to calm her nerves and told herself that she was almost there. The Horsemen would carry her message to Anastasia. From there, it was up to the Queen to save herself. It galled Cypress, gnawed at her, the fact that she could do no more. But it *was* a fact. She was dead. Gone. There was this one last duty, and then eternity.

There were few other souls waiting with her, so she watched the Horsemen go about their business as she waited. She was seated in an alcove off a main hall and could observe the comings and goings of the people headed to several of the office halls. Few were notable; souls going about menial tasks, carrying sheaves of notes and bundles of scrolls around. Occasionally the vibrancy of a still-living mortal would pass, and once a lesser celestial and an infernal strode by, deep in an unintelligible, bickering discussion.

Of more interest to Cypress were the ... *other* Horsemen. She marked a few of them; her spymaster's intuition never quite shut down. The Pale Horsemen were the messengers of Nox Valar as a whole and the Monarchy in particular, but many suspected their remit was broader than that. Sitting in the heart of their operations, she had to believe the rumors were true. To her trained eyes, there were divisions within divisions here. Most Horsemen that passed were exactly what they seemed. But every so often, one would walk by that tickled her perception in the exact same way that she would once have marked an enemy spy.

One such agent came down the hall. Cypress tried to catalog why she was able to mark him out among the others. His dress was not notably different than the messengers and menials, and he wore no particular badge of office, save for a small notepad that he was methodically flipping back and forth through. It was something in his bearing, she decided, his calm awareness. She was sensing him habitually scanning his surroundings, always taking in more than he put out. In life, she would have marked him for further investigation. Hells, she might have even tried to recruit him.

The agent she was studying was carrying on a conversation with another crimson-haired woman, older than Lizabeth with a scar that marred—

Cypress's breath caught in her throat as High Herald Vessa Theramay's gaze snared hers. For a horrible, agonized moment, she was sure she'd been made. The floor of her gut fell away, replaced by an empty void, and she wanted to curse the entire cosmos for letting her get so close to her goal before snatching it back. *Again,* she thought, as the bitter memory of her death—a blade plunging between her ribs, a gasping, airless, silent agony—sprang unwanted to the forefront of her mind.

But then Vessa Theramay's eyes slid away, and the pair continued out of sight without so much as a flicker of recognition. However the Herald had seen through Cypress's disguise before, it hadn't worked now. She was just Lizabeth.

Slowly, oh so slowly, Cypress's heart rate returned to normal.

As the hourglass trickled down, an attendant entered and announced that Cypress's number was up. She followed him from the waiting area down one of the near-identical halls, into a small office. There, a bored-looking Horseman sat behind a desk and motioned her inside. Something about him was odd, and without the contrast of other souls milling around, it took her a moment to realize what it was.

"You're alive," she blurted, taking a seat across from him.

The man was young, dark of tone, and had a boyish charm to him. He roused as he looked to her—to Lizabeth—and flashed her a brilliant white grin. "I'm afraid so," he confirmed. "What can I do for you?"

"I... sorry, I guess I didn't expect that. I knew there were some living folks in the city; you just don't see them much."

"Quite alright, miss...?"

"Lizabeth." She brandished young Liza's coy smile, the one that had made half the court swoon.

"Good to meet you, Lizabeth. My name is Carlow, and I work for the Monarchy. Now, I know it takes quite a while to get an appointment here, so why don't you tell me what you're looking to accomplish so I can get that done for you, eh?"

Cypress flushed. She wasn't entirely sure if it was an affectation of her Lizabeth persona or her own nerves. "I'm sorry, Mister Carlow. This has, in fact, been a long time coming, and it's very important to me. I need to send a message to a dear friend of mine who's still alive. She's in quite a lot of danger."

"Good that you're here then." Carlow raised his brows. "First, I need to ask you some questions..."

What followed was a series of questions that almost exasperated Cypress. What color was the sky where she was from? Major landmarks? Topographical features? What were the largest religions or cults in her region? Names of family lines? How many moons were in the sky? Major constellations? Number of oceans, if known, or number known?

Carlow went on like that for nearly an hour. For every question Cypress was able to answer, there were two she didn't even understand, and the ones that she comprehended didn't make sense to her. Finally, she stopped him.

"Carlow, I'm sorry, but I really don't know why you're asking me all of this." She huffed in the disarming way Liza used to whenever she wanted to tell off one of their tutors without getting in trouble—a knack Cypress and Anastasia took much longer to develop.

"I know it can be a bit baffling," Carlow chuckled, his tone understanding. "But try to understand: we carry messages from the citizens of the Crossing to planes all over the cosmos. There are Horsemen here who have worked together for decades and never visited the same worlds as their colleagues. These questions," he tapped the sheaf of papers where he'd been jotting down her answers, "get cross-checked with the Codex of the Mortal Realms to make sure I'm heading to the right place. Then we make sure that I'm the right person to carry your message—I wouldn't do too great in the Plane of Fire, would I? But we'd find someone who would—and *then* I head off."

"Is there no faster way?" Cypress asked. "As I said I'm just… I'm worried about my friend, and we haven't even gotten to my message."

"It only takes a day or two at most, I promise. Probably less, in your case. Based on your answers so far, I'm pretty sure you're from one of the prime material planes, same as me. But we need to be sure. Better to spend a few minutes now than waste days on the wrong plane and have to start over at the back of the line, eh?"

Cypress conceded the point and apologized for her impatience. Carlow resumed his questions, filling in form after form of trivia and minutiae that would, little by little, narrow down exactly who and where "Lizabeth" was trying to reach.

"That should just about do it. Now, it's time for your message. You can provide me with a written transcription or dictate it to me, as is your preference. Unfortunately, I do have to read it, either way."

"Oh?"

"Function of the Crossing, I'm afraid. Most of the physical substances here are manifestations—memories, emotions, energy. If I try to carry a sealed letter you wrote out of here, there's a chance it won't... well, exist. So, in most cases, we strongly advise that the Horseman hear the message, and I can transcribe it in the material world once I get there if you prefer a written delivery. In any case, I can assure you that your privacy will be respected as much as these constraints allow, with the Monarch's guarantee."

"I see. In that case, I'll dictate it."

"Whenever you're ready." He dipped his quill in an inkpot and held it poised over a fresh page. She eyed it with skepticism. He laughed to himself and explained: "It helps me memorize it."

Cypress began:

Dearest,

By the time this letter reaches you, you'll no doubt be aware of my untimely demise. Know that while the circumstances yet elude me, I write this knowing my fate is clear. The measures I've taken to ensure this message's delivery in spite of it have been grueling, and do not bear dwelling upon. But I undertook this labor gladly through my sorrow, as I cannot bear the thought of petty jackals seeking the skulk about and undo the fragile prosperity we have—you have— finally brought to Alta. The skulking is mine to do. I shall endure no competition.

Cypress's eyes misted, and she had to collect herself. Coming to grips with her passing had been an ongoing process, but manageable. It wasn't too unlike being alive, most of the time. But speaking to Anastasia about it, whom she may never see, or touch, or speak to again… that was harder.

She continued:

Your time to act is short. Here is what I know.

The conspirators seek to elevate Kaskill to your throne. Yes, that sniveling little weasel. I am certain that the plot was not his; he's not got the brains nor the audacity for that, but he went along with it well enough. I suspect he realized that a puppeted royal figure-head was the most he could aspire to in life. Have him stabbed for me.

Your inner circle—you know the six besides myself that I'd bestow that name on, despite your insistence that there are no more than four—are with you. Beyond them, all the court is suspect. Most will wait to see which way the wind blows. I regret I was not able to ferret out the true vipers before I committed this message. Seek aid from Anthe and Duke Vorril. You don't trust them, Ana, but I do, and I'm right.

The solidarity of the army cannot be guaranteed. Some of the old guard have never forgiven you, and Kaskill will be making promises to others. I was able to satisfy myself of Durskin, Keller, and Pondé's loyalties. Their divisions will follow them. Recall Pondé to the capitol under some pretense at once; they are your new generals, as soon as you can make it fact. Set them to the task of pruning the ranks beneath them of traitors at once.

Of the conspiracy's heart, I know too little. Langrin is caught up in it, that much is sure, but his house is a fractured one. I had thought to turn his sons' ambitions against his, if only I had more time. Anthre may yet succeed.

Houses Paeter, Thistwoller, and Mida are rotten. Liddriver may yet stand with you, if you get to them first. The rest of the High Lords are suspect.

My soul aches with the knowledge that I'll not see you again in this life, and that I will not be by your side to weather this storm as we have so many before. And I wish my parting words need not contain quite such a list of chores!

But we knew what life we were to lead. Remember Liza's last words. I trust you, too.

Yours, forever. Your dour tree.

Anastasia would immediately question the veracity of the letter. Cypress was proud of how she'd trained her to conduct her royal duties with the appropriate amount of paranoia. She had been deliberate about her phrasing throughout: the jackals, stabbing Kaskill, the "chores" of the throne, Liza's words—all turns of phrase they'd used in private. Well, save the stabbing, which had started as more of a joke about Anastasia's thrice-removed miserable worm of a cousin, but felt more like a fervent wish to Cypress today.

But the last phrase would convince her queen, if nothing else did. Years ago, Anastasia had giddily found an old tome on "symbology in dendrology." It was so archaic as to be practically unreadable, but what had excited Anastasia had been the entry on cypress trees. They were symbols of the afterlife, they'd read. Markers of the underworld, beacons of mourning. Anastasia had giddily called her a "dour tree" whenever she'd wanted to get a rise out of her for the rest of that summer. Cypress had hated it. But eventually, as the two grew older, and closer, and their lives more complicated by the minute, she'd come to cherish having that one, dumb, private joke that meant nothing to anyone else.

Carlow finished writing and read it back to her. Cypress scrutinized his reconstruction but found no errors. She gave him strict instructions to deliver copies of the letter to several nodes of her spymaster's network: dead-drops, trusted protégés, and royal couriers who could be counted on to do their duty. The letter would reach Anastasia, one way or another.

She could have had Carlow deliver a verbal message, a bewitched dream, or one of several other methods the Horsemen were practiced in, but this was better. Anastasia would question any of those and dismiss them as frauds or imaginings or potential espionage. But she would trust a letter, laced with meaning, sent through Cypress's own network of redundancies and checkpoints. Because if she could have, that's how Cypress would have sent one.

Carlow gave her a peaceful moment to collect herself as he finished the requisite paperwork and compilation of delivery instructions. If he found her message remarkable, he didn't show it.

"Now, Miss Lizabeth, we're all set. There's only the matter of payment left."

"Of course," Cypress said, setting herself. "I was led to believe that payment had already been arranged through a mutual connection?"

Carlow's brow furrowed, and he looked at her skeptically for the first time. "Oh?"

"Here." She frowned and fished around in her pocket for the medallion Dimereial had given her. "I was told to present this to you."

She expected to pull out the simple silver medal on its leather strap. But when she glanced down, she saw it wasn't the nondescript disk the angel had given her, but instead a fractal, shifting, shimmering thing of impossible geometries that folded, twisted, and turned inside themselves and—

She found she could not look away, even as looking at the bundle of impossibilities was giving her a migraine and burning her eyes to behold. Carlow said something, then shouted in alarm, and Cypress was dimly aware of her form shifting. Lizabeth's features melted off of her, replaced by Anastasia's, then Loren's, and on and on, one after another, all the faces she'd worn in the Crossing. As her mind struggled to break free of the hypnotic un-thing in her hand, she was speaking, expounding in the midst of the Pale Horsemen a litany of all the crimes she had committed to reach this place, from her break-in at the Bastion of Endings to the pettiest memory traps she'd set to try and catch anything to barter her way up the line in on her own.

Some part of her registered that Carlow was no longer the only one in the room with her, that hands were grabbing her and wrestling her to the ground, but she hardly felt them. The object that had been the medallion was gone now, lost in the room or slipped back into the ether whence it came, but the painful shapes it had made were still seared into her vision as agonizing afterimages. She was pretty sure people were shouting, now, making demands, but she couldn't find a way to answer them.

Instead, she heard her own voice say with calm, even sincerity, "My name is Cypress Monroe, and I am a memory thief."

CHAPTER 24

"Oh, how I do love an impossibility!" Manuel tittered, practically dancing in his oversized robes as he circled Rasa again. He was a petite man, rail-thin and hunched, who was bursting with uncontained enthusiasm *all... the... time.* This lap, he was double-fisting a set of intricate arcane doodads made of, as far as she could tell, a completely nonsensical assemblage of brass, crystals, and string. One of the crystals tumbled wildly where the strings suspended it in the brass frame as if it were a magnet exposed to a rapidly oscillating opposite until it became hopelessly tangled. Manuel tossed it over his shoulder without looking at it and rummaged around in his shoulder sack to produce a different, even more obscure implement.

Borssa huffed as the knotted gizmo crashed to the floor, muttering a minor incantation while flicking their trunk at it. The device was whisked away and placed neatly on a shelf by unseen forces. They then went back to their third cup of tea with Secan.

Roscoe, who had been the second to volunteer for Borssa's summons behind Manuel, was somewhat more erudite, calmly asking Rasa probing questions as he sketched out a circle of glyphs and runes around her. She was reclining on a couch Borssa had plucked up with one hand and moved to one of the Belfry's arcane laboratories, staring up at the half-dome ceiling above. Whenever Manuel seemed in danger of trodding on Roscoe's work in his enthusiasm, the latter reached out and deftly redirected his companion without pausing his work. Manuel didn't seem to notice.

"What's impossible about this?" Rasa asked, as Manuel shone a bright light into her eyes and examined them with a many-lensed contraption he'd strapped to his head.

"The fact that you exist, of course!" the aged wizard declared with glee.

"Dear old Secan told you something of the workings of the Sunless Crossing, yes?" Roscoe asked her as Manuel distracted himself once more, now shining the light at her palm and attempting to examine how much of the glow emerged from the back of her hand.

"Some, yes. Things aren't always a sensible distance from each other. We live here for a long time until we pass on or return to the living world, because we're dead souls. Though I don't remember being alive."

"And there's the rub." Roscoe tapped the tip of his nose before gently course-correcting Manuel again. "When a soul comes to the Crossing, Rasa, how does it form a body? How does it know what to look like, how to feel? We are, after all, dead. Your physical body was left somewhere back in the material world, wherever you met your end."

"I ... don't know?"

"Few really take time to think of it, sadly. Such a *waste* of an afterlife." Manuel heaved an exasperated sigh before he scampered out of view again.

"We're made of memories, Rasa. Fundamentally," Roscoe continued, as if Manuel hadn't spoken. "When a soul lands here, it's a spark. A bundle of energy. But when the gods built this place, they decided—"

"There you go with that divino-generative notion again, Roscoe," Manuel chuffed. "*My* thesis remains that, *if* a so-called GPOBDGLC—that's 'Greater Power or Other Being Displaying God-Like Capabilities,' you see—even if one or more GPOBDGLC's *were* involved in the creation of the Crossing, the underlying structure of metaphysical—"

"*There is some debate on the details,*" Roscoe reasserted himself, "but that hardly matters in the introductory lecture, does it, my friend?"

Manuel huffed, shrugged, grinned, and disappeared. Manuel was a lot, Rasa decided.

"Regardless of the finer points. A soul can't just float about here like that for long. The Crossing demands we exist as close to our corporeal state as is practicable, so the soul must form a body around itself. But the materials of the Crossing are finite and limited, and the soul certainly did not arrive with anything from which to construct a flesh-and-blood being. So, what are we made of?"

"I ... had not considered it. I suppose I assumed 'magic.'"

Roscoe nodded, marking another rune on the floor and pacing to inspect his work in Manuel's wake. "Not wrong, but imprecise for the situation at hand. No, Miss Rasa, we are formed of our memories made flesh. Your soul recalls how it saw itself. It remembers how your limbs moved, and so you have limbs that move that way. It recalls the face you wore, and that is what we see. It recalls how it interacted with the weave of magic, the air and breath of life, and the tastes, smells, and sights inherent in having a mortal body. The Crossing does not recreate us; it empowers your soul to manifest its memories of itself."

A frozen bead of fear began growing in Rasa's gut. "What happens if you lose your memories?"

"You unravel!" Manuel declared, measuring Raven's head with a five-pronged set of calipers. "It's really a fascinating process. The soul begins to flay and fragment until—"

"It ain't pretty," Secan offered from across the room, sipping his tea. "Those things that attacked us in the Fields? Could be some o' them were unraveled souls, one time or another."

"Just so," Roscoe agreed. "All souls go through a small amount of it over a long enough time period. Memories fade, become less sure. You'll see many in the city who appear less substantial. Faded. For the most part, this is harmless. But if a soul suffers a severe trauma, like being 'killed' in the Crossing, it can cause a loss of those memories. The soul becomes less able to encase itself in its own identity, less sure of what it is. If the damage is too severe, it becomes catastrophic, and all that's left is a twisted abomination that knows only its own pain and that it's missing something—which it will attempt to violently replace with pieces it tears from the rest of us. To no avail."

"Am I unraveling?" Rasa looked wide-eyed at Secan, but Manuel slid into her field of view, very close.

"Ah, and there's the impossibility, you see. You have no memory, yet, if you had no memory, you could not be you in the first place. How can that be? We don't know!"

Manuel trotted away to rummage through a toolbox he'd brought in at … some point, and Roscoe once more stepped in.

"There's a few possibilities we're working through right now. First, we know that you're, in fact, dead. And I believe we've now confirmed—Manuel, yes…?"

"Yep!"

"Alright, we're now certain that you're indeed a mortal too. Nothing too surprising about any of that so far. Next theory. You lost your memory before death. Seems like that's the only way we get close to where we are now. But there's a problem with that."

"What?" Rasa's tension was beginning to ease, but only a little. At least it seemed like she wasn't going to turn into one of those things in the Fields, not yet.

"Doesn't make any damned sense," Manuel spat. Roscoe rolled his eyes.

"Usually, in cases like that, the soul isn't affected when it gets here."

"Brains can get scrambled all they like. They're meat, see." Manuel tapped on his noggin. "If the soul needed the meat in perfect working order at the time of death, nobody would come through on this side properly. Lotta folks die because their brain meat gets roasted, chopped, bopped, sliced, diced, or turned into pudding. Soul doesn't need it." He paused. "I'm hungry."

"Those of us who study this agree on that essential point, yes," Roscoe clarified as Manuel distracted himself digging in his pockets for a snack. "The soul doesn't need the chemical, mechanical stuff of memories stored in the mind. The ... meat. It uses something more fundamental, truer. Some of us think it's how the gods see us—"

"Hogwash!"

"Or how the soul most recognizes itself. The point being that if your memories were *destroyed* before your death, you'd have them here. At least the ones that mattered. Which makes us think they must be present, but suppressed somehow."

"Still usually a meat issue," Manuel said between bites.

"True, true. Amnesia, especially due to spellwork, can simply be a cutting off of one's conscious mind from the deeper memories within. But that doesn't usually transfer to a soul in the Crossing."

"Never."

"It would seem at least *once*." Roscoe gave his companion a level look. Manuel opened his mouth to argue, crumbs dribbling free, but Roscoe cut him off. "Perhaps we simply compile the data now, yes?"

Manuel closed his mouth and nodded. Still chewing, he produced a large tome that was *much* too big for the pocket he'd pulled it from, plopped down on the floor, and began recording all his esoteric readings inside. Rasa saw him flipping between pages that featured intricate, many-layered diagrams and charts where he dutifully scribbled the data his strange tools had been furnishing.

Roscoe bid her to lie back and be still for a moment, and then stepped out beyond the perimeter of his rune circle. He chanted a steady stream of unintelligible syllables, and Rasa felt the air in the room *thrum* with the energies of harnessed ether. The light in the room intensified, and she watched as flickering embers of arcane energy flitted above her in a subtle dance. She imagined she could see them riding the eddies and currents of an invisible ocean, its surface patterns revealed only through the sum of their motions.

Soon, the lights faded, and the gathered energy ebbed out of the room. Roscoe told her she could move about as she liked, and she joined Secan and Borssa for another cup of honeyed tea while the odd pair of wizards compared their findings. They could hear them bantering with one another; despite Roscoe's more composed outward demeanor, after a few minutes, it became clear to Rasa that he was enjoying the investigation as much as Manuel.

"I suppose there's only so many ways to interpret that," Roscoe muttered, looking over Manuel's extensive notes.

"I concur, I concur. Assuming we're not entertaining a deviation in the primary governance of—"

Rasa turned to regard Borssa and Secan as the "bellflies" continued their debate.

"This tea is delicious, Borssa," she told the elephant-folk.

"Thank you, Rasa. More honey?" They proffered a small, crystal jar full of amber liquid, and Rasa gladly added another dollop to her cup.

"Really, how are you getting that stuff?" Secan asked. "Mortal food is so damned expensive anywhere I see it."

"As I said, we have a club," Borssa explained. "We vote on what we want to buy every couple of months, and everybody chips in. Then I go to the merchants with a big group order. Only took a couple of times before word got around and they started bidding against each other for *our* business."

"Hells." Secan chuckled. "It's kinda genius, Borssa."

Borssa looked away. "It was actually Ori's idea, Secan. We just put it into practice."

Secan grew quiet.

"I'm ... sorry," Rasa began. "I've never asked. Who was Ori? You all seem to know her."

The Shepherd didn't look up from his tea, and Borssa gave him a piteous glance before answering. "Ori was a dear member of the Belfry for many years, Rasa. A good friend, and something of a genius when it came to researching, reverse-engineering, and transcribing spells."

Rasa furrowed her brow. "Did something happen to her?"

Borssa hesitated, but Secan broke his silence. "S'okay, Borssa. It was a good thing." He turned to Rasa, and she saw the most peculiar sorrow in his eyes. "Ori was one o' my first souls, Rasa. Right after I became a Shepherd. We hit it off and kept in touch after she got her bearings here in the city. Real quick figured out that she fit right in here at the Belfry."

"Oh, didn't she just?" Borssa sighed wistfully. "I'd only been here a decade, then. Wish I'd hit the ground running half as fast as Ori."

"Anyhow. We got … close. Carried on for years. You'll be surprised how they fly by. You're gonna think this place will drag you down, but if you find something to keep you busy… Anyway. That's how I got to know these folks. They put up with me visitin' Ori and asking clueless questions whenever I was passin' through."

"Where did she go?" Rasa asked, confused.

Secan clammed up again. Borssa patted his arm with one massive hand. "Everyone in the Crossing is going somewhere, Rasa. Sooner or later. Her time came, and she was off to her final afterlife."

"Shepherd's job is to get you where you're going," Secan whispered. "It was good. We were all happy for her. She… she earned her rest."

"Secan was Ori's Shepherd," Borssa explained. "Took her to the threshold."

"Got to say goodbye." Secan's voice was hoarse as he cracked a sad smile. "That's when she gave me my gift. Borssa here met us on the route, lugging a trunk full of Ori's favorite scrolls. Must have taken her months to put together."

"At least," Borssa confirmed. "She knew when her time was, Secan. She made arrangements."

"Ori said I'd put them to better use than anyone she knew." Secan laughed. "Reckon she'd be thrilled with how our little trek has gone down, eh? Saved our hide a couple times, now."

"That wasn't all she left, you know."

Secan was quiet for a moment. "I know, Borssa. I haven't forgotten. Just needed some time."

Rasa felt a pang in her heart at the loss writ on her Shepherd's face as he talked about Ori, an echo of sympathetic pain. She didn't have any parallels to draw on, but … there was something deep there that she recognized, and she wished she could change it for him.

"Sorry, Secan. I didn't know."

He held up a hand, shaking his head before she'd finished. "No worries, Rasa. No worries. Been a couple of years now. It's good to be back here. Good to talk about it."

"Think they're getting close to a point over there?" Secan asked, nodding to Manuel and Rosco, who were still chattering away.

"Anything on that order would have had other—" Roscoe was saying.

"Of course, Roscoe, I'm aware. So, the only possibilities left are—"

"We know she's mortal, though, so that eliminates—"

"Gentlemen?" Borssa's thunderous conversational tone boomed through the laboratory, and the two hunched bellflies turned to regard the tea party. "I have no doubt your full paper on the matter will be fascinating, but we do have a subject here who deserves a preview."

Roscoe looked embarrassed, Manuel unabashed, but he nodded. "Quite quite quite. You're certainly an interesting case, Miss Rasa."

"I try, I suppose," Rasa said with deadpan resignation.

"We are relatively certain that your memories were, in fact, suppressed. It seems likely to have occurred within days of your demise, possibly even minutes. But not through any biomechanical malady or psychic trauma," Roscoe said.

"Not at all, not at all," Manuel concurred. "It is our working theory that you have been *cursed*."

"That so?" Secan's brows shot up.

"Indeed," Roscoe confirmed. "And not by some paltry hedge witch. We can only see the outlines of the enchantment on you—that's what we think we're seeing, anyway—but it's powerful."

"Quite, in order to afflict a soul all the way to the Crossing," Manuel concurred.

"That dictates a number of variables," Roscoe continued. "The bottom line is that the curse is almost certainly not arcane in origin."

Borssa snorted in surprise.

"I don't really know what that means." Rasa frowned and looked askance across the tea set. The Shepherd shrugged, and Borssa gestured impatiently for their colleagues to get on with it.

"There are a handful of possible—"

"Divine, Miss Rasa," Manuel cut him off. "What my companion is dancing around here is that you were almost certainly cursed by a *powerful* wielder of divine energies in the final moments of your life, locking your memories away where even your soul couldn't consciously reach them. Perhaps a GPOBDGLC took a dislike to you."

"That might explain the hammer," Borssa said. "Harbinger iconography. Her robes are similar too."

"Don't know much about them." Secan looked to Borssa.

"It's an odd little cult," they answered. "Influential, but insular."

"I ... was one of these Harbinger people?" Rasa asked.

"Very possibly," Borssa tapped their trunk thoughtfully. "But if I were you, I'd want to know what 'wielder of divine energy' cursed me before I went to their temple and asked."

"Is there any way to remove the curse?" Rasa asked Roscoe and Manuel.

"Something like this will be a process," Roscoe explained. "If we simply try to scour it out with brute force, then there's every chance we do more damage than good."

"Like giving yourself a haircut with a torch," Manuel offered. Rasa stared at him, uncomprehending. "Are … haircuts not a concept you've retained? *Fascinating.*"

"We need to chip away at it, then pry it loose," Roscoe said. "I think the best way to do that would be to stimulate your underlying memories somewhat, before attempting anything more direct."

"How do I do that?" Rasa asked.

Manuel beamed. "You're going to love this."

CHAPTER 25

"He's fucking *back!*" Thrace burst in, stomping over to Pel Solimo's desk.

"*Today* you decide to use the door instead of skulking around?" Pel asked him, exasperated.

Thrace followed his handler's gaze to the chair beside him. "Oh, hi Vessa."

"Good to see you again, Thrace." Vessa Theramay smiled at the soul stitched.

"The Covenant of the Stitched is supposed to be clandestine..." Pel scolded, though it was obvious neither of them were listening.

"How's things at the birdhouse?"

"Bastion of Endings," Vessa corrected deftly, "and a bit hectic at the moment."

"Ah, here on official business then?"

"I believe I was being investigated for a bit, but we've moved past that."

Thrace shot Pel a look. "Pel!"

"Really? *You're* going to lecture me?"

"It's *Vessa*, Pel. Don't be that guy."

"I am not a 'that guy.' I was following a trail."

"It really wasn't a big deal, Thrace," she offered.

"He was so much less of a stick in the mud when you two were tog—"

"Thrace!" Pel exclaimed. Thrace rolled his eyes but dropped it. Vessa winked at him and mouthed: *I know.*

"Who's back, Thrace?" Pel pressed, desperate to regain some control over his office.

"General Edwin double-fucked Harson."

"Terrible middle name," Vessa muttered.

"Where did he go?" Pel asked.

"He was alive!"

Pel stopped thumbing through his notebook. "Oh, fuck me. When?"

"Had to be the day he walked out of here. Got resurrected right after we talked to him. It hadn't even been long enough for us to follow up with him yet, so it slipped through the cracks."

"And he's dead again already?"

"Must have been a hells of a trip, right?"

"What was that, a couple *days*? Do we know what he did while he was alive?"

"Not yet. I've got a couple of the kids digging into it."

"Thrace, how many..." Pel turned to Vessa. "You should know that the Covenant of the Stitched agents do not technically have the authority to requisition Horsemen resources or personnel without approval—"

"It's Vessa, Pel. She knows how it works."

"How do *you* think it works?!"

Vessa leaned back in her chair and smiled. "I do miss this."

Pel and Vessa brought Thrace up to speed with the events at the Bastion of Endings.

"Our thief took a crack at the birdhouse?" Thrace let out a low whistle as they finished. "Bold. *Fuckin'* bold. I wouldn't want to wade into that place even if Pel took the handicaps off."

"I'll take that as a compliment, Thrace," Vessa said.

"I'd still fuckin' clean you all out, you know," the stitched added. "Just saying, it'd probably suck."

"Sure, Thrace. Sure."

"We do not need to have this debate again," Pel cut in.

"Of course, of course. We all know the truth." Thrace blew a raspberry at Vessa, who returned the favor. "Now, a shapeshifter, you think? Not just a polymorph or a glamor?"

"That's what it looks like," Pel said.

"Positive," Vessa added. "Illusion wouldn't have made it through the door. And we've got measures against basic transmogrification magic throughout the compound. It'd be possible for someone to avoid those if they knew where they were, but what we've reconstructed of our intruder's route in and their hasty escape, leads me to believe they likely did not have a comprehensive layout of those defenses. Indeed, they walked right through several. The most likely explanation is a true shapeshifter, or some variety of doppelgänger. Maybe a really, really odd strain of mimic, or something similar."

"What are the unlikely options?" Pel asked, flipping his notebook open.

"Thrace, that's probably more in your department," Vessa said.

The stitched steepled his hands and leaned forward, letting his consciousness fall into itself.

Thrace was no longer who he'd once been. That part of him—that thrashing, angry, malicious *thing*—had been subsumed by degrees into a gestalt consciousness long before he'd ever fallen in with Pel and the Horsemen. Each new soul he took in to sustain himself diluted him by bits and pieces, each personality and new memories adding to those before. The hateful thing he'd been when he came to the Crossing never would have agreed to join the Covenant as one of the

Monarchy's pet monsters, and would have ripped Pel asunder rather than allowing himself to be bound to a Horseman and contained. *That* thing—the deepest, original Thrace—had done deeds here and in the planes beyond that even now would condemn him to destruction should Pel ever learn of them.

That was no longer what he was. But it was still there, that first, dark Thrace.

And *he* knew things.

Thrace felt the subtle fraying of his psyche as he tumbled through old, shadowed memories that prickled like thorns as he stirred them up. Arcane tomes, forbidden lore. There were vile things there, ready to be brought out, but those weren't what he sought today. He reached for trivia, arcana—transmutation, illusion, enchantment, the many things he knew of more common magic, and found what he needed.

Even as he withdrew, that inner voice whispered of all the ways those simple spells could be twisted and used to vile, violent ends. Of how a clever illusion or mild metamorphosis could be bent toward torment and depravity. The times he'd done so. How delicious it had been.

He pushed it down.

"Vessa's right," he confirmed, rousing. Pel and the High Herald had sat silently while he delved through his minds, having seen it many times before. *If only you knew, Pel. You'd end me right now. I think I'd let you.*

"Humor me," Pel insisted.

Thrace shrugged. "At a certain potency, transmutation magic might as well be reality-bending. That would circumvent detection. But anyone wielding that kind of firepower probably wouldn't have needed it. We're talking about folks who could have just kicked in the front door and turned Vessa's guards into a fine mist. Doesn't fit the evidence."

Pel nodded, jotting it down anyway. "And?"

"Dragon, maybe. Middle-aged?"

"I don't think I would have gotten away with stabbing it," Vessa countered.

"Fair. Which rules out most of the rest of that list. Greater celestials and infernals, couple weird outsiders; most of the things that could have tricked your wards wouldn't have needed to bother, and definitely would have dusted you when you tried to poke them."

"Almost definitely a shifter then," Pel conceded.

"Makes the most sense. When shifters change, it's intrinsic; they become what they shift into in every way that matters. Slips right by things designed to trigger against magic. But the ability is not so robust that it can't be disrupted by a concentrated defensive ward, and they're personally fragile enough that getting stabbed and slapped around once their cover was blown would have sent them running." Thrace nodded, more and more convinced of his reasoning. "Like Ves said, there's a couple of varieties that fit the bill, but they're all working on the same general principle. We can probably assume that it's a soul that wound up in the Crossing, so that narrows it down a bit. Not many dead mimics wandering around here."

"Alright. That's a start. Maybe we can work up a list or something."

Thrace scoffed. "Shifters are rare, Pel, but this is Nox Valar. There's still going to be five figures' worth."

"Do you have a better idea?"

"Depends," the soul stitched looked to Vessa. "Sometimes the best place to start is 'why.' Any idea why someone went after you in particular?"

Vessa shared a significant glance with Pel.

"This office is secure." Pel nodded.

"I need this to stay between us." She met Thrace's eyes. He'd always found the cleric so much more *intense* when she did that. Vessa could be jovial, quick-witted, even silly … but when she locked him with one of her High Herald stares, Thrace remembered why she held the office she did. "Just us three. Understand?"

"I can keep a secret, Ves."

If you only knew.

"I told Pel the Bastion was expecting a visitor. We think they were killed before they were able to visit the Crossing. That's true." She made sure he wasn't making notes. Thrace thought Pel's fingers looked restless when still. "But it's more than that. This person had … information. It's vital we get to them before anyone else."

"What kind of info?" Thrace asked.

Vessa hesitated, as if still debating whether she'd said too much already. Thrace saw the moment she made up her mind. "We think someone in the Monarchy is compromised. Someone high up."

"That's not possible," Pel said on reflex. He didn't sound like he believed his own denial though.

Vessa gave him a level look. "Don't be naïve, lover mine."

"Think that might be connected to our thing?" Thrace asked.

"If… if we accept the hypothetical. Which is a *big* 'if.'" Pel sighed. "Then yeah. That would explain how someone could be manipulating arrivals and departures without getting caught."

"Well, shit," Thrace spat. "That puts a wrinkle in things."

"My people are still searching," Vessa told them. "If we find anything, it may be best to coordinate out of the Bastion."

"We can ask the Horsemen and the Guard to be on the lookout—"

"No, Pel. This does not leave this room."

"Vessa, we can still—"

"No, I'm with Ves on this one," Thrace cut in. "Even on the outside chance that someone in the Monarchy is caught up in this, we can't risk tipping them off. Decent chance one or all of us suffers a terrible accident in the line of duty before we do anything useful."

"I… fuck. Alright, point taken. For *now*." Pel rubbed his temple. "But I don't like it. So, barring anything overt: any idea what to do next?"

"Yeah," Thrace said. "I'll go ask my new patron if they've heard anything."

They both stared at him.

"Oh, I signed a contract with a devil. Well, half-devil. Decent sort. Needed to lock her into some honesty and confidentiality clauses."

"*Thrace!*" Pel was agog, leaping to his feet to loom over the desk at him.

"*Pel!*" Thrace shouted back, matching his tone.

"That's got to be the stupidest, most short-sighted—"

Bud, if you only knew how I got here…

"Idiotic, moronic, half-brained, reckless, compromising—"

"Pel."

"What the hells am I supposed to tell Karson? Huh? That my stitched, whom *I am responsible for*, went off a-and-and what, signed a deal and now he's working for—"

"Pel!" Thrace shouted, but he wasn't the one who got Pel to break off his tirade. Vessa's hand on his forearm had been what did it.

A rare smile tugged the corner of Thrace's mouth. He'd always liked them together.

"Hear him out, Pel," the Herald said. Though she shot Thrace a side-eye that clearly stated, *this better be good*.

"It's a soul deal, guys. And I've got souls to spare."

The normally even-keeled Pel was starting to regain control of his breathing and slumped back into his chair. Though the throbbing vein in his forehead was a worrying sign.

"It's not my first time dealing with an infernal contract, you know. Not even my third."

"Can... can you even *do* that...?" Vessa asked, working through what a soul exchange might mean for a soul stitched.

"Won't be pleasant. But yeah, as long as I'm topped up enough when the bill comes due."

"How long?" Pel asked, voice flat.

"Six months. Long enough that—"

"Yeah, yeah. I get it." Pel rubbed his forehead. "Fucking hells, Thrace. At least talk to me about it next time."

Despite himself, Thrace felt a pang of sympathy. At least, the majority of him did.

"Sorry, Pel, really. But I still think it was the best course of action."

"Tell me."

"Madrigal. You know her?"

Pel pulled a different notepad off a shelf behind his desk, but didn't open it. "Small-time backroom dealer. Runs some contraband through her place, but balances it out by keeping her circle civil. Makes sure a tip finds its way to us whenever someone gets out of line. Management thinks it's a net win, so we leave her alone."

"Yeah. Locked her into a mutual aid situation. She realized that whoever we're after might catch her in the crossfire. Bad for business. She's going to feed me intel. I'm going to make sure she stays clean on this one."

"Win-win," Vessa observed.

"That's the plan."

"Sure. Sure. Why not." Pel sighed. "So, we can get something from her, do you think?"

"Already did. That's how I found out about the General. Asked her to keep an ear out about him. Sent me a message an hour later."

"Great."

"Hey, it's not nothing. We know he's probably going to get siphoned up into a brand-new afterlife any second now. I've put in a flag with the Shepherds to make sure he doesn't get raptured before we at least know where he's going."

"We're not going to get approval to stop him."

"I know, but we can at least know when, where, and who. It's better than nothing."

"Yeah, that's fair."

"After this, I'll go ask Madrigal if she knows anything, or knows anyone who knows anything, about the Bastion. See if there's a shifter in the memory market scene we don't know about."

As Thrace finished the thought, pounding footsteps came rushing down the corridor outside, and another Horseman came crashing through Pel's door.

"The fuck, Carlow?" Thrace demanded.

"Solimo, come quick!" Carlow panted, ignoring Thrace and Vessa. "I've got someone in my office confessing to all sorts of shit, and she's polymorphing constantly!"

Pel rushed out of the room with Carlow, and Thrace heard other Horsemen running as the alarm spread.

"Are you fucking kidding me?" Thrace threw up his hands and looked at Vessa. She shrugged and moved to follow Pel.

CHAPTER 26

Cypress tried to focus, but her vision swam, and a wave of nausea washed over her. Morphic afterimages of impossible shapes undulated in her mind's eye, and the vision of them hurt to even try to recall.

She couldn't remember ending up here, wherever "here" was. She was in a dark room, lit only by the dancing lines of light cast from a single torch through the barred window of the door. She learned more about her space through her other senses. The stone floor was rough and cold, pressed into her cheek. She felt pressure against her shin and realized that there was a chair behind her that she might have fallen from. A metallic coolness shrouded her ankles and wrists, paired with the rattle of chains as she groaned.

With great effort, Cypress pushed herself over and tried to rise. She made it far as her hands and knees before a dry heave wracked her body, the cognitive poison still tumbling through her memory, leaving her woozy and drained. She felt as if her inner ear couldn't align, like "up" and "down" kept reversing on her.

The door squealed on rusted hinges, and torchlight flooded the room. She found herself looking at a puzzling mismatch in the light. Anastasia's hands were splayed on the stone, propping her up, but strands of Lizabeth's crimson hair draped down around her. She was caught between her old friends.

Uh-oh.

"Let's get her up," a man's voice said above her, tone neutral and detached.

"Yeah, yeah." There was a scrape of wood on stone, and leather-gloved hands hooked her armpits, and her world spun as a dark figure hoisted her back into the chair.

Cypress gripped the edge of the seat as best she could and managed not to slide right back off again. She willed herself to focus, to gather her wits. It was a struggle, but the mental disruption was fading in agonizing increments.

"...with the basics," the measured voice was saying. It belonged to a plain-looking man who leaned against the far wall, notebook in hand. He was middle-aged, a bit bald, a bit gone to seed, but Cypress clocked his sharp gaze immediately. Her years as Anastasia's spymaster had given her a sense for people, and that sense prickled as she took him in. His demeanor was a calculated act to make people dismiss him; he was in control here, and he knew it.

"Do you know where you are right now?" the nondescript man asked.

Cypress shook her head, though she had a few guesses. Best to let them frame the situation. It might tell her something she could use.

"You're in the custody of the Monarchy," the man told her.

"The Horsemen," Cypress guessed. His eyebrow shot up, but he didn't confirm it.

"The 'Monarchy' is the important bit." His companion cut in. He was a sharp contrast to his partner; a gaunt, avian face framed in long dark hair and dressed neck-to-toe in black. He paced the cell, circling the chair she was seated in.

"You were apprehended following an incident during a messenger appointment, during which you confessed to a number of serious offenses. Do you remember that?"

"Vaguely," she wheezed.

"Why did you do that, miss...?"

"Lizabeth."

"*Liar.*" The dark-dressed man *tsked* in her ear. "I can smell lies, friend. Best not whet my appetite."

Cypress chuckled despite herself. He glared at her. "Something funny?"

"Just... 'smell lies.' No, you can't. You've got a truth charm set into the floor." She gestured with her chin to the faint, circular impression in the room's stonework. She may not have noticed had she not awoken right next to it. "Guessing you activated it, which is why you're playing tough and looming over me. Weird that your buddy is staying outside the circle, though, since I wouldn't know if he lied to me. But you would. Maybe there's something he doesn't want you to know."

The dark-haired man whirled with a snarl to face his partner. "That so, Pel?! Keeping secrets from me?"

The two locked eyes for a tense moment. Then they burst out laughing.

"Good flip. Bit rushed. Don't really have any rapport to trade on." The black-clad man told her, tone approving. "Solid instinct though. Been awake ten seconds and you're already trying to turn your captors against each other—but we're not a back-alley gang, lady."

Cypress shrugged, though her vertigo made her regret it. "Worth a shot."

"Why don't we try your name again?" the first man, Pel, asked.

"Told you. Lizabeth."

"No, see—" He flipped through his notepad, stopping on a page with a dramatic flourish. "According to our the Horseman, Carlow—you remember Carlow, right?—this Lizabeth person was a green-eyed, red-haired woman who spoke in a higher register. You've got red hair, blue eyes, a darker complexion, and a deeper voice."

"And there is the matter of your rapid shape-shifting the entire way from his office to this cell," the closer man added.

"He's Pel. What's your name?" Cypress asked him.

"Oh, delightful." He grinned as if she was an opponent at a game board who had just tried an interesting stratagem. "Deflect the line of inquiry, mine for innocuous personal details with an innocent question most people would answer on reflex. And then we've started answering *your* questions."

"Just want to know who I'm dealing with."

He leaned down, putting his eyes level with hers. She noticed that they were two slightly different shades of gray. "Thrace, my dear. My name is Thrace. Now, sit and wonder why I bothered to tell you that."

Because it doesn't matter if I know your name, but you'll gladly let me wonder if you're playing some intricate mind game by telling me. She almost scoffed.

"Your turn," Pel insisted.

"I told you. Lizabeth."

"Liar, liar, *li-ar*," Thrace teased in a sing-song tone. "Maybe we just get the neuromancers, Pel. Have them go delving."

Cypress was only half-listening as she scrambled to reconstruct what had happened. She'd been there, speaking to Carlow, dictating her message to Anastasia. She'd done it. She'd *finally* done it. And then she'd reached for Dimereial's payment...

A migraine flashed behind her eyes, and she almost fell off the chair again. Thrace's hand caught her. "Little tipsy there, eh?"

The sound of Pel's notebook snapping closed made her look up. "Thrace, why don't you give us a minute alone." He phrased it as a question but spoke it like a command. Cypress recognized the tactic. It was a rehearsed signal; they were going to try a different approach.

Thrace stalked out of the room, closing the door on his way. After a moment, a spark of candle-flame flickered to life in the darkness, dancing on the tip of Pel's finger. He walked around the room, lighting recessed sconces. After a moment, their warm, cheerily dancing light chased the gloom from the chamber, and it felt markedly less like a dungeon. Another tactic Cypress recognized.

Pel dragged a chair over from the far corner and positioned it in front of hers. He sat and fiddled with his notebook.

"You're going to wait for me to break the silence first, so let's get that part over with," Cypress told him.

"You've done this before?" A slight smile creased the corner of his mouth.

"Both sides of it."

"What am I going to do next then?"

"Give me an open-ended question to see if I'll give anything away."

He laughed at that, tipping his stylus toward her in a mock salute. "What would you have to give away, Lizabeth? As far as I know, you were visiting the Horsemen for a legitimate appointment."

"I was."

"Who's Cypress?"

"I am." The words leaped unbidden into her mouth, surprising her, as if invisible fingers had reached down her throat and torn them through her lips. Her headache flared, nearly blinding in intensity, then subsided. *What the fuck?* she thought.

"Good to meet you, Cypress," he said, either unaware of her inner confusion or not wanting to comment on it. "I'm Pel Solimo. I'm an agent of the Godless Monarchy."

"You're a Pale Horseman too," she ventured. "One of the investigative branches."

"Ah. The whole 'secret agents in plain sight' story. I've heard those rumors as well. Never put much stock in them. But listen," he leaned forward, speaking with an earnestness that was so convincing she entertained that he may even have believed it, "I *am* with the Monarchy. But we're not all fire and brimstone. That's what guys like Thrace are for, sure. But they keep guys like *me* around to make sure cooler heads prevail. My job isn't to indiscriminately drop the axe on every minor infraction in Nox Valar. That's impossible, even for us. Like sweeping a beach."

Cypress matched his gaze but said nothing. She was still trying to figure out why the *hells* she'd given him her name. Did they have some compulsion on her? She didn't think so. But that swirling, undulating un-thing that Dimereial's medallion had become...

"My job, Cypress, is to sort *through* the noise. See, folks like you get into a bit of trouble here and there all the time. Usually, it's not worth our attention. You don't cause much harm, and you shuffle off to the great beyond quick enough, in the scheme of things. That's all I'm trying to do here. Get through the noise and focus guys like Thrace on the *real* problems."

"And what are those?" His line of questioning wasn't making sense to her, and she didn't like that at all.

"That's what I'm hoping you can help me with, in fact." Pel beamed at her as if they'd just shared a joke. "See, you called yourself a memory thief. And I happen to be looking for a shape-shifting memory thief. Isn't that something?" Cypress began to protest, but Pel held up a hand for silence. "Hold on,

Cypress, before you try to spin a story. I think we can help each other.

"It hasn't escaped me that you walking into an appointment and having an … episode … is the most convenient way I've ever wrapped up a case. Really seems like the kind of thing that happens when a bigger fish needs to organize a fall guy. Serve up exactly what I'm looking for on a silver platter, and then we get distracted or stop digging. But I'm not like that, Cypress, and that can be a good thing for you. Do you understand what I'm saying?"

Cypress nodded. She was reaching similar conclusions.

For whatever reason, Dimereial, the so-called Angel of Redemption, had set her up.

"Let's start at the beginning. How did you get tied up in stealing memories? It's not a skill most people come to Nox Valar already having."

Presumptive close, Cypress noted. He'd phrased the question so answering it at all would confirm her guilt. She wouldn't play into—

To her horror, that same feeling of having someone else's words torn from her throat and forced through her lips reasserted itself. "I had to get a message to the mortal world as soon as possible. I realized how valuable memories were once I got here, so I found someone in Anywhere to teach me how to steal them. I used that to trade my way here."

Pel frowned. "Cypress, we can talk like professionals here, I think. I know what a lie by omission sounds like. Can you treat me like I'm not new at this, do you think?"

I'm not! Cypress wanted to scream. *I didn't say that!*

Instead, against her will, she continued.

"I'm trying to save Anastasia's life. I needed to get her a message as fast as possible. I realized that trading in rarer, harder-to-get memories was worth more. So I thought that if I could get a high-ranking cleric from the Road to Eternity, that would do it."

"We'll get to that, Cypress. But right now, I need to know who else you were working with, or I can't help you do anything."

"But the Bastion was a bad idea. Their wards hurt my ability to shift. I thought I could make it through the appointment today, but it was longer than I expected. I lost control."

"So you managed to get the Coin you needed even after you failed at the Bastion? That's lucky, isn't it?"

"I was out of time. And I was afraid you would catch me soon after that. I traded everything else I had to get here."

"Let's go back, Cypress. We know there's more involved than just memory theft. How did you know who would be resurrected when?"

What?

"I just need to get a message to Anastasia as soon as possible."

"I understand, really. I can talk to some people about getting a message to your friend if you cooperate. But if you don't answer my questions honestly, there's nothing I can do."

I'm trying! She wanted to scream, cry, bite, spit. But even her body wasn't behaving. Whenever she willed herself to do anything other than sit still and continue her nonsensical confession, a debilitating sense of disorientation overcame her, and she had to fight her way back to lucidity. And the whole time her mouth kept running of its own accord.

"Cypress, I'm being honest with you here," Pel was saying, obvious annoyance in his voice. "There are a lot of ways we can find out what you know. I'm the nice option. I'm the one who gives you a message home in exchange for your help. Thrace is going to take a shot at you if I can't get anywhere, and he's not going to offer anything. He's going to take. And Thrace is *still* one of the nice options down here."

Cypress looked at him with glassy eyes, hoping he could at least get a sense of her inner turmoil.

"I think you got tied up in something bigger than you realized, Cypress. Somebody is messing with the Crossing. Messing with afterlives. That isn't the kind of thing we can let go. That's the kind of thing it *is* my job to hunt down. And right now, you're my only lead. So either you're going to help me run this down, or the powers that be are going to take you out of my hands and give you to someone—some*thing*—that will do things to you that I won't. Please."

"My name is Cypress Monroe," her voice said as she screamed in her mind, that non-dimensional, corrupting pattern twisting her thoughts around its incomprehensible, spiraling edges. "And I am a memory thief."

CHAPTER 27

"**N**ormally I'd warn ya that this was going to be unlike anything you'd ever seen, but..." Secan began. "Y'know."

Rasa laughed, appreciating his humor as they followed the long staircase down, down, and down some more. She felt as if the warm, dim corridor descended deeper than they'd climbed to enter Nox Valar, and yet it never seemed like a difficult trek. She chalked it up to more strange tricks of perception and distance that plagued the Sunless Crossing and decided not to dwell on it.

"The key to success here is polite declinin' of invitations and a steady walkin' pace," Secan went on. "You're going to be approached by all types of folks and critters with something to offer. The safest ones are after more Coins than you've got. The dangerous ones are going to offer to take you on credit. You don't want that. Hear me?"

Rasa nodded in the affirmative, amused at her Shepherd's obvious discomfort. He'd given her some version of the same warning multiple times on the way here, and now the reiteration had become a self-soothing exercise. It was clear that Secan wished to be anywhere other than Paradise.

A distant corner of her mind wondered if she ought not to be more anxious about wherever they were heading, but she could only shrug and carry on. Everything she could remember had been a forward march into the unknown. She had Secan to give her context. And she had Raven's comforting weight bobbing along at her back.

She'd be fine.

They emerged from the staircase onto an opulent, expansive mezzanine festooned with lavish furniture, secluded alcoves, and buffets of food. Curious, alluring beings prowled the space or lounged about, their hungry stares tracking the trickle of souls emerging from entrances like the one they'd just walked through. Several angled to approach them, but Secan juked their path and quick-stepped to avoid interception. Rasa followed close behind him with some bemusement.

They had almost reached the stairs down from the mezzanine when Secan's serpentine evasive pattern failed. They rounded the corner of one cluster of tall-backed, semi-private seating areas just as a figure emerged from within. Secan practically knocked into her and recoiled with a muttered apology, though Rasa doubted that her timing had been accidental.

"No need to worry, darling," the creature purred. Rasa had to crane her neck up to look her in the eyes. She appeared to be cast entirely of polished jade, glass-smooth, and swirled with subtle inclusions of lighter or darker patches. She shone translucent toward her extremities, and her entire body was etched with a flowing filigree of glittering gold designs.

She looked like the gargoyles Rasa had seen throughout the city, but after a moment, she reassessed that notion. There was something less terrestrial about this woman, more fluid and ethereal. Her eyes glittered in the low light in a way unlike the animate stone of the Nyxian gargoyles, and when she spoke there was a softness in her lips that belied a different root.

Secan had told her that they would encounter an abundance of fiends in Paradise, and Rasa decided this must be one of them. Four enormous horns swept back from her brow, and a pair of batlike wings were tucked behind her, decorated with jeweled piercings down their ridges. An abundance of jewels and the full-body golden filament were her only adornments, a fact that caused Secan to visibly blush and avert his eyes. A slender tail *snip-snapped* back and forth as she examined the pair, like a cat would idly twitch as it watched a flock of birds it hadn't yet decided to chase.

"We're in a bit of a rush, ma'am," Secan stammered, attempting to step around the towering succubus. A translucent jade wing stretched out in front of him, its wide span entirely blocking his path.

"Well, I certainly don't approve of *that*," she chided. She spoke with a soft accent that Rasa hadn't come across in Nox Valar. Her voice felt as if it had *weight* to it; the words oozed into Rasa's ears like a spoonful of Borssa's honey. "Paradise is meant to be savored, sweetling. Join me for a cup of tea."

"W-we really can't, miss. We're here for an appointment."

The emerald wing wrapped around Secan and pulled him in close, and the fiend's molten-gold eyes flicked between him and Rasa in a conspiratorial fashion. Rasa tensed, ready for... she wasn't sure what, actually. She'd been led to believe that violence within Paradise was both unlikely and extremely ill-advised.

"I know who you are, Shepherd," the demon murmured into Secan's ear, lips nearly brushing it in a lover's confession. "You're here to meet *me*."

They were ushered inside the seating area she'd appeared from, which turned out to be a collection of cushions, chaises, and sofas surrounding a low table, all lit by a perimeter of candelabras. The table was covered in a spread of meats and cheeses, the aromas of which struck Rasa and set her mouth watering. The entire area was surrounded by a ring of privacy screens draped with additional layers of silks and gauzes. Other infernals were lounging within, stone- and gem-skinned men, women, and androgynous figures of stunning proportions and varying levels of dress, but none had wings like their host. She dismissed them with a wave, and they slinked away.

"Sit, sit," she insisted. "Call me Menthissa. Please, enjoy the snacks. My treat."

Secan perched on the edge of a sofa, tense as a bowstring. Rasa frowned at his discomfort, but couldn't bring herself to share it. The one thing she'd been able to rely on since arriving in the Crossing was her sense for imminent danger, and Menthissa wasn't triggering that response in her. Not yet anyway. She kneeled on one of the cushions in front of the table, Raven's haft settling against the small of her back. Seeing no reason not to, she plucked up a morsel and popped it into her mouth.

It was astonishing. The only thing she'd had that approached it had been the fruit in the Atonement Grove, and perhaps the sweet indulgence of Borssa's mortal-realm tea and honey. But that fare had left an entire spectrum of taste unstimulated. The meats and cheeses on Menthissa's table were rich, creamy, and *savory*, and Rasa found herself heaping more onto a serving plate on impulse.

Secan watched her feast with concern. "We were supposed to head down several rings," he ventured, tone wary.

"True, true," Menthissa granted. "But you don't want to do that, Secan."

"I don't? We don't?" He tried to hide it, but the use of Secan's name had alarmed him.

"If you want to go, I won't stop you," she told him. "But I'll advise you to hear me out before you decide. But first, a little privacy." Menthissa snapped her fingers, and the gauzy curtains around them suddenly hung from solid stone walls, and all light and sound from beyond vanished.

"I heard bellflies had made an appointment with Ixixi down in the possibilities ring," Menthissa continued as if nothing had happened. "Ix is competent, don't get me wrong, or it wouldn't be on the payroll. But it was an unusual sort of request, so I decided to drop my good friend Borssa a line and see what was going on. They told me a bit that intrigued me, and I offered them an upgrade. They accepted on your behalf."

"We're supposed to believe that you're a friend of Borssa's?" Secan asked, incredulous.

In response, Menthissa snapped her fingers again, conjuring a gold-lined, black-iron teapot on the table in front of her, with a set of cups and saucers to match. The teapot was just beginning to whistle. "Honey, or sugar?" she asked.

Rasa looked at the pot and couldn't help but crack a smile. "You're kidding."

"Borssa knows where to get the good shit." Menthissa returned her grin. "And let me anticipate your next few questions, Shepherd, and save us some time. You are incurring no debt by meeting with me; in fact, I am repaying one. Aside from our shared social interests, the Guild owed the Belfry a favor. Borssa offered the chance to settle that account, if you two accept it. As I said, you are welcome to refuse my services in favor of Ixixi's, but I can say without ego that you will receive a lesser result."

"So ... you can help with my memory too?" Rasa asked between bites.

"Yes, Rasa. I can get your memories stirring, per the bellflies' request. And a good deal more besides, if you want to negotiate for additional services." She blew a kiss at Secan.

"I-I think we should just stick to what we came for, miss Menthissa," he said.

"I'll leave that offer on the table for a bit, sweet Shepherd. You really should think about it. I don't work the floor much anymore. Not everyone gets a chance to see why I got moved up to management."

"Secan, is there a reason we should not accept this person's help? It seems to me we came here to see a fiend one way or another," Rasa asked.

"That's ... true enough. I suppose I'm wary of sudden changes in a place like this."

"If it makes any difference," Menthissa sipped from her own teacup, the steam condensing on her gemlike skin as it drifted past her face, "I had planned to meet you at Ixixi's booth first, but there is the small matter of the assassins surveilling it." She shrugged. "I thought this would be easier. Less disruption to the business."

Rasa and Secan locked eyes. Rasa's hand twitched toward Raven's haft, but Menthissa broke the tension by reaching over and placing a cup in front of each of them.

"Calm, lovelies. No one can bother us here. Once our business is done, you're on your own. But I don't care for interruptions while I work. Sugar, Shepherd? You never answered."

"Who are the assassins?" Rasa asked. "What do they want?"

"Not my problem, not our deal. The Guild of Vices dabbles in information brokerage from time to time—who doesn't— but that's really more of an Anywhere thing. Paradise is focused on ... *sensations*." She dragged out the word as she poured Secan's tea.

"Honey," he told her. She passed him a delicate crystal container that didn't match the rest of her set. Sure enough, it was a twin to the one Borssa had used in her office.

Rasa took hers with milk and sugar, just to see how different it was. Underneath those, Menthissa's preferred blend had more spice and verve than Borssa's muted, mellow brew. She decided that, if she was going to be stuck in Nox Valar, she needed to explore this apparent cabal of tea aficionados further.

"To business then," Menthissa announced, refilling her cup and focusing on Rasa. "You're dealing with some malady of the memory, apparently due to some bastard lightspawn. The bellflies seem convinced that removing this blockage will go better for you if it is done in parts; soaking the ground before we dig to soften it up, as it were. You didn't ask, but Borssa did. I concur with their findings. And the stimulation of memory is something of a specialty in Paradise—one I am very, very skilled at."

"What do we do?" Rasa asked.

"We've already started, love. Find a comfortable spot and lay back. Keep that hammer nearby."

With a shrug from Secan and no small amount of trepidation, Rasa picked one of the chaise lounges and lowered herself into its plush cushions. She reflected on the fact that she'd gone from a constant, slogging fight in the Fields to laying down while getting magically prodded in every corner of Nox Valar, all in the span of a few days. If nothing else, the afterlife had *range*.

Menthissa moved to kneel behind her head, the infernal's towering stature putting her well above the arm of the chaise. She appeared upside-down in Rasa's field of vision; a beautiful, alien sculpture of jade and gold.

"Memory is a fascinating thing. Experience and thought and perception locked up in lumps of malleable, unreliable flesh," Menthissa began. Her golden eyes flared with arcane power as she looked Rasa over, tracing filaments of something that only she could see. "Mortals always describe memories as stories, as if you were re-living a scene. But your bodies do *so* much more without your conscious mind."

Jade fingernails began to trace their way from Rasa's temples across her brow, around her skull and face. They left little electric trails in their wake, whirling lines of tingling energy that lingered just below the surface of Rasa's skin for several seconds.

"Think about the tea you just had. The milk, the sugar. Did you enjoy it?"

Rasa arched a brow at her. "I did, yes. So?"

One of Menthissa's fingernails dug into her skin when she answered, and Rasa felt a jolt shoot through her face, through her mouth, through her tongue. It was like she was drinking the tea again, the herbal spice sitting at the back of her palette balanced by the cool smoothness of the milk, the sweetness of the sugar... but there was more there. The sugar led her to Borssa's honey, the mellower tones, which in turn called up another taste, more distant. *It was a lukewarm cup, left on the table too long, but she choked it down anyway, the precious leaves hard to find and too good to waste...*

"Wait, what was that?" she asked, startled. She tried to wince away from where the demon's nail had drawn a small trickle of blood from her cheek, but Menthissa's fingers might as well have been an iron fence. She felt the blood flash-drying and drifting away as ash as it dribbled away from her, but she didn't care. "I remembered... I almost remembered... there was something there!"

"Sense memories are among the strongest pathways your little brains forge; the hardest to break. A mortal forgets more days than it remembers, especially its larval years—but the right smell, the right taste, the right pattern, and a moment can spring back crystal clear." Menthissa's fingers circled back to their starting point and began their circuit again. Rasa felt as if some of them followed the same winding paths as before, while others forged entirely new ones.

"What I'm going to do is ... *focus* you on different sensations. Different senses. Different emotions. We're going to flood those old pathways and see where they lead. It won't bring all of your memories back at once. But it *will* crack the foundation of this wall someone put in your head. Now, lie very still."

Menthissa's grip tightened into a vice, and she drove her nails into Rasa's skull.

CHAPTER 28

"**N**o, no-no, let's not go this way," Thrace muttered to himself, though his compass's needle stubbornly refused to change directions. *Damn.*

He'd been following Cypress's trail from the Bastion of Endings for an hour. She was skilled, he had to give her that. Even injured after her narrow escape and leap from the wall, she'd managed to plot a path that led her through double-backs, overlooks, and choke points, plus brushing the outskirts of some of the busier spaces in Nox Valar on the way. Had someone tried to tail her from the Bastion at the time, there was an extremely good chance she'd have lost them, or at least spotted them, before she gave any indication of her final destination.

None of that mattered now that she was in custody. A pinprick of blood, drawn so that it did not reduce to ash, was all that he needed. With that, a known starting point, and a simple ritual he'd learned in his youth, Thrace had been able to thaumaturgically tie a compass to the path she'd taken during her escape. Pel could spend his day trying the soft-sell interrogation if he wanted. Thrace was going to find out where their captive had been operating from.

Problem was, it was leading him back to familiar ground.

"Don't turn left. Don't turn left. Don't turn—fuck." He groaned as the needle swung left at the next intersection.

"It's fine. Probably going to pass right by. What are the odds that... oh, thrice-fuck and double-damn you."

The needle was pointing straight at the front door of Madrigal's.

"Fuck you," Thrace cursed at the compass. The compass did not reply.

He stomped through the front door, then away from the main tavern and straight over to the dusty, disused, uninviting side door. He didn't need to glance at the compass to know he'd picked right. The door was enchanted; subtle work that even he *might* have missed if he hadn't been paying attention. The wards laid over it gave it a patina of unremarkableness; even now he found his attention wandering when he walked toward it, his gaze sliding off and away as something whispered deep in the back of his mind that this was the wrong path, the *boring* path, that he was wasting his time and the main room of the tavern was much more likely to contain what he was—

It might have worked on another. Hells, it had probably worked on him the first time he'd walked into Madrigal's without searching for the backroom.

But he wasn't just any soul poking around Nox Valar, and his psyche was not so easily influenced. Well, his original one, anyway. He'd been trained, and more than that, he'd *practiced* resisting such influences, often under deadly circumstances.

Which is why it was so frustrating when he found himself walking into the common taproom again.

He snarled, turned on his heel, and marched toward the blasted door.

"*I am Thrace the gods-damned reaver,*" he told the door, which seemed unimpressed. "Ember wizard of the Silent Order.

Doom of the Brass Legion. Lord of the Hollow Mountain. And I will *not* be dissuaded by a—*gods damnit!*" Thrace shouted into a startled taproom he hadn't realized he had re-entered.

"Alright. Alright. New fuckin' approach," he growled, leaving the taproom once again to stand in the hall. This time, he didn't try to approach the door. He didn't even look at it. Instead, he closed his eyes and focused inward, toward the tiny burr now lodged deep in the amalgam of souls that comprised Thrace in this new, strange phase of his existence. When he had isolated it with his mind, he seized it, clamping down with a vice of willpower and channeling his energy toward it.

"Oh, my dearest patron, I beseech thee," Thrace chanted when he was sure he had a firm metaphysical grasp on the contract that linked him to Madrigal. "Do me the boon of opening this door, and I won't knock a hole in your fucking wall."

Thrace waited, glowering at the wall. Less than a minute later, he heard a soft groan of wood, and the door swung open.

"Start talking, Madrigal." He pointed an accusatory finger at the half-devil, who looked ... amused. "What?"

"'*Doom of the Brass Legion,*' huh?"

"Ah. You heard that."

"I did, in fact."

"Great."

"Never heard of a Brass Legion."

"Well, I doomed them. So."

"Clearly they weren't hiding behind my door."

"Listen, lady, fuck you. This is serious."

"We're listening, Thrace."

Thrace opened his mouth to snap something back, but hesitated as he registered the rest of the room. The elaborate circles set into the floor toward the back marked this as the place Madrigal had blindfolded him through on his last visit, as expected. What he hadn't counted on, though, was the table.

Thrace had been a mighty wizard once. Many of his powers were lost to him now; scoured in the un-making of his death, diluted by the necessary melding of less-arcane souls it took to sustain him in the Crossing, or deliberately shackled by the Godless Monarchy as a condition of their tolerance for his service.

But despite all of that, he still had gifts enough to See.

Gathered around a card table in Madrigal's backroom was a collection of infernals. Some, like the other half-devil, the boggart, and the insectoid, Thrace was familiar enough with. A hulking, furry thing took up one flank of the table, rumbling at him with a quivering snarl on its fanged maw. Thrace didn't know its kind, but it appeared to be some hyper-carnivorous offshoot of one hellish evolutionary tree or another, nothing terribly exotic.

Opposite the fang-brute was something else; a spindly man his Sight read as a thing of shadows and pain, something more primordial than the fiends it shared the space with. Here, now, it sent a shiver through Thrace's spine, and he thought that even at the height of his powers a lifetime ago, he'd have opted to give that thing a wide berth.

If this room turned violent, Thrace was in trouble. In his prime, he might have blasted his way out. Now, if Pel had been there to peel back the Monarchy's shackles, he might stand a chance; but on his own, it looked grim. The boggart, as a thing of fears and mind games, would be simple enough to neutralize with the right defenses. The insectoid and the half-bloods were dangerous, but unlikely to take tremendous risks if he proved he could maim one of them. The brute might get him, if it was as fast as it appeared strong. And he didn't even know how to do the calculus for the strange, shadowed old man.

Despite the unexpected audience, he did not think violence was imminent. Fiends were self-serving, and even without his nominal contract to Madrigal, there was little to be gained by attacking a Covenant of the Stitched agent, except for the ire of the Horsemen.

No, what gave Thrace pause and made him question his Sight was the table itself.

To mortal eyes, it appeared as a simple stone table, longer than it was wide and lined with felt or velvet to make manipulating cards easier. But if he opened his eyes up to include his hard-won wizard's senses, there was something else to it. The table was … he didn't think "massive" was the right word, but it was close. It was an anchor, a tremendous weight of darkness that squatted on the Crossing like a menhir marking some unknown tomb.

"What in all the hells is that thing?" he asked in a low voice.

"Depends which one of them you're talking about," Madrigal said matter-of-factly. "Wouldn't push the tall guy too hard about it though. He thinks it's rude."

In that horrible moment, Thrace realized that Madrigal had no idea what he was referring to.

Okay. Okay. Focus, Thrace, some deep part of his fractured mindscape urged. *Whatever we're looking at, it's kept for a while. We have a more immediate problem.*

With deliberate effort, he turned from the black-hole mass in his Sight and focused his attention on Madrigal. "Shapeshifter. Memory thief. Start talking."

Madrigal opened her mouth to speak, but Thrace felt a tug on the kerel that was their contract. She frowned, no doubt feeling the same pull: their deal had compelled mutual truthfulness on this subject. It had been the entire reason Thrace had signed it.

"You. Are. *Kidding me,* Mads!" The purple half-devil at the table stared at her scarlet counterpart with bewilderment and no small hint of delight. "You contracted with a Horseman, of all people, and he *got* you? Oh, *brava*, sister-mine. This is hilarious!"

"Shut your soul-sucker, Tilla," Madrigal snapped. "*You* don't have to get your hands dirty running this place. Sometimes that means working with the system so all of *you* still get to keep enjoying this little clubhouse unimpeded. So stuff it."

"Ahem," Thrace pressed.

"Yeah, yeah. The person you're talking about is Cypress. Small-time dealer, hasn't been in the city long. Comes in with a trap from time to time, mostly blind catches."

"Mads!" Tilla exclaimed, eyeing Thrace like she might have a fight on her hands.

"*Stuff it fucking full, Tilla.* I'm not an idiot. He's bound too."

"I don't care about the small-time crap that goes on back here," Thrace confirmed, addressing the conclave of fiends. "Even put it in the contract. I'm working one specific case, and Madrigal's stays off the books as long as I get what I need. So settle down, and I won't need to pull the wings off you."

The infernals bristled, but Thrace allowed his mask to slip a bit. For a fraction of a second, to those attuned to energies beyond the physical, Thrace the soul stitched agent of the Godless Monarchy was replaced by who he once was: the Blackfire Lich, dread incarnate, who had dispatched fiends and worse with a word.

They weren't stupid. They knew he wasn't that entity anymore, not really. But in his experience, most infernals were pathologically selfish, and they couldn't be sure he wouldn't be able to disintegrate, banish, or maul one of them before the others stopped him.

Tilla shut up.

"As I was saying," Madrigal continued with a final glare at her kin, "Cypress plays it safe, mostly. She's after a meeting with the Horsemen more than anything, as fast as she can get it."

"Ironic."

"Yeah, well. She's trying to get a message to the living. Time-sensitive, from what I gathered."

"What about?"

"Not sure. We get along, but I encouraged her not to share too much with this crowd. You know."

Thrace arched a brow. "Awful kind of you."

Madrigal shrugged, embarrassed. "Cypress is a decent egg, Thrace. Gets her hands dirty because she needs to, not because she likes it. I honestly think she'll be done as soon as she gets her message out."

"Interesting."

"If I'd known she'd be involved at all, I wouldn't have taken your damned contract."

"You can't expect me to feel bad that a devil got the raw end of a deal this one time."

"You can shove your pity right up the same hole you can shove that tone, Thrace. You should feel bad for Cypress. Whatever she was up to, it was because she thought she *had* to do it."

Thrace considered her words. It was a different angle to approach the interrogation, if nothing else. But Madrigal's reaction was telling him as much about her as it was about the shapeshifter. "You actually give a shit about her, don't you?"

He felt the tension on their contract fade. Apparently, that line of questioning wasn't strictly relevant to what was stipulated there. Still, Madrigal looked troubled, hesitating. *Perhaps her human side asserting itself,* Thrace mused.

"Don't just ash Cypress when you see her, Thrace," she said. "If she got tied up in something like we talked about the other day, she'd probably try to help you fix it."

"Good news and bad news, then. She's not ashed, but she's not helping."

Madrigal frowned as she went through the implications. "Ah. Well, fuck."

"Cypress done anything unusual recently? Break her patterns?"

Madrigal huffed, glowering as he sensed their contract compel her to answer again. "Showed up bloody and beat down a couple days ago. Hex was messing with her shifting ability. Cut a deal to get patched up and went on her way as fast as she could."

"Where to?"

"Anywhere. Bought a ticket."

"Say why she was going?"

"Remember that angel I mentioned last time we spoke?"

"Dimmerel. Redeemer guy."

"*Dimereial*," she corrected.

"Pel's the fucking note taker. What about him?"

"Cypress went to meet him. She was one of the ones he met with in the circle here."

Pieces were beginning to fall into place in Thrace's mind. He wasn't sure what the picture was, yet, but he was beginning to see its outlines.

"Alright. Two things. One, you're going to need to give me all the information you have on who else Dimer-all was meeting."

"Dimereial. And fine."

"Two, you're coming with me," he told her, ignoring the susurrus the order caused in the room. "I think Pel and I can use your help. And I think Cypress can too, if you can get through to her."

CHAPTER 29

"She's in the city?" Vessa Theramay demanded as she swept into the Bastion's armory before the other Heralds even had a chance to acknowledge her with a proper salute. Six of them were there already, changing or making final adjustments to their war gear.

"Sighted an hour ago, High Herald," Thomlin answered her. "I sent word as soon as I heard."

Vessa grunted an acknowledgment as she discarded her formal robe, kicked off her street boots, and stripped down to her undergarments. Armory attendants rushed to present her with her gambeson and plate mail.

"Where's Rine?" she asked as she shrugged into the heavy fabric, and the attendants began the process of strapping her into the metal plates over the top of it. Those who had been on duty were already encased and set to the task of helping the attendants prepare the weapons of their compatriots. Two others, like her, had been out of the Bastion at the time the messaging spells reached them and would need a few minutes to don the heavy, black-and-red plate of the Proclaimer Sect. Vessa had practically sprinted from Pel's office, promising to circle back and compare notes after her mission and his inter-rogation of the peculiar shapeshifter.

"He's received word and is returning to Nox Valar," Thomlin told her, "but the trip will take several hours at best speed."

"We're not waiting," Vessa ordered. "Seven Proclaimers should be enough. Have him regroup at the Bastion and gather a relief force, just in case."

"Yes, High Herald." He made a gesture in the air, a trail of arcane sparks following his fingertip. Then he spoke to himself, subvocalizing as he relayed her message into the spell. After a moment, he nodded. "It is done."

Vessa assessed who would be with her. Thomlin, the next most senior among them, had acquitted himself well as the organizational nexus while she was away from the Bastion. He was a competent lieutenant and facilitator, but she'd never seen him tested in battle. Three of the others, she did not even recognize, all faces that had come to the Sunless Crossing well after her. Leldi and Kurac were there, which she took comfort in. The twins had never shown a particular interest in lead-ership, but they were two of the most capable duelists she'd ever encountered, Leldi practically an artist with her deadly war pick and Kurac wielding a pair of long-bearded axes like a hurricane.

They were all Proclaimers, true, the elite fighters of the Harbinger ... but they were all so *young*. She'd dispatched Rine with the most experienced of their order, expecting the greatest hardships in their hunt would be faced in the Ashen Fields, and certainly not anticipating a need for Proclaimers within Nox Valar. It had been years since she'd had to take to the field herself, not since...

Well, not since the last time she'd been tangled up with Pel and Thrace on something. The pair were practically an omen unto themselves.

"Was she with anyone?" Vessa asked Thomlin.

"Unidentified man, possibly a Shepherd. Last seen heading into the House of Bereavement. Haven't emerged yet."

"I don't know it."

"Low-rent bar," Leldi offered in her thick accent. "Cheap drink. Dark enough ta' flatter whoever yer drinking wif."

"And now we all have a stunning insight into Leldi's social life," Vessa quipped. They laughed, Leldi hardest of all. *Young or not,* she reminded herself, *they're still Proclaimers.* They would do what needed doing.

"Listen up," she commanded as the attendants secured the buckles of her gauntlet onto her pauldron. "We are not the town watch. I will not waste our time with stirring oratory. We're seeking a dark-haired woman in Harbinger colors, carrying a raven-patterned maul. We do not know what state she's in, or how she or her companion will react to us. Any questions?"

"Could ye possibly give us aney less informashun?" Kurac asked. "Feels a bit like we're goin' in o'er-prepar'd."

His joke was muffled as Vessa lowered a winged great helm over her head. Then she hefted a shield bespoke in raven iconography from one attendant's arms, and took Calamity, her masterwork morningstar, from the hands of another. The head of the weapon was gold-inlaid steel forged in the shape of a starburst, each stylized streak of fire tapering off to a wicked point.

"Let's go," she commanded.

Of all the things that were scarce in the Crossing, animals were perhaps the most unexpected omission. There were no insects, no birds, no dogs or cats—and no horses. But as the squad of Proclaimers met twice their number of standard Heralds in the Bastion's sally port, they deployed their alternative. The squad leaders distributed shadow gems from the

Bastion's supply to each member of the force, and they used them to summon smoke-shrouded steeds of darkness. Most took the standard form of cavalry chargers, massive midnight horses bred for armored combat that were familiar to many of the Heralds in life. The twin Proclaimers, of course, summoned oversized rams and were pleased with themselves about it. The other Proclaimers laughed as the rams snorted and bucked, casting cautious sidelong glances at Vessa and Thomlin to make sure the antics weren't going to bring down their rebuke.

Vessa hid a grin behind her helm's faceplate. She had well earned her position of leadership within the Bastion and was proud of her station... but sometimes she did miss the camaraderie of the rank-and-file.

Thomlin took point and directed the formation through the city, bringing them to the street outside the House of Bereavement. Leldi's assessment was accurate; it looked like a public house that, even with the nigh-infinite time the Crossing afforded her, Vessa would never have thought to patronize. Their mounts faded like shadows at dawn as they dismounted, and after they established that their target had not been sighted leaving, Vessa ordered the standard Heralds to form a loose perimeter.

There was no subtlety in a squad of Proclaimers in full war gear, so they didn't bother feigning any. The streets before them soon cleared as word spread, and Vessa had no doubt that word had already been sent to the Guard. But they were sanctioned agents of one of Eternity Row's temples. They may be watched, even shadowed, but the Nyxian Guard would not rush to confront them without cause.

Vessa ordered Leldi to take the lead as they entered the House, given her familiarity with the layout. The taproom managed to make even the ubiquitous marble of Nox Valar look drab and run-down. Every surface in the place was caked in a film of ash tracked in by generations of souls, stained with various fluids, or more often, both. Vessa's Proclaimers dredged up small dust-clouds as they walked, fanning out to scan their way through the establishment's patrons.

The House of Bereavement's arrangement was simple. A long main room made up the bulk of it, with a bar island running down its center, stacked high with wine barrels and shelves of dusty bottles. To one side, a set of stairs led up to a secondary seating area that overlooked the main hall.

The place was practically empty by Nox Valar standards, which only meant that there were still a few tables that weren't taken. Still, the crowd was subdued. The House was not a boisterous bar where souls came to party away their time. A sullen air hung over this place, a sense of profound resignation and acceptance of futility. Souls muttered as the Proclaimers filtered through the tables and benches, but none addressed them. A bored elven barkeeper watched them with disinterest, not even bothering to question their appearance or intentions. The squad formed a loose line across the width of the House, scanning each face as they went, making sure no soul could slip by them unnoticed. Vessa couldn't help but wonder what Leldi saw in the place; though knowing Leldi, she'd probably stopped at "cheap booze" and didn't think to examine it further. Some habits take the dead a long time to break.

As Vessa mused on that point, the twin in question came to a slow halt. The Proclaimers had made it about halfway into the House, and the search line stopped as they reached parallel.

"Somethin' ain't right 'ere, 'igh 'erald…" Leldi began.

All hells broke loose.

Even before she'd finished her warning, Leldi whirled and buried the spike of her war pick into the forehead of a creature that sprang at her from beneath the nearest table. Vessa caught a flash of a fanged, twisted horror before it burst into ash that washed over the Proclaimer.

A great weight slammed into Vessa's side, knocking her from her feet. The force was such that she didn't even try to stand fast, instead allowing herself to fall with the momentum of the blow, letting her armor absorb the worst of it. As she recoiled from the hit, she turned to face her attacker. It was a bipedal thing, technically, though as it stalked forward it hunched and skittered along on its scythe-bladed forelimbs. A wicked, serrated beak snapped at her as it drew closer, and she saw it coiling its hind legs for another pounce.

Vessa wasn't going to give it a chance. She pointed Calamity and spoke a word, invoking the gifts the Harbinger had granted for her lifetimes of service. A lance of searing light burst from the head of the morningstar, battering into and *through* the beast's chest. A crackling stench of ozone and wood smoke filled the air in the wake of her spell, and a pile of ash drifted to the floor.

A dozen feet away, she saw Thomlin speak another word and punch his fist into the air. A raven medallion mounted to his gauntlet flared, and a wave of violet un-light washed through the room. As it hit, the passive patrons of the House of Bereavement vanished, the woven magic of the mass illusion destroyed by Thomlin's countermeasure. Much of the ash Vessa had taken for poor housekeeping was revealed to be what it was: soul dust, spread everywhere.

Kurac bellowed in defiance, and Vessa saw him chopping and cleaving his way through a crowd of blackened horrors to reach his sister. She drew up her will and reached for another spell—

And felt the power torn from her, shredded before she could invoke it into being as some unseen foe unraveled her magic.

"Caster!" she shouted, searching wildly. Everywhere she looked, she saw undead horrors and aberrant monstrosities laying into her Proclaimers, but no sign of a hostile mage. One was there, she was sure of it.

A thing that may once have been three or more men, their jaws unhinged and gnashing beneath blank, lidless eyes, and their bodies fused together in a warped parody of life, barreled toward her. It knocked tables and chairs aside in sprays of wood and ash as it ran, its gait a loping thing brought on by a mix of mismatched limbs.

Vessa snarled at it and charged, shield held high. She angled her first contact with the undead so that her shield deflected the monster to one side, and as they passed, she already had Calamity swinging down to crush its flank. The weapon flared with radiant light as it made contact with the warped thing, charring undead flesh even as she drove the spiked head into one of the amalgam's deformed skulls. It burst like a rotted watermelon, showering her with viscera that flash-burned into an ashy film against her holy armor.

The monster staggered, but she gave it no time to recover as she pursued, ramming the edge of her shield into a soft-looking bit of flesh, and following it up with a powerful overhand strike. The creature went down in a burst of ash and light.

An arrow thudded into her back, punching through layers of armor and driving her to one knee. She screamed.

Then one of the Proclaimers she didn't know reached her. This one had a hammer strapped to their belt but wasn't wielding it. Instead, each gauntleted hand was engulfed in magical power; their left wreathed in fire, their right covered in dancing arcs of lightning. "Above!" they shouted, loosing a gout of flame toward the House of Bereavement's upper balcony. The spell sputtered and died in the air as the unseen enemy countered it, but the Proclaimer was ready, unleashing a thunderous *boom* of lightning with their other hand, even before the flames had fully died. Vessa heard unfamiliar screams from above.

Thomlin joined them while the unknown Proclaimer re-ignited their fire spell and blasted away. "Bad luck, High Herald," she heard sympathy in his voice. Then he reached down and grabbed the arrow shaft lodged through her armor—*agony*—and brought his sword down, breaking it near the head—*excruciating*—before helping her to her feet. She could feel the arrowhead, punched through her armor and gambeson, still jabbing at least an inch into her lower back, but there was nothing for it right then.

Vessa took up position beside the elementalist Proclaimer. "Good work!" she shouted in encouragement, looking at Thomlin askance.

"Proclaimer Orld, High Herald! Just joined us a fortnight ago!" Thomlin informed her before he unleashed an arcane storm of razor-sharp sleet from his outstretched palm, pummeling another horror-beast and reducing it to ash.

"Duty persists!" Orld shouted in greeting, clapping their hands together and loosing a cone of plasma in front of themselves, disintegrating a swath of the house's furniture and at least two monstrosities hiding among it.

"Don't it fucking just though?" she replied, eschewing whatever traditional reply Orld no doubt expected of a High Herald. With a feral laugh, Vessa added her spellwork to the mix. Spears of flame leaped from her weapon, streaking out to splash against a number of monsters bearing down on Kurac.

The twins were farthest in and in danger of being mobbed by sheer numbers. They fought like paired whirlwinds, Leldi covering her brother's back with her shield while landing precise, annihilating blows with her pick, and Kurac an armored storm of singing ax blades that kissed every beast that came within his reach. They were holding back the tide by a hair's breadth. Any mistake from either would doom them both.

"The door!" Thomlin bellowed, directing the two Proclaimers farthest behind to secure their escape route. Vessa saw them about-face without hesitation, battling their way back toward the entrance. There, not fifty yards away, she saw the Heralds stationed outside frantically trying to fight their way in to assist them, though they were faring far worse than the elite Proclaimers. The taproom's doors were a choke point they'd yet to secure, meaning they could only come at the monsters in twos or threes with precious little room to maneuver. They would need relief from the embattled but more mobile Proclaimers inside if they wanted to breach the entrance without taking horrific losses.

A lance of hellish green light scoured Vessa's vision, and she watched in horror as Thomlin was unmade before her eyes; plate, cloth, and flesh turned instantly to dust as the beam bore through him. For a gut-churning second, he pawed feebly at the hole in his chest before falling to his knees. He was ash before he hit the floor.

A figure stepped from the folded light of an invisibility spell and stood before her, glaring them down. He was clad in filigreed plate armor enameled in blacks, grays, and whites. His faceplate was up, revealing a bald, grizzled visage with a tremendous scar that marred one eye. Vessa saw with growing dismay the crackling *power* that wreathed the figure, tendrils of energy coursing through the runic etchings of his armor and radiating off him like body heat. He lowered a gauntleted hand, his knuckles encrusted with emeralds that still glowed with the same sickly energy that had felled Thomlin.

"Bear witness, Harbinger." The man spoke in a voice worn by age but hardened in righteous determination. "I have seen the truth, and I offer it now to you. Throw down your weapons and no more need suffer this day."

"Who inna fuck is 'e?" Kurac shouted, still locked in ferocious melee.

"I was Edwin Harson," the man offered, his tone calm and measured as if his audience wasn't battling for their afterlives. As he spoke, one of the quadrupedal monstrosities circled him, protective. He scratched its head, and it nuzzled in like a dog to its master's touch. "I have done such ... terrible things. But I have been given a gift. I have been given Truth. I have been given Purpose. I am Redeemed."

"I do not know you, and yet you brought us violence," Vessa snapped. "You attacked us unprovoked. Butchered this tavern. Cavort with these things. And you speak of redemption?"

The General held up a grasping hand, and a miasma of darkness formed in his grip. It coalesced into the shape of a sword, a flat cutout of void-dark nothingness that looked like a mistake in the tapestry of the world. The Proclaimers bore grim witness as he held the blade aloft, and streams of ash began flowing across the floor and converging. As the piles grew, they began to take on grotesque shapes akin to the other monsters that had attacked them.

"He's making those things out of soul-ash," Vessa breathed in horror.

"We are about the great work, Herald. You shall not interrupt it."

Orld scoffed behind her. "Not much point negotiating with madmen, Herald."

"Agreed." Vessa raised her shield and readied Calamity.

"So be it," Harson declared. "You are known to me, heralds of the carrion god. Vessels of the omen. Proclaimers of woe. Let us see if even you may be *redeemed*."

CHAPTER 30

Cypress was alone.

After Pel tried for hours to get her to divulge any-thing about her activities, hours of Cypress knowing she had been betrayed but finding her throat closing, voice failing, and thoughts fragmenting whenever she attempted to tell her interrogators as much, she had been moved deeper into the Onyx Requiem. She had been hooded and carried by blank-helmed guards when they moved her, so she had no sense of how far they'd gone or where in the massive structure she'd been placed.

Below, probably, she thought. *Far, far below. To rot.*

She'd only glimpsed the narrow cell they'd put her in for the scant seconds after they'd chained her wrists to the wall, pulled the hood from her head, and closed the door. Then there was only darkness.

It was absolute; no light peeked in from around the heavy door, no window let the Crossing's gloom give even a hint of illumination to the stone tomb they'd locked her in. Feeling what she could reach of the room told her nothing: smooth stone walls and a matching floor. She could not reach the door, nor the mountings of her chains. There was a single block positioned beneath her, a low, immovable stool. If she sat on it, the manacles held her arms up above her head. She supposed that was how she was expected to sleep. Otherwise, she could stand straddling it with little trouble, as it was narrow enough. She could stand on it, if she chose, but didn't see how it would help.

She was there for ... hours? Days? Minutes? She did not know. She was not sure which horrified her more. When she was alive she could have marked the passage of time by feedings, by thirst, by waste, or by bodily processes, but all of that was void here. The dead might eat, drink, and be merry, but they were still dead. They *could* persist without for a very, very long time. What toll the lack would take on her sanity remained to be seen.

In a grim moment, there in the dark, she wondered if she could escape the cell if she ashed herself. If her soul weren't too frayed, it would reform and fall to the Fields again, as it had when she first arrived. Though if it was too damaged, she might come back as ... something else. It was a risk.

Not that it mattered. She didn't see a way of doing it, short of bashing her head into the wall. Which would likely knock her out before anything else. And there had always been rumors about the extent of the Monarchy's powers in the Crossing. It stood to reason that if they wanted a soul confined, they could ensure it stayed that way.

She wondered if she was still sporting a strange fusion of Lizabeth's and Anastasia's features. That had been ... odd. Possible, but unusual, and not something she'd ever done without serious concentration. Whatever had happened in Carlow's office had scrambled her. She tried shifting now, thinning her wrists and hands to child-sized, seeing if she could slip free. The manacles must have been enchanted too, as they expanded and contracted right along with her.

Cypress hung from her chains in the dark. It was so pitch-black that her mind struggled to fill her vision with noise; she thought she could see the pattern of stone in the room, the strands of hair—Lizabeth's red, or Anastasia's black?—that she could feel framing her face. She imagined lights, sounds, anything to fill the void. She imagined moonbeams and summer breezes and Anastasia's laughter, just in the next room.

When the tears rolled down her nose and fell to the floor with a soft *pat … pat … pat …* she was not sure if she imagined them.

"Delicious." A rasping voice rumbled from opposite her. It was no more than a whisper, but it broke the eon of smothering silence like a thunderclap.

Cypress recoiled, pressing herself back into the wall and straining to see something, *anything,* in the nothing. No one had entered, she was sure of it—she hadn't fallen asleep, had she? And she knew she was alone in the cell when they put her in. Nothing could have stayed so silent, so still, for so long; not when she was so desperate for even the slightest stimulation.

A candle flame lit the room, dawning like the sun.

An enormous, mangled grin filled her vision, inches away, stretched across a grotesque parody of an old man's face.

"Azlaru. Has come. For. A visit."

Cypress fought down her panic at being so close to the … *whatever* Azlaru was, alone. "H-how are you here?"

"Azlaru. Is. Bonded to. The Cypress." He chuckled, puffs of putrid breath washing over her and making her eyes water. "The Cypress. Is. Never. Alone. So long as. The Cypress. Owes. Azlaru."

Cypress couldn't hold back a horrified tremble.

"What do you want?" she whispered.

"Your. Suffering. Here is. *Exquisite.* So much. Loss. Sorrow. Hope. *Devoured.* Betrayal. Futility." He sighed in blissful satisfaction, as if describing a gourmet meal. "Azlaru was. Right to. Watch. The Cypress. Such. Potential. Realized."

"So you're just going to sit here and bask in my misery now?" Cypress spat, rage flashing deep within. "Fuck you."

"Azlaru. Would enjoy. This feast. For only. So long." He *tut-tut-tutted* her in reproach. "Variety. Is the spice. Of misery."

"Go then. This is it. This is all you're getting."

"No. It is. Not."

For a horrible moment, Cypress feared the demon meant to inflict misery of his own. But Azlaru continued, "The Cypress. Owes. Azlaru. Azlaru cannot. Collect. If the Cypress. Stays here."

Cypress snapped her gaze up to meet Azlaru's gigantic, yellow eyes.

"Ah. Hope. The marinade. Of. Suf—"

"Yeah, I fucking get it. Get to the point."

She wasn't sure if he looked befuddled or pleased at her interruption. She decided not to bother trying to figure it out.

"Azlaru. Would like. To play." He gestured, and she realized that they were seated at a table—the card table at Madrigal's, in fact, except that she could not see anything beyond its surface and her opponent, lit as if by a handful of low-burning, unseen candles. All space beyond was as black as her cell.

She found her hands were free and rubbed her wrists. A deck of cards sat on the table before her.

"Cut," Azlaru said.

She did so, and the cards slid away from her of their own accord. "What's the wager?"

"Azlaru. Wagers. The means. For. The Cypress. To free. Itself."

"What does that mean? You can get me out of here?" Maybe he already had. But she doubted it; this table was some trick of perception. It had to be.

"Azlaru. Can unlock. A door. As the Cypress. Should already. Know."

She stared at him, trying to decipher his meaning. Then, a realization dawned on her. "The Bastion."

"A simple. Lock. A few. Tumblers. Shifted. And so much. Delight. Unfolds."

Cold sweat trickled down her spine as she realized she had not been alone since her first game with this creature, not truly. He knew... what did he know? How many faces had he seen? Her movements? Her methods, her thoughts, her fears?

Anastasia?

"But. The Cypress. Does not. Want. Azlaru. To simply. Unlock. A door."

"I don't?"

"The Cypress. Could. Escape. The Requiem. With difficulty. But it has. Been marked. *Branded*. The Monarchy. Lords of. Cattle. Will follow. The Cypress. Will never. Lose them."

"Then what are you offering? *Exactly?*"

"The Cypress. Cannot. Speak. On how it. Came to be. Here. Can it?"

Dimereial's pendant flashed through her mind, a knot of distortion in both reality and her mind. Even thinking about the angel made her tongue twist, her thoughts muddle.

"It is. A *geas*," Azlaru explained with a sneer. "Crude. *Inelegant*. A coercion. Made manifest."

"It seems like your kind of thing to me."

The table vanished. She was in the cell again, hands chained back. Azlaru loomed so close that the tip of his bulbous, warty nose pressed into hers. "The Cypress. Will not. Insult. Azlaru."

Then she was back at the table, and he was seated opposite her again. She fought to catch her breath.

"Azlaru. Will forgive. Because the Cypress. Still does not. Understand."

"I'm... I'm sorry..." she whispered. She was so exhausted, so tired of being vulnerable.

"Has Azlaru. Ever. Compelled. The Cypress?"

She considered for a moment. "No," she admitted. "No, I suppose not."

"Azlaru. Does not. *Force*." he explained. "Azlaru. Presents. Opportunities. And. Choices."

She began to see what he meant. "Choices when my other options are terrible. But choices. Yeah. I get it. Forcing it would ... spoil it, I guess."

"*Delicious*."

She shuddered.

"Azlaru. Will break. The betrayer's geas. If. The Cypress. Wins."

"And if I lose? I don't have much to bet here."

"The Cypress. Has. So. *Very*. Much. Left to. Lose."

Cypress considered what she knew of Azlaru. Even during their first game, he had been coaching her to understand him—but never for her benefit. Everything he did was to increase her potential for... for misery. For suffering.

"Why do you pay so much more for certain memories?"

Azlaru blinked and tilted his head. He hadn't expected that question, but she felt like she was onto something.

"Love. Sex. Intimacy. Anytime someone comes into Mads's with a memory that centers on those, you outbid the room. You let everyone think it's because you have some... I don't know, voyeuristic side. But it doesn't fit. So why?"

That broad grin began to stretch across his face. "Azlaru. Thinks. The Cypress. Understands."

"You aren't after the memory," she concluded, following her logic. "You... you get something from it being *removed*, I think. You consume it or destroy it or whatever it is you do, but the real prize is leaving the void in some poor soul where there used to be joy. Love."

"Take. The moments. Of. Togetherness. And the soul. Becomes. More alone."

"But you don't overpay for any memories of companionship, or family. Just between lovers."

"Potency." Azlaru shrugged. "And because. The others. Want them. More. Their denial. Amuses. Azlaru."

Cypress thought for a moment. She had a terrible idea.

"I can wager my memories. Of Anastasia."

Azlaru leaned closer, his shoulders fully over the table's edge.

"Delicious."

CHAPTER 31

*S*weet, soft music drifted to Rasa's ears as the towheaded man plucked the lute strings. He turned to her, smiling, as the breeze picked up—

The wind bit hard, cutting through her cloak and straight to her bones. The spray off the ship's prow was like a cloud of icy needles against her face, but she dared not look away. If they didn't find—

It was here, somewhere! It had to be! She would find it even if she had to tear this entire house apart—

It was a modest home, two rooms and an outdoor privy, but it was warm in the winter and airy in the summer, and her parents had—

Tears fell as she watched the soil pile on her father's coffin. She felt so hollow, so lost. The plague had come, just like the raven-folk had predicted, but no one had—

Speak the warnings. Heed no doubt. Duty persists in the darkest hour. Proclaim the truth. Proclaim—

A Proclaimer fell before her, helm stove in by the tremendous impact, blood and bone spraying from his faceplate in a gruesome crimson splatter. She raised Raven, ready—

She took the hammer, humbled. She would do it proud, she resolved. Hers would be a noble entry in the Book of Deeds. She—

The other children found reading tiresome, but she begged papa to show her the words again. Every night, he took out his precious box of letters and helped her through them one word at a time. She asked to see his "special letters," the ones only momma read, but he laughed and said no, and that some letters were boring and only for adults—

She threw her head back and moaned, legs shaking as ecstasy shot through her like sugar-coated lightning. The man from the tavern seized her hips and pulled her closer, and she could taste their sweat on his lips when—

The air by the cliffs smelled of salt and sea life, the crash of waves on the rocks below an ever-present churn. She laughed as she ran through the tall grass, chasing—

Rasa gasped as she came to, arching her back to press against Menthissa's grip, but the fiend held her head down. Her pulse was a battle-drum, and her chest heaved as she gasped for air. Methodically, Menthissa withdrew her jade claws from the bloody welts around Rasa's skull.

The persistent ring cut off abruptly as Secan put the hand-held bells down. "A good one," Menthissa commented. "A bit of music can take you down all sorts of roads. Even if the user's sense of rhythm is all wrong."

"You said I was doing fine," Secan muttered to himself. Rasa's head was throbbing, and she felt as if she was caked in blood and ash.

"A-again," she croaked, grappling for breath. "Put me down again. It was clearer that time. I saw... I saw..." Already, she couldn't remember Papa's face, or the tune the man played, or...

"Hush, sweetling," Menthissa stroked her hair, pushing it back from where it stuck to her sweat-sheened scalp. "Your mind has to rest now, or we do more harm than good. This was a good start. The bellflies should be able to begin chipping away at that wall now. If you'd like another session with me, Borssa can put you in touch." She smiled as she traced a nail down Rasa's bloodstained cheek. "Be warned, love. I don't come cheap."

"Thank you for your time then, miss Menthissa," Secan offered. As she got her bearings, Rasa noticed that he was white as a sheet. Perhaps Menthissa's ministrations had not been pleasant to observe.

"No thanks are needed, Shepherd. This was debt repaid. But you, too, would be welcome to reach out again." Menthissa rose and stalked around him as she spoke, collecting the bells and other props she'd had him using to assist in the rituals. One jade batwing stretched out to partially embrace him as she circled around the chamber, tracing around his figure before trailing away and retracting. "I'm so curious what you would ask me for. I'm sure we can come to some arrangement."

Secan looked wide-eyed at Rasa. She was too preoccupied trying to solidify the fading-dream flashes of memory in her mind to tease him.

"Alas, sweetlings, our time is up." Menthissa snapped her fingers, and the stone walls around them were replaced by the gauzy curtains of Paradise's mezzanine again. "Before you go, I will remind you as a member of management that all forms of violence are *strictly* prohibited within the grounds of Paradise, except, of course, within our sanctioned experiences."

"What are you—" Secan began before a storm of crossbow bolts ripped through the curtain wall around them.

They were saved from the initial assault by luck and the heavy furniture. One bolt splintered the lounge that Rasa still sat upon, deflecting its trajectory enough so that the point of it missed her leg by inches. She dove to the floor, snagging Raven on the way, and dragged Secan down too. More impacts thudded into the wood and cushions around them. Several struck Menthissa and simply shattered, leaving her unmarred and showering them with fragments.

"Little children," Menthissa snarled. "You really should read the rules."

The devil clenched her fist and Rasa felt a surge of power *thrum* through the space, followed by the sound of screams that cut off abruptly with a chorus of breaking bones.

"The Guild of Vices would like to remind all patrons that—" Menthissa began, interrupted by a final bolt smashing into her temple, snapping her head around. *"Really,"* she growled, raising her hand in the direction the shot had come from. There was a rush of air as a man was violently pulled into view, propelled by an unseen force into Menthissa's waiting grasp. He wore light armor, layers of fabrics and wool, and a shroud over his face. Black and white heraldry Rasa didn't recognize adorned his chest and shoulder. He kicked as Menthissa held him by the throat with one hand. Then, with snakelike speed, she plunged the fingers of her free hand into his eye sockets. A gurgling, miserable screech escaped him as the fiend used the handholds as leverage to rip his head and spine from his torso.

Rasa fought down bile at the sight, and Secan audibly retched. What happened next shocked her more than the violence, however. As blood and viscera sprayed from the corpse, it began to decay before her eyes. Menthissa discarded the limp form, disinterested. Rasa watched in fascinated horror as it bloated, shriveled, and desiccated before finally disintegrating into dust that seemed to fall straight through the floor. The man's armor and clothing remained in a disheveled pile where he'd fallen. The entire process took mere seconds.

"Gods help them, they're alive." Secan breathed.

"The Guild of Vices," Menthissa repeated as if nothing had happened. "Would at this time like to *stress* to all patrons that violence within Paradise will absolutely not be tolerated. You have been warned."

She turned on her heel and began to stride away. "Paradise ends at the steps, sweetlings," she announced without looking back. "Have fun."

Slowly, deliberately, Secan and Rasa stood. He reached to his scroll bandoliers and pulled two sealed rolls of vellum free. She held Raven loose, ready, but did not raise it to charge. Instead, they scanned the mezzanine in silence, assessing.

Half a dozen other piles of discarded black-and-white clothing lay scattered in a semicircle around the ruins of Menthissa's lounge. Another half dozen figures still stood, crossbows trained on Secan and Rasa, but clearly unwilling to tempt the wrath of the Guild again. Behind them, the lesser incubi of the mezzanine prowled, eager to catch another infraction now that their mistress had left the room.

"You see the stairs from here?" Secan asked her, voice low.

"Yeah."

"Pick a clear path?"

She frowned at the debris from the initial volley, and the would-be assassins beyond. "Kinda?"

"Hells. Whatever you do, don't raise a finger to these fellas until we reach the steps."

"I figured that out when she ripped that guy's head off, Secan."

"I don't think they're gonna fire at us for now."

"They saw the head too, I'm guessing."

"*Hells.*"

"You take me to the nicest places," she quipped in a tone of forced joviality.

"Alright. Alright. On my mark. Stairs. Fast as we can. Up and out. We'll try and make it to the street. Less chance they'll want to cause a scene there."

"We could just stay here forever."

"The Guild removes you if you're not patronizing their services at least every hour."

Rasa looked at the fallen pile of clothing and wondered if Menthissa and company defined "removal" as anything more gentle. "Well. Fuck me. Let's do this."

She heard him take a steadying breath. The bustle of Paradise was a distant thing, the revelry unimpeded by this small disruption in one corner of the carnival of carnality. But around them, there was a tense hush, as every party waited on a knife's edge to see what the next move would be.

It was Secan who broke the dam.

There was a *rip-snap* that Rasa took to be him tearing one of the scrolls open, and she saw a flash of light in her peripheral vision. "Now!" Secan barked and took off at a sprint. She joined him and saw a nimbus of invigorating golden light surrounding their limbs as they ran. She was baffled to find her footsteps felt lighter, her mind swifter, and her muscles singing with euphoric joy at the exertion. She bounded over the ruined furniture without a thought, eating half a dozen yards with each loping stride. Their assailants and the staff of Paradise remaining in the area appeared to be moving through molasses, reacting with exaggerated sluggishness to their escape.

One of the would-be assassins loosed a bolt at them, and she traced its path as if he had thrown it rather than shot it from a crossbow. It was a simple enough thing to dodge; and before it had even crossed their path, the incubi of the mezzanine were on the poor fool. One slammed a marble fist into the back of his head with bone-snapping force, and the man fell limp to the ground. To Rasa's horror, he did not begin to decompose—even as the demons snatched his rag doll form and turned to abscond with him, he was still alive.

The remaining men in black-and-white rushed to follow, but could not compete with the speed Secan's spell had given them. As the duo reached the grand entryway that led to the base of Paradise's stairs, Secan whirled and brought his second scroll to bear. Even as they began to climb, the spell contained within flashed to life.

She had to grasp the handrail as the treads beneath her morphed and buckled, and the sound of grinding stone echoed up the long stairwell. A wall of bedrock bisected the stairs just past the entry, growing up to fill the gap at Secan's direction. As the scroll's magic faded, the way to Paradise was completely blocked.

"Run!" Secan bade her, taking the steps at double-time. "That ain't gonna hold for long!"

Halfway up the steps, time seemed to run back toward normal, and Rasa almost collapsed as she hit a wall of debilitating lethargy. Secan stumbled, catching himself with his hands, wheezing and panting for breath. The feeling began to abate after a moment, but Rasa still felt a bone-deep weariness dragging her down.

"Only problem with that spell," Secan panted, starting a slower, methodical climb up. "You still gotta pay for it."

"I think we are in the clear," Rasa offered, looking back. The lights of Paradise were still obscured by the new wall.

"As long as nothing is waiting for us ... at..." Secan's voice trailed off as he looked ahead. Rasa followed his gaze and frowned.

Judging by the dancing light and shadows shining from above, the tavern they'd entered Paradise through, a dump named the House of Bereavement, appeared to be on fire.

"As long as nothing's waiting for us at the top." Secan sighed. "That's what I was going to say."

CHAPTER 32

"**M**ake your. Requests."

"We're doing requests?" Cypress asked. Across the table, the sole island in their endless personal void, Azlaru nodded.

"Azlaru. Enjoys. This element. Of the game."

"It's not part of the game." While it was common in back-room games, the request-and-veto practice was more of a house rule.

"If Azlaru. Wanted. To play games. At the House. Of the Dawn. Azlaru. Would."

"Fair enough, fair enough." Cypress held up her hands, thinking. "Advantage roll."

"Vetoed," he rumbled. Cypress was surprised, but not disheartened. Taking an extra roll would have benefitted him as much as it did her, but apparently Azlaru wasn't interested. "Azlaru. Requests. Twist round. Price set. Before roll."

Cypress mulled the proposition. In theory, it helped both of them: before the final reveal, there would be a round in which they could buy additional cards from the deck by increasing the pot. But she was beginning to understand a little more of what drove Azlaru, and through that lens, spotted the trap for what it was. She needed exactly one thing from Azlaru, whereas he would delight in tempting her. If she allowed that to be on the table, he'd try to entice her into emptying her mind to secure the win...

"No. Veto," she said. Azlaru grunted. "My next request: ghosts are high."

He tilted his head at her, quizzical.

"Pride," she explained. It also meant he couldn't request infernals high, as the accepted system barred players from directly contradictory requests.

Azlaru laughed, a *chuff-chuff* sound that invoked a sense of shoveling grave dirt. "The final. Request. Is Azlaru's. One-card stud."

Cypress nodded; her veto spent, she had no choice but to accept. The first card in each of their hands would be dealt face-up for the other to see. Combined with the dice draw of Purgatory Poker, it could lead to a massive advantage for one's opponent if you wound up with a short hand. But that was how it would be.

"Ante," Azlaru rumbled. "Azlaru. Bids. The removal. Of. The lying. Angel's. Geas." As he finished speaking, a token, a small disk of absolute, perfect darkness, coalesced on the table between them. It was a marker of the fiend's promise.

Fear clutched Cypress's heart as she looked inward. She knew what she had to do. Even if it broke her.

"I wager a memory—*ah!*" Even as she conjured up the memory in question, she was overcome with vertigo. In a flash, she was *there,* in that moment...

"Ostov is on his deathbed. It'll be any day now," Anastasia said, *the edge of worry straining through even her typically unshakable composure.*

"We knew this was coming," Cypress told her. *She wore the same face she always did around the palace: a stranger they'd seen*

on a trip as children, a beautiful young woman from a faraway land. Ostov had thought it important for his great-niece's … peculiar … friend … to have a more palatable persona for the court to know her by.

"There's knowing and then there's happening!" Anastasia cried, massaging her temples. "A couple of months ago, we still thought Mastin was just stuck on the frontier somewhere. Not… not…"

"It's you, Anz. It's going to be you." Cypress put her arm around Anastasia's shoulders. "I'm going to be right there with you. The whole way. Always."

Anastasia nodded and leaned into her shoulder, letting herself be held. She laughed softly. "Last chance, Cy. We can run away, right now. You and me, like we always said."

"I still think we'd be great highwaymen. Pirates. Something like that." Cypress nodded. "There's a problem though."

"What?"

"I think you'd make a better queen."

Anastasia's eyes glistened as she held back tears, but after a moment she fixed Cypress with that dazzling smile. "Then your first royal command is to shut up and kiss me."

An amber token the color of candlelight joined Azlaru's on the table.

"Deal."

Azlaru's cards distributed themselves of their own accord. One glided across the table to rest in front of each player facedown. They were swiftly followed by one face-up card a piece: Azlaru showed a king of gargoyles, and Cypress a six of ghosts.

"Order," Azlaru announced. "Evens. Or. Odds."

"I call odds." A glassy black pyramid tumbled across the table and came up showing a two. "Well. Looks like you go first."

"Roll." He plucked the die back up and let it fall. It skipped toward her, landing on a three. Three more cards whisked themselves into Azlaru's hand. Cypress picked up the die. Its edges were sharp, with tiny, scalloped serrations, like it was made of chipped obsidian. But every dimension was even, and she detected no irregularities in its balance—not that she'd expected any. She believed what Azlaru had told her after their last game: he didn't cheat. He wanted her loss, her suffering, to be real. He could risk losing because he could always wait for the next game, whereas every time she played, her back was against the wall.

Cypress threw the glass die. It bounced once, twice, and settled.

A single card slid itself across the table and joined her hand.

Wincing at the setback, she reached for her now-two hidden cards ... and hesitated. She laid her hands flat on the table.

"Interesting." Azlaru rumbled, yellowed eyes fixed on her. He, too, had ignored his cards.

"You said it last time," Cypress explained. "The cards aren't the interesting part of the game. You are."

"Azlaru. Raises." Another dark coin began to swirl into being on the table, forming as if siphoned from the prevailing shadow around them. "The angel. Will be. Alerted. When the geas. Is. Broken. Azlaru bids. Two hours of. Delay. For the Cypress. To prepare."

Cypress nodded. "Call."

She was so nervous she would be found out that she had switched faces five times and thrown up in a closet. The palace was so much bigger than she'd expected, she did not understand how the folk who lived here found their way around.

She'd been scolded by three different adults for the state of her dress, which she frantically explained as the result of a slip and fall in the mud. She could wear the forms of the other little girls she'd seen coming and going through the gates, but there was nothing she could do about their fine dresses and fancy hairstyles.

Her nose gave her some sense of direction as she scampered through the servants' corridors, following the mouth-watering scents of baking bread and spices.

"Jackpot!" Young Cypress whispered as she peeked through a door and found a treasure trove. The pantry was crammed full: loaves of bread sat cooling on one shelf, cured meats hung from hooks beneath another, and there were entire crates filled with fruits, vegetables, hard cheeses, and more.

As quietly as she could, she closed the door behind her and began stuffing her satchel full. She was careful not to take too much of any one thing, spreading her thievery out so as to, in her mind, raise less suspicion.

She was almost finished, her satchel full to bursting, when she spotted a pair of eyes watching her from behind a crate.

"Eek!" she squealed, stumbling backward, and falling right on her prize, scattering produce everywhere.

"Ermph!" A raven-haired child startled from her hiding place, mouth stuffed full of a freshly pilfered sweetloaf.

Panicked, Cypress did what came naturally to her: she shifted, switching from the girl with golden curls she'd seen waiting for a coach with her family to the red-headed boy she'd watched struggling to ride his first horse as he followed his instructor around the palace walls.

"Wow!" the other girl exclaimed, bread falling from her slack-jawed mouth. "How'd you do that?"

Cypress's lip quivered with fear. "Please don't tell on me! I'll leave! I was just hungry!"

The girl frowned, then picked up one of the buttered rolls that had fallen from Cypress's bag. She sat down cross-legged in front of Cypress and offered it to her. "I'm Anastasia," she said. "Wanna be friends?"

A bright token the color of a summer sky appeared on the table next to her ante.

Azlaru drummed his bony spider-fingers on the table, his gaze never wavering from Cypress.

She met it.

"Raise." Azlaru declared. "The means. To leave. This place. The Cypress. Will escape."

"Rejected."

Azlaru tilted his head so it was nearly perpendicular. "Explain."

"I don't need to be a fugitive. That wager is worthless to me."

"Azlaru. Can. Give. The Cypress. Power. To fend off. The Monarchy. Of Fools."

Cypress shook her head. "I would accept a lesser bet: the means to walk out of here and present my story to that investigator unimpeded. With the geas broken, preferably before your delay wears off."

Azlaru considered her words, stroking his pointed chin and nodding. "Azlaru. Will. Wager. This." A dark coin appeared on the table. "Azlaru is. Curious. What morsel. The Cypress. Will offer. To call."

"I have a final bet in mind." Cypress took a steadying breath. "But it comes with a rider."

"A. Condition?"

"Yes. I'll bet all of my memories of Anastasia. I won't remember a single moment with her. They're all yours. But leave my feelings for her. I'll know exactly what I lost." She met his rancid gaze. "That way I suffer as much as possible."

"Azlaru. Was right. To choose. The Cypress. It is. Most. Interesting." His horrific grin blossomed and kept growing as he spoke. "What is. The. Rider?"

"Before I place this bet, and regardless of the outcome of this game, you personally, have to guarantee the delivery of my message to her. The message I left with the Horsemen. I know you saw it. You will ensure it is delivered immediately, in the exact manner I asked of them. And you will take no detrimental action toward its recipients in the process."

"This. Also satisfies. The conditions. That allow Azlaru. To call on the Cypress. For a favor."

"That's correct," Cypress said. "Mutually beneficial."

"The Cypress's rider. Means that. The Cypress cannot lose."

"Oh, I can lose plenty," she snapped, her eyes misting up as she grappled with what she'd just offered. Every moment, every laugh, every fight, every kiss. "I stand to lose *everything*. I'm offering you the chance to see me suffer *forever*; do you get that? But. But you'll do that one thing. You'll make it so *all of this* wasn't for *nothing*. That's the deal. Take it or I'll fold right now. You can have your two memories and leave me to rot in a cell, and you'll never get your favor."

Azlaru's grin stretched wider and wider.

"Azlaru. Chose well. Indeed. Azlaru. Accepts."

Cypress braced for the whiplash of being drawn through every memory, every moment with Anastasia all at once, but it didn't come. There was only a blur, a brief sense of displacement and a ringing in her ears, and the fading echo of Anastasia's voice, as it had been the very last time she'd seen her:

"...*love you too, Cy.*"

A third token, pure white, joined the pot.

"Choose. Your. Cards." All but two of Azlaru's cards flitted away into the darkness. He kept the king of gargoyles and one of the untouched face-down cards.

Cypress flicked away the six of ghosts, leaving only her two unseen cards. It had to be that way. She trusted blind luck more than she trusted her ability not to give something away if she looked, if she let Azlaru dissect her while she hemmed and hawed trying to fit the six in with whatever else was there.

"Show." he said.

Heart in her throat, Cypress flipped her cards.

She held a king of infernals and a king of ghosts.

Azlaru showed the king of gargoyles and the king of celestials.

She stared at the cards, uncomprehending. Her mind was blank. She couldn't process it; her heart was pounding—

The next noise she registered was the clink and rattle of the chains falling away from her wrists in the dark. The *clack* of the cell door's lock. And a low, steady, rumbling laughter that seemed to come from inside her head.

"*Ghosts. Are. High.*" Azlaru's voice echoed from nowhere. "*Good. Game.*"

Dazed but with a growing sense of elation, Cypress scrambled to the open door and sprinted down the hall.

CHAPTER 33

A shimmering wall of moonlight flared into being as Vessa raised her shield, deflecting a deadly beam of caustic death that leaped from the Harson's fingertips. She clung to the spell with all her willpower, keeping the gossamer-thin protection between the remaining Proclaimers and their foe, but only just.

"*Submit*," the armored dreadnaught commanded, and Vessa's knees almost buckled under the sheer weight of the word. She kept her stance but heard Orld stumble behind her before being helped to their feet by Leldi.

"He's drawing from somewhere!" Orld snarled as Harson canceled another of their evocations with a contemptuous flick of power.

"I'm aware!" Vessa snapped. Edwin Harson must have been a capable warrior to begin with, but the man they faced now was clearly channeling power beyond his ken. The black-and-white armor he wore was heavily enchanted, but the Proclaimers could feel the energy coursing through him like an arcane furnace.

The problem was, there wasn't an awful lot they could *do* about it.

Kurac was gone, felled by a column of sickly blue fire after charging their foe. His twin Proclaimer had lost her arm, and war pick, and was now doing her best to shield their flank from the remaining monstrosities that stalked them through the House of Bereavement. The other Proclaimers were lost. Vessa believed there may still have been some Heralds outside, fighting to get in, but with a wave of that black sword, Harson had raised a fresh wave of monsters from the soul-ash that covered the tavern and they had lost their beachhead by the door. Vessa had not seen any sign of her Proclaimers since.

Vessa held Calamity high and belted a litany of holy invocations to the Harbinger, beseeching her god for aid. In the Crossing, this place removed from all and yet so much closer to the divine than the mortal realms, such summons were not trivial, doubly so when uttered by one of the Harbinger's chosen representatives in Nox Valar.

A pillar of silver fire punched through the roof of the House of Bereavement, showering Harson in chunks of rubble and a torrent of divine fury. Vessa lost sight of him in the wash of light and debris. The remaining unraveled shrank back from the blast, as if stung by the radiance of it, retreating to the corners and shadows of the House. The respite was welcome, but would last mere moments.

Vessa, Orld, and the battered Leldi surged forward to press the advantage, spreading out to flank Harson's position. As the light faded, his silhouette began to emerge ... standing. Unbowed.

Unharmed.

A glowing aegis in the shape of folded angel's wings sheltered him from all but the most trivial pass-through of the attack, which he staggered through. A warning couldn't even pass Vessa's lips as he lashed out, taking Leldi full in the chest with a whipping cord of coruscating flame. The wounded

Proclaimer cried out as it burned through her armor. She stumbled and fell, dissolving into ash as she struck the floor.

With a contemptuous snarl, Harson pointed his sword where the Proclaimer had fallen. A twisted, many-legged thing of gristle and bone reconstituted itself from her ashes, gnashing at the air with half a dozen mouths.

"Damn you!" Vessa shouted, charging at Harson and smashing Calamity through the blasphemous half-formed creature as she passed. He roared in return, his cold composure discarded in the heat of combat. That wretched blade, a tear in reality shaped like a sword, met Calamity's blazing swing with a parrying length of pure absence that hissed and sizzled as the weapons touched.

Orld struck Harson with staccato lightning blasts as the combatants broke apart, but each bolt grounded itself on the former general's infernal weapon. The rent in space seemed to eat the energy wielded against it, removing the magic wholesale from the tapestry of the Crossing.

Harson struck back, two battering blows that Vessa caught with her shield. But though the blade turned aside, some essence of it continued as if she wore no shield nor armor at all. Vessa cried out in surprise as something bit deep into her arm, and she felt blood gushing from the wound and soaking her sleeve. Crimson welled in the joints of her plate mail.

"What is your purpose here?" Vessa shouted as she bit back her pain. "What can possibly be worth this?"

"No price unpaid, Proclaimer!" Harson bellowed, striking with fire from his free hand. Vessa countered it, but barely. "The work will wash away sin, choke, and starve the engines of suffering that underpin the cosmos! Who am I to deny that? Who are *you*?"

He charged as he spoke, swatting aside a storm of frost from Orld. Harson swiped that ethereal nether-sword through the air, and another clutch of twisted beasts began to drag themselves into being on the House of Bereavement's floor. They snarled and set upon the elementalist, who backpedaled while cursing furiously.

Then Harson was upon Vessa again, who eschewed her crippled shield-arm in favor of meeting each strike with a screeching opposition from Calamity. The blessed and ensor-celled morningstar seemed better able to deflect the warping blows of the black blade, though it was not a weapon made for precise parrying and swordplay.

She managed to bind Harson's slash in the spikes of Calamity and punched out with her shield despite the flash of pain and spray of blood it cost her. The blow connected with Harson's helm, and he staggered, but not enough. Vessa tried to lever the blade out of his grip, but its edge rippled and mor-phed, breaking the bind and sending her scrambling to avoid his counter-blow. He slashed twice more, then again, and again, advancing all the while and driving her back in a losing defense.

She felt her heel butt against the House's central bar, and in a moment of grim realization knew she had nowhere left to retreat. Harson raised his sword again, and Vessa prepared to defend as best she could.

A hammer blow tore the general from his feet.

A black-haired, soot-streaked woman in the remnants of Herald's robes stood over him, her face twisted in a screaming rictus of rage and defiance. She wheeled a great maul carved in the likeness of a raven through the recoil of the first blow and brought it around and down again, crashing with tremendous force against Harson's enchanted armor. The blow rang with a deafening discharge of energy as the magical wards buckled under the strain, and the general skittered back across the floor.

The woman snapped her gaze over to Vessa, assessing whether she was a threat before returning her focus to Harson.

In that moment, Vessa gasped as a knot of conflicting emotions tugged at her heart.

She had her grandmother's eyes.

A roar of fire and a wash of heat ran over them as a swarm of flaming projectiles ripped through the air, scattering among the clusters of monsters where they erupted amid the surprised cries and death-shrieks of the horde. Vessa looked first to Orld, who had been badly mauled and backed into a corner, but the beleaguered Proclaimer was looking to Vessa in confusion as well.

Then she spotted a stranger, a lanky man with a walking stick slung across his back, holding the remains of a spent spell scroll as it flaked and disintegrated from his grasp. "Rasa! We gotta go!" he shouted at the hammer-wielding woman.

"This one summons the beasts!" she roared in reply, crashing the maul back down on Harson as he fought to stand. He parried with the black blade and her blows seemed sapped as they rebounded from it, as if she were striking a sack of sand instead of a sword.

The stick-and-scroll man drew up alongside Vessa. "You alright there, miss?"

"Had better days," Vessa admitted, pulling herself together. Her arm was bleeding badly, and something in her opposite leg had been damaged in the ensuing melee. She was struggling to hold a decent fighting stance.

"Don't know who you are, but as long as we can agree that the fella wearing the same kit as the living assassins and summoning the freaky things is probably bad, we'll stay on good terms, yeah?"

"Sound logic."

"Alright then. Let's see what I've got left in my bag of tricks." He pulled several more scrolls from a strap across his shoulders and frowned at the seals affixed to them. "Not much, I'm afraid."

Orld fired off another lightning bolt that would have struck Harson square in the side, but even embattled with the fresh newcomer, he still managed to counter the magic with his free hand.

The gangly man frowned. "Might be able to sneak something through if you folks can keep him busy for a second."

"Aye." Vessa nodded, already drawing up her will and channeling it through Calamity. "I think we can do that. Orld!"

Struggling to stand, but with lightning still wreathed around their hand, the last Proclaimer looked to the High Herald. Vessa shucked her shield, letting it clatter to the floor. She held her wounded hand up and began a countdown. Orld nodded.

Three.

Two.

One.

Vessa unleashed a gout of holy fire from Calamity, unfocused and sloppy but still dangerous. At the same moment, Orld fired off a final lightning bolt at the general before collapsing to the floor.

Harson sensed the welling etheric energy in the room and raised his defenses, deftly canceling Orld's lightning as he had so many times already and raising a shimmering barrier against Vessa's stream of wrath. He held the barrier focused around his outstretched free hand while he continued to duel Rasa with his midnight blade.

Harson didn't see the stick-man's scrolls coming.

As Vessa and Orld unleashed their volley and, more importantly, tied up Harson's defenses, the lanky man ripped the seals off of two scrolls, one after another.

He unfurled the first and recited the incantations there, directing a churning ball of ether at the general. It flew across the room as a shimmer, a distortion in the light, and splashed around him as the spell took hold. It caused him no harm, but

Harson's eyes widened in alarm as his movements slowed, his limbs turning sluggish. He looked like he was moving through molasses; after a moment, even his reactions were delayed compared to what was happening around him.

Not that he had long to consider it. Seconds later, the second scroll flash-burned, targeting not the general but Rasa—specifically, Raven. The hammer's head began to glow as she clobbered it into the defenseless Harson, each strike erupting with a blinding strobe of radiance that dazzled Vessa's eyesight and left smoldering craters in his plate armor.

Edwin Harson reeled from blow after blow, falling to his knees. He raised his sword in meager defense, but Rasa brought Raven down and annihilated his wrist in a flash of light. The dark blade fell to the floor in eerie silence; offset by screeching from the monstrous stragglers in the room, who writhed and vanished along with the general's control of the weapon. Rasa swung Raven up and caught his chin on the backswing, a geyser of blood and teeth spraying into the air as he flipped onto his back. Before Vessa, Orld, or the scroll-man had any say otherwise, Rasa brought the still-glowing Raven down in an overhead blow that caved in Harson's chest plate.

The old general fell still and slowly crumbled to ash.

Vessa staggered over to Raven's wielder, whom the scroll-man had called "Rasa" for reasons she hadn't figured out yet. She reached down and secured Harson's wicked sword—whatever the thing was, it had some capacity to conjure those creatures within the city, and Pel would want a look at it.

She put her good hand on Rasa's shoulder in congratulations. "Well done, great-granddaughter. I am so glad to have finally found you."

Emelia Theramay—the girl called Rasa—looked at her in confusion.

"Who are you?"

CHAPTER 34

"**W**hat's all the commotion?" Thrace asked, appearing in his usual seat across the desk without a whisper of announcement. "Jensen's got fifty guys suiting up downstairs."

Pel didn't flinch. He'd been dealing with Thrace's theatrics long enough that his random appearances didn't faze him. Plus, he knew it annoyed the soul stitched.

"Nice to see you back to your usual tricks," he said without looking up from the notes he'd been compiling on the Cypress interrogation. "Not sure. Some kind of dust-up in the next ward. Guard's on the way, but someone got a whiff of our brand of funny business. Jensen's goon squad is on it, so not our problem."

"Fair enough." Thrace shrugged. "Anything new with our prisoner?"

"About the same as what you saw." Pel sighed. "Every time I think she's starting to open up, she glazes over and starts repeating the same thing. I'm letting her stew for a bit while I try to dig up some background I can use. Need some leverage… Don't suppose you turned up anything?"

"Yes, actually. Remember how I said I was going to see my new patron?"

Pel frowned. "Thought you were going to run down the shapeshifter's escape route first."

"Funniest thing happened."

Pel laid his head on his desk and closed his eyes while his bonded soul stitched agent explained to him how the devil he'd signed a soul contract with had, as it turned out, been caught up in their ongoing investigation, and was waiting in the hall.

"Karson is going to have my ass, Thrace," he said without looking up.

"Karson's all talk," Thrace told him in a tone that made it sound like he *almost* believed it. "Besides, it worked out."

Pel roused enough to glare at him. "By 'worked out' do you mean that you, the bonded Covenant agent with the unauthorized infernal patron, have shaky secondhand information that says our single lead is probably a patsy, and we're nowhere?"

"There is the angel," a woman's voice added from the door. A crimson half-devil stood there, her wings and hands folded and her tail flicking back and forth with anxiety.

"Oh, come in then." Pel sighed. "Pel Solimo. This one's *other* leash holder. Allegedly."

"Madrigal. Charmed." She surveyed the furniture and selected a backless ottoman to perch on, to better accommodate her nonhuman limbs. "Thrace tells me you've locked up a friend of mine. I'm here to change your mind about that."

"Your 'friend' practically turned herself in. Keeps confessing, in fact."

"About that," Thrace interjected. "Madrigal here thinks Cypress got duped by a rogue celestial. Dimmerang."

"Dimereial."

"Whatever. I think we can flip her and put together a plan to go after the big fish."

Pel gave Thrace a level look. "And why wouldn't we just grab both if he's involved? Are we contending that Cypress *isn't* a memory thief? That's enough to keep her in the void cells indefinitely, at the very least."

Thrace held up his hands. "Not saying she's off the hook. Just saying that it looks like there might be some extenuating circumstances on this one."

"Explain."

"Thrace gave me a general outline of your broader concerns here," Madrigal chimed in. "Someone messing with resurrections and crossings over. That's not Cypress, Mister Solimo. She's a shifter and a damn good sneak, but no major arcana behind her."

"I am so thrilled that Thrace has brought you up to speed," Pel said, glaring at Thrace. Thrace made a rude gesture. "But Cypress is still part of the scheme. We can look into this celestial too, but—"

"If we've got a renegade angel in the mix, then I don't think—"

"We've already gone so far off book with your antics that there's no way I can justify—"

"Since when are you such a hardass, Pel?"

"Since when are *you* the bleeding heart, Thrace?"

"Hey there, Cypress," Madrigal addressed an empty corner of the room.

Confused, Pel went to query the infernal as to what the hells back-alley dust she'd been smoking. But before he could form the words, something dropped from the periphery of his vision; it was as if one part of his office had been sectioned off with a curtain that exactly matched what it concealed, and he only noticed the change as it was torn away. There, disheveled and worn, stood a tall dark-haired woman with the same face he'd first seen Cypress wear.

Everyone was still for a beat, save Madrigal's casually twitching tail.

Thrace whirled, and Pel could feel him drawing in eldritch energy in preparation for a spell. For his part, Pel dove for the door, ready to sound the alarm. Madrigal caught him by the collar and hauled him back with inhuman strength, clamping her free hand over his mouth, even as her outstretched wing blocked the view between Thrace and the escapee. Enraged, Pel dove within his mind and began the memetic rituals that would unshackle Thrace from the dampening wards that kept him contained. He and Thrace could handle a single infernal with some effort—but an unleashed Thrace could swat her like a fly.

"Wait wait wait wait wait!" Cypress shouted into the fracas. "I came here by choice! I want to talk!"

Thrace looked at Madrigal. She nodded, and the stitched began to unwind by degrees.

"Tentatively," Thrace began over Pel's muffled protests. "Let's say we're willing to hear you out.

Pel bit Madrigal's hand. She looked annoyed.

"Better let him go, Mads," Cypress said.

Madrigal dragged Pel bodily over to one of his office chairs and placed him in it. "Sit. Behave."

Cypress took a steadying breath. "As you're all aware, my name is Cypress Monroe. I'm a shapeshifter. And until very, very recently, I was placed under a geas by an angel named Dimereial that prevented me from discussing him or the details of my activities in Nox Valar."

"That little shit," Madrigal snarled. "How'd you slip it?"

"And while we're on the subject, how did you get into my office?" Pel added, pulling a notepad from his pocket. The circumstances were less than ideal, but if his previously clammed-up prisoner was suddenly ready to talk, he'd let her.

"Same answer to both. Won a game of cards."

"What?" Thrace asked.

"Wrong question," Madrigal added. "Against who?"

"Azlaru."

Madrigal's eyes widened, and Pel clocked the recognition in Thrace's face as well.

"Do we have a security breach?" Pel asked his partner. "More than the obvious one in the room."

Thrace slowly shook his head. "Not as far as I can tell. At least, no more than we did yesterday. Or will tomorrow."

"Thrace, I need you to not be fuckin' cryptic today."

"That ... name. Got a look at him earlier, under my Sight. He's not an infernal."

It was Madrigal's turn to look surprised. "He's not?"

"It's not so much that he *isn't*, it's that he's also *more* than that. Older. I don't have a good answer. But if he had a secure link to our shifter here, there's a really, *really* short list of things that would have stopped him from using it. And none of them are built into the void cells."

"Thrace, those cells can hold—"

"I know what they can do, Pel. I said what I said."

Pel collected himself. This whole case was spiraling, fast. Every part of him was screaming to escalate it up the chain, let Karson and the brass make the call if they wanted to take it out of his hands, or at least bring in the serious firepower the Horsemen could call upon for a high-caliber disaster. Thrace was a heavy hitter, but their job was fundamentally about fact-finding, apprehension, and crisis aversion. This was firmly into damage control territory, bordering on open conflict. They weren't equipped for it.

But Vessa's warnings weighed heavily on his mind. Maybe more so than if they had come from another source, he had to admit, but Vessa was rarely far off the mark.

If someone in the Horsemen, or worse, higher up in the Godless Monarchy was involved in whatever this scheme was, escalating the issue was the worst thing he could do.

"Fuck," he groaned. "Fucking hells. Alright, Monroe. You got out. You came to see us instead of running. Noted. What do you want to tell us?"

"That the angel Dimereial has been orchestrating a memory theft operation throughout the Sunless Crossing. He approached me within a month of my arrival in the city. He led me to believe his cause was noble, if not legal—that the targets he assigned to me were all people who had done horrible things, and by excising negative formative experiences from their minds it was enabling them to reevaluate their lives and possibly improve their prospects for an afterlife."

"Even if that worked, it would still be a capital crime in Nox Valar," Pel pointed out.

"Yeah, well, he had leverage too." Cypress's gaze fell. "I died with information that would save my home. My family. Dimereial told me that he could guarantee the information was passed along to the living before it was too late, if I helped him. That's why I came here. I was done. It was supposed to be my final payment."

"He sent you in here with a geas to turn yourself in and become the scapegoat?" Madrigal asked. "Fucking dickhead."

Thrace was looking at Pel. "Really makes you wonder how many times something like that's happened."

"Might have been a rush job after the Bastion. But yes," Pel agreed. He knew they were thinking the same thing.

There was a strong possibility that other pawns like Cypress had been marching themselves in only to be quietly disposed of by a different Horseman.

"Gentlemen, I was a royal spymaster, so when I say I understand the desire to cover every angle of this, I'm speaking as a professional. But I'm afraid there's an urgent wrinkle to our situation right now."

The hairs on the back of Pel's neck stood on end. "Oh?"

"I have it on good authority that in about ninety-seven minutes, Dimereial is going to realize my geas has been broken. And then he or someone he trusts is going to try to kill me as quickly as possible."

Thrace locked eyes with Pel. Pel nodded, and Thrace went to the back of the room. A series of cabinets were built into the wall, subtle panels with inconspicuous hardware.

Thrace flicked a latch on one, revealing a tiny metal barb. He pressed his thumb into it, drawing a drop of blood through his gloves. A glyph resembling outstretched, feathered wings appeared on the cabinet door as internal tumblers rattled open. From within, Thrace plucked an obsidian rod and dagger, and a handful of other implements carved in the glassy black stone. He closed the cabinet and placed them on Pel's desk.

"Crossing obsidian," Pel explained to the others. "Enchanted to the hells and back. Literally. This wouldn't be the first time the Horsemen have had to stand against a celestial."

Madrigal looked at the spread with equal parts intrigue and apprehension. Pel assumed her inhuman senses were giving her some idea of what the simple arsenal could do. "Only works in mortal hands, I'm afraid."

"I think I'm fine not touching that stuff, Horseman."

"Even a rogue celestial isn't going to be cocky enough to come at us here, so close to the Requiem," Thrace ventured. "Even if he gets her, his cover's blown. He'll get hounded out of the plane."

"We don't know if he's already got people inside," Pel countered, letting Thrace connect the dots without saying too much in front of Cypress and Madrigal. "How many, how they'll make their move, when? If he knows where Miss Monroe is at all times, it's a huge disadvantage to try to stay here and wait for his move."

"Fuck," Thrace conceded. "The birdhouse? Ves's people seem to be outside of whatever this is."

"Might be our best option." Pel stood. Madrigal eyed him but allowed it. "Miss Monroe, you're still in custody, but given the apparent circumstances, we may be able to come to some arrangement on the matter of your charges in exchange for your assistance right now."

Cypress nodded, a look of resignation on her face. "Promise me my message gets delivered, Mister Solimo, and you have my full cooperation."

"We can certainly discuss—"

"Done," Thrace said, extending his hand. She shook it.

Pel threw his hands up. "Patrol. I'm going to ask to be reassigned to street patrol just to be rid of you."

"Welcome to the team." Thrace grinned at Cypress. "Pel plays at being the put-upon straight man, but secretly he appreciates that I speed things up."

"In the spirit of teamwork then," Cypress looked to Madrigal, "I have a suggestion."

CHAPTER 35

"Sit, sit, we can speak freely here. My chambers are warded against eavesdropping," Vessa insisted, ushering them inside. Rasa—Emelia, if this woman was to be believed—saw an office appointed with functional, comfortable furnishings, and chose a seat.

This Vessa and her companions had aided Secan and herself in the ambush they'd found leaving Paradise, and thus had earned some measure of trust in her eyes. Further, the High Herald claimed to know Rasa, and that was not an invitation she nor Secan were prepared to ignore. They had allowed themselves to be led away from the ruined tavern, riding steeds of smoke and shadow with a decimated contingent of Heralds before the authorities of the city converged on the scene in force.

On arrival at the fortresslike temple the Heralds called home, they'd been given cursory first aid and healing magics for their most grievous wounds, but Vessa had insisted they reach the innermost sanctums before a detailed discussion could be had. She indicated a desire to speak to Rasa alone— not something Rasa nor Secan were thrilled with, but curiosity had won out over pragmatism, and they'd acquiesced.

Vessa carried a basin and a basket of cloth towels over. "To clean off the grime and soot," she explained, using one to mop the worst of said remains off the parts of her armor she could. Rasa accepted a rag and mopped up her face and limbs before the water got too soiled.

They worked quietly for a moment, and Rasa surveyed the room. Behind a large desk loomed a carving of a cowled figure, flanked by ravens. It tickled her mind as she studied it, a haunting sense of familiarity that swam through the faint etchings Menthissa's treatment had left in the pathways of her mind.

"What did you say this place was, again?" she asked.

The red-haired woman frowned at the question, worry in her eyes. "This is the Bastion of Endings, Emelia. Do you really remember *nothing*?"

Her words were compassionate, even concerned, but they evoked a flash of anguish in Rasa's fresh-churned psyche; a shame that something precious had been lost while in her care, the bitter regret of failure. Without context, she could not define the scope of it, and so was lost amid feelings she lacked the tools to grapple with.

Seeing her turmoil, Vessa stopped her scrubbing and put a gauntleted hand on her shoulder. "I'm sorry. That was my own frustration shining through. Let's go from the top: what do you remember of how you came here? Or why?"

Rasa relayed all she could of her journey through the Crossing, starting with her soulfall and meeting Secan. Vessa sat across from her, listening intently and occasionally refilling a crystal glass with cool water whenever Rasa finished hers. She smiled as Rasa described the bellflies, and leaned in close as Rasa explained their visit to Paradise.

"You've had a unique path through the Crossing," she said as Rasa finished her story. "The Bastion owes the Belfry a debt for their aid. And your Shepherd, too, has gone above and beyond his duty. I'll see to it they all know they have made friends of the Harbinger's faithful in this."

"What, exactly, is 'this?'" Rasa asked. "You say you know me. I'm sorry. I wish I knew you, I really do."

"It's okay, Emelia. 'Rasa' for now, if you prefer." She drummed her fingers on her knee. "There's really no other way to start this. My name is Vessa Theramay. Your name is Emelia Theramay. I'm your great-grandmother. I believe I died somewhere around two and a half decades before you were born. It's a pleasure to meet you."

Rasa stared at her. There were faint resemblances; the curve of her chin, the tilt of her brow, other subtle features—and there were areas where they were nothing alike. Her copper hair, for one, and her very human, rounded ears. Rasa supposed that given three generations and at least one part of elven blood removed, she could believe the claim.

"I wish I had more to say, Great-grandmother. Truly. This must be frustrating for you as well."

Vessa nodded, accepting the point. "Hardly the family reunion I'd hoped for, but such is the way in the Crossing at times. We will simply have to build our relationship fresh and come what may as your memories return."

"You indicated that you were expecting me here? I was condemned to die?"

"No! The opposite, in fact. You were intended to visit us as a living mortal, through a powerful portal spell. It's not common, but not unheard of. I'm sure you've noticed the occasional non-dead around the city, yes?"

Rasa nodded. Secan had pointed a few out, the majority of them being around the Nyxian Guard's barracks, but always those donning the Guard's armor.

"It's dangerous in that the Crossing is … very unkind to mortals who perish here. You were set to take on the risk in service to the Harbinger. You had valuable information that had ramifications for both Nox Valar and the living, and we did not trust other ways of communicating it."

"What information?"

Vessa hesitated for a long moment. Rasa saw her make up her mind about something. "I think it's important to tell you this in case your memory does recover. We suspect there might be some … corruption among the Godless Monarchy. Do you know who they are?"

"Secan has mentioned them. Not really."

"In brief," Vessa began, clearly picking her words with deliberation. "The Sunless Crossing is a between-space. A liminal plane of souls with a less-than-simple path to their afterlife."

"Right, that's what I've been told."

"What many don't realize is that this makes the Crossing *important*. Powerful even."

Rasa furrowed her brow. "How so?"

Vessa rolled her hand in a contemplative gesture. "You'll be missing some context for much of this until we can bring more of your memories to the fore. Your theological training in particular. In summary, souls are a very potent source of power for some entities. The influence of gods can wax and wane with the number of their followers, for example. Archdevils will shackle, dominate, or even consume souls to fuel their machinations. And there are innumerable other things in the cosmos that would find some use for a teeming plane of lost souls. Temples like the Bastion, not the least among them."

Rasa nodded and continued scrubbing the soot from Raven. Her words made sense, though she was at a loss for the implications.

"The Godless Monarchy is in essence the government of the Crossing," Vessa continued. "It makes the laws, brokers arrangements between groups that would war with each other on every other plane, and cuts deals with gods and devils, all to keep things … civil."

"The Monarchy are potent too then, if they can enforce such things," Rasa observed.

"They are, in their way. Few individuals within their ranks are so mighty; the Monarchy is made of mortal souls, mostly. Dead like you and I. But as an institution, they can give even deities pause, especially within the Crossing itself. They've amassed an incredible amount of raw power here—magics and relics and armies and so on—but they hold even more… well, *political* sway, for lack of a better term. There are *many* gods that would rather see the Crossing in the Monarchy's hands than open to exploitation by a rival. Or worse, an infernal. And the same logic holds in the Hells, for the most part."

"I think I see." Rasa nodded as she worked, buffing weeks of fighting from the intricate carvings of her prized hammer. "With the Crossing under the Monarchy, everybody gets their steady stream of souls as expected. And if someone tries to disrupt that balance, the Monarchy has all these other forces ready to back them up."

"Just so," Vessa confirmed. "And the Monarchy has existed in that state for eons, now. Stewards of countless souls, an entire plane, and constantly making trades and deals with heavens, hells, and more that none outside the Monarchy have any knowledge of. It's entirely possible they could stand up to entire pantheons on their own if they had to."

"And you suspect…"

Vessa's face was grim. "Someone within the Monarchy is working against the Crossing. I don't know who or why yet, but the signs are there. And even the threat of instability within the Monarchy is enough to put me on high alert."

She was still missing much of the context, but her ancestor's demeanor was dire enough that a chill ran down Rasa's spine. "And this had something to do with my death?"

"The Harbinger, my god—*our* god—is the Lord of Omens. We deal in prophecies, turmoil, disasters. Part of that means we delve into certain mysteries. Seek information others would not think to search for or care to find. You were about some of this work with your companions."

"And I found something, I take it?"

Vessa met her eyes. "You were first to raise the alarm. Someone, or a group, within the Monarchy is trying to corrupt the workings of the Crossing to their own ends."

"Ah." Rasa considered her words and their implications. "That might be the kind of thing that could get me killed and my memories erased, it seems like."

Vessa winced. "Seems like."

"If it wasn't for the memory loss, it would have been a good plan," Rasa mused. "If they killed me to silence me, I take it there was some provision to make sure I wound up in the Sunless Crossing, regardless?"

"I'm sorry, Eme—Rasa. Your life may have been lost to my oversight. The consensus was that, because stopping you that way would have been pointless, you were relatively safe on the mortal side. Our security focus was here, where we thought you'd be in the most danger." She sighed. "I've never heard of a spell that could carry memory loss from the living to the Crossing. That's ... unfortunate. And new."

A knock, soft and tentative, came from the door.

Vessa frowned. "Enter," she commanded. There was a sound of locks magically disengaging when she spoke the word.

"H-high Herald." A young man in unflattering robes shuffled in, holding a sealed parchment.

"Ah, Loren. A message?"

The boy gulped. "Yes, High Herald."

"Excellent." She stood and, to Rasa's surprise, produced a loaded crossbow from behind an end table. She leveled it at Loren. "You know the new rules."

Loren sighed and walked over to the carved wall behind the desk at a slow, deliberate pace, with the crossbow aimed at him the whole while. He placed the parchment in the stone raven's beak and flinched.

Nothing happened.

"Fantastic. Thank you, Loren. You're dismissed."

"Heed, High Herald." He left the way he'd come. Vessa didn't stop aiming at him until the door locks re-engaged.

"We had a bit of a security breach the other day," Vessa explained. She stowed the crossbow and strode over to the message, still hanging from the raven's beak. "This crossbow is only temporary while we reinforce our more elegant defenses to prevent it from happening again. We take that kind of thing seriously here. Oh, it's from Pel."

"Who?"

"A friend. I'll introduce you soon. I know it wasn't planned, but you're family, and a celebrated member of the faith, so we'll get you a place to stay here while we figure out..." Vessa explained as she walked back to her seat, breaking the seal and unfolding the letter as she went. "Oh."

"Is something the matter?"

Vessa handed the note to Rasa. It read:

Vessa,

Need your help. Immediate. Meet us in Anywhere. Bring anyone you can trust.

Expect a ght. Less than an hour.

Hurry.

—Pel

"It appears I shouldn't doff this old armor quite yet," Vessa said.

"Does this have anything to do with why I was supposed to come here?"

"I'll be honest with you, Rasa, I don't know. It might. There are a lot of pieces moving right now, and I haven't figured out how they all fit together yet."

"I see."

"I'll return shortly. I'll have one of the Heralds see to your quarters, and your Shepherd is welcome to recuperate here for as long as—"

"No." Rasa stopped her. "I'm coming."

"Emelia, we just found you."

"And I have been fighting my way across the Crossing for the entire interim. My intervention saved you in that tavern. I am sure you are eager to recover the information I may have locked away in my mind. So am I. But both the bellflies and the demon in Paradise agreed that the fastest way to do that was to stimulate my memories through familiar experiences. And this," she hefted Raven and rested it across her shoulder, "is the only thing I connected with when I arrived here. I *know* fighting, Great-grandmother. I saw flashes of Heralds in my memories. Proclaimers. Tell me, how did I know that name? Was I one of your number?"

Vessa frowned, but nodded. "Yes, Emelia. Rasa. You were. And a damned good one, from what I know. You did the family proud in your life."

"No reason to stop now, is there?"

Vessa hesitated for a moment, then laughed. "As stubborn as your grandmother. Fine. Let's tell your Shepherd we're heading out."

"I bet he comes."

"Why would he do that?"

Rasa was already at the door, unbolting the locks and throwing it open. "Secan! Bring Stick!"

CHAPTER 36

Today, Anywhere was a jungle.

Cypress stalked the winding trails of the marketplace, of shack and booth and tent and table set between enormous tree trunks, the cloying, dark damp of the jungle floor plastering Anastasia's hair to her scalp beneath the hood. A fine mist punctuated by heavy, pattering drops filtered down from the canopy far above.

Some of the vendors she recognized from past visits; certain stalls that she always seemed to see regardless of their position in the market of the day. Others were new to her, built into hollows in the trunks or atop platforms between the trees themselves; undeniably part of Anywhere and yet inconceivable how they might move to any other setting.

Cypress stuck to the shadows, slinking through crowds and behind tufts of undergrowth that Anywhere had not deigned important to remove. She was practiced at this sort of thing: moving quick but smooth, so as not to linger in anyone's awareness, nor create enough disturbance to draw focus. The key, as she had always explained to her trainees, was to walk like you were heading to a rendezvous that you were barely on time for.

294

The crowds of Anywhere were as eclectic as ever. Infernals, celestials, gargoyles, and souls of all kinds perused its fare. She spotted the familiar faces easily enough, though. The Pale Horseman, Pel, circulated past her every few avenues. His grim partner, Thrace, was less obvious, peering out at her from one clutch of shadow or another. Had they been following a layman, Cypress estimated they likely would have gone unnoticed. But clandestine surveillance was her domain, and she would have spotted their efforts even if she had been unaware of them ahead of time.

The others were more conspicuous, and Cypress had advised them to keep a greater distance from her. Madrigal, as an infernal, blended into Anywhere easily. There was no contrivance there; when Cypress spotted her, the half-devil was making a purchase. The new faces Cypress had concerns about. Vessa Theramay was known to Dimereial, and her presence could blow the element of surprise, but Pel had insisted that she and those with her be folded into Cypress's hasty plan.

Given that they were operating in a lawless clandestine marketplace and couldn't be sure any Pale Horsemen or Nyxian Guard they summoned wouldn't be in league with Dimereial, Cypress had admitted it was probably worth having a gaggle of battle-clerics on hand. Even if they were as subtle as a building demolition.

Cypress was feeling a level of tension she hadn't experienced since her first missions as a novice spy. Azlaru's grace period had ended an hour before, and every sudden movement in the market crowds had her jumping as if the angel were going to emerge and smite her down.

She made her way to the edge of Anywhere. It wasn't a visible thing, but a feeling deep in the root of her soul. The jungle continued; the faint trail through the growth, the distant animal calls, and the ever-present patter of rain all extending past the market's border as they should have. But to Cypress, the edge might as well have been a neon line, a wall of fire.

"Hello, dear sleuth."

Cypress stiffened and turned to find a cowled old man, hunched and walking toward her with a cane.

"You're not the only one who can change their face, Cypress," he said in Dimereial's voice. "I admit I'm impressed you slipped free of the Horsemen, but you always were swift and sly. It's what I like about you. But tell me: how did you break my little charm? *That* is something I would dearly like to know."

"D-Dimereial," Cypress said. "Listen. I'm leaving. I don't want any part of this anymore."

"Leaving?" His chuckle might have sounded benign to a passerby, but to Cypress, it was patronizing. "Not that way, certainly. And not through the Crossing, with the Horsemen looking for you. Come with me, dear sleuth. I will escort you somewhere … appropriate."

"Dimereial of the Twilight Chorus," Pel's voice boomed from behind him. The plain, unassuming Horseman stood alone in the middle of Anywhere's avenue, staring at the angel's back. In one hand, he clutched the obsidian rod; it stood as tall as his chest, its point dug into the jungle floor. In the other, he held an unfurled scroll. The insignia of the Horsemen was emblazoned on it for all to see, and he presented it like he expected Dimereial to turn and read the writing upon it. "Archon of the Hall of Tempered Innocence, *divinus hospes* of Nox Valar. By the authority of the Godless Monarchy, you are named *damnatus legatus*. You are hereby censured. You will submit to custody so the extent of your crimes may be determined."

"Ho! You cut a *deal,* dear sleuth?" He laughed again, but there was no mirth in the sound, only bitter contempt. The visage of a withered elder melted off of him like candle wax. To Pel, he said, "I'm afraid there has been some mistake, Sir

Horseman. I compelled this thief to turn herself into you, that much is true, but anything beyond that—"

"You will have time to plead your case," Pel cut him off. "The truth will be found, angel. Submit or be bound." Cypress couldn't help but note how empty Anywhere seemed all of a sudden—the throngs of customers and illicit merchants avoiding Pel like minnows around a shark. No doubt the Guild of Vices was already hard at work ensuring this incident didn't disrupt their broader operations.

"Submit, he says?" Dimereial laughed. His robe boiled away in a wash of ardent light as his wings unfurled, and he finally turned to face Pel. "How twisted you all get in the Crossing. One taste of true authority and you forget your place in the cosmic hierarchy... But we're not in Nox Valar, are we, Horseman?"

"My authority stands through the length and breadth of the Crossing, angel. Even here." Pel, for his part, did not flinch. Cypress found the scene surreal: the banal, administrative investigator, staring down a contemptuous angel. "Thrice I command, and be done. Submit."

"No."

A wave of pure white light, silent save a faint, high reverberation, rippled from Dimereial and crashed against Pel. The scattered plant growth between them simply evaporated, unmade and rendered into constituent particles that drifted away on the wind.

Pel's jacket, a garment Cypress had never thought to look twice at, flared with arcane power. Interwoven glyphs etched in gold and starlight silver blazed on the leather, and Dimereial's wave of annihilation stopped against a shimmering sphere of power that protected the Horseman.

"Insolent," the angel spat.

With a flick of her wrist, Cypress palmed the obsidian dagger and plunged it into his back, then broke the blade off with a twist. Veins of black-purple contamination shot across his perfect skin like cracks in shattered glass.

Dimereial whirled and backhanded her, the blow shattering her jaw and sending her slamming into a tree with enough force that she felt her ribs crack. Bleary-eyed, she saw him stagger, saw him cry out with rage as he reached for another blast of ardent energy to end her, only for it to ground out against the Monarchy-enchanted weapon now burrowing into his back.

Thrace had told her only to show the weapon if she saw an ideal opening. She hoped that counted.

Pel slammed his obsidian rod into the ground, and the air filled with a low *thrum* of near-infrasonic reverberation that made her heart flutter even through the pain and adrenaline. Dimereial recoiled from the note with obvious agony, attempting to take flight, only for his wings to spasm as the dagger blade's wicked magic spread.

Pel struck the note again, and Dimereial collapsed to one knee, clawing at his ears with such force that brilliant, glowing white blood seeped from around his nails.

"Submit!" Pel demanded.

"I. Said. *No!*" Dimereial roared.

And then he reached outside of reality and tore something free.

Cypress's eyes struggled to focus as Dimereial moved, as if she couldn't quite determine what or where to look. He reached his hand out and contorted it in some agonizing, impossible way. When he pulled it back, he drew something with it: it looked like a spear, or the cutout of where a spear should be. It was taller than him, topped with a slender serpentine blade and crossguard. But the entire thing was pure black, without depth or variation. It was a hole, a void, terrible and impossible to look upon.

As he gripped the alien weapon, Pel struck the tone again. It rang out, but Dimereial did not respond as before. His flesh trembled, his feathers shaking as if in a gale wind, but he did not recoil. He hauled himself upright with the haft of the dark spear, glaring purest hate at the Horseman. Pel rang the rod again, but Dimereial stood tall. He pointed at Pel, and a lance of light leaped from his fingertip.

Thrace caught it.

One moment, Pel stood alone. In the next instant, Thrace was before him, the angel's spell burning unheeded into the soul stitched agent's gloved palm. A shockwave radiated from the impact, sending brush and dirt flying in all directions.

"He asked nicely," Thrace snarled. "My turn, fuck-face."

Shock threatened to take Cypress, but she felt a surge of cool energy spread from her ribs, up her neck, and into her jaw. Her bones knitted themselves together with a grinding lurch, the muscles and tendons popping as they rearranged themselves.

Armored hands rolled her over, and she looked up into the face of Vessa Theramay. "On your feet, shifter," the cleric said. "Nice job with the dagger."

"Glad to be on the same team," she groaned. "Now what?"

Vessa grinned, unslinging the quiver of bolts from Pel's office and a crossbow to go with them. Each bolt in the quiver was silver, etched with a scrolling pattern of runes, and tipped with a spike of the same polished Crossing obsidian as Pel's rod and the dagger she'd plunged into Dimereial.

"The boys brought the Horsemen's whole celestial-containment kit. You a good shot?"

"Decent."

"You're done being bait then. Wait 'til he's bogged down and take your shot."

Cypress slung the quiver and nodded. "So be it."

CHAPTER 37

"*Thrice I command, and be done. Submit.*"

Rasa exchanged glances with Secan and the fiend, Madrigal.

"Sounds like our cue, kids," the half-devil said.

Secan looked … worried, Rasa realized. Despite her words to her great-grandmother, she knew it was well beyond his remit as her Shepherd to follow her this far. Yet, with nary a minute of convincing, he had indeed grabbed Stick and followed.

She grasped his shoulder and met the taller man's eyes. "Luck, Shepherd."

"'Course, Rasa. You too. Be a damn shame to come this far and not see it through."

"We need to get out there," Madrigal insisted. Rasa was not sure of her, yet, but she hoped the half-devil would prove to be somewhat like Menthissa, the other fiend she'd dealt with. Menthissa had pulled people's spines out with a gesture. That seemed useful.

Rasa pulled Secan down into an embrace, striking him twice on the back. Hard. He coughed.

"Thank you for everything. My friend."

Then she hefted Raven with one hand, clasped her other around Madrigal's forearm, and the two of them took flight.

It was a sensational thing, flying. Rasa had to stop herself from whooping in sheer exhilaration as Madrigal beat her wings and lifted them, carrying them above the rows of stalls and weaving through the trees.

Rasa felt the *wrongness* as they neared Anywhere's edge; an unshakable certainty that to venture farther was to invite disaster. She would rather have let go and fallen to the jungle floor below than allow Madrigal to carry her across that threshold, but thankfully the half-devil had no intention of doing so. They banked and paralleled the border, rising to just a few feet below where the canopy branches became dense and lush.

Madrigal squeezed her hand twice, signaling that she'd spotted their quarry. Rasa saw them a moment later: the Pale Horsemen, Thrace and Pel, engaged in a protracted duel with an angel, spells and light flashing between them in a blistering display. She saw her great-grandmother quietly rousing the shapeshifter, Cypress, just beyond the battle. Cypress sprinted away a moment later, flanking the fight and darting to cover. Vessa joined the other Proclaimer that had been in the House of Bereavement earlier, and the two armored figures began a cautious advance through the brush.

"Hope you're sure about this," Madrigal said.

"Don't miss."

Madrigal dove.

The rain-soaked wind rushed at them, and Rasa found herself grinning with manic delight. Madrigal flared up just above the level of Anywhere's stalls, sending them hurtling along with tremendous speed. They were approaching the battle from Dimereial's flank, perpendicular to Thrace and Pel, and opposite where she'd last spotted Vessa.

As they streaked past the last tents and into clear view of the angel, Madrigal banked and let go.

Rasa rocketed toward the celestial, putting every ounce of power and rage she could behind Raven.

He caught the blow with the black spear; a nauseating un-thing that could have been part of a set with General Harson's sword.

Rasa felt like she'd hit a wall of soft clay, or worse, half-molten wax. She managed to land on her feet, Raven locked with the crossbar of his spear. Her nerves screamed with both the unexpected stop and the eldritch wrongness of the force arresting her, and she bellowed in defiant agony.

"Crow kin!" Dimereial snapped. His eyes were wild, trails of foul black fluid streaming freely from them, but she saw recognition when he looked at her. "Finally, you hold still long enough for me to end you properly."

Rasa had a flash of familiarity—of those eyes looking down at her in a blood-soaked room as life left her body, staring impassively as she sank into the cold and dark.

"You," she growled through gritted teeth. "I'm going to pull your fucking feathers out."

A shard of silver flashed past, punching through one of Dimereial's wings in a gout of white-and-black blood and whistling off into the trees. He screamed, and the distraction was enough for her to leverage Raven and slip his guard. She had no position to strike, however, and so leaped back to gain distance.

Fire lanced down from above, a storm of brimstone-scented rays as thick as her wrist that exploded across the angel's back and wingspan. Dimereial staggered.

And laughed.

"Oh, of course!" he bellowed at Madrigal's wake. "Thus it ever was that the hells did hide behind the feeble flesh of mortals! Face me and know destruction, Madrigal of the Black Bells! Let us rid the cosmos of one more blot of—"

A geyser of darkness engulfed his head.

No, Rasa corrected even as she scrambled back. *Not darkness*. It was black like smoke, but flickered like flame, and the heat raked at her skin even a dozen feet away.

The darker Horseman, Thrace, was advancing on the angel. "You talk too fucking much," he said, reaching toward Dimereial and making a tearing motion. Another blast of shadow-flames erupted from the air, clinging to his skin like paste and burning ferociously. "Gloves are off, shitbird. I get to *play* today."

Dimereial strobed with light, casting the burning ichor to the ground. "Oblivion is too good for you, Blackfire. Some things are beyond redemption."

"Yeah? Well—" Thrace hurled another storm of the stuff at him, which he deflected with his spear. "Fuck you too, guy."

A chorus of lightning and sunfire slammed into his back as Vessa and Orld made their presence known. Dimereial shrugged it off, too preoccupied with protecting himself from the Blackfire Lich unleashed, but they persisted, raining strike after strike of evocation magic into him. Rasa re-engaged, harrying his flank whenever he turned his focus to deal with the magic users. She was under no illusions—a celestial was not a creature she had good odds of beating to death with a hammer—but Raven was something special. Whatever had bound her to it, kept it true in her mind through scouring, oblivion, and death itself, it held power. When she struck, angel-flesh bruised. And so she struck, again and again and again, refusing to be ignored, and refusing to allow him to direct his wrath too readily at another.

Thrice more, silver bolts whipped through the fray, blasting sprays of celestial blood from his wings. Each time, the glowing hot-white blood was clouded more and more with darkness, the same ever-black void that formed the spear.

"**_Enough!_**" Dimereial screamed, loud enough that Rasa's hearing vanished, replaced by a high-pitched ringing that slowly ebbed back toward function. A wall of pure force slammed into her, and she flew as if struck by an enormous invisible hand. She caught a flash of the Proclaimers tumbling in a jumble of glinting armor, and saw Madrigal sent crashing earthward. Thrace, awash in an aura of blackfire, was knocked to one knee, but was the only one of their number who held his ground.

She landed in the dirt near the other horseman, Pel. His leg was shattered, bent at impossible angles. She crawled closer, trying to assess his damage and get a sense for her own. She was battered, but intact. He was out of the fight, and likely to be ash if he stayed put.

She struggled to her feet and dragged him away by the collar.

"My staff," he croaked, pointing to the obsidian rod that lay in the dirt beside Raven. She snatched both up and shoved them into his arms so she could continue to move him. He moaned in pain but helped as best he could. As Thrace and Dimereial continued to duel, she pulled Pel around the trunk of a tree as thick as an oxcart, trying to at least get him out of direct sight.

She found Secan waiting there, Stick in hand.

"I'll be honest with you, Rasa," he said, looking at Pel's injuries with alarm. "I don't really know how to kill a celestial. Seems hard."

"What have you got left?" she asked.

He showed her two scrolls, both identical. "Last of Ori's stock. More of an escape plan than a weapon, I'm afraid."

Pel gripped her arm, grinding his teeth through agony. "Thrace can't win," he told her, matter-of-fact. "Not alone. Maybe once. Not anymore. He'll burn himself up too fast."

"I am open to ideas."

Pel thrust the obsidian rod into her hand. "Horseman weapon. Made to subdue celestials. Don't be fancy. Just hit the prick with it, and it should stun him. Give Thrace an opening."

Rasa looked at her friend once more. "Will those get me close?"

Secan was grim. "How close?"

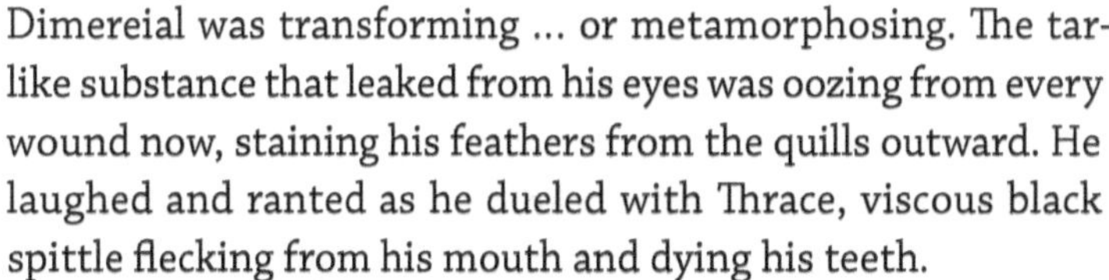

Dimereial was transforming ... or metamorphosing. The tar-like substance that leaked from his eyes was oozing from every wound now, staining his feathers from the quills outward. He laughed and ranted as he dueled with Thrace, viscous black spittle flecking from his mouth and dying his teeth.

The spear, that wicked un-thing plucked from nowhere, was now grafted to his hand, and a subsonic buzz shook the air with every thrust and slash he directed at Thrace.

The Blackfire Lich held his ground, crafting weapons of coruscating shadow that engulfed the shadow spear with each parry and tried to greedily crawl their way up its haft to devour the angel's skin. They succeeded often, but were greatly diminished by the time they reached him, as if most of their power was sapped directly into the spear's void.

"I am about great work, lapdog!" the laughing angel ranted manically. "The Monarchy of Rejects have squandered their charge, cast their lot with damnation, and told us all to be thankful for their efforts. *It is madness!*"

"You're not one to lecture on madness, fucko."

"Better dire action than to revel in sin and call it glory!" Dimereial lunged. Thrace backpedaled and blocked the strike with a conjured dome of blackfire, but a gash still blossomed on his arm, spraying thick blood that turned to ash in mid-air. "Do you not see? Do you not *care?* We have the means to *correct* the balance! The Crossing is a filter, a tool, a mechanism by which the cosmos might be fully, *finally* cleansed, had the feckless Monarchy only the will to use it."

"Keep talking, birdshit," Thrace countered with a lance of blackfire that scoured a furrow across the angel's chest.

"I'm going to see if your cobbled-together patchwork of a soul can be put to use," Dimereial raged, slashing with the spear. "I've never tried to raise a soul stitched with this before. I wonder what will happen?"

"You ready?" Rasa whispered.

"As I'll ever be," Secan replied.

Above the din of the melee, the sound of two scrolls opening in the treeline was easily lost even to superhuman ears.

Rasa readied the obsidian rod. It was lighter than Raven, more slender. It felt fragile in her hand—but there was nothing for it. Secan clamped his hand on her shoulder.

There was a moment of vertigo, and a sensation of displacement as the jungle warped around them, just for an instant.

Then they were less than a foot from a surprised, enraged, lunatic angel.

Dimereial, angel of redemption, was faster than any mortal could hope to be.

Dimereial, corrupted renegade, ravaged with blackfire, lightning, divine wrath, hellfire, and Monarchy-crafted weapons designed explicitly to butcher celestials like him, was not *quite* fast enough.

Rasa bashed his spear arm with the obsidian rod, which rang with a visceral note of satisfaction as blackened angel-blood sprayed from splintered bone. She rode the recoil into a backhand that took him across the chin, and then followed it up with two more blows about the head. Disrupted, the black spear fell to the jungle floor, and deprived of its power, Dimereial sagged.

"Now!" Rasa barked, throwing the rod down. Secan slapped the other scroll, already activating, into her hand. With the other one, she reached out and grabbed a fistful of oily feathers.

The teleportation scroll finished its casting, dragging Rasa and Dimereial twenty yards deeper into the jungle. Right up to the border of Anywhere.

"What the fuck did I say?" Rasa asked, ripping the feathers free with a satisfying tear, and kicking the stunned angel across the line.

Rasa, as did every soul who ventured into Anywhere, knew one thing about the invisible, undeniable border of the Crossing's impossible market. You did not cross it.

Dimereial demonstrated why.

The silence was the first disturbing thing. The angel staggered, casting about as if he had lost sight of her, lost sight of any of them despite being only feet away. She could see his mouth forming words, but he made no noise: no speech, nor his crashing about through the brush.

Something slashed at him, tearing a jagged gash in the belly of his robes that welled up with corrupted blood. He clutched it, glancing furtively around, and Rasa realized that he had not seen his assailant.

A chunk was torn from his wing and he whirled, striking out, but connecting with nothing. Next was a fist-sized hunk from his calf. Then a gash opened up on his face.

They got faster, but never more deadly.

Rasa stood and bore grim witness as Dimereial was picked apart by unseen terrors, ripped to literal shreds for as long as his celestial constitution could bear it, lashing out and screaming at nothing all the while.

Finally, when he seemed on the verge of death, or whatever passed for death among angels, something plucked him from the ground like a mangled ragdoll. She caught one glimpse of horror in his eyes before he was dragged away with frightening speed, disappearing into the vast jungle beyond Anywhere.

EPILOGUE

"Thank you for meeting me." Secan stood politely as Rasa—Emelia Theramay, he reminded himself—reached his table. He was cleaned up from his latest trek through the Ashen Fields, but still in his typical traveler's garb. Emelia was bedecked in fresh cream-and-crimson robes of the Harbinger, complete with a shining breastplate and bits of a chain shirt visible as she moved. They were tucked into a quiet reading nook high up in Exora's Belfry, but he had no doubt there was a contingent of trusted Harbingers nearby as bodyguards. Vessa Theramay was not taking chances with her kin's safety in Nox Valar.

He pulled a chair out for her, and she rolled her eyes and dragged him in for an embrace. "It's good to see you, Secan," she said. "How have your excursions been?"

Secan chuckled as they took their seats. "Nothing as exciting as bringing you in these past few months, I'll tell you that much. Tea?"

Rasa beamed as Secan handed her a cup from his newly acquired antique tea set, a lovely thing of subtle, smokey ceramic grays that had been oft-repaired in the *kintsugi* style in some time long past. "Borssa said you'd joined the club."

"They let me keep my set in their office while I'm in the Fields."

Rasa found Secan's preferred blend fitting; the mellow tones of Borssa's undercut with a faint, bitter drop that was more than offset by the sweetness of any honey or sugar the drinker added, or smoothed out with milk.

"Borssa said you're making some progress?" he asked as they drank.

Emelia shrugged. "Some. They and great-grandmother have worked out a regimen between the bellflies and Menthissa. I can recall flashes now. Moments from my life. But I'm still missing almost all of the context. I can identify some people by comparing what great-grandmother's told me, but I don't recall *knowing* them."

"Sounds frustrating."

"Sometimes," she admitted.

"Anything on … you know?"

"The 'big mystery?'" Emelia shook her head. "Not yet. We're hopeful."

"Ah."

"How long are you in the city for?"

"Actually, that's why I called on ya." Secan slid a large book across the table, flipping it open for her to see. Its pages contained diagrams, runes, and intricate notes written in a tiny, precise hand. "Borssa's been holding onto this for me too. It was Ori's. She left it for me."

"I'm not sure I follow."

"It's her spellbook," he explained. "One of them anyway. Borssa says there's a whole set, but I should start with this one. The 'introductory material' they called it, if you can believe that."

"Start with?" Emelia smiled.

"Yeah, I, uh… well." Secan flushed, rubbing the back of his head. "Figured since I ran out of Ori's scrolls. Should maybe learn to make my own. Or learn some tricks so I don't need them. You know."

"That's great, Secan."

"So, I'm going to be taking some time out of the Fields. Arranged it with the Shepherds. I'll still head out when they really need me, but I'm going to be in the city a lot more. Here, mostly. Studying. And I thought that I'd let you know that I'd like to stay in the loop on your … matter. Borssa and the others too. Help out where we can."

"Couldn't imagine doing it without you." Emelia beamed, reaching over the table to squeeze his hand. "Vessa wanted me to convey the gratitude of the Bastion for your help before. Again. And I second it—I've got a bit more of an idea of how the Crossing works now. I don't think many Shepherds would have done what you did."

"Eh, was nothing." Secan waved dismissively. "In my view, Shepherd's job is to get you where you're going. You just had farther to go than most."

"Anything?" Vessa Theramay asked, locking the door behind her and checking the wards. They were deep beneath the Bastion of Endings, in a little-used vault that she'd spent the past weeks reinforcing with every manner of protective magic Pel, Thrace, and the Heralds could muster. Plus some rather *expensive* consultations from the bellflies and the half-devil, Madrigal. Finally, their work had started in earnest.

"Thrace's handwriting hasn't gotten any better." Pel was standing at a desk pushed to one corner of the room, looking over a sheaf of scrawled notes. "The gist of it is 'they're fucking weird.' He's got some ideas on what to try next, but he's got to gather some supplies."

Vessa frowned and looked toward what the vault had been converted to contain. In the center of the chamber stood two pillars, each surrounded by layers upon layers of physical, magical, and divine protection. Upon one pillar was General Edwin Harson's sword, and upon the other lay Dimereial's spear. Both were voids; pure-black, weapon-shaped cutouts in reality.

"Thrace is sure of one thing though," Pel told her. "Dimereial didn't make these. He doesn't know who could have, yet, but it wasn't a celestial."

"Hells."

"We're not sure yet."

She gave him a deadpan look.

"Joking," he offered. "Little humor to lighten the mood."

"Where is our favorite former lich, anyway?"

"Meeting with his new patron and protégé."

"And how are we feeling about that?"

Pel looked from the notes to the vexing mystery weapons in the middle of the room, and Vessa couldn't help but note the worry lines on his face.

"On paper, against it," he said. "Between you and me? We're only just getting started, and we're going to need all the help we can get."

"I do love these little reunions," Mads said, closing the final circle and plunging the room beyond into darkness.

"How's the wing?" Thrace asked, a picture of innocence.

"The wing is fuck you, you existential rag doll, that's how."

Cypress failed to suppress a snort of laughter. If the heckling they'd gotten from Tilla as they entered Madrigal's back room was any indication, the devilkin had plenty of reasons to be rethinking her arrangement with Thrace.

But damned if the two of them didn't come up with the best derogatives for one another.

"Thrace, did…?" she asked, anxiety cutting through.

He was nodding before she continued. "Yeah, Monroe. Good news on that front. Took a while to confirm without drawing any attention, but your messages got through to Anastasia. She's got a long road ahead, but Carlow thinks she's gonna come out on top."

Cypress's sigh of relief came from the bottom of her soul. "I don't know what you told him. But thank him, if you can."

"Weirdest thing, actually. He didn't deliver the message. Someone beat him to it. So he just poked around to see what was happening and reported back."

Cypress looked at Mads, then at the spot outside the circle where she knew Azlaru sat. "Well. That's great then." She swallowed.

"Must have been a hell of a game, Cy," Mads said, brows raised.

Thrace followed her gaze and frowned. "Ah. Careful with that one, Monroe. Pel's already less than thrilled that we've got a pact with hot wings here."

"Yeah." Cypress hadn't yet broached the topic of her impending favor to Azlaru. *Technically,* she was a fugitive, not a Horseman, and so she hadn't tipped her entire hand to her unlikely new compatriots yet. But the only ones who knew she was on the lam were Pel and Thrace, and whatever hidden hand they were trying to uncover. And they'd worked out an arrangement.

"Can we speed this up?" Mads asked. "I've got paying customers coming soon, and I'd rather my pet Horseman not be around to scare them off."

"You first then," he said.

"Fine," Mads said. "The Dead Hands lost a thief yesterday. Looks like he tried to breach the wrong estate. Funniest thing, though, is someone else picked up the score."

"Which was…?"

Mads snapped her fingers, and an ancient leather tome appeared in her hands in a flash of fire. It had been water-logged at some point, stained and warped badly. The leather was a peculiar color, deep purple-black, from a source Cypress couldn't identify.

"Old ass book. Mostly illegible."

"Why do we care?" Thrace pressed.

Mads waved her fingers and the book flipped itself open, coming to rest on a badly degraded spread.

What was still visible, however, was a drawing of a familiar spear, rendered in pure black. The edges of other weapons were visible around the lost portions.

Thrace whistled. "Fuck, alright. Good find. I'll take it to Pel and Vessa, see if we can reconstruct anything useful—"

"We had another idea, actually." Cypress stopped him. "The Dead Hands went after the book on contract."

"For who?" Thrace pressed.

"Let her finish, rotbreath," Mads snapped.

"We don't know yet," Cypress continued, ignoring their bickering. "But we know they're down a thief and on the hook."

"Think we can press them?"

"Better." Cypress grinned. "How much do you want to bet they'd love to recruit a shapeshifter?"

THE CITY OF THE DEAD TEEMS WITH INTRIGUE—
CYPRESS, RASA, AND THE REST WILL RETURN IN BOOK TWO!

BOOK CLUB QUESTIONS

1. Cypress takes a lot of risks to achieve her goal. What did you think of her gamble(s) with Azlaru? Would you have taken the bet?

2. The tension between good and evil, and how they're defined by each character's perspective, is a through-line throughout the book. How would you define the fiends like Mads or Tilla in terms of good and evil, compared to Dimereial? Or Thrace?

3. If you found yourself in the Sunless Crossing, would you seek out a job like Secan or Pel? Pursue your passions, like Borssa? Or something else?

4. Where do you think the black weapons Harson and Dimereial wielded came from?

5. Thrace saw *something* when he looked at the table in Madrigal's. What do you think it could be? Were you

frustrated we didn't find out in this story, or intrigued at the possibilities? Both? Neither?

6. Vessa and Pel have some history, as did Secan and Ori—what do you think of these relationships that form after souls enter the Crossing? Do you still think you would seek out that kind of intimacy there, or leave that to your mortal life?

7. General Edwin Harson goes through several very radical changes when we see him: first, as a bitter, brutal man, then confused and ashamed after his memories are altered, and finally as a converted zealot to Dimereial's scheme. Do you think removing a key memory would alter your personality? Do you think that's true for anybody?

8. Toward the end of the book, we learned about the Godless Monarchy and a possible broader scheme beyond Dimereial. What do you think the conspirator's objective is?

9. Living mortals in the Crossing are taking an enormous risk. What do you think it would take to convince someone like Carlow to take a job there?

10. Cypress's love for Anastasia is her clear driving force—do you want to learn more about their history? How about what's happening in the living world now?

AUTHOR BIO

Chris "C. D." Corrigan is an author, artist, and game designer from Virginia. A lifelong sci-fi/fantasy addict, Chris started writing his first novel at age thirteen. It was terrible. He has improved slightly since then. When he's not writing, Chris is usually working on something for Relict RPG, the tabletop system he developed. He currently lives in Virginia with his wife and their pets, the latter of which have very strong opinions about when Chris is allowed to work on the stupid computer and when he's supposed to be feeding or walking them.

If you enjoyed this story, be sure to check out *Tattered Pawns*, Chris's debut novel!